LUCY
Or, A La

Here is the sprawling, sensual tale of a
spirited young country lass who defies
convention and confounds London
society in determined pursuit of the one
man who has won her heart. . . .

LUCY EMMETT

Or,

A Lady of Quality

Anita Bronson

FAWCETT CREST ● NEW YORK

LUCY EMMETT: OR, A LADY OF QUALITY

Published by Fawcett Crest Books, a unit of CBS Publications,
the Consumer Publishing Division of CBS Inc., by arrangement
with Coward, McCann & Geoghegan, Inc.

ISBN:0-449-24212-9

Printed in the United States of America

First Fawcett Crest printing: December 1979

10 9 8 7 6 5 4 3 2 1

'For my daughter Siobhân
with love.'

Can love be controlled by advice?
Can madness and reason agree?
Oh, Lucy, who'd ever be wise
If madness be loving thee?

Let sages pretend to despise
The joys they want spirit to taste,
Let us seize old time as he flies,
And the blessings of life while they last.

Dull wisdom but adds to our cares,
Bright love will improve ev'ry joy,
Too soon we may meet with grey hairs,
Too soon may repent being coy.

Then, Lucy, for what should we stay
'Til our best blood begins to run cold?
Our youth we can have but today.
We may always find time to grow old.

Anonymous
(ca. 1770)

CHAPTER I

A Child of Fate

*In which the reader becomes acquainted with the
circumstances surrounding Lucy's birth.*

Ragby, Leicestershire.   **January 1772**

The parson had warned the villagers of Ragby that the
Almighty would send a hard winter, and a hard winter it
was. Snow had fallen from late November and snow was
still falling in mid January. The "Entire Heart of England,"
including the tiny thatched village of Ragby, was locked in
a grip of mercilessly cold weather.

Roads, such as they were, little more than rough tracks
for farm wagons and staging coaches, were impassable.
The snow had drifted so deep it almost entirely covered
the stone walls that surrounded the neat patchwork of
fields. The tall oaks of The Charnwood Forest alone stood
above the deep, crisp, white carpet, their ancient, gnarled,
brown fingers reaching toward a leaden sky.

For the first time in the memory of the oldest inhabitant
of the village, and he claimed one hundred years of life,
the pond at the centre of the village green had frozen solid
with ducks intact, locked in ice, their vulnerable rears
rudely exposed to a cutting North wind. As soon as their
plight was discovered, the poor surprised birds had been

rescued by several stalwart volunteers who had smashed the ice surrounding them and carried them quickly to the Hare and Hounds Inn. There, before a huge log fire, ducks and volunteers were thawed out. The stalwarts stayed to drink warm ale; the ducks marched back to the pond. Wiser now, they did not venture near its surface but sat about at its edge, waiting for Divine Providence in the shape of a thaw to restore them to their former sailing glory.

Country folk woke cold, shivered all day and retired to their straw mattresses at night, still deathly cold. Great log piles carefully stowed beside each house began to dwindle, and animal fodder was fast running out.

Farmers like Roger Emmett, tenant of Ridge Farm, near the Charnwood, cast worried eyes on their hungry livestock. Spring was still weeks away. Cattle, their bones showing sharp through their dull hides, stumbled about frozen fields. Ewes, heavy with hoped-for spring lambs, moved about exhaustedly, searching in vain for any nibble of greenery.

Ridge Farm lay about half a mile from the village. It was a modest establishment—a small stone and thatch farmhouse, a stable with hayloft above and a large barn with a vaulted roof inside and thatched outside.

Farmer Roger Emmett was a fine tall man of blond Saxon origins, a veritable giant in Ragby terms, well over six feet high out of his boots. His family had lived at Ridge Farm since feudal times and had survived many hardships, but the past few months had sorely tested all his inherited tenacity and optimism. On the morning of the twentieth of January Roger opened his eyes to a pale silver light filtering into the farmhouse from the bitter landscape outside. The fire in the inglenook had died down during the night and Roger felt chill and reluctant to rise. He reached out for the warm, ample body of Margaret, his wife, who had shared his mattress for twelve years, but found instead of her welcoming flesh the sturdy shapes of his two young sons—Toby, aged ten, and John, aged eight—their fresh faces snug with sleep. Roger groaned. Margaret had evidently risen to milk the cows, and before making her way to the barn, had tucked both her sons in beside their strong father to keep them warm.

"Here's a fine waking for a lusty man," Roger grumbled to himself as he sat up and searched about for his leather breeches. "Looks for a wife and finds two lads." He crept stealthily out of bed so as not to wake the boys and pulled his linen shirt well down to obscure his private parts from his sons' curious gaze, should one of them wake and peep, and then, dragging his breeches behind him he strode, shivering, over to the inglenook. He displayed his backside to the little warmth from the fire and dressed quickly, pulling a leather waistcoat over his shirt, and on top of that, a long brown fustian coat. Then he sat on the settle and forced his chilblained toes into his big boots.

He breakfasted on a slice of meat cut from the ham that hung from a hook in the beamed ceiling and drank a good pint of warm ale from the copper pot Margaret kept close to the fire for him in such weather. Breakfast over, he pushed open the oak door of Ridge Farm, kicked snow away from the step with his boot, and found three hens dead as nails, frozen stiff at his feet.

"Meg?" roared Roger. "Meg?" His wife, her head wrapped in a woollen shawl, appeared at the barn door, his sheepdog Simpkin beside her. "What is it?" she shouted back, and Simpkin bounded across the deep drifts to welcome his grouchy master. Roger patted the dog's nose and let it sniff at the hens' corpses. "Look at this here, will you, wife," he said, as Margaret joined him near the door, "that's a fine how dee do." Margaret looked down at the birds and raised her astonished eyes to meet Roger's. "Well, I'll declare!" she exclaimed, putting her hands on her wide hips, "I only let them free from the barn a little while since—I was about to feed them." The rest of the Emmetts' chickens were by now clucking around Margaret's skirts, anxious to escape the fate of their friends.

Roger bent down, lifted them and handed the unlucky victims of the frost to his wife. "In the pot with them, dammit. But this is about the size of it. If this cold continues we shall be on the parish, begging, as God is my

9

witness, and if I lie—well—may I be struck dumb here, and my boots burned under me."

Margaret held the three birds by their legs and laughed, kissing her husband fondly. "Now go on off with you, Old Misery Guts, and stop complaining, things will turn for the better on another day." He caught hold of her arm. "Have you finished the milking?" he asked, slipping a strong arm around her waist and pulling her to him. "Aye, I have, but I have more to do besides, don't you fret." She grinned up at his bright blue eyes. "I know what you want, Mister Emmett, and you'll not have it this morning—for that takes two, and I shall be missing." He squeezed her tight. "Oh, and will you be missing this afternoon then, too?" he asked. Margaret frowned. "This afternoon? Well I may just be able to accommodate you, Sir, between plucking these fowl and cooking the supper . . . but it will depend on my humour, of course." Roger smiled and patted her belly. She expected their third child in August. "You keep warm, Mistress Emmett," he said fondly, "for when I return I shall expect a big bite from you."

Roger buttoned his coat to keep out the wind, whistled Simpkin and was off across the farmyard, out through the gate, and walking up the track towards the big field near the Charnwood to inspect his ewes. He climbed over the stile and jumped down into the field, calling to the dog to follow, and was soon among his small flock of sheep. His good humour was quickly soured again when he arrived at the centre of the beasts to find that three ewes had miscarried and that a host of black, yellow-eyed crows, always quick to take advantage of any gift from mother Nature, were tucking into a bloody breakfast at his expense.

This was too much for Roger's spirits—three less lambs to sell at the May Fair at Melton. "Now see," he yelled to Simpkin, "I am already a good nearer begging on parish than I was when I left my house—I should have stayed in my bed." While Simpkin raced around, barking and growling, sending the black doom birds into the air, Roger stumped about inspecting what remained of the miscarried lambs and cursing violently. He looked up at the sharp-beaked birds circling above, shook his powerful fist, damned their glossy wings and swore to shoot the stuffing out of them at the very next opportunity. Then he sighed, resigned himself to his loss, whistled Simpkin to heel and strode off up the sloping field towards Charnwood Forest. When farmer and dog had departed the crows once again settled on their prey.

The gypsies had made their camp at the top of Roger's big field, close to the forest, their gaudy yellow, red and green-painted wagons pulled well under the branches of the sheltering oaks. While Roger had been inspecting his ewes the gypsies—or Egyptians as country people called them—were setting about rekindling their fire. Sturdy and dark-skinned women, garbed in bright flannel and with heavy shawls of woven multi-coloured hues thrown across their shoulders, were setting off into the forest, the gold earrings that marked them as Romanies dancing in their ears. They would gather wood for the fire while their men saw to the shaggy ponies that pulled their pretty travelling homes.

The gypsies had not asked permission to camp in Roger's field—there was no need. A wise countryman would not risk saying no and falling foul of a Romany curse, and Roger Emmett was certainly a wise man.

The ponies had lain all night in the snow and were now stiff in the joints from long, damp hours of darkness. Roger could see the swarthy, wild-looking men holding the beasts by their bridles, running around the top of the field with the ponies trotting beside them, steam pouring from the animals' flared nostrils and from the open mouths of their masters to mix with the icy morning air. Roger could hear the men calling to each other, and the sound of hoofs beating on hard earth. They made a grand, colourful spectacle against the lifeless spread of white fields and brown forest. And to add to the brightness of the gypsies a great scarlet ball of a sun climbed slowly into the heavens, flooding the land with its rosy pink light, setting the icicles sparkling on walls and the frost on hedgerow, the heavy snow on bough and fields, shimmering, twinkling and glittering as though the Almighty himself had repented his

11

harsh weather and thrown to earth a veritable shower of diamond dust as a gift to cheer the hearts of men.

This miracle bauble hung in the sky above the Charnwood and as it gained strength, served to warm the dark-eyed faces of the gypsy women, who were bent double lifting stout branches felled in the Autumn gales, their long, black hair, rivalling the crows' glossy wings, falling about their shoulders. These were strange, primitive women who gathered wood for the communal fire early on that January morning—women who sprang from a race foreign to the country people, whose way of life ran contrary to their own settled habits. The gypsies lived beside, but never with, the farm folk. They belonged in no one place. Their language, culture and lore kept them apart—aloof and respected, but feared, too, for their powers of perception and foretelling the future. And Esmeralda Lee stood apart even from the other gypsy women, separated by two qualities from the rest of her kind. She was supremely beautiful and insatiably curious.

While the other women kept close together, gathering the kindling and talking in their deep, musical voices, Esmeralda walked alone, deeper into the wood. She was tall, her pale olive skin lighter than that of the other women. Her black hair curled in heavy coils to her waist. Her eyes were chestnut brown, wide, thick-lashed, her nose narrow, long and straight, with delicately curved nostrils. Her red mouth was full-lipped and sensual. Although no more than seventeen years old, her body matched the perfection of her face. Her shoulders were broad, her breasts large, rounded and firm, and her hips, under the layers of red flannel petticoats, swelled outwards from a narrow waist. Hers was, in fact, the form that men, when dreaming of the sublime female, are given to draw in the air with their worshipping hands.

At seventeen, Esmeralda was prime for marriage, of the right age for childbearing. In May, when the gypsies reached the Welsh Border, she was indeed to be wed with great celebration to one of her own kind. The band of Romanies camped in Roger Emmett's big field were carrying her, a proud possession, across the country from the lowlands of Norfolk, across the Midlands of England, to the Marches of Wales. There, after the Spring Fair in Llangollen and the sale of her father's best ponies to raise a dowry, she would marry the man chosen for her when she was an infant of three years, lose her closely guarded virginity, become the mistress of her own bright-painted wagon, and soon bring forth many handsome children to swell the Romany tribe.

All this would surely have come to pass had the gypsies not had to camp in the field behind Ridge Farm, because the snow made their progress impossible. Had Esmeralda Lee not been in the Charnwood on that morning in January 1772, had she not met Roger Emmett, then Lucy Emmett would never have been born. But fate, or coincidence, or whatever we call that strange force that governs lives, would have it so. Esmeralda's brown eyes met Roger Emmett's blue ones and in an instant Lucy Emmett, a child of fate or coincidence, was seeded, to bloom upon the world later in that year.

Roger had entered the forest through a break in the low stone wall with Simpkin hard at his heels. The bright glow of the sun had not fooled Roger. He knew that a "red sky in the morning is a good shepherd's warning" and more snow would follow hard on the sky full of glowing promise. He would have turned for home earlier, except that the previous afternoon he had laid six iron traps under the snow. He was certain that during the night rabbits, in their desperate search for any piece of green to sustain life, would have ventured out of their snug burrows. If his luck turned, perhaps in a couple of those carefully set traps he would find the booty they had been laid to catch, and good rabbit pie would grace his supper table on the following evening.

Roger's luck had turned, for out of the first trap he pulled a doe rabbit. She was warm, still alive, her heart beating feebly through the soft grey-brown fur. She had all but torn one of her hind legs off, trying to free herself. There were vivid crimson spots of blood on the snow and when Roger released her from the trap her brown eyes stared up at him, wide with fear. Roger ignored the message. He snapped her neck, quickly and cleanly, then with great satisfaction tucked the limp carcass into the big pocket Margaret had sewn into the lining of his fustian coat. Big heavy snow clouds were beginning to roll ominously across the sun, but Roger felt jauntier now in spite of the cold. Here was his first success of the day. He would not return home empty-handed, at any rate, even if he didn't find another rabbit.

He thought of the fire at home, of warm ale, a pipe full of tobacco and Margaret's ripe flesh. He felt his loins go hot as coals, looked down at his dog and growled at the amazed animal. "Simpkin," he said, "I know just how you felt, you mad packet, when you stayed away days and nights for that bitch-on-heat at Sycamore farm, and you didn't let a bit of snow stop you neither, did you, you devil?" He laughed and ruffled the dog's fur. "Her a full bred pointer and all. Throwing half sheepdog pups, aye, and everyone knew whose door to lay them at. Still, I don't blame you. Each dog must have his day, as the saying goes. Find a bitch of your own kind, though, next time, my friend. I don't want to have to make little seamen of any more mismatched pups, and be called a murderer by my boys."

Esmeralda was cold in spite of her red flannel petticoats and her thick green cloak. Her feet were bare and her toes numb. The rest of the women had turned back to the camp long since, carrying heavy loads of wood, but Esmeralda was given to dawdle, watching the squirrels, with dusty red coats, running quickly down the trunks of the oaks and pausing, their fluffy tails in the air, trying to remember where they had hidden their treasure troves of acorns the previous Autumn. Esmeralda knew how to be very still and quiet, so as not to alarm them; she would watch them race off across the snow and return bearing the hard little nuts and disappear into welcoming holes in the thick trees. She carried a twig in her hand as a token of the errand she had been sent on and used it as she walked along to poke about in the dense snow-covered bracken, for Esmeralda was in search of a hedgehog, those tiny, prickly creatures that slept all winter long. To the gypsies they were a mighty delicacy to be wrapped in mud and baked in the fire. When the hard mud was broken off, away would come the spines, and the flesh was always tasty and sweet. Esmeralda's stomach was empty, and the thought of baked hedgehog warmed her a little, but the wind was growing bitter, forcing tears to run in hot rivulets down her frozen cheeks. She looked up through the trees and saw more snow waiting to fall. Hedgehog or no hedgehog, she must return to the camp and shelter.

She was just about to turn back when she felt something bite at her ankle, and a searing flame of pain caused her to drop the twig she was carrying. Real tears sprang from her eyes and she fell to the ground in agony. She turned and looked at her left foot and saw the relentless jaws of an iron trap locked hard about her ankle. It held her fast. She was about to follow her first impulse and attempt to wrench her foot out of the hideous contraption when her instinct told her the trap would not relinquish its hold without taking with it most of the flesh that covered her shapely leg. She must try instead to loose the catch that had sprung at the side of the trap and she started frantically to shovel at the snow with her hands to reach it. She was sobbing with pain and fright. What if she were to be crippled, lose her leg, or even die from loss of blood. She was too far away from the camp to be heard by her father or her brothers. Esmeralda's vivid imagination did nothing to help her plight for the more frantic she became, the weaker she became.

Roger and Simpkin heard the shrill cry of pain at almost the same instant that it escaped from the girl's lips. They were only a short distance from her and Roger, now flushed with success, was just pushing the body of another rabbit into his coat's capacious pocket. When the dog heard the cry he froze, pricked up his ears in a perfect imitation of the pointer bitch he had coupled with so recently, and pointed his twitching black nose in the direction of the sound. Then he turned and looked quizzically at Roger. "I don't know *what* it was, as God is my witness," said his master, "go off and see."

Simpkin didn't need a second order. He was off like a

bullet shot from a gun, bounding through the snow, for all
the world like a fox with the entire hound pack of hell in
full cry behind him. Roger quickly resprang the trap and
followed.

Esmeralda reached the catch but her fingers were too
cold to release it. She lay down, moaning with exhaustion,
and watched the blood seep from the wound in her ankle.
She tried clapping her hands to warm them, she blew on
them, she pressed them hard against her body until she felt
them hurt, but they would not warm and remained useless
to her. She sobbed for her father, for her mother, for her
three brothers, even for her grandmother who had been
dead before she was born. She was about to call on the aid
of her great-grandmother when she heard barking, and
pushing back the tumble of tangled black curls she looked
up to see a big grey and white shaggy sheep dog leaping
like a hind towards her through the snow, his soft pink
tongue lolling, his ears flapping with excitement, his tail
wagging in a transport of delight. He sniffed at her hands,
her face, and then her injured foot. He trotted around her
three times, then sat down on his haunches, cocked his
head on one side, and looked puzzled. This was no rabbit,
this was no hare. He had better wait for orders from a
higher authority.

The authority appeared a second later. Esmeralda, her
arm around Simpkin's neck for warmth, looked up and
saw a blond giant of a man stalking towards her through
the trees. His long flax coloured hair had worked itself
loose from the ribbon that held it at the nape of his neck
and blew about his face and shoulders in the quickening
wind. His big hands were blood-stained and the brown
coat that hung unbuttoned beat against his body like the
wings of some huge bird. He travelled in long, loping
steps, kicking the powdery snow into flurries with his high
leather boots. More snow was falling now in the shape of
big lacy snowflakes that settled on Esmeralda's black hair
and clung to the abundant lashes shading her lovely eyes.

Roger Emmett came to an abrupt halt and looked down
into those wondrous eyes, and he was trapped himself. He
stood staring down at her, his arms hanging limply at his

16

sides. Simpkin watched him, hoping for some sort of movement, for quite a long time. Then, at long last, Roger scratched his head, shook it several times, and grinned at his dog. "Go *on*, I don't believe it," he said, "I did not think to catch such a quarry in my life, as God is my witness, I never did. No, I never did." He sat down next to Esmeralda and looked at her foot. She began to cry again. "Ah now," said Roger, "don't weep, maid, I'll have you free quicker than a saint can get to heaven; just be still." He took a piece of blood-stained linen from his coat pocket, bent, released the catch quickly and gently lifted the girl's damaged foot free. "I shall be a cripple," wailed Esmeralda, "and no man will want me then."

"You need not fear on that score." Roger grinned. "No man wanting you, indeed." He wrapped the stained linen about her ankle carefully. "You'll not be a cripple," he said. "You were wise not to pull. The wound is not deep and it will heal quick with the right care." Esmeralda tried to stand but could not, so Roger lifted her into his arms and looked down into her face. "You are a true beauty, maid. What are you? An Egyptian girl?" Esmeralda nodded. "I thought you was. Yes, that's what I thought you was as soon as I saw you, to tell the truth."

The snow had reached blizzard force. Roger's eyes were blinded by a stinging curtain of ice. Esmeralda clung close to him, her head tucked into his broad chest. "Well, what in God's name are we to do with you?" he asked. "This snow is as thick as lentil soup." He whistled to Simpkin, and the dog ran around in front of him. "Now, my old friend, what's to be done here, eh?" In Roger's long experience, a man was always wise to rely on a sheepdog's instinct in such weather, and when Simpkin made off through the forest Roger followed close behind, confident Simpkin would find the nearest shelter. He did, true to form, though he had to chase out a stag and his wives before he and Roger could carry the girl to shelter. "Ah, you would have thought twice about tangling with that fine fellow if it was the rutting," Roger said to his dog, nodding after the departing stag. "He'd have tossed you over the moon, and that's a fact." Simpkin had led them to the ruined hut of a long dead forester. The roof had gone but a great holly tree, heavy with red berries, had taken its place and the ivy that grew up the crumbling walls mingled with its branches to keep out the snow. It was warm inside. The bodies of the stag and his wives had softed the earth and the good animal smell of the creatures scented the air.

Roger Emmett laid his charge on the ground and sat beside her close to one of the walls. His dog lay down across the entrance as a warning to the stag not to return. "Well," said Roger, after a moment, "this is about the best place for us until the weather clears a bit." He watched the girl as she unwrapped the blood-soaked linen from her foot and peered closely at her ankle. It was a very nice-looking ankle, and the hot blood rushed to Roger's face. "It's not too bad, is it—considering?" he asked Esmeralda. She smiled at him. "No, Sir. A lot of blood. It will be better in no time." He nodded then laughed, watching her bind her foot and loosening a button on his waistcoat. "I was worried," said Esmeralda, "for I am to be married in May."

The girl's green cloak had fallen open and he could see the swell of her breasts beneath the shawl wrapped tightly over her short, laced bodice. Her skirts were bunched up, revealing a slender calf above her wounded ankle. He tried to look away, but his greedy eyes unwrapped her, and he groaned as he thought of the bountiful softness he would find if he could allow his hands to do what his eyes had already done.

He coughed and tried to speak normally. "What do they call you, maid?" he asked, watching her rearrange her petticoats layer by layer.

"Esmeralda Lee," she replied, stealing a glance at him. "And you, sir?" she asked, undoing the shawl and settling it more comfortably round her shoulders, revealing two full curves above the top of her bodice.

Roger drew a deep breath. "Roger Emmett. I am the tenant of the land hereabouts. I pay my dues to Squire Billy Royalston." He said this hoarsely, for Esmeralda, her clothing rearranged more to her satisfaction after her unusual journey, was moving closer.

A voice somewhere in Roger's head told him three or four times that he was old enough to be her father, but the voice was faint, and easily ignored. "What do you want to know then, Esmeralda Lee?" asked Roger, his heart almost bursting the remaining buttons of his waistcoat. 'I want to know," said the curious Esmeralda, "what you have in that great big pocket in your coat."

Roger closed his eyes as the gypsy girl's exploratory hand moved over the lower parts of his body in search of an answer to her question. "Aha," he murmured, as he felt his breeches stir, "That is a very secret pocket." Esmeralda pouted and frowned. "Oh," she cajoled, "I long to see what you have in your very secret pocket," and she tickled him a little to coax an answer from him. Roger sighed, shook his blond head from side to side, as an exquisite pain pricked him where a man most likes to be pricked. "Oh no," he groaned, as the pain grew into a mounting torment. "Oh, no. You will tell."

Esmeralda, in her childish ignorance, understood nothing of the man's discomfort. She pressed her sweet lips to his cheek, then brushing them against his ear, whispered, "No, Sir, I promise not to if only you will..."

"Rabbits," yelled the agonised voice of the frustrated farmer. "Rabbits," he repeated as he threw the astonished girl to the ground. "Rabbits," he groaned as he pulled up her petticoats and found warm, round buttocks bare to his rough hands. *Oh, rabbits,* he thought as he struggled with his breeches and it was of the rabbit that he thought again as he parted her legs and felt the soft down between her thighs. He mounted her and groaned, pushing his hard tongue into her soft mouth. He felt her stiffen, trying to keep her secret from his urgent body. As their gaze met once again he saw the doe rabbit's pleading message in Esmeralda's dark animal eyes. "Oh, no," wailed Esmeralda. But it was too late. Roger Emmett entered her sealed body and the secret was gone forever.

Meanwhile, some way off in the forest, Esmeralda's

19

father and brothers were moving slowly through the driving blizzard, calling to her in anxious voices that echoed through the trees. "Esmeralda," they called, shielding their faces with brawny arms and peering vainly through the sheet of snow. "Esmeralda Lee," roared her desperate father and shot his loaded blunderbuss into the sky. It was the dull bang of this weapon that alerted Simpkin, back at the forester's hut, and it was the dog who alerted his master, now lying at Esmeralda's side. Simpkin growled, low and fierce, causing Roger to raise his weary head. "Bang," rang a shot again, and now both Roger and Esmeralda sat up, the girl's huge eyes widening with horror. "Oh, the heavens," gasped the girl, "that is my father's gun. If he finds us here together he will kill us both. For I was to keep myself for marriage in May." Roger wrestled with his breeches and Esmeralda with her many petticoats, as frantic as she had been while trying to free herself from the trap.

"Esmeralda?" Now the girl heard her father's voice and so did Roger. Some of her terror transferred itself to him. It was not a sound to bring tears of joy to a man who had just taken a treasured daughter's maidenhead. *It seems,* he thought, as he laced the front of his breeches, *that I have two choices open to me. I can stand and have my head blown off or I can run like a thief.* He took Esmeralda's hand. "Forget I was here, for your own sake." She nodded, gladly, willing him to go. He and Simpkin ran through the break in the forest wall, raced across the big field, vaulted over the stile and onto the track that led home, and did not pause for breath until both leant panting against the gate of Ridge Farm. Which, for a man nearing forty years, and a dog possessed of only average-length legs, is a feat that requires more than mere stamina to achieve.

It was warm in the farmhouse. Toby, the eldest boy, was blowing at the fire with a pair of bellows, causing the logs to leap into flames. John was playing with some little wooden horses his father had made for him the previous Christmas and Roger's handsome, red-haired wife was standing beside the long, central trestle table, plucking the fowls for the pot. Roger shut the heavy door behind him, allowing Simpkin to slip in out of the snow. Both dog and man looked breathless, to Margaret, who had expected her husband earlier. Simpkin skulked over to the fire, head down, tail curled between his legs, and lay in a guilty-looking heap before the fire. Margaret looked at the animal, then at her husband who stood, panting, with his broad snow-covered back to the door. "What ails you both?" she asked, wiping her hands on her apron.

"Nothing ails us, woman," replied Roger, finding it impossible to meet her eyes.

"Ho—nothing," said Margaret, pointing at Simpkin who looked for all the world as though he had committed a mortal sin. Roger crossed to the fire and sat down in the inglenook, stretched out his boot, and administered a sharp prod at Simpkin's rear. The dog instantly sat up and attempted to look more cheerful. Toby and John each took one of their father's boots and started to pull them off so that he might warm his feet by the fire.

Margaret was still looking at Roger with her hands on her hips. "What kept you so long, man—I was worried out of my mind. Such snow falling!" she said, pouring warm ale from the copper pot into a pewter tankard and handing it to him. "I could not see my hand before my face when I ventured out to look up the track for you."

"I was all right," said Roger, sipping the comforting ale.

"Yes, all right you say now, but what of me at home here? Did I know you were all right, Mr. Emmett? I will answer for you. No, I did not know you were all right." She pointed towards the door. "There is weather that has made worm meat of younger, stronger men than you, I swear. There are all manner of chills and miseries to be caught, without a fine, stout fellow staying abroad in such weather. Tempting Providence, I say." She knelt before him and rubbed his frozen feet with her warm hands. "But do not listen to me, pray. I am happy to worry myself to a frenzy on your behalf." She looked up at him, and her bright blue eyes softened. "There," she said, "rest, man, you look worn to the marrow."

Roger was worn to the marrow. He expected at any instant to hear a pounding on the stout oak door, and the sound of a gypsy blunderbuss rending the peaceful air inside his home. Margaret perched herself on his knee, and slipped a round arm about his neck. Roger cast a worried eye on the door. "Why are you staring at the door?" Margaret asked.

"There is a draught from it," Roger said.

Margaret rose, crossed to the door, and pushed the roll of sacking that kept the wind from whistling under the door against it. "There," she said. Roger stood up and reached for his short clay pipe from the mantle and filled it with tobacco from his leather pouch. "You know what I intend to do?" he asked, pointing the stem of his pipe in her direction. "Though I have lost three lambs today, wife, and will be so much poorer come May?"

Margaret shook her head.

"I intend," said Roger Emmett, "to carry you to the May Fair at Melton and buy you the finest bonnet any woman ever had, as God is my witness."

"Ah, do you so?" said his wife, as she felt his arms about her waist. "And what has brought this about?" He moved away from her, and put his hand into the big pocket in his coat. "Rabbits," he said, throwing the limp, furry bodies on the table.

Later, with his stomach full of chicken stew, he sat by the fire, convinced no vengeful gypsies would now burst through his door, and watched Margaret, her head bent over her quilting, on the other side of the inglenook. *Mm*, he thought to himself, puffing with deep satisfaction on his pipe, *fresh gypsy wenches are all well and good, but for a hard-working man there is no woman better than a hard-working wife*.

Two days later came the longed-for thaw. The country was suddenly released from the grip of ice. With the easing of the weather, the Romanies departed and Roger was a completely easy man. February passed and in March the verdant green grass began to grow, providing food for the Spring lambs that skipped about the fields. The people of Ragby village were endlessly busy sowing seed and making ready for a good summer. In May, Roger took Margaret as he had promised to the Melton Fair, and when they returned she wore a splendid straw bonnet over the frilled white cotton cap that covered her red-gold hair. Roger Emmett had a good day at the fair; and when he looked at his pretty wife beside him on his cart, he felt himself a very lucky man.

In August, he became father to a small daughter, who was, at the end of that month, to be christened Lucy at the village church. Three days after the birth of his daughter his neighbours turned out to help the Emmetts with the haymaking and Margaret joined them in the fields, her new baby tied tight to her breast with a linen wrapper. She laboured alongside the other men, women and children, walking behind Roger and the other farmers who had cut through the grass with long scythes. She would lift the hay and turn it to dry, her sons beside her, stopping only to eat and drink and feed her infant from her milk-filled breasts. Roger, the sweat dripping from his brow, wielded the scythe against the gray-green crop, felling scarlet poppies, blue cornflowers and yellow and white round-faced ox-eye daisies with the gleaming blade. Now and then he would stop and sharpen the scythe with the whetstone he carried in a pouch on his belt, would look over to his wife, see her bent back, and hear the plaintive mewling of his new daughter. They worked through the day from early morning until the sun sank behind the ridge, and the birds themselves thought of sleep. It was a fine time for all and the earth was bountiful.

But then a shadow fell over their lives. Their little daughter died before they could christen her and was laid in a small coffin in the warm, brown earth of Ragby churchyard. The Parson, a lean young man who was reputed to be very clever—though no one knew, for he and his sister had only recently come to Ragby—stood beside the little grave in his cassock and surplice and read the words of the burial service through his long, pointed nose. "For dust thou art, and to dust thou must return," he intoned, over the bowed heads of the mourners.

Margaret was inconsolable. For days she sat on a stool beside the door of Ridge Farm, her hands folded in her lap, her eyes full of unshed tears. Roger and his sons would leave for the fields in the morning, kissing her sad face, and return in the evening to find her still in the same place. Her breasts, full of milk with no child to drink from them, became taut, and sore. Mistress Alice Westwood, the midwife from Ragby, was called in to bind them. The old woman tried hard to cheer Margaret but there was nothing to be done for her.

Margaret mourned the loss of her little daughter more than she might have had she been a younger woman. But time was passing for her and she felt the absence of her baby more acutely for that. On the third day of September, 1772, Roger Emmett woke to find the place beside him in his bed empty for the first time since the death of the child. He sat up, concerned, looked across at Toby and John, who had run in from their beds in the hayloft, and asked, "Where is your mother, in God's name?"

The open door answered his question. Margaret threw it wide. She was singing, "Oh, someone stole my heart away, riding on a cart of hay, I looked up and he look down, handsome, sunburnt..." She smiled at Roger. "No," she said, "I shall not give you the satisfaction of knowing who stole it away." She was carrying a wooden pail of milk, warm from the cow, and set it down on the table. Roger sat up and looked at her. She dipped earthenware bowls into the milk, and handed one each to her sleepy-eyed, tousle-headed young sons. "What's this?" asked Roger hopefully. "Up with the lark again, and singing like one, too?"

She crossed to her husband, and handed him a bowl of milk. "Drink the milk," she said, "come along, Mr. Emmett, there is still corn to cut, I believe—or have you taken to your bed?" Then she sat on the table, spread her hands on the surface, looked around the room, and exclaimed, "My, my, Mistress Emmett, look at the dust that surrounds you."

Roger smiled to himself. All would be well after all. His wife was still with him.

Over the following days while Roger and his sons worked to bring in the corn, Margaret set about such a spree of brushing, dusting, polishing, a-pulling out of furniture and a-washing of linen, treading it in a big wooden pail until her feet were sore, that any stranger passing Ridge Farm might have been forgiven for thinking that King George himself was due to visit. She hung all her washing to dry in the warm sun on the hedges and when it was dry carried it in, burying her nose in the fresh, sweet piles, and then smoothed it with the heavy irons she heated beside the fire, folded it carefully and stowed it in her coffers. When she had finished with her home she started on the yard, the barn, and the stable, much to the surprise of cows, horses, chickens, ducks and geese. It was only at the finish of all this activity that she was able at long last to climb alone up to the hayloft, throw her apron over her face and weep and wail, like women before and since, for the daughter she could never have.

On the evening of the sixth of September that same year Roger Emmett was walking slowly back home from a hard day's work in the fields. He wore a work smock over his leather breeches, and in his hand he carried his reaping hook. Toby and John, with Simpkin hot on their heels, had taken a shortcut home across the fields. Roger was bone weary, his hands raw in places from hours of toil and his back, that had been bent double all day, was aching. As he made his tired way home he thought of all the work that was to be done in preparation for the next winter once he had finished with the harvesting. Hurdles were to be mended and walls rebuilt. Pigs must be killed for the bacon and hams Margaret would cure. The thatch on the house and barn would need a thatcher to be paid, and that was no small matter.

He shook his head, and sighed. "One thing follows on another all the time," he said out loud. "You are no sooner done with one than, blast me, another jumps out and says Boo, but that is the way of it all. I doubt there's an answer to it." He was often given to philosophising when alone at his labours. He used to tell his friends, after a drop of ale, "Just because a man is not educated, it does not mean he may not think, if he's got a mind to do it with." Roger nodded and grunted to himself. Yes, that's what he'd do when he'd eaten his supper. He'd take himself off to the Hare and Hounds Inn at Ragby, swallow a good drop of ale, and share some lively company. That should restore his spirits.

The sun was just beginning to set. It was a red sky—a good shepherd's delight that boded well for the next day. Hot, dry weather, good for harvest. "If it holds," said Roger Emmett, "I will lay in a good harvest, and as God is my witness, I will put a coin in the plate at Michaelmas. I may even give Parson Brown some elderberry wine." He shocked himself at his generosity, and pulled himself up short. "No—a coin in the plate will suffice." He was not over-fond of the new Parson and his sharp-tongued sister. He had seen enough of their thin clever features of late.

Roger sang a little song as he trod the last few weary steps. "Solomon Grundy, Born on a Monday, Christened on Tuesday, Married on Wednesday, Took ill on Thursday, Worse on Friday, Died on Saturday, Buried on Sunday, and that was the end of Solomon Grundy." Suddenly, Simpkin appeared in a hole in the hedge. He had been home and back to Roger again. He raced up to his master, smiling his wide dog smile.

"Have you come to meet me, my old Simpkin, then?" said Roger Emmett. It was only a short distance home now, and Simpkin ran about, sniffing the grass at the edge of the track, chasing birds that tried to settle in the hedgerows, and racing after the odd stick Roger tossed for him, barking at nothing in particular, just to show that he was a lively dog still and fit for anything that might show itself.

This display of efficiency set Roger laughing in spite of his weary bones, and when Simpkin ran ahead of him in great excitement, panting and growling and blowing through his nose, then disappeared quickly into the deep ditch that lay at the edge of the track, Roger thought it was all part of the game, and whistled him sharply back to heel.

But the usually obedient Simpkin did not reappear though Roger could hear him scratching and whining in the distance. The farmer quickened his step; the dog might have a hare trapped and a hare was a good supper, especially jugged. He walked through the long grass, and looked down into the ditch. There, under the bright-berried hawthorn hedge, lay a woman, her face obscured by a profusion of black, curling hair. Simpkin sat at the woman's side and looked up at Roger, whining through his sensitive wet nose. Roger felt the blood drain from his face. He stood staring at the lifeless-looking figure. He did not need to see the face—he knew it was Esmeralda Lee. He descended into the ditch and looked closer. Her green cloak and red flannel petticoats were torn to shreds, her bare feet, dusty and bleeding, bore witness to many miles of walking across hard country. There on her left ankle, under the grime, was the scar his trap had made in her sweet flesh on that January morning.

Roger, his eyes bright with tears, knelt beside her and turned her limp body so he might see her face. Her head lolled against his shoulder, her eyes were closed. There was the gypsy face that had so captivated him and he held once again the body he had enjoyed for such a brief moment.

But Esmeralda's glory was gone. She was frail and thin. The body he held in his arms was the body of a wraith. But Fate had another blow in store, for as Roger drew aside the torn green cloak he found the reason for her sorry state. Her belly was full of child, and by the look of it a child soon to be born.

Roger set the girl down again and walked away from her. He sat at the edge of the track and covered his face with his hands. The child was his—he felt it. There had been no May wedding for Esmeralda Lee, there had been only shame. She had been cast out by her father and must have walked clear across the land, carrying the child back to the man who had sired it.

He walked back to her, his heart now pounding and knelt, pressing his ear to her breast. He felt her heart, but it was faint and he could hear her breath rattle in her lungs. He knew the sound well. Her lungs were full of fluid. The girl had consumption. Then he put his hands on her belly—a farmer's hands, sensitive to quickening life. The child inside her moved, and it was the movement of that child that moved the heart of Roger Emmett. He lifted Esmeralda Lee in his strong arms for the second time and carried her to shelter.

Margaret had washed her pretty red hair that morning in water from the well. She had donned a fresh apron, made butter and cheese, fetched her bread, new-baked, from the village baker and now, at the end of her busy day, had set the table for supper, with a loaf, butter, cheese and sweet apples laid on wooden trenchers and a big jug of buttermilk besides. Toby and John were seated on a wooden form by the long table. All Margaret needed now to complete her triumph over adversity was to see her good man seated and well fed.

Roger stood outside the door of Ridge Farm with Esmeralda in his arms. The girl was dying, that was certain. Had it not been for the child he would have hardened his heart and left her in the ditch, rather than have to risk hurting Margaret with the truth of what delayed him that January morning in the Charnwood. Margaret had suffered enough. But here inside the gypsy girl beat the heart of his child, so he looked his fate straight in the eye and called to his wife to open the door.

"Oh, Mr. Emmett!" gasped Margaret when she opened the door and saw her tall, broad-shouldered husband and his burden framed in the door. "Whatever have you brought me now?" Roger did not reply, but simply carried Esmeralda to the straw mattress he and his wife shared and laid her gently down. Margaret stood beside him and looked down at the girl. She thought she must be the daughter of a neighbour who had been injured in some way and that she would have to tell the bad news to some grief-stricken mother. But the face on the mattress was the face of a stranger, and although that was a relief to Margaret her soft heart was moved by the miserable condition of the girl she saw before her.

She looked at Roger. His eyes did not meet hers. "I found her in the ditch under the hawthorn hedge. There is a child well on the way. Her petticoats are wet and there is no dew. I believe her waters have rushed from her," said Roger. Margaret knelt and lifted the girl's thin hand.

"Poor, poor little bird," she murmured, then looked up at her husband again. "What is she, do you think? A tinker, or an Egyptian? See the golden rings in her ears—she has no ring on her finger. The girl bears a bastard, that's for certain, poor, unfortunate child."

Roger felt weak now. He had used all his strength to carry the girl home, but he felt weak also with guilt and remorse. Margaret crossed to a polished chest, lifted the lid, and took out a thick blanket of wool, covered the girl with it, and sent her two curious sons back to their supper. "Draw the curtain," she said to Roger, and he pulled the thick curtain that separated his and his wife's sleeping quarters from the rest of the house.

"What's to be done?" Roger asked. His wife was examining the girl, her hands travelling over the full belly under the blanket, and then, pulling the cover back, she lifted the layers of filthy petticoats and revealed a vivid crimson stain spreading slowly across the ticking cover of the mattress. The girl's belly had begun to heave. Margaret covered her again, looked up at Roger, her eyes startled. "We must call Mistress Alice Westwood directly. The child is at the very hour, it seems."

Roger turned away, his shoulders hunched. Margaret took his hand. "Now come, man. Sit and eat. You have used all your strength today," she said, pulling out a wooden form for him. He sank down and put his elbows on the table, buried his head in his hands. Margaret patted him on the shoulders and looked across at Toby who was just finishing a bowl of bread and buttermilk. "You, Toby Emmett," said Margaret sharply, "go and fetch the midwife from Ragby, without delay." Toby's milky mouth fell open with astonishment. He swallowed the last morsel of bread with a gulp and stood up. "Why?" he asked. "Are you breeding again?" He caught a quick, light cuff on the ear. "Do I *look* as if I'm breeding again, heaven help me?" she asked, and caught him by his collar, dragging him towards the door. She opened it and pushed him out into the darkening evening. "Tell Mistress Westwood your mother bids her hurry to Ridge Farm. There is work for her to do here. Say that." His mother looked stern and Toby was worried. The last time Mistress Westwood had come to Ridge Farm a tiny coffin left soon after. Sensing his worry, Margaret kissed him. "There is nothing to fear, I promise—now quick, lift those strong legs and run!"

Toby did run, like the wind itself, across the farmyard with Simpkin bounding beside him, through the gate and out along the track towards Ragby, his fair hair flowing about his full-cheeked young face. The crows in the Charnwood Oaks rose in a black cloud from the high trees, their wings beating against a closing night. The crows followed the track of a vixen and her pups through the forest, waiting for the weakest of her young to stray from her, when they would quickly swoop and remove its almost blind young eyes. Margaret, standing at the farm door, heard the cawing of the birds of the Charnwood and looked over towards the forest. "John," she called to her youngest son, "bring the pail and fetch water from the well. We must have hot water." John walked past his mother, carrying the pail, and she patted his golden head, her eyes still watching the crows circling through the high trees. "Plenty of water now. We must fill the iron pot." She watched the boy attach the pail to the hook on the long chain, and listened as he turned the handle of the winch, sending it clanking down to the cool depths of the well below. "When you have brought in the water, better see to the fowls," she said. "Secure them well. I can sniff a hungry vixen abroad tonight, and we will lose some should she choose to call."

She turned back into the house. Roger sat motionless at the table, his food untouched. "Who would blame the vixen," she sighed. "Not I, upon my word, for she kills only to feed her young." She walked across, and drew back the curtain, looking down at the thin form of the girl her husband had brought to her home. "I don't know who you are, girl," she whispered, "or who is responsible for your sorry condition. But under my roof you are my child, and I am your mother." There was much to be done. Margaret bustled to it, laid sacking under the girl to save the mattress from more stains, ran out to the wood pile and fetched a short thick piece of wood for her to bite on when the time came.

Esmeralda had started to toss now, her head flailing from side to side, still unconscious. Margaret, knowing that this must be her first labour, because her belly bore no marks of stretching on the skin, felt that her travail might for this reason, as well as her weakness, be prolonged. Roger was pouring water from the pail into the big iron pot that hung above the fire. Margaret sent John for more logs, took up the bellows, fanning the fire until the new logs crackled into life, and soon the small farmhouse was as hot as a furnace.

Mistress Alice Westwood came in later, all of a bustle. She was closely followed by a breathless, red-faced Toby, and an inquisitive John, who had waited outside the door for his brother's return. "My word," gasped Mistress Alice, her face puckered with exertion. She plumped her broad rear down on the wooden form by the table. "Oh, my dear legs. If I wasn't all of a bounce, drawing the poultry, when this great hurdy gurdy monkey whisked me off like a kidnap." She glared at Toby. "Dragging at me and jolting me so much I swear I've spat my very heart out a dozen times along the way." She patted her grey hair with a plump, pink hand. She was as round as a pumpkin and as wide as a double barn door. Her dress was of dark green starched cotton, over which was a white apron of the same material. Upon her head she wore a muslin caul cap tied under her several chins in a neat bow. About her waist was a wide, black ribbon and from this ribbon hung the small leather pouch in which she kept the tools of her trade—chiefly, a tiny silver crochet hook and a pair of silver scissors with handles of tortoiseshell. Both instruments were used for a multitude of purposes on the quick and the dead.

"This sprat," she said, pointing at Toby, "is the very freshest ever, I swear." She laughed. "I said, 'What ails your mother?'" Here she tweaked Toby's shirt out of his breeches. "'Ho,' he says. 'I think she's breeding again, though she denies it!'" Mistress Westwood threw back her head and laughed, sending all her chins swinging. She nodded at Margaret, wiping tears from her eyes. "Breeding," she repeated. "Like an old husband himself. 'Lord,' I said, 'Toby Emmett. Your mother was not breeding yesterday when I met her at the wayside cobbler. This is a very sudden business. Do they make a child in a night at Ridge Farm?'" She exploded again into gales of laughter, wobbling like a jelly on the wooden form. "Oh, Lord, and when I'm almost through the door, this one," she pointed at John, "catches my hand, and says, 'Please spare the babe this time, Mistress Westwood.' As though I had aught to do with your little maid's death. As though I were the very murderer of infants." She wiped her watering eyes with her hand. "Oh, my heavens above, what a pair of rips." She wagged a short fat little forefinger at John and Toby, who stood before her, red with an agony of embarrassment. "You men," she said, "you'd have a body laughed out of mind."

Margaret smiled down at her sons and put her arms about them both. "Well, the two remaining are fine chicks, though, Mistress Westwood."

The old woman nodded. "Aye, grace of God. Two good ones. I'll be pulling the fruit from their wenches soon, by the look of them, if I'm spared."

She sighed and sniffed, undid the bow under her chins, and tied her cap more securely. "Now then." She looked at Margaret, her eye eagle sharp, ready to be about her business. "Now then, Margaret Emmett, what ails you here?" And she stretched out her hand and placed it firm between Margaret's legs. Margaret blushed, but it did not deter the old woman. "You look well enough, or is it the milk still in that bothers? Well, I have said it and I will say it again, if you let the husband nibble at them, it will never go away. Fie on you, Roger Emmett, playing the baby." She poked Roger with her finger.

Margaret took the old woman's arm and helped her to her feet. "Now then, Alice," she whispered, smiling back at Roger who was by now blushing himself. "We have a girl here," she said, leading the midwife towards the curtain, "who is in urgent need of your skills." She drew back the curtain and Alice Westwood's eyes rested on

Esmeralda. Toby and John had both crept along behind the women.

"Take those snouts back to the table," snapped Mistress Westwood, turning on them like the flagship of the British fleet. "And you," she said sternly to Roger, "go off with you outside, and smoke a pipe. Be grateful that is all you have to do this night."

Roger walked outside and sat on the stool by the door. He was soon joined by the boys and Simpkin, the four of them fugitives from Mistress Westwood's grave and cutting work-to-be-done tongue. Roger filled his short clay pipe from his tobacco pouch and lit it with the taper John had carried for him from the fire. Soon he had a good glow going in the bowl and its pungent smell mingled with the smells that hung in the night air. He leaned back against the wall of the house and looked up at the silver crescent moon that moved across the velvet sky, sniffed the sharp dung smell of the farmyard and the sweeter smells of hay and corn from the shorn fields. He thought of Esmeralda and his secret, and felt his throat tighten. It was as if he had now a great weight on his shoulders that could never be lifted and the sigh that left the depths of his chest was a deep one. Toby, John and Simpkin were at his feet. Next to Roger, Simpkin was the most hang-dog of the quartet. He had not had any supper. He lay in a sulk at his master's feet, his black nose resting dolefully on his paws, a small worried frown marking the space between his ever-alert brown eyes. Perhaps there was never ever to be supper again? He groaned, lay on his back with his feet in the air, played dead to gain sympathy, but found himself ignored. The folk at Ridge Farm had other things on their minds.

Mistress Alice Westwood's eyes were wide with amazement as she listened with bated breath to Margaret's account of how the girl who now writhed in agony at her feet had been found. "Why, here in Ragby! What next? The dear Lord preserve us!" she exclaimed. "Here, well, who would give the tale credit? Why, the whole village is alive with gossip at anything untoward. No person alive or dead can pass through Ragby unnoticed." She knelt beside the girl with some difficulty because of her bulk, put a soft

33

hand on her brow and felt the cold sweat. "Oh, dear, dear, dear. This is a sorry business. She is in a mortal state, Margaret, I'm afraid. What is she, think you? An Egyptian?" Margaret shook her head. "God alone knows, Mistress Alice, for I don't, that's certain. She wears the earrings, she is dark enough In the hair." Mistress Westwood quickly unlaced the girl's bodice. "There were Egyptians here at the year's start, were there not?" Margaret nodded and frowned. "Yes, in the big field near the Charnwood, but they left directly the thaw set in."

Something of a memory from the back of her mind tried to come to the fore, but now Mistress Westwood had her ear pressed close to the girl's chest. The old woman sat back and shook her head until her bonnet threatened to fall clean over her eyes. "She breathes very bad. I swear the poor girl has consumption. Her lungs rattle like dry poppy seeds with every breath." She snapped her fingers. "Dear Lord above us, I have no laudanum about me. You have none, I suppose?" Margaret shook her head. "Oh, well," said Mistress Westwood, "we must soldier on without it. This is a rare state to lie in childbed in. But it is so with many of these wayside sort of women. Why, I hear that in Melton last month they took one off the High Street to the Poorhouse and she and the child that followed both died of inflamed lungs within the week. Aye, that's the way of them. The quack, Fitzmaurice, told me the girl was taken by a Recruiting Sergeant on his way to London. She followed after him, but he would have none of her, so the poor creature set to walk to Lincoln, far gone as she was."

Margaret sighed. "The poor waif to die in such conditions."

Alice Westwood shook her grey old head again. "Better to die in them than live in them," she said, "and that's the Lord's own truth."

She looked sternly at the girl, rolled up her sleeves, and said, "Now, let's to it and see how things are inside." She lifted the woollen blanket off the girl's body and drew up the petticoats. "Oh, yes," said Mistress Alice, "now here's a show of blood, and this clothing is wet." She parted the girl's legs and pushed her hand into the writhing body, almost past her wrist. Esmeralda groaned hollowly. The experienced old woman felt about carefully for some time. "Aye," she said, at length, "aye, I feel the child's head here, and the bag has burst itself, for sure. Hush, hush, my duck," she murmured soothingly as the weak girl groaned again. "Mistress Alice will have this tadpole from you, never fear."

She removed her hand and took a piece of clean linen from Margaret to wipe it. "She is only beginning," said the midwife. "The head is only the size of a crown. She has much pushing to do still, God help her." She leant across the girl and covered her again with the blanket. "Hush, duck, and keep warm," she whispered kindly as Esmeralda moaned with pain and threw off the blanket, her eyes fluttering as though at any moment she might become conscious. Margaret and Mistress Alice moved closer. The old woman took her hand. "There, my precious," she murmured, "here I am to hold your hand, see." She felt the girl's thin, cold fingers grip her plump warm ones. Tears filled her old eyes. "You hold hard to me, child. I'll sit close, never you fear."

Margaret bent over and touched the gypsy girl's thin cheek. "Now see," whispered Mistress Alice, "here is Margaret Emmett, whose good man found you." Esmeralda's dark eyes opened. "See, sweetheart, here is the kind Mrs. Emmett." For an instant the cloud that covered the girl's eyes passed. She looked up into Margaret's caring, honest face, and there was a moment of comprehension. She gripped the midwife's hand tighter and tried to raise her weak head, but even this simple movement proved too much, her strength ebbed, her head fell back and her eyes once again became dull.

Margaret Emmett's heart tightened with pain. There had been something so hopeless in the girl's expression that she felt she wanted to draw away from her. It was as if she herself knew that every contraction of her frail body brought her death a little nearer. Her lips were moving now, but soundlessly. Margaret put her ear close to the girl's mouth, hoping that somehow she might find the strength to at least communicate her name, but the only sound Margaret heard was the terrible, dry consumptive rattle that escaped from her diseased lungs.

Mistress Alice took her aside. "She cannot live," she said quietly. "It is simply not possible. I doubt also that she can bring a live child to this world and that is the truth, as I see it."

Margaret looked down at the thin body on the mattress. "There is nothing to be done, then?" she asked.

The old midwife patted Margaret's hand. "Nothing," she replied, shaking her grey head. "We must wait, and let the Lord take her, how and when he will."

It was almost two o'clock on the morning of the seventh of September and Margaret Emmett and Alice Westwood still sat beside Esmeralda. They wore thick shawls about their shoulders, for they were both tired, and despite the fire in the cottage they were both chilled by the prospect of death that hung in the air about them.

Toby and John had not been able to persuade her husband to join them and this early hour saw the man sitting on the settle inside the inglenook, gazing into the fire, his heart heavy. Suddenly, he heard from behind the drawn curtain in the corner of the room a piercing long wail of pain that went ringing around the low-beamed ceiling, searing the peace that had been before. He was on his feet in an instant. Then, as the cry was repeated, he crouched on the floor, covering his ears with his hands to shield himself from the awful sound. Behind the curtain, Esmeralda's time had come. Mother Nature took her and shook her wasted body in a remorseless grip. Mistress Westwood, used to the ways of the Earth Mother, quickly threw off her shawl, rolled up her sleeves again and set to work with her. She thrust the short piece of wood between the girl's teeth; the agonised creature bit so hard, blood poured from her mouth. Margaret gripped the girl's shoulders, for she was tossing terribly, biting on the wood and shrieking through her clenched teeth as the strength of her labour grew, Margaret couldn't hold her down, try as she might. She stood quickly and drew back the curtain to see her husband crouching on the floor like a frightened animal. "Roger," said Margaret urgently, "you must come.

I cannot hold her, she is almost torn in two with pain." He looked up at her, his face chalk white. He stood, bowed his head to his wife's plea and followed her to the mattress.

Roger gazed down at Esmeralda. The eyes that had beguiled him were open wide, but wild and sightless. He knelt beside her and pressed down the heaving shoulders. It took every ounce of his considerable power to hold her and stop her rearing. "Hold hard, Mr. Emmett," commanded the midwife, "God knows, it will be a miracle if this child is born at all."

Margaret watched the midwife lift the girl's legs and hoist them over her broad shoulders. She was to work, both her able hands employed in her task. Here was a life coming and she must bring it, by hook or by crook. The sacking that covered the mattress was red with gore but now, between the girl's gaping thighs, Margaret saw the sticky dark hair of a baby's head appearing, growing rounder and bigger with seconds that now seemed to fly, after such a long time waiting.

She felt her heart leap. "Oh," she cried joyously, "I see the child's head. The hair is dark and so abundant." Roger felt his heart move in response to his wife's joy. Now all misery was forgotten. The wonder of creation was being repeated in that small farmhouse near the Charnwood.

Mistress Alice placed her fingers at both sides of the baby's temples and, with careful turning, helped its face into the world. There in her capable hands lay the ancient mask of the newborn, its eyes tight closed, preparing to leave the warm protective body of its mother. Next came the shoulders and almost at the same moment, it seemed to Roger and Margaret, the rest of the child slipped quickly and easily out, and arrived, pink, wrinkled, and wriggling upon the mattress.

"Oh, dear God," gasped Margaret, feeling for her husband's strong hand. "See, the little child is born. It is a sweet tiny maid." Roger looked past his wife and saw the perfect almond slit between the plump, round legs. The child writhed about now, limbs kicking, feet and fists flailing, still held fast to its mother by the thick throbbing cord. Then he felt Esmeralda go limp. Her head fell to one

37

side, her eyes were shut now. He removed the piece of wood from her bruised lips. He could hear her breathing—it was faint now, and shallow. He looked over to his wife and Mistress Alice. They were busy with the baby. He saw the bright flash of the midwife's silver scissors as she cut through the thick cord and tied it tightly close to the baby's round stomach with a piece of waxed twine.

"There, Rosebud," she said, "we want a pretty button. We must be neat." Then she caught the slippery body by its ankles, hoisted it in the air and whacked it smack across its wrinkled little rump. The squealing and howling were deafening. Roger laughed and covered his ears. "Oh, good God, what a jangling," he said as Mistress Westwood quickly wrapped the yelling infant so tightly in linen that it was quite immobile apart from its noisy little mouth. Then she handed it to Margaret who planted a big kiss upon its curly head and handed it to Roger so that he might lay it beside its mother.

Roger Emmett cradled his daughter in his arms, holding in her the biggest secret of his life. He rocked her gently in his arms from side to side, murmuring to her in his deep voice, touching the tip of her little pointed chin with his work-worn fingers. "You are a little beauty," he whispered, rubbing his nose against her soft cheek. "A little beauty, as God is my witness," he whispered again gruffly, the tears pouring down his rough, weathered cheeks. He laid the child beside the motionless Esmeralda, whose own life was now slipping quietly away, stood, looked at his wife, his blue eyes full of grief, walked quickly away from the bed of labour, opened the door of the farmhouse and stepped out into the dark countryside.

"What ails him?" asked Margaret, worried by the look that her husband had cast her.

Roger was striding up the big field toward the Charnwood. Simpkin, surprised to see his master about so early on an Autumn morning, followed him with some curiosity. Dawn was some time away and the whole land, wrapped in a dark cloak under a moon paling to make way for the sun, was at peace, for those few animals that roamed at night were soundless, stealthy predators. It was only as Roger Emmett entered the Charnwood that the still night air came alive, rent by the shrill squeaking of the hundreds of bats that weaved and whirled in their curious deliberate way through the tall trees. Simpkin trotted on before him, his nose pressed close to the dewy moss and bracken, his tail wagging in hope of sport.

After a long walk, Roger found at last the forester's hut and sat down beside the crumbling walls with his dog beside him. Inside, hearing the man at his door, the great, many-antlered stag turned his solemn wary head, ready to protect his wives and young that lay close beside him. But Roger Emmett was no threat to any beast that morning, for he simply sat, his blond head sunk against his chest, and wept long and loud, his powerful body and strong, broad shoulders wracked with hoarse sobs. Later, when the first bird raised its voice to greet the sun, starting the joyful chorus of song that greets each new day, Roger Emmett raised his face to an awakening sky and stopped weeping. But back at Ridge Farm, as the day opened its arms to receive the glorious choiring of the birds, Esmeralda Lee, her beauty now restored, sent her last tremulous breath high into heaven to join them.

CHAPTER II

An Ill Wind Can Bring Good

*In which the reader is informed as to Lucy's childhood
and the above saying is put to the test.*

At a very early hour that same morning of the seventh of
September, 1772, Mistress Alice Westwood and Margaret
Emmett sat one on either side of the inglenook, their knees
spread wide and their skirts raised high to allow their
usually hidden parts full advantage of the fire. In their
hands they held pewter tankards of warming ale, and
though the night's business had taken its toll, their
conversation was tense and urgent.

Esmeralda's body was covered now, ready for burial,
and lay hidden by the curtain in the corner of the room.
The baby, sleeping the deep sleep of the new-born infant,
was tucked up snug in Margaret Emmett's linen chest,
close to the fire. Mistress Westwood glanced down at the
baby and sighed. "Yes, you could suckle it, Margaret
Emmett. But heaven help me, perhaps the best way for all
would be to let it go the same road as its unfortunate
mother, for the good Lord above knows what manner of
creature it will be if it lives." She took a long sip at her ale,
wiped her lips and shook her head. "You are a goodly

woman, Margaret, and we both have soft hearts for children, but truly, if that child is badly sired—and so it must be, for who but a beggar of the roadside would couple with a girl like that?—then I warrant you as I sit here breathing today, it will bring nothing but trouble to this house."

Margaret's eyes were troubled as she looked down at the sleeping baby. "Ah, but Alice, it is a sweet little wench, though."

The old midwife nodded. "Aye, upon my word, I have not seen better, and I have brought many. I did not think to see it so robust, to be true. I did not think it could live after that tussle, but this is only the start of it. All babes are pretty things. What are they, though, when ten or fifteen years? Scamps and naughties. Thieves at twenty, in Bedlam at twenty-one, hanged at Tyburn at twenty-two. These tales come through the quack, Fitzmaurice, from London itself, where all manner of hotch potch, pimps and bawds abound, some of them country born, some well-sired, upon my life, not wrenched from a creature found in a ditch—no, many born good have turned to bad ways. You have heard them say a bastard brings bastards, have you not?" The midwife drained the last of her ale, stood dropping her skirts and smoothed down her soiled apron. "Now, think well before you take it to suckle. Practicality is all in the end. It is well to know beforehand what you are raising, lest you whistle up a storm."

She nodded curtly, then, seeing the longing look Margaret cast in the direction of the child, patted her hand kindly, "Dear, dear, I know how it is with you, woman, but think hard now. Think on your man and your sons, and what you may lay in store for them." She crossed to the door, pulling the shawl borrowed from Margaret close about her shoulders before venturing into the chilly morning air. "I will see Parson Brown on the way to my home, and tell him of the girl. There is a sum set aside each year from Squire Billy for the burying of paupers. The sexton must open the big grave."

Margaret followed her to the door, and opened it.

"About payment, Mistress Alice," she ventured timidly.

Her old friend waved her hand in distress, "Do not speak of payment, in God's name, or I shall go all of a flop. I am in enough of a bother as it is, my heart. This was no joy for me, you know. I am one for seeing a happy end to a birth, not one such as this." She wiped her eyes with the corner of the shawl, sniffed, and patted her bonnet. "Oh, I declare," she tutted, "if I didn't almost forget them." She felt about in the leather pouch at her waist and took something from it, caught hold of Margaret's hand and pressed into it the two gold earrings she had taken from the dead gypsy's ears. "There with you," she said, "do what you will with them. For there is enough carrion about. Lord, how long would it be before the sexton had them from her, think you?" She wagged a ferocious finger in Margaret's face. "Why, there is more precious metal and jewels pulled from graves in this land, I'll be bound, than was ever seen by a king at a Coronation, and if that's not good God's own truth, he can have my tongue now, I'll not complain."

Margaret looked down at the gold earrings and closed her fingers tight about them. She watched Mistress Westwood wobble off through the gate towards Ragby and closed the door, then crossed to the fire and looked down again at the baby. "Oh, you little imp," she laughed, for now it was smacking its pink lips together and turning its head from side to side in search of a nipple to nuzzle.

Margaret sat back on the settle, Esmeralda Lee's gold earrings in her hand, looked down at the little stranger in her linen coffer and shook her head. "What's to become of you, you ill-born little thing?"

Mistress Westwood was nearing Ragby. The tiny village was rousing itself; she could hear the ring of iron on iron from the smithy. Obediah Boost the smith was at his anvil early. Women were throwing open the doors of the low thatched cottages, cows were being driven to be milked, mooing in low, complaining voices, anxious to be relieved of the milk that burdened their heavy, swinging udders. Dogs ran about, chasing the ducks on the green, and along went the landlord of the Hare and Hounds, rolling a barrel before him so that one of its iron hoops might be repaired at the forge.

Mistress Alice quickened her step—she had business with Parson Brown. "Good day, good day, Mistress Alice." Fitzmaurice, the quack, was riding slowly towards her from the village on his arthritic old nag, Cleopatra. He wore a long black frock coat, now turning green with age, and upon the greasy dark hair that covered his grinning skull of a head an equally antique tricorn hat. "Whoa ho, who hup, Cleopatra, my beauty," he called, as though he was reining up a veritable stallion. The bored animal crawled to a halt. He lifted his hat and twirled it theatrically in the air. He smiled broadly at Mistress Westwood, displaying a mouth full of rotting teeth.

He pulls others' teeth with alacrity, she thought. *Is he too cowardly to pull his own?* though the vision that sprang to her mind of Fitzmaurice with a pair of pincers firmly fastened to one of his own molars, rolling about in the dust made her smile back up at him. "Why, good day, Quack," she replied, and raised her arm in self-defence as he immediately tried to persuade her into buying one of the many panaceas and elixirs in the pannier baskets that hung before him across the lame nag's back. Fitzmaurice travelled that county and beyond, visiting fairs and villages where he would, for a financial consideration, cut corns, pull teeth, trim hair, apply leeches or bleed any one of the unfortunate populace who might fall into his unsteady hands. He carried a sign with him: "CORN CUTTER TO THE QUALITY. PURVEYOR OF ALL MANNER OF COSMETIC WASHES, HAIR DYEING LIQUORS, PROLIFIC NOSTRUMS AND TINCTURES TO SWEETEN THE BREATH." The last was a product of his trade that Fitzmaurice might well have benefited from himself, for his breath stank like an old pig byre. *A mixture of unhealthy innards,* thought Mistress Westwood, covering her nose with her hand, *and evil drinking,* this being rumbo, or perhaps the gin which the quack absorbed throughout the day in great quantities.

"There is nothing you can sell me that I have not bought

44

before and found wanting," she said sharply, "and don't, pray, tell me that you are now possessed of a phial containing the Elixir of Eternal Youth, for I am too late for that, as the Almighty well knows." She raised her pudgy fist at him. "And if you, you knave, don't stop tippling you will tip top over arse and snap that head from your neck one day, mark my words." She was just about to march on her way into Ragby and the parson when she remembered that Fitzmaurice was the man to ask for any information regarding wayside girls. Because of the quack's itinerant habits he was regarded by the country folk as a human newspaper. She looked up at him, placed her hands on her broad hips, and said, "Now, you raggedy, drunken old crow, do you know aught of a girl who passed this way last afternoon, about seventeen years, by my telling—long, black, fine-curled hair, advanced with child—looks like an Egyptian?"

Fitzmaurice thought for a while. "Not a squint-eyed hunchback?" he asked.

Mistress Westwood huffed impatiently. "Now, would I or would I not have said the child was a squint-eyed hunchback if it were a squint-eyed hunchback? Lord save me, you drunken old fool. All that you look on is crooked, and it's no wonder." She turned angrily from him but he caught her arm. "Well, now, Mistress Westwood. I may not know the girl you speak of, but here's a tale for gossiping wives. A wench, no more than twelve years, is gleaning in the fields with the rest of 'em, when she groans, puts her hand to her back, lies under the hedge, and gives birth there to an infant before anyone knowed it. This is the nip of it—the babe is full term, but only six inches long in all." He wriggled with glee and rubbed his hands together.

Mistress Westwood shook her head. "Humph, here's another tall tale come to us."

Fitzmaurice grinned wide, tapped one of the panniers, cocked his head like a jackdaw. "Ho, Ma'am. I have it in here. Would you care for a glimpse of it; you being a lady in the medical way yourself?"

Mistress Alice clapped her hands in horror, but

Fitzmaurice continued on his grisly way. "I have lain it on my scales, and it weighs no more than a pound of walnuts altogether. The girl must have starved herself in the hope her condition would not be discovered. Anywise, discovered it was, for her father laid about her with a flail for bearing a bastard. But it's an ill wind that blows nobody any good, as the saying goes, that's true now and will be true hereafter. I gave the father a coin for the object—I am well pleased."

Mistress Alice was outraged. "You buzzard, Fitzmaurice. An ill wind is good wind to you. What will you do with the poor mite's body, I am afraid to ask?"

Fitzmaurice laughed, "Why, I am now to deliver it to the taxidermist when I visit York. Later, when his work's done, I shall display it on my stall at the fairs, for it will be a wonder for all to behold to see a child so perfect formed but yet so small. Aye, that will send eyes a-rounding and a-goggling."

Mistress Alice shook her head sadly. "These poor girls suffer so from careless tupping. The one I spoke of is now lying dead at Ridge Farm, but the babe lives on for the present, though 'tis my belief it were better dead than to live in a world with such as you abroad."

Fitzmaurice's eyes widened with interest. He was just about to question the old woman further, but she was well on her way into the village, shaking her head, the muslin cap bobbing.

A very short while later, Fitzmaruice climbed down off Cleopatra's back, shuffled up to the door of Ridge Farm, and knocked twice. Margaret opened the door. When she saw the bent, black figure of Fitzmaurice she shook her head. "Oh, now be off, quack, I have no money to spend on cures and frip fraps. I am a busy woman with no time to gossip today." She tried to close the door, but Fitzmaurice's buckled shoe prevented it. He slid through the door and into the cottage. His eyes, beady and bright now, fixed first on the curtain drawn across the place where Esmeralda's body lay. He was there in a trice with the curtain pulled back and then he quickly drew away the clean linen sheet that covered the dead girl. What a feast

46

was there for Fitzmaurice. He bent down, a deep sigh of pleasure escaped from his lips. "Oh, now here it is, the very thing," he whispered to himself and caught hold of the girl's profusion of black curls, running his dirty, scrawny and greedy hand through the abundant tresses, his breath catching in his throat with excitement.

Margaret took hold of the quack's arm. "Now come, man, leave the poor child. She is dead. There is no more to be done and no more to trouble her."

Fitzmaurice turned and looked at Margaret, lifting Esmeralda's hair. "This is of value. Let me fetch my razor to it, and I will pay you well."

Margaret was shocked. She pulled Fitzmaurice away, "You will not take her hair as I live."

"There are wig makers who will pay for such fine quality tresses. Why send it to the worms when it can be worn again to give pleasure to a lady or a gentleman?" said the quack. "Now come, Mistress, you are not a wealthy woman to turn a little windfall away." He felt in his frock coat pocket and pulled out a bag of coins, jangled them so that Margaret could hear the coins rattle. He looked about him. "Here is a house that could well use repairs," he said. "And here," he said again, touching Margaret's patched petticoat, "is a well-looking woman who could walk grand in a new bodice or skirt."

Margaret pulled her petticoats from his grasp, her eyes wide with fury. "Here," she shouted, "is a woman who would rather walk naked than rob the dead to collect a shower of silks and satins. Now jump on your nag, quack, for I am becoming angry!"

Fitzmaurice smiled. "Ah, Margaret Emmett, you are a difficult woman. But no bother, the sexton shall benefit later, I warrant you, and his wife will wear the new bodice for all your foolishness." He put his money away and walked across to the baby sleeping still in the linen coffer by the fire. "What of the brat?" he asked, hovering over the child.

"What of it?" snapped Margaret Emmett, her eyes blazing, her own bountiful red hair falling from under her cap. She stood, legs apart, both hands on her hips, and glared at Fitzmaurice. "The child surely has not enough hair yet to be shorn?"

Fitzmaurice grinned back at Margaret. "Ah, but it is well known that the fingernails of the newborn, ground to a powder, are aphrodisiac in virtue," he said, feeling under the tight linen wrapping that held the baby's hands tight to her body. He was just about to feel the warm little fist and inspect the fingers when he felt a blow of such force across his bent back that he was almost felled. Margaret Emmett wielded her birch broom about his head with such ferocity that it was all the fellow could do to make his way out into the yard. She whacked him solid about his shins and shoulders and about his ears, sending them ringing and singing "Hallelujah" on their own account. He was on his mare quicker than he had ever mounted in his life, sober now as a hanging judge. And Cleopatra, feeling the blows too, made off through the gate of Ridge Farm in a very good imitation of a gallop.

"There," shouted Margaret Emmett after the departing pair, "call again and afford me the same pleasure." She turned back to her home like a virago, threw her broom clear across the house and slammed the door. "Now," she said to the sleeping baby, her face triumphant, "let them send in the entire King's troop with bayonets fixed and I shall deal likewise with them." Then she sat on the settle, threw her petticoats over her face and howled until the very thatch on the roof was almost blown away.

Up in the hayloft, among the warm hay Toby and John had roused their heads late for them. Alerted by the sound of the departing Cleopatra's hoofs on the hard dirt of the road, they woke as young boys do, instantly, and in a second were fighting about who should be first down the ladder. Toby, being the elder and the stronger, won, but not before his nose had been well pummelled by John's furious fists. They were down the ladder and running pellmell across the yard, shouting, wrestling and playing tag, when they were joined by Simpkin who had run before his Master in at the gate. Boys and dog burst in at the door of Ridge Farm, to see Margaret Emmett bent over the trestle table with a baby laid before her on the

48

polished wooden surface. The three came to an abrupt and breathless awe-struck halt and stood aside as Roger Emmett lowered his head and walked in at the door.

What a sweet sight met his blue sorrowing eyes at last, for there stood his fine wife washing the child carefully with warm water and patting the creases under its fat little arms and between its legs, for all the world as though it was her own child. She cooed softly to it as she worked, wiping the blood of its birth away from its tight curls and Roger saw the child's hair shining now as Margaret, twirling each curl about her finger, arranged them like a little woven coronet around its head. Then she wrapped it in a white shawl that she had knitted only a short while before for her own daughter, so sadly laid in the ground, and smiled down at the baby's little unfocussing eyes, framed by feathery dark lashes. Then she laid the child carefully down again on the table and looked first at Roger, then at Toby, then at John, who moved almost on tip-toe towards the table and peeped at the child.

After some time, Toby looked up at his mother. "Is this ours?" he asked.

Margaret's eyes met Roger's. "Well," she said softly, "I was asking your father, of course, before entirely deciding on the matter." She stood twisting her hands together in a sort of agony. "It is for him to say, Lord knows, for although I should have the care of it, it is Mr. Emmett here who has the word about such matters in this household." She looked again at the baby, and then at Roger, who turned his eyes from her, bent his head and put his rough finger on the baby's button nose, laughed to himself, shook his head, and looked back at his wife.

"Oh, it is indeed, is it?" he asked, looking grim, "Mr. Emmett who has the say about such matters in this household, is it? This is good news to hear. The man who shall have the work to keep it fed and sheltered has a say about such matters as who shall live under his roof." He turned his back on his wife. Margaret's heart fell almost to the pit of her stomach as she looked at her husband's stern back—she couldn't see his face. She lifted the baby and held it close.

49

"Well, boys," she said to Toby and John, "if this is to be the way of it, you better pack bundles and join me at the roadside begging for I'll not remain without this child."

Roger was smiling broadly now. He turned and looked at Margaret. She had handed the baby to Toby to hold, had taken her bonnet from the hook behind the door and was resolutely tying the ribbons under her chin.

He loved to tease her and his eyes shone with laughter. "Oh, I see," he said, "here is a family to be broken now, for the sake of that whelp?" He caught hold of his wife's arm. "Is that the way of it, then, Mrs. Emmett?" he asked, looking down into her furious face.

"Aye," she said breathlessly, "I'll take my chance with the children on the roads, I'll not stay with a man..." But she didn't finish for she was hoisted into the air by her husband, gripped firmly by her waist and danced all the way about the room.

"Hey!" shouted Roger Emmett to his sons, "see what an ill-tempered fierce little besom I have to bear with?" He swung her high in the air and stood her on the table. She was smiling now with some satisfaction. "Off with the bonnet," said Roger, and she slowly began to untie the bow.

"Does this mean we are to have a maid after all?" asked John.

Roger grabbed the baby off Toby and held the little girl high in the air, looking up at its tiny pointed face. Then he held it close to his broad chest and said, "We are. We are to have a maid, after all, and this arm," he said, shaking his right arm towards the ceiling, "shall work like the very devil for her, as God is my witness. Now, dammit, let's to our breakfasting. The day swings on and there's no good comes of crying over milk spilt long ago."

The same day, Esmeralda was carried to the church-yard at Ragby and buried in the paupers' grave. The Emmett family, joined by Mistress Westwood, said earnest prayers for her soul and shed as many tears for the lost girl as if she had been one of their own. But although Esmeralda's death had deeply troubled Roger Emmett the

50

delight he enjoyed at having a little daughter so unexpectedly deposited under his roof more than made up for the sorrow. As soon as the funeral was over, it was back to Ridge Farm and to work for him. He went into the barn and lifted up the rocking cradle that had been in use at the farm since long, long years before he could remember, and carried it into the house again. He had last carried it in when Margaret's child had been born some weeks previous but carried it out again when she died, as the sight of the empty cradle distressed his wife. It was dusted up now again with great care, a soft goosedown mattress set inside, then it was carried to the inglenook and the new baby was laid inside. Later that day Roger and Margaret sat by the fire with Toby and John beside them. Margaret had just finished feeding the child and was lacing up her bodice again when Toby piped up.

"I have been giving this matter a lot of thought," he said, looking at his father.

Roger Emmett raised his eyebrows and looked down at his son, who sat beside him on the settle, a sort of blond-miniature of himself. "Aw, well," said Roger filling his short pipe. "Thinking is no bad thing if you have a mind to do it with, that's what I say."

He watched his wife lay the baby over her shoulder and pat its back to bring the wind from it. "What have you been giving thought to?" he asked Toby, who was still frowning.

"Well," said the boy, "what are we going to call it? We got to call it something. We can't go about calling it nothing, can we?" John agreed. They watched their mother lay the baby down in the cradle and cover it carefully.

"Well, it's your mother who has the naming of wenches in this house," said Roger Emmett. "I had the worrying of naming you boys."

Margaret Emmett smiled. "Oh, now," she said, "I'll put paid to the worrying and thinking at this instant, for I named the child as soon as she was born."

Roger looked at her in amazement. "Did you so,

ma'am?" he asked. "Oh, I see." He nodded. "And might I be a bold man, risk my neck and ask what you called the wench as soon as she was born?"

"Lucy," said Margaret, "for she has come to take the place of the Lucy we lost. That's her name for you—Lucy Emmett." As though in answer to her name, the little Lucy opened her mouth and wailed. Margaret had lifted her and held her tight. "Ssh, ssh, Lucy Emmett," said Margaret, rocking her gently.

Roger pointed towards Margaret and nodded at his sons. "You mark my words," he said, "the woman will have that wench spoilt to a pout."

By the time she was one year old, Lucy Emmett had her father wrapped so tight around her finger that she only had to pucker her mouth to be picked up. She would wake first in the morning, pull herself up in her cradle and peep out over the rim, looking down at her father, who slept on the mattress beside Margaret. If his eyes did not smile back at her she would set up such a plaintive wailing that the poor man would have to rouse himself and lift her into bed beside him to quiet her. Then for a while she would lie contented, gurgling to herself and watching her fat toes waving and wriggling, talking to herself in the language babies use before they have to communicate more complicated needs. Margaret would scold Roger for spoiling the child, but he would say, "Well, then, woman. What am I to do, eh? Let the little chit break her heart weeping for me?" He was, if the truth had been known, secretly pleased by Lucy's devotion. As time passed, next to Simpkin, she became his closest companion—so close, in fact, that she sometimes clung so fast about his neck, her legs wound around his waist, that he was forced to button up his big fustian coat with her inside it and march out into the fields like a man with two heads.

By the time she was three, there was no doubting that she was "the prettiest and brightest little wren in the whole county, if not in the world," according to Roger. She was as brown as a berry and would run behind him as he went about his work, her feet bare in all weathers. The mingling of dark Romany and fair Saxon blood was very favourable to her looks, for Roger Emmett's "little mongrel," as he would call her when they were alone, had inherited her father's bright cornflower blue eyes. But the rest of her was all Esmeralda. There before him, as a constant reminder of his one lapse from being an entirely faithful husband was the tiny Lucy, with the mass of glorious black curls, promising to be more of a beauty, if that were possible, than Esmeralda herself.

This thought often kept Roger awake at night. "There will be trouble with that little maid," he would say to Margaret, half asleep beside him in the dark hours. "There will be all the toms in Christendom after her."

Margaret would sigh and turn across and pat his shoulder. "Aye, Roger Emmett, she is but three years old yet. Worry me again ten years from now, there's a good man."

But Roger would fret on. "Let them howl out here," he'd say threateningly, "I'll shoot the tails off them all."

As Lucy grew, so did Roger's worries. She was spirited and curious and into everything about the farm. She would attempt all manner of feats, causing the hair on Roger's head to grey. Once, when the thatcher was at work on the barn in the Springtime, Roger walked in at the gate and heard her call him—"Yoo hoo, Roger Emmett!" He looked about in vain for a sight of her. "Here I am, sir," shouted Lucy and the poor man's heart nearly jumped clean from his mouth when he looked up to the barn roof to see a radiant, excited Lucy skipping along the central beam, waving her arms at him.

"I told her to come down, Mr. Emmett," said the thatcher, "but the wench says it is all right, she has been there before after bird's nests without using a ladder at all."

"Meg," yelled Roger Emmett.

"What is it?" asked a tired Margaret, coming out of the house.

"Look here at that wench," said Roger pointing up at Lucy dancing along the top of the barn.

Margaret nodded. "Aye, I can see her. She will either climb down or fall down, either way she will be down," said Margaret, going back into the house, by now used to Lucy's devilry and Roger's worrying.

But Roger always fell for Lucy's tricks. He went to the barn, stood at the foot of the thatcher's ladder, pleaded with her to come down until he was almost voiceless. In the end he climbed the ladder to reach her and arrived on the top of the roof, only to find she had climbed down the other ladder on the other side of the barn and left him breathless and foolish perched on the barn while she skipped about below, calling "Yoo hoo, Roger Emmett!" But later she made up for it and would fill his pipe like a dutiful little daughter, sit on his knee by the fire and pull out his grey hairs one by one, saying with each hair that she pulled, "Here is one for the tinker and one for the tailor, one for the soldier, one for the sailor, one for the beggar man and one for the thief." Roger would sit patient while she tweaked at his hairs. "Aye, there's one for every soul in the county," he would say wryly. "Who put them there, eh?"

Lucy's life was not all play. As she grew, so did her work. She took charge of the hens, collected the eggs from under them while the shells were still warm and before the rats could get to them, carrying them to Margaret in her little wicker basket. She helped with the milking, learnt the whims of the cows and would put them in good humour by singing to them while she drew their milk. She worked in the house and in the fields and was prepared by her parents to be a good wife and helper to an honest countryman some day.

There was no question of Lucy learning to read and write. These skills were not essential, neither could Margaret and Roger afford the cost. Reading and writing and schooling was for the few, quality people mostly, whoever they might be. For though she heard quality people mentioned all the time, Lucy never seemed to meet any. The country folk who could not read and write had a way of their own of writing bills for work. The hurdle makers and other skilled men would take a piece of wood and carve a straight notch for every hurdle or other article that had been made, then a different shaped notch for the charge, and a farmer, like Roger, would pay according to the number and shape of the notches.

Every man had his own mark, his sign. He would put his mark to a legal document read to him by a lawyer—though, for the most part, as Roger said, "It is well to keep clear of lawyers. They are concerned to send a transaction wrong, and muddled. Then you pay them for unmuddling it." Roger Emmett's mark was an acorn with a wedge shape under it. The acorn signified the oaks of the Charnwood. The wedge was the symbol of the ridge from which the Farm took its name. Most transactions, however, were simple and between men who knew each other well. Then they spat on their palms and shook hands—the spit and the handshake sealed the deal.

There was a lot of spitting and handshaking at the district markets. There was the market at Melton every month—this was Lucy's favourite. She would sit beside her father, with Toby and John in the big cart behind them with whatever they had to sell, and Roger's horse would pull the load to Melton at a good pace, depending on the weight it pulled. When it was beasts they were selling, it meant a long wait at the sheep and cattle pens for their turn to auction their animals. The pens were erected around the town clock in the Central Square and as a man's turn came to sell he would run up the steps of the clock, his animals would be pointed to, and the bidding would begin. Roger Emmett would stride up the steps, stand tall, lift his staff, and shout his name above the yelling, haggling men below, and the cries of the stall holders and street traders.

"Here I have ten fine lambs," he would say, looking about at the faces of the farmers. Toby and John would prod the lambs with crooks to make them look lively in the pen. "Now, friends—who will bid first for my lambs? Come along now, good stock. Look closer—these lambs must go today. Here is a bargain not to be missed." Simpkin would be sent among the animals and would nip their heels, causing them to break into moaning baas and thus draw more attention. Then, if it was a good day, the farmers would lean over the pen, look close at his animals, and approach Roger. The haggling would start—hours of it. Lucy would sit up on top of a pen, listening to the men arguing and haranguing, watch her father make off to the inn with a client to strike a bargain and often return later with no bargain struck at all. She would smile as she saw her good father looking at men he had known for years with disgust, horror and disbelief.

"No," he would say, as the man made yet another offer, "no—as God is my witness, that would be *giving* the beasts away. Why man, if I sold the ten at that price I'd not get back the value of one ewe." He would walk away shaking his head. "No, that's my last word on it," he'd say, then walk back. "What would you have me do?" he'd say, catching hold of the farmer's sleeve again in case he lost interest. "Give them as gifts?"

Then the men would climb into the pen. There would be a lot of looking at animals' teeth, inspection of feet, prodding at their rears, opening of eyes and peering down into ears for sign of disease. But at long last men who had arrived with voices and lost them about their business would spit on their palms and shake hands. There was the bargain, struck at last.

They would retire again then to the inn, good friends, to gargle a pot of ale. Lucy learnt more at Melton Market that would be of use to her later in life than she realised. She never saw anything worth having that was not fiercely fought for and she herself became a shrewd judge of what was worth having, after sitting on those pens for a few years.

It was at the Melton Markets that Lucy learnt to read her first few words, and it was Fitzmaurice, the quack, who taught her, for his own ends. By the time she was twelve years old, Lucy was showing all the signs of growing into a fine young woman. Her breasts were just beginning to bud under her cotton bodice. In a few short years her body, like Esmeralda's before her, would round and swell outwards into seductive curves. But at twelve, only at the start of her blooming, she still had a look of childishness that was most appealing. The face that shone out from the mass of tousled black curls was bright, intelligent but also innocent.

This was the attraction she held for Fitzmaurice. Innocence was a commodity that could rarely be bought, for once bought, it was gone. He was always on the prowl for new objects of interest to draw people to his stall, and the shrivelled body of the stuffed infant had now ceased to attract.

Lucy was fair game for any new venture, so she took over the quack's stall on those market days when he retired now and again for a quick tipple. "Corn Cutter to the Quality." Those were the first words she learnt to read, after much tuition from the quack, who could read nothing more than his own sign himself. She examined the posters pasted to walls, and the words above the shops, watching out for "quality." She was unsure what a purveyor of quality provisions was, but knew that Miss Parson Brown bought her tea at his shop. And once she puzzled for a long time over the poster announcing the sale of quality East India goods, lingering near it to hear what these might be. There was that word again: "Quality." Lucy would repeat it over and over again. "Corn Cutter to the Quality," she would mutter to herself before she fell asleep at night. "Cutter of Quality Corns," she whispered, with something like awe. She knew a man who had the care of quality feet, and felt herself to be quite a body to be reckoned with.

From the quack she earned her first payment and lost a little of her innocence for it. While he made off, his tooth-pulling and leeching laid aside to sip gin and wrangle at the inn, she would join the other traders, sword and fire swallowers, puppeteers, chair menders, knife grinders and brass-buttoned, loud-mouthed sergeants, who, to the accompaniment of fife and drum, would call on country lads to take the King's Shilling and join the King's Dragoon or some other regiment. Lucy would grit her teeth with reckless determination, climb on a box and, holding a pot of one of the quack's mysterious potions in her hand, raise her young voice above the tumult and call, "Hark ye, hark ye, good people! Here is news for sufferers from all disabilities. Here I have in my hand a strange and wondrous potent unction, from out the east, that may with

57

confidence be applied to any part of the body or extremities of human or beast. The secret of this extraordinary cure for a multiplicity of ailments was whispered to me by a dying Fakir that I by chance happened on during one of my extended journeys to the far corners of the inhabited and uninhabited globe." Here, to gain more attention, she would wave the pot in the air dramatically. "Ladies, do you fear the loss of your complexions? Does age touch you and wrinkle your skin? I can vouch myself for the magical properties of this miraculous panacea. A daily application will restore you to your former youthful glory. Look at me, ladies. I am living proof—I shall be thirty on my next birthday," she would say. By now there would be a flurry of women around her, wanting to believe. Jars would fly hot from her hands.

But it was to the men that Lucy most appealed as the old quack well knew. They would stand close to her, gaping, catching glimpses of her rounding young breasts. "Gentlemen," she would say, in less strident tones, "do you suffer from impotence?" From the back of the crowd would come the inevitable, "Just come to me, my chicken, and I shall show you whether or not I suffer from that complaint." There would be gruff growls of agreement and laughter. Lucy would look quickly around to make sure Roger was out of earshot—or worse, her two big strong brothers, Toby and John, now grown men themselves—to start a fight. When certain she was safe she would continue. "This remarkable unction contains, among other ingredients, an age-old cure for that most distressing of disabilities. Only apply a little smitchin of this to the offending member, and within minutes you will find it revived and alert."

"I've got a member here that's been alert this half hour!" would shout the raucous voice from the back, to the loud cheers of the rest of the men.

No matter how many pots of ointment she sold, her payment was always the same—one penny. This infuriated Lucy. She would stamp her foot at the quack, beat at his hard, bony chest, follow him about, calling after him, "Unfair, unfair! I have today made you a fortune and for my pains I am paid a penny." But nothing she could do would shame the drunken leech into paying her more. As the pennies on market days was all she earnt and the sole source of her earnings she was bound to continue in his employment. "At this rate," she would complain to Roger and her brothers on the long ride home, "I will be one hundred years old before I have a satin bodice, and buried in it I shall be, by heaven." She would look down at the penny that she held in her hand, spit on it, and put it carefully away in a pocket hidden among her petticoats, pull down her pannier skirts and scowl, toss her head. But in a short while she would have regained her cheerful temper.

Simpkin died not long before Lucy's thirteenth birthday. He had lived almost sixteen years, a great and wonderful long life for a dog. He had been retired except for light work some time before he died, his place being taken by a gold and white bitch called Dolly. There was such weeping from Lucy, Roger, Toby and John when Simpkin was laid to rest in the warm earth behind the barn that Margaret enquired if she would walk to York, "to collect his Grace the Archbishop to conduct the service?"

Roger was somewhat consoled for the loss of his old friend by Dolly, who was an affectionate little bitch and quick to learn the vagaries of his temperament. She also delivered four pups, three of which Lucy sold, with some reluctance, adding to the store of coins in her pocket. But she kept the one who needed special care. He was patched black and white, had one blue blind eye, and one seeing brown eye. Roger declared him useless, Margaret complained that he walked sideways and got under her feet, John and Toby laughed and made fun of him, but Lucy Emmett adored him. "Time will tell," she would shout, waving an angry fist at her jeering brothers. "Have no fear, this sharpy knows what he's about, he will learn soon enough." But again she would fail for the thousandth time to train the dog to beg or even to come to heel. The foolish animal would shamble about, bumping into doors and walls, falling into ditches and tripping over anything that might lie in its way.

"As God is my witness," said Roger Emmett, "that same is the only hound I have seen in my life who will miss seeing a horse but will see an ant to trip over well enough."

Lucy had in the end to give up training him and took to carrying him about in her arms in case he would come to grief. The dog was not such a fool—he would lie in her arms, looking at her with his one good eye, secure in the knowledge that he would for the rest of his life be kept in idleness. Lucy called him Mr. Magpie, for his black and white colouring and also because of the country superstition that if you saw a magpie in the morning you must say, "Good morning, Mr. Magpie," then you would have luck all day.

Along with Lucy's thirteenth birthday, as the winter of 1784 turned into the spring of 1785, came the collection of toms and young bloods about the farm that Roger had foreseen, when she was a tiny girl. While the stage rutted up in the Charnwood, antlers locked in clashing combat, snorting and bellowing as hopeful young males fought seasoned old ones, in an attempt to take wives of their own, the very same pageant was enacted on Roger Emmett's doorstep. But at Ridge Farm, the round-faced, hopeful, downy-cheeked lads who came to sniff out Lucy had not only Roger's grizzly old head to lock with but there were his two strapping broad-shouldered sons besides. Roger, Toby and John, with Dolly at their heels, arrived back at Ridge Farm after a day's lambing to see Lucy with Mr. Magpie asleep and useless at her feet. She leant against the gate post, her eyes turned downwards with proper maidenly propriety, but her full red lips turned upwards in a smug and almost satisfied smile, while before her circled yet another hopeful swain, thumbs dug deep into his breeches pockets, all of a swagger to show her what a rough and a tough she could have if she were wise.

"By God!" roared Roger, his face outraged and turned almost black at the sight. "Look at this here, lads," he yelled, reining himself and his sons up sharp. "Hoi!" he bawled, "what's your business, eh, you damned swanker—."

60

The poor boy's ardour was quickly dampened when he saw Farmer Emmett and his sons pounding towards him. He turned on his heels and made off like a comet with tail firing down the track to Ragby whence he had come with such high expectations.

"You must talk to that wench," said Roger Emmett, flinging his fustian coat down on the settle. "Talk to her, woman," he shouted, grabbing for his pipe. "Or, as God is my witness," he said, putting it in his mouth with such vigour he bit the stem clear in two, "she will be tupped, taken and torn up by one of those loiterers." He threw his pipe in the fire.

"I have spoken to her," said Margaret, reaching for another clay pipe and filling it. "She knows what she's about, never fear. It's all innocent pleasure and sport to them, the young. Now stay your frantics, man. You know well how it is, you were such as that youth yourself once."

Roger nodded. "I was," he said, taking the new pipe from her. "That's where my worry springs from."

He sat down to supper that night a very uneasy man. His concern was not only to do with Lucy's continuing a maid. *Here's another wonder to worry over*, he thought to himself now, looking across the table at his two sons. *Why haven't those two whips caught themselves a wench apiece?* Toby was now twenty-three and John twenty-one. Both handsome, well-built and hard workers. Roger scratched his head and looked up at Margaret and Lucy who were feeding the men first with trenchers of mutton and potatoes. Margaret Emmett looked at her husband's frowning face, and sighed. "Oh, eat, in God's name, Mr. Emmett," she said. "I have never in my life known such a one for bothering."

Roger speared a potato with his knife, pushed it into his mouth, then waved it at his sons. "Now, see you here," he said, nodding at the pert Lucy, who was all of a flirt still because of her memories of the suggestions made by the boy at the gate. "We have one here who is drawing looks and more beside, shamed she should be too, for it is too young," he said, glaring at his bright-eyed daughter. "But what ails you two studs, eh? What are you two about? Or is

61

it business so private it may not be spoken of? Dammit. I thought to have seen you both hot and hitched by now, as God is my witness. Lord, I have half the buck rabbits in the county after her," he glared again at Lucy, who smiled coyly back, "as though she were the only female fit to fancy from here to Timbuktu. But I have seen several itchy wenches in Ragby fit to tickle."

"Have you, indeed!" retorted Margaret, putting his ale by his trencher. "You are an old buck indeed to be looking for wenches."

Roger snorted. "Not for me, the God above, for these two," he said. "Though I'm not past the taste for a bit of tickling myself, as you well know," he slipped his arm about her waist, "depending on the humour of the party to be tickled, of course." Margaret smiled at this reference to her spirit. "It cannot always be relied upon to be sweet," said Roger, patting her rear. "A man always has to watch where he puts his finger and how the breeze blows first for fear of having it bitten off."

Margaret snacked him about the ear. "Ten fingers, five on each hand, say whether that's the truth or no," she said, "and look, sir, you have all yours." She lifted his big right hand and waved it before his eyes. "Anyway, leave well alone with the boys. Let's have no more talk of tickling, for they are men now. What they are about is their concern."

Toby looked at his father. "I have been thinking about it," he said at last.

"So have I," said John. Then they continued with their meal.

"Ah, well," said Roger. "Praise be, from thinking of it the next step is to the doing of it, dammit. That is good news indeed."

But as Spring became Summer Roger's hopes to see a quick marriage for his sons dwindled in spite of all the girls who cast come-hither looks at both young men at the fairs and in the village. Neither Toby nor John seemed keen on taking up any offers. When Roger walked into the Hare and Hounds in the evening men would ask him, "Any sign of a coupling for your hearties, then, Roger Emmett?" Roger would shake his head and make some excuse. "You know how it is," he'd laugh. "They be about it all right, but they keep mum. Oh, don't worry, they'll spring it on me some day. There'll be weddings all at once, you wait and see."

But it was obvious to Roger that they needed a prod. "Hoi!" said Roger, prodding both his sons sharply in the ribs one day as the three of them rode through the village on the cart. "Now, there's a couple of likely flaunters for you." He winked towards a group of girls. These "flaunters" populated the village green on summer afternoons and evenings, decked out in sprigged cotton and ribbons and bows, giggling, twiddling with their hair, and wriggling their bottoms, their eyes bright in search of husbands.

"Hey," Roger growled. "See, they look this way, lads." He winked again. "Ho, ho, come up," he shouted to his carthorse, and pulled it to a halt. "There, I'm reined up, get down boys, and be at it, or the best will be taken." He pushed both his sons headlong off the cart, bent down and whispered. "See, the maid in blue and the other, smaller, in yellow?"

Toby and John looked towards the blushing girls. "Catch them," said Roger, "for they are well built and will pay you handsome in rolling. Now it may be they will whine and say nay, straight off. But listen, lads, don't heed them—that means yes in my experience." He lifted the reins and slapped his horse into a trot, turned his head and called back, "To it, you rascals, come home when you will."

"Where are my brothers?" asked Lucy Emmett with a frown, when Roger walked in at the door later, grinning like a cat who has just drunk a cow dry of cream.

"About a man's business, that's where they are, maid," he said, lifting her in the air, kissing her nose and dropping her on the floor. "About what they should be about, I say," he said, wopping Margaret's rump hard with the palm of his hand as she bent over to lift his supper pot from the fire. He threw off his coat, sat at the table, and winked up at his wife. "Two pretty fillies on the green caught their eye," he said. "They were down off the cart and away after them like the raunchy whippets they are." He took a long swig of ale, wiped his mouth with the back of his hand and shook his head. "Dammit, don't wait up for those two, for it will be a wait past morning if you do."

Two short hours later the door of Ridge Farm opened and Toby and John walked in. Roger watched them as they sat down at the table. "Hey, here's a quick business," said Roger, standing and putting his back to the fire. "Did you not catch them?"

Toby smiled at John; John grinned at Toby. "We caught them, sure enough," said Toby, sitting waiting for his supper. Lucy ran to serve her brothers. Roger nodded, pleased but still puzzled. Perhaps ways had changed since he was a young man. "What is it nowadays?" he asked, "courting only on Sundays?"

There was a pause while the boys tucked into their food. Roger felt that another prod might be in order. "Well, what was it? So quick agreed? Is the date set then, all at once?" He leant eagerly towards them, clay pipe jabbing the air.

John looked at Toby. "Mine was nothing of note when you got down to it, was yours?" he asked.

Toby shook his blond head, his mouth full of swede. "No," he replied, "the trip was not worth it, to tell true, for when I got to the nut of her it was not as sweet as had been promised."

Lucy strode up to Toby and John, tossing her mane of black curls. "Why search for nuts in foreign parts," she said, setting down their ale before them, "when there are nuts to be picked at home?"

Roger was shocked by this forward display. "Hey, Miss," he said, "speak when you are of an age to understand what you speak of. Nuts, indeed!"

Lucy tossed her head again. "Fiddle faddle," she said. "The boys are right. Those wenches are decked out well enough, but pull the feathers off 'em, and beneath you find scrawny sparrows. Wait, I say, till I have my satin bodice, then the world will see a different sight. What is promised is what will be found, I warrant you, or my name's not Lucy Emmett." She flounced off, tossing her head and swinging her hips like a very "flaunter." Toby and John watched her, and blushing red as poppy heads. Margaret Emmett was quick to see her sons blush, but Roger was aghast.

"Hey, Miss," he bellowed, "let us see less of that sort of parade here. You have years yet before you take to waggling." He looked at Margaret, his eyes wide with disbelief. "This is a fine thing," he said. "This is how things swing here, is it, while I am about my work."

The following evening Roger made off to the Hare and Hounds with John and Toby.

"Well, heaven be praised for that," said Margaret, shutting the door behind them. "Here's peace for me at last." She sat down in the inglenook with her quilting and set about sewing another patch. All was quiet, just as Margaret Emmett liked it. Lucy was lying on the floor before the fire, grooming Mr. Magpie. He lay flat out and fast asleep while Lucy searched behind his floppy ears for fleas. Margaret Emmett watched her, and shuddered. "Oh, the Lord," she said, "how you abide that hound and its crawlies beats me. Loathsome thing!" Mr. Magpie sighed and turned on his back, looked sadly at Lucy with his one good eye.

"There, now," she said to Margaret, "he heard. Have you no care for his feelings?" She kissed the dog's nose. "I will have no one speak ill of you. Have no fear, you are my treasure, are you not?"

Margaret Emmett laughed and shook her head. "What will you do when you marry?" she asked. "No man will abide that thing near him, I swear!"

"I shall have no care for a man who has no care for my dog," said Lucy. "I tell you, Madam, that would be a pretty fine man who would turn such as this helpless soul away." She turned Mr. Magpie over again and stroked him.

Margaret laid aside her quilting and said, "Come here, close to me, Lucy Emmett." She patted her knee, Lucy scrawled across the floor and sat at the mother's feet, her head on her lap. Margaret stroked her hair, lifting the great bunches of black, crisp curls, feeling the same glorious abundance that had graced Esmeralda's beautiful head.

She sighed. "There are things we should speak of, Lucy," she said. "Time moves on for us all—we grow older and, we hope, wiser." She turned Lucy to face her and looked down in the girl's eyes. There, staring back at her, were the eyes of her husband. She had never told Roger what she suspected, but it had become clear to Margaret Emmett as Lucy grew that there was Emmett blood in the child. In spite of the dark gypsy looks there were those bright blue eyes and the same tilt of stubbornness to the chin so typical of Roger and her two sons.

"Now," said Margaret, at last, "we must talk as women together." Lucy groaned. "Aha, yes we must. I know we have talked before, but it is the way with these things that they keep coming about again to be talked of." She took the girl's hand. "Now—this casting your eyes about for a buck...Oh ho," she said, as Lucy was about to deny it, "don't say the bucks only cast the eyes and you are all innocence. I've seen you. There is such a thing as a look that travels a mile, I can tell you, and speaks a thousand words at a glance." She laughed. "Oh, the bucks come a-chasing, but 'tis the doe that does the calling, I know." She chuckled. "But there comes a time, sweetheart, when care must come. You know I am not the mother that was given you by Nature, but there is the saying 'She who rears is she who cares,' so until such a time as you are of an age to care for yourself, listen hard to me. There is no more sleeping in the loft with Toby and John."

Lucy jumped up, her face outraged. "Oh, why, Madam? Why so?"

Margaret looked sharply at Lucy and nodded. "I *thought* that's the way the wind blew. I saw it straight off. Well, Miss, because I say so, that is why."

Lucy stamped her foot.

"It is here in Ridge Farm where I can see you nights. For you, Miss, sniffle and stamp," said Margaret Emmett, "I want no fights between those buffs of boys, for that's the way it will go."

Lucy opened her mouth to protest, but Margaret said, "That's the last word," and Lucy shut her mouth.

Later that night, as Lucy slept on a mattress in the

inglenook with Mr. Magpie, and Toby and John slept in the warm hay in the loft, Margaret Emmett turned to her husband at her side and whispered, "Mr. Emmett, you must promise not to shout if I tell you something."

Roger cocked his ear. "What's that?" he asked gruffly, "what's to be told at this time of night? Lord, women! They have all day and they must mutter to a man in bed."

Margaret smiled. "I can tell you why those sons have not taken a wench to marry."

Roger turned over, caught his wife in his strong arms, squeezing the breath out of her. "Well—come along, woman, I'm here—hot and handy for you. Tell quick or I shall be to business," he said, slipping his hands under her shift. "Oh, my," he groaned, "here's a time to choose for talking. Here am I at attention for you," he murmured, biting her throat, then, heaving himself on top of her he lifted his shirt and prepared to mount.

Margaret Emmett smiled up at him and sighed. "Shall I say, or will it keep?" she murmured, wriggling and opening her legs to accommodate him.

"Oh say," groaned Roger Emmett, preparing to enjoy his wife's soft hospitality.

"'Tis Lucy they desire," said Margaret, feeling the tip at attention touching her deep inside.

"Ho!" yelled Roger Emmett, ascending almost to the ceiling with shock, the tip now weak and limp, no longer at attention, although the rest of him was.

"Hush," said Margaret, sitting up quickly and covering his gaping mouth with her hand. "You'll wake the girl."

Roger had been just about to shout again, but his voice died in his throat. He sat as still as a marble monument. In his head he heard the rattle of all his skeletons as they danced out of his cupboard. He covered his face with his hands and pressed hard on his throbbing temples.

Margaret shook her head and lay down. She knew the reason for his panic, but he would not say and she would not ask. *If he will not tell me and come clean with it after all these years*, she thought, *then the silly man deserves to suffer*. But after a little while her heart softened and she patted his cold behind. "I have spoken to the wench," she whispered, just before falling asleep, "now you do the man's part and see to your horny studs."

"God help me," groaned Roger Emmett. "You no sooner are done with one thing than another comes leaping at your throat, dammit."

Lucy Emmett sat up and wiped her sleepy blue eyes. The sun was shining in at the windows and she could see the sky outside was as blue as the eyes that looked on it. Her parents still slept. Lucy tiptoed softly across the room so that she would not wake them, opened the big oak door, slipped quickly out into the fresh morning and closed it quietly behind her. She skipped across the yard, lifting up her petticoats, ran in through the door of the stable past the weary old carthorse, shinnied up the ladder and crawled through the loose golden hay in search of her brothers. They lay side by side, strong, brown chests bared to the sun gleaming on their skin through the gaps in the thatch. She was between them in an instant, snuggling close to them, sniffing at their hay-smelling hair. She pulled the still sleeping John's arms around her waist and curled herself up in the curve of Toby's body. "Oh," she whispered, wriggling with pleasure.

Toby yawned, then opened his eyes and found himself looking straight into the wide, blue, dark-lashed eyes of his sister. He gasped. "Ssh," said Lucy, putting her finger to his lips, "or we shall have visitors." She kissed him on the chin and snuggled closer.

"I thought you were not to come here again," Toby whispered.

"At night," said Lucy, "naught was said about the mornings." She giggled. "They will not know. They sleep, both of them." She poked John in the chest. "Wake, you frowsty," she said. He woke, startled, then grinned.

"What's this, Miss?" he asked.

Lucy laughed. "Ssh—don't shout," she said, kissing him, too, and brushing her cheek against his bristly chin.

John caught her quickly around the waist and rolled her under him in the hay. "Oh, great to-do's," he said, "here's

68

Lucy Emmett, back again. What do you want Miss—cut and come again?" he said, pressing her down in the hay and lying flat on top of her so that she was powerless to move.

Lucy pouted. "Now you have me flattened—how am I to speak if I am squashed like a shrove pancake?" John grinned down at her and shook his red-gold head. "Push me off then if you will. Eh? Or are you too weakly now, uh?" He rattled the pennies in her pocket. "Here's loot for a satin bodice, by God," he said. "Let's have it from her and make off for a spree!"

Lucy's eyes widened with temper. "Hold off," she snapped, "Touch the pocket and the hens shall have your eyes."

John laughed and laughed long. "Mincey, mincey," he said, teasing and tickling her, until she shrieked. "Pennies a-plenty here for the taking—I'm at them." He wrestled with the struggling Lucy who was determined to hang on to her pennies whatever else she might lose.

"Ah, bully boy," snorted Lucy, "take a poor maid's pennies—that's about the size of it," she yelled, biting his hands.

Toby took hold of his brother's arm. "Aye, hey, come off," he said. Things were coming too close to what he desired himself. "Come off, leave her. She is no match for you."

John shook himself free of his brother's hand. He jingled Lucy's pennies. "I have the pocket," he cried. "Now I shall have the petticoats beside."

Toby, seeing his sister's tail coming into view, grabbed his brother around the neck with an arm like a vice, for he was much the stronger, and hauled him off. "Now," said Toby, throwing his brother down, "do as I say—hold off."

John looked up at his brother whose eyes were red with anger. "What's this pulling off?" he yelled, his own eyes flashing. Lucy dragged at her clothes and made to get up. "Lie still!" said John.

"Get up!" commanded Toby.

"Lie still," said John.

Lucy wrapped her arms about herself and crossed her

legs about her pennies. The two young fellows glared at one another, snorting like young reckless bulls, then John ran at his brother and butted him sharp in the belly with his head.

"Damn!" shouted Toby. He caught John by the scruff of the neck, hurled him across the loft, and lifted Lucy into his arms.

"Right, swine!" snarled John, "put that wench down and walk with me to the yard. Fists up, that's what I say."

Toby put Lucy down. "With pleasure," he growled, "for I'll take you and pummel you till your nose darts through the back of your head." Then he spat clear across John's feet.

"That's it," said John, looking grim. "That's done it. March, friend. Go to it, for my blood is up well and true now."

Lucy had seen them both fight at the fairs for payment, but this was a different matter. Here was something to worry at—glaring, and snorting and huffing and hitching of breeches and a shrugging of broad shoulders. She peeped out from behind Toby's back and saw to her horror John, knees bent, advancing on Toby with a bright, sharp-edged, reaping hook glinting in his hand.

"Oh, mercy," wailed Lucy. She darted from behind Toby, reached the top of the ladder, shinnied down it, badly grazing her knees on the downwards journey, ran through the stable door, yelling "Help!" across the farmyard. "Help. Help! Help. . . . Murder . . . Death and destruction come to us all at once." She threw wide the door, flung back the curtain, jumped astride the astonished Roger, gripped one of his big ears in each of her hands, thumped his head up and down on the mattress with furious urgency and shrieked breathlessly, "Bust me. Will you to it now, or the brothers' giblets will fly!"

Giblets did fly. Lucy's. After racing to the loft and separating his two snarling sons, Roger hitched the bawling Lucy over his shoulder, marched into the barn, slammed the door, threw the bolt, hurled her—rump to the air, head to the ground—over his broad knee, sending her pennies tinkling from her, and thwacked her round

70

rear so hard her hair stood on end. "Here's a stroke for every year of your life, so hold hard, there's a dozen more to come."

Lucy wailed and yelled, weeping very rivers of hot tears onto the straw-covered floor. "Oh, you, monster, brute, you—now I have the truth of it," she sobbed. "Now I find what you are at last, now I know your ways, Mr. Smiles Kindly at Strangers but Beats his Daughter," she wept, as he set her on her feet again, both her hands held to her smarting rear. "See," she said, wiping her eyes and pointing to the straw on the floor. "See—now all my pennies have rolled away and I shall never find them again. Now I shall have no satin bodice in my life—for your cruelty. But have no fear, sir, the world will hear of this injustice." She burst out again into a fury of loud sobbing, walked out the barn door, still rubbing her backside, howling like a hurt cat, into the farmyard, where an anxious Margaret, John and Toby waited to see the result of Roger's firm hand that had been so long coming.

Lucy stamped her foot and glared at them. "Now are you happy?" she shouted. "Happy to see me beaten? And with no pennies?" She threw herself face down on the hard earth of the farmyard, beat her fist on the ground, and shouted in the voice reserved for selling ointment at Melton Fair.

"Beaten, Good Lord. Beaten for nothing. For as God is my witness, I am innocent of all things." Then she fell to little hiccoughing sobs.

"Aye," said Roger Emmett, coming out into the sunshine, spitting on his sore right hand, and shutting the barn door behind him. "Innocent. So cried Eve, when she followed Adam from the Garden of Eden." He watched her stand up and wipe her eyes on the corner of her grubby petticoats. She sniffed, then brushed the tumble of black curls from her forehead. Her head was down. Her shoulders hunched. Although he couldn't see her face, he knew her lower lip trembled.

Margaret, John and Toby had turned away. None of them could bear to see Lucy's spirit so crushed. Roger felt sorry, hurt himself. He walked across to her. She looked so

71

small, so woebegone. Standing before her, he put his strong hands on her shoulders. Turning her towards him, he looked down at the tousled head and sighed.

"Well, Lucy Emmett. I never thought to see this day dawn," he whispered. Lucy tried to turn away from him. But he tilted her chin with his forefinger, forcing her to look up at him. "What have you to say?" he asked gently.

Lucy felt her heart quicken. She looked up. Blue eyes met blue eyes. At an instant Lucy and Roger were again locked in combat. Roger couldn't believe it. The girl's eyes were defiant, her chin jutted, she was not contrite. She pulled away from him, her hands clenched tight into fists. Her eyes flashed.

"Well. What would you have me say?" she shouted.

Roger Emmett stamped his foot so hard he almost displaced the bones of his spine from his seat clear to the nape of his neck. "Dammit!" he yelled. "Are you not repentant, wench? Do I have to take you and whack you again?" he bawled. "Do I? Is that what I must do to get an apology?"

Now it was Lucy's turn to stamp. "You may beat me ten times over," she hissed. "Nay, sir, one hundred times, you may beat me. But first I demand to know why I was beaten at all?"

Roger's mouth fell open. He was furious. The veins stood out on his forehead. He felt all the blood in his body rush up to his scalp. "Why you were beaten at all?" he asked hoarsely, his voice breaking with rage and amazement. He clasped his hands behind his back and proceeded to march up and down before Margaret, Toby and John, who stood by, bemused spectators.

"The Lord's Wounds! Do you hear that, you lot of gogglers?" he yelled at them. "What do ye say to that, then, wife? Eh? Did you ever hear the like of that, then?" He glared at Margaret. She lowered her eyes, trying hard not to smile.

"Ssh," she hissed at her sons who by now were convulsed with laughter at the dramatics.

Roger Emmett was doing a war dance of sorts. "I get no

answer from the wife then," shouted Roger. "Hear me, woman! Across the country there are girls such as this one here—he pointed at the defiant Lucy—"who go running about in a dutiful fashion, doing as they are bid, with not a whit of questioning. But does that same apply here? No, it does not. Here the wench questions the father. Yes, here at Ridge Farm things have swung in a different manner, by God! Here the wench tilts at the master of the house."

There was silence. Except for the birds' song and other country sounds. Also, the stifled laughter from Margaret and her two sons. Margaret peeped through her fingers, and watched her husband pace up and down on one side of the yard and Lucy pacing up and down opposite him.

Then the girl stopped and turned on her father. "Well?" she persisted. "Well, is there to be no answer for me then, sir? I am not to be told why I was beaten. Aye," she sneered, "I thought that would be the way of it. Damn me."

Roger swung round. "That's enough of the cursing, by God!" Marching across to her and catching hold of her arm, he glared down at the angry little face, that glared back up at him. *Bold and defiant still*, he thought.

"Right ho, Miss," growled Roger. "Now then. You ask for a reason. Right. What, pray, Miss Fancy Flounce, were you told by your mother regarding sleeping alongside those boys in the loft?"

Lucy glanced quickly over to Toby and John who were both studying their boots. Then she looked back at Roger. He grinned and nodded. "Ah. Yes. 'Tis as I thought. That slipped your mind, did it? Along with the memory of how to be a dutiful child." He let go of her arm. "So, Miss. There's the reason for the beating," he said triumphantly, wagging his finger under the tip of her nose.

Lucy placed her hands on her hips, and narrowed her eyes. "Ah, but Sir," she said equally triumphantly. "I obeyed you to the letter. For I slept beside the hearth all night. 'Twas only the morning coming that took me to the hayloft. I do not remember you forbidding me to say good morning to my brothers." She smiled at him, the picture of

73

innocence. "For if you did forbid that, well, I am at a loss, I swear. For I cannot remember your doing so. Upon my life, and my dog's, that's the truth."

Roger was speechless. He shook his head slowly. "Well," he said, after some time. "That's it, I'm done for. Stumped. There's no dealing with the waywardness of it. It's too far gone in cussedness. As God is my witness, I'm done with it. The youth of today is beyond my understanding. The Lord knows how this poor world will continue with the likes of this wench in it. There is no order, no respect left. Nor obedience." He strode over to his wife. "I am giving up," he said solemnly. "No man could remain in command with this lot about him," he continued, his eye travelling to Lucy, then to John, then to Toby. "Oh," he groaned, "God help our country should it look to these for service."

Margaret smiled and patted his hand. "Come," she whispered. "Leave well alone." She looked across at Lucy who stood, with ramrod straight back, legs apart, her arms folded across the front of her bodice, ready for another bout with her father.

"You know she will not apologise," said Margaret to her husband. "The girl's pride is sore hurt. She knows well enough she is in the wrong. But Mr. Emmett, I tell you, as I live and breathe, her temper is much the same as your own. Hot as hell, but quick to fall as it is to rise. She will come with apologies when she is ready."

Roger turned and looked at Lucy who was now marching purposefully towards the barn. "Where are you off to now, miss?" he yelled.

Lucy swung round and fixed him with a hard stare. "I'm off for my pennies," she shouted. "I'm not so easily parted from them, upon my honour." She disappeared into the barn, slamming the door behind her.

Roger shook his fist after her. "Well. If she's not the very devil," he said. But there was a hint of pride in his voice.

Lucy spent the rest of the day hunting for her lost treasure. She combed through the hay on the barn floor, until she was as sure as she could be that every precious coin was found and deposited back in her pocket. It was

74

late in the day when she returned to the farmhouse, hot cheeked and grubby.

Roger was warming his toes by the fire. Margaret was busy cutting up vegetables for the evening meal. Toby and John were discussing the crops they should sow, which fields should be tilled, which should remain fallow. None of them looked up.

Lucy slipped in quietly and shut the door. Then she tiptoed over to where Mr. Magpie was asleep in the Inglenook and sat beside him. She took him into her lap and tickled his fat belly. The dog lolled against her arm, his eyes tight shut in an ecstasy of sensuality.

Roger watched and smiled, then he yawned and reached for a clay pipe. Lucy was at his side straight away with a lighted taper to set to Roger's tobacco.

"Thanks," he murmured, puffing contentedly at the glowing bowlful.

Lucy blew out the flame and returned the taper to the mantle. She glanced at Roger from the corner of her eye. He was grinning at her. She felt her heart melt like candle wax. She smiled back, her eyes filling with tears. Then she bent her head and whispered in his ear, "Mr. Emmett?"

Roger inclined his head closer to her lips. "Mm, then. What is it? Speak up," he said gruffly. He felt her slip her arm about his neck, her soft cheek against his rough one. He waited.

"I am sorry," she whispered. Roger was moved. He knew what it cost Lucy to apologise. He felt tears prick his eyes and he coughed.

"Aye. Well, let's say no more about it," he said, patting her hand.

Almost before he could draw a breath, she had thrown her arms around his neck and was sitting on his knee, weeping so hard he felt sure she would never stop.

"Oh, I am sorry I am such a trial to you," she sobbed. "You took me from nowhere and reared me as your own, but I am nothing but a misery to you, a rod to your good back. Oh God help me to grow from these hot ways."

Roger hushed her, patting her quivering shoulders, and smiled across at Margaret. "Oh, come, come, Lucy

Emmett. I wouldn't have you other than you are, that you know well enough," he murmured. "And as for the hot ways, spirit is not a thing to be grown out of. The best have it and need it in this harsh world, God knows."

Margaret crossed the room and kissed the weeping Lucy. "There, there. All is forgiven and forgotten now," she said, trying to comfort the girl. "We all love you well, that you must know."

But Lucy sobbed on, "Oh, how could you love a thing as forward as I?" she cried.

Margaret laughed, brushing the tears from the girl's cheeks. "Why, sweetheart," she said, "do you not think that we have had more joy and fun from having you than we ever would have had without you? As for your coming from nowhere, why, I believe the good Lord himself sent you to comfort me for the loss of my own girl child and a comfort you have been. Now, that's crying enough or you'll have the whole house full of salt water. For your brothers look like blubbing and both your father and I are not far from it." She wiped her eyes on her sleeve. "There, that's better," she said, seeing that Lucy was trying to smile. "Think on the satin bodice. For when you are of an age to wear it, I have something for you to wear with it that will become you very well." She kissed Lucy, and thought of Esmeralda's gold earrings, put away so carefully in her linen chest all those years ago.

How like the mother she's growing, Margaret thought. *Such strange gypsy looks. But with such blue, blue eyes.*

Roger drew Lucy close to him, and rubbed his nose in her sweet hay-smelling hair. He too was thinking of Esmeralda. With pity, but with gratitude too, for giving him such a delightful daughter. "Time enough yet for my girl to grow to a woman," he said. "And to wear satin bodices. No matter when the time comes, I tell you, 'twill be too soon for me."

Lucy left his knee and sat on the floor at his feet, her back resting against her father's knees, her face lit by the warm glow of the logs burning in the fireplace. She shut her eyes, listening to Roger drawing contentedly on his pipe. She could hear Margaret working away at her

76

cooking. John and Toby's voices reaching her, seemed to come from a great distance. She was tired. But at peace with the family again and it pleased her not be at odds with the people she loved. She thought of her natural mother, tried to visualise her. Margaret had told her of how she was born. Told her that her mother had been beautiful but poor.

She remembered the beggar women she had seen on the country roads, thin, half-dead creatures, their hands always outstretched for alms. She shivered. It was bad to be poor. *Was my mother a beggar woman?* she asked herself. She had seen such a woman once, beside the road one day, suckling a dying infant at her empty breast. That was before she had ever earned a penny, or she would have given every coin she possessed to see the mother and child plump and well fed. She opened her eyes and looked across at Margaret. *She is aged early by hard work*, Lucy thought. Then she sighed. *We are poor*, she thought. *But yet, not so poor as the beggars.*

"Oh, anyway," she said out loud after a time. "The satin bodice appeals less now."

Roger raised his eyebrows. "What has gone amiss?" he asked. "We have heard nothing but talk of satin bodices for a good twelve months together." He laughed and ruffled her hair.

Lucy stood up. She put both her hands behind her back, and her back to the fire. She nodded thoughtfully, in a very good imitation of Roger when he had a lot on his mind.

"Satin bodices are pretty enough things," she said. "But I have been thinking that it is not a wise way to spend hard-earned money." She was frowning now. Looking about the farmhouse, she looked at her brothers and thought of their labours. How they worked hard from dawn until dusk. Of her father, his back bent, his hands callused by hard work. Of how he complained in the winter when the rheumatism hurt his bones, though more often than not he made light of it.

"No," she said. "There is no return for a satin bodice. For bust me, the very instant you part with the money, what have you? A useless frippery." She tossed her great fall of ebony curls with businesslike determination. "The thing to have is property, and livestock," she said.

Roger's eyes widened. Margaret, Toby and John were astonished.

"Property and livestock?" Roger said incredulously. "What's a wench such as you talking of such things for, dammit? Buy the satin bodice. Catch a farmer who owns his farm and is not a tenant like me. Marry him, and you shall have all the property and livestock you desire."

Lucy shook her head. "Ah, no," she said. "For that would not be truly mine. It would be my husband's." She knelt at his feet. "I would have some of my own. So that I might do as I please with my own chattels. Without having to ask my husband's leave. I have thought, sir," she went on "to buy a ewe with my pennies. One small ewe only to start with. If I may borrow from you a ram to tup her, then soon, by my reckoning, I shall have a flock."

There was much hilarity at her plan. Toby and John almost fell off their seats, they laughed so long and hard.

"There, Roger Emmett," said Margaret. "Stand by with the ram. For this wench is to be a farmer."

"Oh, the heavens!" said Roger, grinning wide. "Here's trouble for me. Stick to the satin bodice, Miss, or you will put me on the parish. I would not care to compete with you at the sheep pens. For I know well which of us would leave Melton market the richer." He winked at Margaret and tapped Lucy's head with the stem of his pipe. "Here's a wench could sell a pair of boots to a fellow with no feet," he said.

Lucy sat on his knee. "What if I were to breed the best sheep in the country, Sir, and made us all a fortune. What if I bought you a farm of your own, made gentlemen of you and my brothers? Why, I can just see my mother sailing about decked over like the Queen of the May in jewels and silks. We should all be rich, by God. Why, we should have satin bodices to put on the sheep each morning and throw away each night. What do you say to that?" she asked Roger.

Roger nodded. "Well 'twould not be such a terrible thing. I dare say I'd get used to it, given time. No more dues to the Squire, did you say?" Lucy was beside herself with excitement.

"You follow me exactly," she said. "No more dues to Squire Billy, and land of your own, sir, as far as the eye can see." Roger leaned back in his chair, stretched out his legs and puffed away at his pipe.

"Ah, well," he said. "There's all my worries solved for me, wife. All I have to do now is remain lolling in this fashion and wait for the maid here to make me a fortune." He looked into Lucy's eyes, his own twinkling with amusement. "How long before I am hob-nobbing with the King?" he asked.

Lucy jumped off his knee, and ran across to Margaret. She threw both her arms around her waist.

"He thinks I'm jesting," she said. "But you know I mean to make it all come true. Don't you?"

Margaret nodded. "We all know that you want to make it come true with all your heart," she said. "But, there's enough dreaming for one day. There's men here to feed, cattle and fowl to be seen to and you must work by me. So roll up the sleeves, let's to it now. Tuck all the dreams back in that little head."

CHAPTER III

What's To Be Done with Lucy Emmett?

In which a solution to the above question is found satisfactory to everyone but Lucy.

It was during the week immediately following Lucy's sixteenth birthday that Margaret Emmett fell ill. At first it seemed nothing to worry Roger, and the rest of the family. It began as a slight discomfort, a little weariness, and Margaret rarely complained. Even when she had to stop in her work and sit for a moment, her eyes clouded with pain, she would laugh off Lucy's concern.

"'Tis nothing, girl. Old age catches at me, that's all." Then she would bend her back again to her tasks.

Before Christmas came, though, she was forced to take to her bed. She lay under a blanket on a straw mattress in the inglenook.

Lucy tended her by day and night, keeping the fire well supplied with logs from the woodpile, and trying to tempt her mother with food. But Mistress Emmett could not eat. Christmas came and went with no celebration, for by then the worst was clear. Her plumpness was gone, her skin hung loose over jutting bones. Her complexion, once rosy and country fresh, had faded to a grey pallor. Before the

New Year, she was so weak she could not raise her head to take even the merest sip of water.

Lucy did her best to cheer the menfolk, but all hearts at Ridge Farm were heavy. There was no physician in Ragby, so Roger took the horse to Melton and fetched one. It took almost four hours, through driving rain and a screaming wind to reach him, and the ride back took longer. The physician had been reluctant to return with him. Roger was obviously only a poor tenant farmer and the doctor wasn't sure he would get his fee.

His diagnosis when he had examined Margaret was vague. "Something attacks her that is in its nature a wasting disease," he muttered. Then he covered her again, and looked around him with distaste. "I would suggest as treatment alternate hot and cold baths. But this place is so riddled with drafts that she would take cold at once. I suppose you could not carry her to a Spa to take waters?"

Roger lowered his eyes. The physician sighed.

"Well, then we are left only with laudanum for the extreme pain and have you some beef?"

Roger shook his head. The only meat left was a litte fat salt bacon. The physician sighed again. He wondered sometimes how these people survived to any age at all.

"If you could come by some beef," he continued, "I would suggest that it is boiled and rendered to an extract, then fed to her several times a day."

Lucy watched Roger pay him with the last of his money. He had paid his half year's rent to the squire at Christmas time. Now he would be left with nothing and they still had to purchase laudanum. She knelt down at Margaret's side and laid a hand on her brow. It was damp, and beaded with perspiration, though the rest of her body was ice cold. Her mother opened her eyes and tried to smile.

"Tell that good man not to waste further money on the physician," she whispered. "It is useless. He cannot help me."

Lucy shook her head, trying hard to hold back her tears. "Don't say so," she said. "We will have him visit often now. We will follow his instructions and in a short while you will be well again."

Margaret took Lucy's hand, "Lucy Emmett," she said softly. "I am content to put myself in the arms of the Almighty. I have lived longer, and in better health than I ever hoped to. Now you must tell your father to rest himself and cease fighting what is inevitable." Then she shut her eyes, and fell once again into the blessed unconsciousness that took her increasingly.

The physician had donned his cloak and hat, picked up his apothecary's box and was about to leave again for the journey to Melton.

Lucy took hold of his arm. "I have money to buy laudanum," she said. "And more will be found if you will visit again."

He frowned at her, noting her anxious face. There were dark shadows from lack of sleep beneath the beautiful blue eyes. He took a small purple glass bottle of laudanum from his box and handed it to her. "I cannot visit again this week."

Lucy's hand tightened on his arm. "But what of my mother?" she asked.

"If the weather changes, then I will endeavour to make the journey," he replied. "But in truth, child, the roads are rutted and miry and I fear my horse will fall lame if I ride him over such ground. You must administer the drug when the pain becomes insupportable." He glanced across at Margaret. "If she dies before I call again, send word to me, will you?" He opened the door, then held out his hand for payment. Lucy handed over all but two of her pennies and opened the door for him. He tied his cloak tight around his throat, to keep out the wind, and left.

Toby and John sat disconsolately at the table. Roger sat silent opposite them. Apart from Margaret's heavy breathing and the crackle of the fire, there was no sound. Lucy stood by the door and looked across at the three men, so sunk in misery.

"There must be something to be done," she appealed. "Surely there is something that can be done for her. We are not helpless in this, are we?"

Roger stood and walked slowly to the inglenook. He looked down at his wife, and slammed his fist into the wall so hard Lucy heard his knuckles crack.

"I must stand and watch my good woman die through lack of funds," he groaned. "Because we are poor there is no help for us. We are blown along, like chaff before the wind."

Margaret lived one day longer. On the second day of that New Year a grave was dug for her, in the heavy dark clay of Ragby Churchyard.

It was a sad, hard day for the Emmetts. For Lucy, who was entering the seventeenth year of her life, it seemed the last day of her childhood. The sky above was heavy with lowering rain clouds. The wind from the north was keen, touching the bones of the living with chill, harsh fingers. Crows and rooks, leaving the sheltering churchyard elms, wheeled above the heads of the little group of mourners.

Lucy stood close by her father and brothers beside the grave. Her head was covered by a black woolen shawl, her bare feet cold against the new-dug damp earth. She watched as Margaret's coffin was lowered into the yawning hole, to lie forever beside the body of her infant daughter.

She was numb with grief, beyond tears. Glancing at Roger, she saw his weather-beaten face a still, grim mask, his blue eyes dulled with loss. He took up a handful of clay and threw it upon the coffin, just before more clay from the sexton's shovel covered it completely.

"I heard a voice from heaven say unto me, 'From henceforth blessed are the dead which die in the Lord.'" The Parson's voice joined the bleak cawing of the black torn-winged birds circling above. "'Even so said the Spirit for they rest from their labours.'"

Lucy felt Roger's hand grasp hers. Then at last, scalding hot tears raced down her frozen cheeks. "Amen," she whispered.

Grief sometimes travels hand in hand with joy. Winter passed into snowdrop time. With the appearance of the tiny white bells, Lucy felt some of her despondency leave her. Each day the sun grew warmer and stayed longer. It smiled on the soil and coaxed forth the daffodils and primroses, flooding the meadows, woodland and forest with a glory of nodding yellow gold. The yellow turned to

84

hazy mists of bluebells that met the bluer skies. Birds mated and nested, it was Maytime and Lucy's heart sang with the birds. Here again was life quickening about her, echoing the surge of her spirits. Every day that dawned wiped the sadness from her soul.

It was a shock when Roger married again in June. His bride was a woman almost twenty years younger than he. They courted for six weeks only, then she was brought to Ridge Farm as the new mistress.

Elizabeth Thomas was attractive, but quick tempered. Lucy did not begrudge her father his happiness. There was nothing better she could have wished for him, but Elizabeth's coming brought many trials to her and her brothers. Roger so doted on his new bride that he had little time for anything or anyone else. Elizabeth demanded his full attention.

For Toby and John it became a simple matter to keep out of the way. They worked hard, returning to the house only to eat, before retiring to the hayloft to sleep. But Lucy was with her new stepmother all day, and before long they were arguing over the housework and the cooking. Each day when Roger walked in at the door there were complaints from Elizabeth about Lucy's conduct. Roger found himself with two strong-willed, uncompromising females under his roof. Lucy's dislike for Elizabeth grew to hatred while Elizabeth's jealousy developed into a constant shrewish nagging.

It was a July day. Ridge Farm basked in a torrid quivering heat. All around, the crops ripened in the fields. The air was still and heavy with the rich scents of summer. Inside the cool farm kitchen Elizabeth was dozing in a chair by the open door. Mr. Magpie, who had been banned from the house, was sleeping at a distance from her, with one eye open ready to escape her foot should she kick out at him. Roger had made off to Melton with Toby and John to buy some sheep.

Lucy had remained behind for a reason. As soon as her father had departed, and her stepmother's eyes had closed, she had raced off across the farmyard, and climbed the wooden ladder to the hayloft. She was wild with excitement for she had an assignation with one of the village boys—Barney Cowper, the wheelwright's apprentice—her first real assignation. Her heart was beating fit to burst.

In anticipation she had washed herself in cool water from the well, and tied a scarlet ribbon through her dark curls. *In anticipation of what?* she asked herself. Arriving in the hayloft, she found a piece of broken looking-glass she kept hidden on a beam, lay on her back and studied her blurred reflection. She thought herself very grand from the neck up, but wished her gown had been less torn and stained, and that she had a pair of slippers instead of her worn boots. She took them off and hid them under the hay; her bare feet, she decided, were quite pretty.

"I am well looking," she whispered to herself. "But I am a bastard, not baptised, I have no property, I am a wench almost seventeen years old and here I am greeting my first comer with not a thing to my name nor yet a gown upon me that one would call decent." But she smiled to herself, too, for she doubted Barney Cowper cared about those things. She put down the piece of glass, sat up and unlacing her bodice she looked down at her pert apple breasts, touching each nipple with her finger, causing them to rise and harden at the touch, and smiled a smug secret smile. She heard a movement in the stable below, and laced herself quickly. Jumping to her feet, she ran to the top of the ladder, knelt and looked down at Barney who looked up at her, his face widening into a grin.

He was a handsome youth of eighteen, with fair curling sun-kissed hair, a fine brown complexion, and just the beginnings of a downy beard. He was broad-shouldered and tall. Lucy thought him the best-looking boy she had ever seen apart from Toby and John. This opinion had often been confirmed by the jealous stares of other girls who watched them exchange smiles after church on Sundays.

She put her finger to her lips. "Be very silent, Barney Cowper," she hissed. "My father's new wife sleeps. But by God, I tell you, she has the ears of a very sharp vixen when she cares to prick them in my direction."

Barney nodded. Then, while he climbed the ladder, Lucy ran back to where she had been seated, ferreted about in the hay until she found at last her piece of looking-glass, held it before her for a second to ensure that her face did not betray the expectant thrill she felt welling up inside her. Then quickly replaced the glass on the beam. Seating herself, she arranged her skirts becomingly around her. Averting her eyes, being sure she looked suitably demure and casual, she waited to greet her suitor.

Barney arrived on the hay beside her, not a whit breathless after his climb. He sat close, and although they did not touch, Lucy felt herself heated by the warm glow of desire that radiated from him. She wondered what she would do if his passion were suddenly to overcome him. *What if he were to fall upon her all at once? But then what if he didn't? Lord,* she thought. *Here's the buck, and I'm all of a bother with worries.*

Barney picked up a stalk of hay. Sucking thoughtfully on it for a while, he seemed deep in contemplation.

Lucy arranged her skirts again, patted her hair, and looked about casually. "It seems," she said, "the weather will remain dry for the harvest."

Barney removed the straw and looked at her.

"Parson has it, on authority from a learned man in Oxford, that the harvest will be a good one," he replied. "My master says he cannot remember such a spell of hot dry weather. Pray God it continues through to September."

Lucy waited for a sign of movement, but it did not come. He just sat there, chewing on the straw, seemingly content to sit that way forever. Her brow puckered into a frown, and she coughed politely, curling a tendril of hair around her finger. "I hear your mistress is breeding again," she said. "I feel so sorry for that poor creature. The youngest is still at the breast. Dear, dear. It will be the ruination of her. I see her often, always swelling, short on money. Ill clothed and ill shod, and your master is a foul-tempered man so they say."

Barney stole a peep at Lucy from the corner of his eye. *I wish she'd stop prattling and come to it,* he thought. He observed the curve of her cheek, the thick glossy fall of lashes that fanned out around the wide blue eyes, and the tumble of shining black curls wound about the scarlet ribbon. Then his amorous glance travelled to the full firm bounty that lay beneath the tight-laced bodice. He felt his colour rise, and something more besides. He caught his breath at the sharp pain that bit him in the loins.

"Aye well," said Barney hoarsely. "That's the way of the man." He rolled over and lay on his stomach. Lying very flat to hide the evidence of his desire. "He's good enough to me. I mean who would blame him for being short of temper with my mistress, for I tell you she whines without end and is a real wall-faced besom. Not comely at all."

Lucy tossed back her hair, and shrugged her shoulders. "How comely does constant breeding leave a woman, in God's name?" she asked. "I tell you, I have better hopes for myself than to be forever swelling like a marrow and dripping milk like a cow."

Barney removed the straw from his strong white teeth, turned onto his back and looked up at her. "But you must have a man, Lucy Emmett, whether you would breed or no, that's for certain. Or will you choose to dry up altogether and die in your bed, a withered stick of an old maid?"

Lucy laughed and lay on her stomach beside him. "Like *The* Miss Parson Brown?" she asked.

"Aye," replied Barney. "That's right. Alone in your bed, for twenty, through thirty, forty, fifty years." He put the straw back in his mouth. Lucy quickly snatched it from his lips and tickled his ears.

"Oh my, what a fate for me," she whispered, widening her eyes.

"A dried-up stick of an old maid," Barney said, "mincing along with your prayer book to church of a Sunday. Then mincing back with your bonnet all of a dither." Lucy moved closer tickling his nostrils with the straw trying to make him sneeze. He tried to catch hold of her hand and take the straw from her, but she foiled him. "With a face all sour, and screwed up like a pickled walnut," he managed to blurt out, just before he sneezed.

Lucy giggled. "Oh, dear, Barney Cowper, then my future holds no promise at all."

Barney turned. She was lying beside him. "Not unless fortune smiles on you and brings a lusty man along to shape your future."

Lucy looked shocked. "What. You mean there is no hope that I may shape it alone?" she asked.

Barney shook his head. "A woman is not whole without a man. That's known for a fact. 'Tis in the Bible. You must have a man, or go mad, or dry up."

Lucy buried her face in the hay. She was giggling. She stopped when she felt Barney's hot breath on the back of her neck. He slipped his arm around her waist, turning her body to face his. She lay against him, her breasts pressed hard against his muscular young chest. She thought she might even grow to love Barney Cowper, if she were certain he would never speak again. She kept her eyes closed, when she felt his full moist lips meet hers. The taste of him was sweet. The smell of him was fresh as the crisp early morning air. She thrilled and quivered as he pushed his knee between her legs, causing them to part easily for him so that he might press his risen sex against her. Trembling as his mouth left hers and travelled along the softness of her throat, she helped him reach the warm dewy cleavage between her breasts.

His body began to move rhythmically against hers, rising and falling slowly. As he moved, something inside her was tightening and loosening again in harmony with his motion. His searching hand lifted her skirts. It moved over the roundness of her thighs. She groaned when it reached the very sanctum of her, feeling a towering rush of desire race through her body. His mouth found hers again, this time hungrily. His teeth caught at her lower lip, biting it, bruising it, until the salt taste of blood made her aware of the pain she felt.

She whimpered and cried out, but he was on top of her, pulling at the lacing on her bodice tearing at it until it gaped, spilling out her breasts. She felt his tongue caress the rosy nipples. Then he bit them urgently. Lucy was melting away under him.

"Oh Barney, stop!" she gasped.

But he was fierce, groaning, biting and kissing her all at once. Finding her strength she heaved him off and rolled away, laughing. Before he could rouse himself to tackle her, she had jumped on top of him, and pushed her knee between his legs until she saw him wince. She laughed again.

"I am a match for you," she said "I have fought often with my brothers and never come out beaten though they are stronger than you."

Barney grinned. "They let you win," he scoffed.

Lucy pressed her knee harder into him. "They do not," she snapped.

He caught hold of her wrists and held them tight. "Oh it's easy to catch a man when he is off guard." He threw her down again. This time, struggle as she might, she couldn't throw him off. "You saucy teasing wench," he said. "I'll show you."

"Oh now come off, Barney," Lucy shouted. "I am given up. See, I lie still." Barney rolled off her, and she would have escaped had he not caught hold of her hair. "Oh" wailed Lucy. "Now you are hurting me." He threw her down, holding tight to her hair.

"I'll call my brothers and set them on you," Lucy screamed.

"Call them," Barney said. "But you'll have to shout clear across the county to Melton. Anywise don't show so prudish, Lucy Emmett, for you are panting as rapid as I."

Lucy was just about to deny this vehemently, when she saw that he had unlaced his breeches.

"Oh my," she gasped, contemplating what she was about to be introduced to. "Hold hard. What sort of spectacle is that to show an innocent maid?" She fought to sit up, but Barney pressed her back to the floor. I looked only for a pleasant social afternoon," she wailed. "I am a virgin still," shrieked Lucy, realising that there was more to be bitten than she had contemplated chewing. "I am intact. I warn you. The wrath of God will come down on you if you take me. Enter me and I shall scream."

But Barney only grinned, saying with quiet determination, "Do not scream too loud though, Miss. Or the whole parish will know you are virgin no longer."

He was just about to mount her, when he felt an almightly blow across his back. Yelling with pain he caught sight of the horror that filled Lucy's eyes. He jumped to his feet, dragging up his breeches and turned to see, not God in his wrath but Elizabeth Emmett, wielding a birch broom.

"Villain," she screamed. "Toad-spawned fornicator."

"Ouch," yelped Barney, trying to lace his breeches, only to be caught by another swinging blow, this time across his seat. His breeches descended quickly to his ankles causing him to meet the floor with his face.

"Here's a couple bent on copulating in the bright light of day," Elizabeth screamed, swinging the broom this time at Lucy who was trying to recover her skirts from about her neck, and her heart from her throat. The broom caught her so hard on her shoulders that the handle broke, and the head of it flew across the loft. For a moment Lucy imagined it was her own head that had been severed.

"You heathen," Elizabeth gasped, contemplating the broken broom. "Do you plan to lay another bastard at Mr. Emmett's door to feed and clothe and grow as Godless and wayward as yourself?"

Lucy was about to answer, but Elizabeth set about her and Barney with the broom handle, beating them both soundly. "Be off," she yelled at the dodging and weaving Barney, who was still trying to rescue his breeches. "Be off, back to your work. But wait on the punishment from your master when he hears of this from my husband. He will tell him, you sneaking, poking, fumbling hound, you." She threw the broom handle after Barney, who had vaulted out of the hayloft and landed heavily on the stable floor below. At last with his breeches secure, he ran back to the wheelwright's house and the terrible fate that would befall him when his master returned like Roger Emmett from Melton Fair.

Lucy had been sitting on a hard wooden stool in the

corner of the farmhouse for a full three hours, when she heard Roger's cart rattle over the dry, baked earth of the yard. Her dress was torn now, her hair disarranged, her shoulders smarted, and her swollen lips had been bruised purple by Barney's fierce kisses. The pretty scarlet ribbon had been lost in the hay. Tears cascaded from her eyes and fell upon her sore bitten breasts. She glared across at her stepmother as she waited for Roger to come in. Elizabeth's face was triumphant.

"You measly wretched bitch," spat Lucy. "Do not look so smug, Mistress. I have only sat patient so long to wait for my father, so that I may tell him of your cruel ways. Worry, for I hear him come now, and he will throw you from this house with only a crust for company, when he sees how sore I am abused, and how miserable you have made my condition."

Elizabeth stood up. "I doubt that, hussy, so I do," she said. "I know my man and I tell you he is the man who will read you the record. For if he does not I am out of here of my own accord. Make no mistake." She marched across to the door, her hands on her hips. "Do not think that I am going to live beneath the same roof as a jitty cat. You are the one who need worry, baggage."

Roger came in, stooping to avoid the lintel. He kissed Elizabeth's cheek fondly. Lucy wiped her eyes with her petticoat, and stood up. Toby and John were not with him. Her heart sank again. She knew her father was easily persuaded by Elizabeth, and had hoped for support from her brothers.

"What's this?" Roger asked, cupping his hand under her chin. "Weeping?"

Lucy wept harder. "Aye," she moaned. "That spiteful shrew you took to wife has beaten me a thousand times in your absence. By God, I tell you I would have taken a scythe, quartered her, and bounced the pieces over the ridge, had she not been wedded to you."

Elizabeth, too, burst into tears and sank down on the settle. "Oh, Mr. Emmett, the horror of her. The shameless, wily ways of her," she whimpered. "My patience and wits have been driven to this. You know how gentle I am by nature. But she would cause a saint to swear oaths and take to dicing."

Roger groaned and crossing to the mantle took down a clay pipe. "Oh, this is ever the tale. I leave for a day, and while the cock's away the hens fall to pecking one another." He found a pipe and filled it from his pouch.

"You have not heard yet what I have to say," snapped Elizabeth. "You'll not be so easy about it then, I warn you."

"Where are my brothers?" Lucy asked.

"Left at Melton," replied Roger. "They have to drive sheep back here."

Lucy glared at Elizabeth. "*They'll* have a few words about this when they return," she said pointing to her bruised shoulders and chest. "Wait, Mistress, till they see the tarramangle I'm put into at your hands. Somebody's hair will fly."

Now that Roger's eyes had become used to the gloom of the house, he could easily see the angry marks on her shoulders. He caught her arm and looked closer. Turning on Elizabeth he asked sharply, "Why did you do this? I know she can at times be wayward, but as God is my witness, there is no need to beat her so severe." He put a protective arm around Lucy's shoulders.

"No need?" shouted his wife. "This object has only taken it upon herself to play the whore in your absence, that is all." Roger looked down at Lucy. She shook her head at the question in his eyes. "You ask her to answer out loud whether I lie or no," Elizabeth insisted. "Ask the false mot whether she didn't have Barney Cowper the wheelwright's apprentice on top of her in your hay, thrusting fit to shame a full-blooded boar. His breeches were unhitched when I came upon them, and she was flat on her back beneath him. Ask her. She knows the truth of it."

Roger's eyes darkened. "Well, Lucy Emmett?"

Lucy lowered her eyes. "He was with me," she started.

"Ah," said Elizabeth. "Now she begins to spit it out. Wait another hundred years and we may yet have the truth." Roger was looking uncomfortably stern now.

"It was not at all as she said though, Sir," Lucy hurried

on trying to stop the storm clouds gathering around her again. "I promise. We were sociable to start with."

Elizabeth laughed scornfully. "Sociable?"

Lucy threw it back at her. "Yes, Mistress, sociable. But that is something that you are not acquainted with between a maid and a young man. You would not think of sociable conversation. No. You think only of copulation and fornication, rutting and coupling—that's the way your mind runs."

Elizabeth laughed again. "Sociable conversation, my rear. Her with her gown about her ears, her legs all of a dangle and him with his breeches down, hard on top about to hit the mark. Had hit the mark for all I know. I heard nothing for the whole time that I stood, except the sound of slapping flesh."

"Had I known you were watching," retorted Lucy, "I'd have called you nearer—then you might have heard what was being said."

"Are you going to stand there, Roger Emmett, and listen to her speak to me in this manner?" asked Elizabeth. "I shall suffer her lewd and cheeky ways no more. Either the party oppisite me is put out," she said, pointing at Lucy, "or I make my way back to my own good family and you sleep alone."

This troubled Roger. She had not threatened to leave him before. "There, there, little wife," he murmured taking her in his arms. "Let's have no more of that talk. I'm sure there is nothing here that cannot be solved by a little give and take."

But Elizabeth was not to be placated. "I have taken enough. What if she is mated by Barney Cowper? What of that? Am I to take her work upon my back while she lies around with a blossoming belly? That's to be my life is it? A scullion to her? Had I known what to expect, I should never have married you. Never, in all honesty."

Roger stood with his arm about her and looked across at Lucy. "Did you couple with that 'prentice?" he asked.

Lucy stamped her foot. "I did not. I am virgin still. I tell the truth," she stormed.

"Huh. Virgin," scoffed Elizabeth. "I doubt you know

the word's meaning. That 'prentice boy is not the first to take you, I warrant. Count yourself fortunate indeed if he agrees to marry with you."

"Listen well, Mistress," Lucy advanced on her. "I am a virgin still, do not forget it. As to marriage, I shall wed when I wish and with whom I wish. I shall not be married at your whim. Forget that at your peril." Then gentling her voice she turned to her father. " 'Twas silly, light sport," she whispered. "You know how it is. I was flirty, he was naughty, things just went wagging further than I meant." She gazed up at Roger, with great blue eyes. "I am so very sorry," she murmured.

Roger found it impossible not to forgive her when she was contrite. The eyes were so like his own. He nodded his head. "Aye. I daresay that was the way of it," he said, patting her head fondly. "Sweet innocent sport, turned a little...well...hot. Yes, nothing untoward in that. But promise that things will not go so far again, Mm? Not until you are wed to a good man. For I tell you, your maidenhead is your fortune, along with your looks. Chastity was invented for poor girls. The rich have their dowries to take to their marriage beds."

Elizabeth was furious. "Oh, Mr. Emmett, you are a fool. An addleheaded old fool, growing sillier with your dotage. Whatever she will say, why, you will believe it. I despair." She ran over to Lucy, pulling at her bodice, revealing the deepening love marks Barney had left around her nipples. "Look, will you?" she cried pointing at the love bites. "Those look as though they were left by a boy intent on sociable conversation, I suppose? Would you have me lift her petticoats? Because I'll wager that there's more silly innocent sport and polite conversation to be seen down there."

Roger's face turned white with anger. "So," he growled. " 'Tis true."

Elizabeth pushed Lucy away from her. "Of course it is true," she sneered.

Roger sat down abruptly as though shoved. "I cannot marry her to Barney Cowper," he groaned. "The boy sleeps among the wood shavings and has not a penny to his name." He looked up at Lucy. "I don't know what to do with you. I mean, watching after you has become too much for me. I'm not as spry as I was, and I cannot be always around driving off these fellows. I don't know what's in you, girl. Why cannot you be like the other girls hereabouts? Hang on fast to what you have to offer till some man of merit bends the knee?"

"How often," shouted Lucy, "must I repeat myself? I am a virgin still, sir."

"Not," shouted Roger, "for very long if you continue in your present ways." He stood up, and clapped his hands together. "Wash and repair yourself Miss. Come on, bustle. This is a matter for the parson."

The parsonage stood behind Ragby churchyard. It was the only house in the village built of brick. It had a tiled roof, unlike the other houses that were thatched with reed and straw, in common with Ridge Farm. In the previous winter, however, the parsonage had been struck by a blast of forked lightning, and one of the tall chimneys had fallen straight through the roof. Parson Brown was hopeful that the Squire Billy Royalston, on whom his living depended, would deign to provide monies for repairs before the Autumn, at least. For the thought of heavy rain pouring through the roof, as well as the damp creeping up through the floors in the winter to follow, caused him to quake in his black gaiters.

He was a thin beaky-nosed man, whose clever features had become sickly and he had grown round-shoulders. He was afflicted by chestiness, which now caused his nose to drip constantly. His sister bore a marked resemblance to him, *the* Miss Parson Brown, as she was known (being unmarried, and taking her brother's title in the absence of a husband) was seated on a straight backed chair, near the window in the parson's booklined study. She was dressed in a severe gown of dark grey wool, ancient and heavy, in spite of the heat of the late summer afternoon. Her hair was pulled into a tight knot at the nape of her scrawny neck. *The* Miss Parson Brown believed in keeping her hands busy (lest the devil should find some work for them to do) and her fingers were engaged in repairing her brother's sadly threadbare black surplice, which was so advanced in age it shone quite green in places, where shafts of sunlight from the window touched it.

Her brother was being visited by the squire's nephew, Peter, who, since the squire had no issue of his own, was considered his heir. Peter Royalston sat at a writing table, toying with a quill pen. He was in his early twenties, delicate and girlish in appearance, with pale skin, and a vacant face. His lips were pursed and rosebud red, heavy drooping lids covered eyes empty of any intelligent expression.

He wore a fine blue taffeta coat, with wide turned sleeves, and silver buttoned cuffs; sage green velvet breeches, laced with silk cord; and pale blue silk stockings that matched exactly the colour of his coat. His shirt was of creamy linen, with flounces at the wrists and a cascade of French lace jabot at the throat. He wore his carrot-colour hair tweaked into a fringe of tight corkscrew curls at the front; behind his head it was gathered into a blue velvet bow. He opened his eyes at last, and gazed fixedly at a damp patch on the ceiling. Meanwhile the parson strolled up and down the room with its globes and maps, holding a leather-bound copy of Tacitus up to his dripping nose, listening like a man hypnotised to the sonorous tones of his own voice.

"*Quadraginta millia cetari cum venebulis.*" He removed a large handkerchief from the worn sleeve of his coat, and with a gesture of grand theatricality swept the gathering dewdrop from the end of his nose.

The room was close, hot and airless. Peter Royalston yawned, pulled fitfully at some of the barbs in the quill and, putting his elbow on the writing desk, propped up his empty head.

"Phut to Tacitus," he whined under his breath. He wished his uncle would abandon these futile attempts to make him take advantage of the parson's reputation for scholarship. After all, he had long since ceased to be a child, and what was the point? Such scholarship was all well and good for those who wished to pursue the life of a Descartes. He shuddered. *Lard. Locked in a wretched* room for years. Or was Descartes the fellow who lived in a barrel? No matter. I desire more entertainin' company, he thought, than Tacitus. The society of people who are like-minded to myself. A life of pleasure and distractions. London society, the dance. The theatre. Levees at fashionable houses. He sighed, dreaming of himself at such functions, dressed in a high powdered wig, and a yellow satin coat. Perhaps he might display a patch or two on his chin and cheeks, as became a gentleman of fashion and breeding. "Would to heavens I could make off to London now," he muttered petulantly to himself.

Peter's father, the squire's only brother, had been a Navy man. Years previously he had met with a gory end during a skirmish with pirates off the Barbados coast. The news of her husband's death had sent his mother into a rapid decline and she survived her husband by only two years, leaving Peter in the care of Squire Billy and his wife Jemima.

When the young man had shown no inclination towards the normal pursuits of the gentry—hunting, hare coursing, whoring, and drinking—the squire had hoped he might prove a hand at learning. Being a person of very small intellectual ability himself, he naturally required that his second-hand heir would make up for the fathomless void in his own education, but Peter had not appeared to profit from his time at Oxford. In vain the squire now admonished his nephew. "You go and see the parson. He's a learned man, they say. He'll fill your head with what clever people know. Stop you being so mopish."

To his horror Peter became even more languid, foppish and uninterested. He lay on the brocade couches at Ragby Hall reading a particular kind of romantic novel very popular with ladies or he would spend much time practising the latest French dance steps, causing the squire apoplectic dismay.

"*This,*" he would shout at his wife Jemima, "is to succeed me? This scented, wilting flower is to lead the Ragby hounds? Strap me! The sop will lead them dragged in a sack behind my horse if he continues thus."

Peter was jolted from his reveries, and the parson from

continuing "*Pro minimento retinens,*" by the heavy toll of the bell at the parsonage front door. The parson shut Tacitus and looked significantly at his sister.

"I will repair to the door, brother," she said.

Peter Royalston yawned again. "Oh Lard," he sighed. "Oh Lard. Was there evah such a taresome day? The weathah is too too oppressive." He reclined in his chair. "It's the very Devil I swear, Sah. Lard. I feel like a limp kerchief, so I do. My whole body is in the very misery of a sweat. I fear a fever. I fear a fever of the very severest nature." He fanned himself with his lily-white hand, watching the parson quickly secure the wig that had fallen over his eyes with the surprise of hearing his doorbell tolled so late in the afternoon.

"Well well," he said. "We have enjoyed a most rewarding afternoon, have we not, with our dear friend Tacitus? Most enjoyable and most elevating to the mind. But ah, me," he sighed glumly. "Since the morrow is Thursday I believe, and I am engaged in two burials of the dead, I fear we may have to postpone our eagerness to pursue the text."

Peter tried to look dismayed. To his horror he must have succeeded for the parson continued. "However. If you inform the squire that I will be pleased to call at Ragby Hall at about eight of the clock in the evening, I will be most happy to discuss with you what we have learned today, and who can say, we may also sport ourselves in an excursion mathematical?"

Peter slumped further in his seat. *Lard*, he thought. *I shall be a corpse for burial myself by then, quite dead from heat and boredom.*

"Enter," caled the parson to a timid tap on the door. *The* Miss Parson Brown entered, followed by a bashful, shambling Roger Emmett, and a suitably demure-looking Lucy, now washed, her hair carefully brushed, and her shoulders covered by a loose knitted shawl to hide the marks of her amorous adventure. She folded her hands, and peeped out from beneath the brim of a flat straw bonnet.

Peter Royalston straightened himself and raised an

eyebrow. He vaguely recognised Emmett as one of his uncle's tenants, but he couldn't remember ever having seen the girl before. He smiled with some pleasure, not at Lucy's abundant charms—they held no attraction for him—but it did amuse him to see the farmer so ill at ease, and he thought he might have some entertainment at Roger's expense if he remained in the study.

"Ah, Roger Emmett of Ridge Farm," said the parson. "What can I do for you, pray?"

Roger had removed his hat, and was twisting it in his hands. "Good afternoon, Parson," he said, feeling very out of place in the book-lined room. Then, looking across at Peter Royalston he touched his forelock. "Begging your pardon, Parson. I didn't know that you had gentry in for company. If I'd known I would never have come."

Peter Royalston sniggered. "Lard, think nought of it, fellow. A cat may sometimes look at a king, don't y'know." He removed a lavender-scented lace handkerchief from his cuff and waved it about under his nose with a great show of surprise and distaste. "Do I smell pigs?" he enquired of the parson.

Roger felt his cheeks flush at this indirect insult. He moved back towards the door, dragging Lucy with him. She too, was bristling.

"I'll return another day," Roger muttered.

"Heavens. Say what must be said, fellow," called Peter. "Lard. You look so mightily uncomfortable. Why writhe longer than you must? Utter. Utter."

The parson drew Roger back into the room, and shut the door. "Stay, Roger Emmett," he said, laying aside Tacitus. "My full attention shall be at your disposal." His sister trotted back to her seat by the window and took up her sewing.

Roger looked at the lady and frowned. "I, er—" he started. Then he twisted his hat almost inside out with embarrassment.

"Come, come. What is it then?" the parson asked.

"Well, Sir," mumbled Roger. "It's 'er. Well, it's *The* Miss Parson Brown, Sir. I don't in truth think that what I have to unfold here is suitable for a lady to hear, who, er, is of such a delicate and spiritual disposition."

"Oh. Rural scandal," trilled Peter Royalston overcome with glee. "How jolly entertainin'."

The Miss Parson Brown quickly laid her work down and, directing a little "tut, tut" towards Lucy, left the room.

When his sister had departed, the parson adjusted his wig, wiped his nose again, and lowering his head as much as he dared, placed his hands, clasped, behind his back, adopting a stance which he regarded as being properly solemn considering he was the authorised representative of God in Ragby.

"Be seated," he murmured. Roger and Lucy sat side by side on hard chairs. The parson waited. Peter Royalston waited. But Roger Emmett said not a word. There was silence for what seemed an age. At last Peter grew impatient enough to enquire.

"This um, rough wench here. What is it, Mm?"

Roger looked at the fop. "'Tis my daughter," he answered. Then, as an afterthought: "Adopted."

Peter looked interested. He nodded, hoping for more information. It came from the parson.

"Born of a wayside woman. A pauper or something like. This good simple man took it and reared it as his own." He peered at Lucy over the bridge of his beaky nose. "I buried the natural mother myself I think. Yes. I buried the woman; six months after I first came here. No name of course."

Peter nodded. "So. 'Tis a bastard?" The parson nodded in reply. "Known as what then?" asked the squire's nephew. "Lucy Emmett," replied the parson. "What ails the chit then?" asked Peter.

"Nothing ails me, thank you," snapped Lucy. She resented being spoken of as though she were not present. "I am as straight as a yard rule."

Peter turned pink and giggled. "Lard, it speaks," he shrilled. "So, hoyden, nothing ails ye? Well, fellow, what of you, eh? What ails you? What was all the bashful shamblin' about, if nothing is amiss? I was after some sport. But 'tis ever the same here. Fields, trees, cattle and men, all as dumb as each other." He yawned again, and looked bored.

The parson popped a lozenge into his mouth to help his pulpit voice. "Now, Emmett," he boomed sucking on the lozenge. "Let us approach the reason for your visit. I take it that you seek advice in matters of a spiritual nature? Or, perhaps the flesh is unruly?" He looked directly at Lucy, who blushed more with anger than shame. Roger blushed too. He was considering how best to phrase the story of Lucy's spree with Barney Cowper. He was also in need of the parson's guidance if he was to keep Lucy a virgin until a suitable husband could be found.

"It's not so simple," he said, looking at Peter. "I am a man of few words, and the matter in hand touches on the wench here beside me." He nodded towards Lucy. "Now she's come out of childhood, as you can see. But in a somewhat rude and wayward manner. Rude and cheeky so to speak."

Lucy was astonished. "Rude, and cheeky?" she asked looking at Roger. He silenced her with a look.

The parson nodded. "Expound further pray."

Roger didn't know what 'expound' meant, but he continued. "See, I have the sole care of the wench since the death of my wife Margaret. Now I have wed again, recent. Well the nub is, I don't know how to put it." He looked across at Peter Royalston. "See I don't know how to speak before gentry. Him being here ties the tongue."

Peter sighed. "Foolish dolt, you may speak freely before me. I am a man of the wider world. I am acquainted with its curious ways. I have been at Oxford, and am only recent returned from Scarborough, and am also a frequenter of that greater metropolis, London. I can assure you, fellow, that my pretty youthful looks, my fresh ingenuous appearance, belie a positive plethora of experience. Speak in comfort, do."

Roger cleared his throat and squared his shoulders. "Well. Right. I'm to it," he said. He stood up and thrust both hands deep into his breeches pockets. "As God is my witness, Parson," he went on, "I'm in a stew, a real stew. I've trouble with this wench here. Now hear me, at heart she's good enough. But, by God, in the head she's hot, and..."

Peter interrupted him. "In the loins is hotter, I'll be bound."

"That's it, sir," Roger said. "You've hit it, bang on the mark. It's damned hot in the loins. So hot, that it's a boiling about with lads as hot as itself." He was about to continue, when Lucy jumped to her feet her eyes flashing.

"That is a great lie. I am not the hot one. Is it my fault if the boys pursue me? I try and fend them off but they run at me so and hide in the bushes, hedges, ditches, stacks to get at me. What am I to do? Fend them off with a pitchfork? Big brawny brutes of boys with arms like oak branches ever ready to grasp me?"

"Sit, Miss," Roger shouted her down. "I am here to speak. You are here to listen."

"What?" Lucy yelled back at him "I am supposed to sit like a blessed monument am I, and hear myself slandered? Well. I shall not. I shall not sit here in silence and hear men discuss my character in such a lewd way." She turned on her heel and was off towards the door. Roger grabbed her arm, and pulled her back to her chair.

"Sit as I told you," he ordered, "and put the tongue back where it belongs, or dammit it's over my knee here and now." Lucy sat down, and bit her lip.

"I think I am come to understand," the parson said. "You are concerned to keep the maid intact until such a time as the act is sanctified by the church. Until in short, the wench is a wife."

Roger was overcome. The parson had got his drift. Not for nothing was he reputed to be clever. "That's it. You have it. Today she has been very near the loss of it. You know what I mean," he winked at the parson. The parson winked back, and immediately shot up in Roger's esteem.

"Do not elucidate further," he said. "What you have intimated is sufficient." He was surprised to find that he was wiping beads of perspiration from his forehead. His nose had completely dried up. He thought this extraordinary phenomenon might conceivably have something to do with Roger Emmett's sultry-looking daughter. His eyes rested on her full red lips, and at once he felt the scalp under his wig heat up. He removed the wig, displaying a boney pate with only a few loose, straggling, grey-yellow hairs clinging to it, wiped the head and replaced the wig. "Yes. Tut, tut, this is a problem," he muttered as Lucy's eyes met his. Again he was aware of that burning sensation beneath his wig. Again the perspiration began to creep down his brow, threatening to enter his eyes and blind him completely. "How to keep it intact," he groaned.

"Oh, 'tis a battle bound to be lost," said Peter Royalston. "These outdoor wenches have no taste, nor yet discretion. Their appetites are coarsened by an excess of air and weathah. They will roll about with any old hearty who barks at em, on my life." He sniffed. "'Tis distasteful to think on, but ill breeding turns evah to loose breeding. That's what I say." He stood up and approached Lucy, peering down at her as though she were a freak in a roadside show. "I doubt if it is virgin still," he said poking her in the arm. "No. It does not look it to me. Its face is knowing, and damme, it's uppity beyond its station," he gasped, having received a blistering look from Lucy. "Whip it," he advised, reeling at the power of the look. "It's bold even. Whip it, whip it hard, swinge it and make it more respectful."

"I have been whipped," Lucy cried out, pulling the shawl off her shoulders to show the bruising on her body. "Whipped almost to death, Sirs, by my father's new wife."

The parson moved closer to conduct a more concentrated examination of the bruises. Lucy felt his hot breath on her cheek. She pulled down her bodice and exposed more of her bosom. He flinched and drew back, shutting his eyes, and then fumbling in his pocket for a book of devotions he muttered something about the devil being an ever patient fiend. Lucy found it hard not to laugh at the parson's embarrassment. But she listened along with Roger and Peter, while he read a prayer out loud.

"Our weakness, strengthen and confirm,
For Lord thou knowst us frail,
That never Devil, world nor flesh,
Against us shall prevail."

He shut the book. Now Lucy's ripening body could not disturb him, nor tempt him again to touch it. But just in case, he sat down and closed his eyes.

"Well," said Roger Emmett. "That's brave-enough verse. But what of my troubles? What's to be done about them? Here's this one and my new wife flying at each other like poultry in a panic, and on this very day she"—he pointed at Lucy—"is caught with a 'prentice boy, in the hay, mounted and ready to ride."

The parson thought it best to gasp in horror. But Peter was richly entertained.

"Caught, mounted and ready to ride," he guffawed. "Oh, I say, what extraordinary waggish language they do use, these hoy polloys. Why one could sweah they were descended from another planet, so strange is their delivery. Haw, haw, haw." He laughed displaying equine teeth. "Haw, haw, haw, 'pon my word. Mounted and ready to ride, and you worry that the hoyden may lose her maidenhead? Lard, yokel. 'Tis lost, departed, gone, that's certain. Her honour, such as it evah was, is vanquished, that's what I say."

"Well, I believe her to be intact still," said Roger. "But 'twill not be long before she's taken. For as you can see, she's uncommon handsome. She signals just by standing still."

Peter sniffed into his handkerchief and peered down at Lucy. "It's a gaudy coloured thing, but too healthy-lookin' by far to be fashionable. It can't hope to make a decent match. I mean. 'Tis a bastard after all, and country bred. Looks country bred too, by God."

Roger grinned and winked at the parson. "Well things may wag different in London or whatever. But 'round these parts we like 'em fine and lusty. Now if I was looking at her myself, I would see it along these lines. Stand up, wench," he said. Lucy stood up. "Here," said Roger pointing at her, "is a wench, of almost seventeen years. True she is a bastard, true she has no dowry. But she is well-built in the hips, wide and round which bodes good for breeding. Her back and legs are strong, which they need be for bearing brats, working, lifting and carrying and so on. Even without her beauty, sirs, this wench would be a bargain for any man. I can vouch for her cooking, and being neat about the place, and she can sew a seam, knit a sock, and suchlike. She remains intact, and..."

"That is open to conjecture," Peter interrupted.

"Well, take it as true," said Roger. "Let's not beat too much about that point. But you get my drift? It's a handy wench, would suit a man with a hot appetite. For who would not be pleased to turn about in bed of a cold night and grasp that to him. What do you say, Parson. Am I right or am I wrong?"

The parson was startled. Had the man read his mind? "Do not enquire of me, Mr. Emmett," he said lustily. "I have nothing to do with the flesh. I keep it, as you might say, at a distance. My mission as you will have comprehended from the many sermons I have preached on the subject being to purge the world of the flesh entirely. Thus bringing spiritual renewance, pure of all sweaty and bestial desires." Roger had never listened to these sermons, too full of lost words for him, but had dozed or planned the next week's work. "But," the parson continued, looking once more at Lucy's bountiful curves, "we are all human things and were I other than I am, I believe I would not complain if she were suddenly to be found by me somewhere about my bed."

Roger smiled with satisfaction, and motioned to Lucy to seat herself again. This she did, though she felt mortified at being spoken of as though she were a mere object, without feelings or opinions of her own.

"So," said Roger. "You see my stew. As she stands she's in line for a good marriage. But without that maidenhead, well the prospects are not so good. I want only the best for her. Though sometimes I think she doesn't believe that." He glared at Lucy, who glared back.

The parson clutched his book to his thin chest. "There must be some solution to this dilemma," he muttered.

When he brought no suggestion forward, Roger spoke.

"Now look ye here, Siree," he said, pushing his hands into his breeches pockets again. "You know her capabilities. Why don't you take her?"

The parson was on his feet at once, his eyes threatening to leave the safety of their sockets.

"Me?" he exclaimed. "Me take *her*? Oh, upon my life, you forget your station."

Roger put a steadying hand on his shoulder. "You mistake me, parson. I don't ask you to marry her. I mean, take her to work in the house for you, as a maidservant. I thought Miss Brown would watch her and tutor her in ways more proper to her sex."

The parson sat down and removed his sodden wig. "That is simply not possible, Mr. Emmett," he replied. "It would not be correct for me to employ such a creature under this roof."

Roger nodded. "I see," he said. "But what am I to do? My new wife won't have her under my roof either. She has threatened to walk back to her family unless Lucy is found another place and soon."

"The boy she was caught with is no match I suppose?" the parson asked.

Roger shook his head. "He's the wheelwright's apprentice, penniless and only a little older than her."

"Not the best match, I agree," said the parson.

"Well *I* like him," said Lucy. "But I don't suppose my feelings matter at all."

"Oh Lard," giggled Peter Royalston, who had watched and listened with vast amusement. "I'll wager a hoyden such as yourself would like anything with hairs upon its chest."

"Well, ho, Mr. Gentry Sir," snapped Lucy. "I don't like you and I wouldn't marry you, if you came calling with one hundred gold guineas in your breeches. As for hair, I'll warrant your chest would be seen to be bare as a pebble, and if outside looks are anything to go by, I'll warrant that your lower part is as weak as your chin."

There was a stunned silence while Roger and the parson waited for the squire's heir to explode.

His mouth hung open in disbelief. "Oh," he gasped, "you are just sore, Miss, because I do not rise to the bait of your looks. Nor will I evah."

"I doubt you could rise to anything, you damned milksop," retorted Lucy. With that she would have kicked him, had she not been caught and held fast by Roger. Peter retreated behind the writing desk.

"The wench is quite demented," he quavered. "Mad. I sweah it would have attacked me. Did you hear how it abused me? The words, the behaviour." He sank down on his chair. "Lard, to speak so to a person carefully reared, and to hear it said by a mere bastard. Ditch bred to boot." He shut his eyes and fanned himself with his handkerchief.

But Lucy hadn't finished. "All I wish to say," she shouted, pulling Roger's hand away from her mouth, "is that if you are gentry, Sir, and representative of your class, well, give me Barney Cowper any day."

Peter Royalston let out a shriek of rage. "Give me an apology," he shrieked. "Or I shall see you in the stocks, a target for rotten fruit."

"Apologise," hissed Roger in her ear. "Apologise, or lose me my farm as well as my wife."

"Righto, Sir. But you know well enough how this will choke me," she whispered. She moved towards the Squire's nephew, lowered her eyes, and made a curtsy. "I apologise, Sir. I was quick and froward. But I am not couth, being unused to the company of gentlemen as you can see."

"Indeed I do see," said Peter. "You are not forgiven, though. You are merely ignored."

Lucy curtsied again. "I thank you most humbly then, sir, for ignoring me," she said.

The parson fell to clapping his hands together with a great show of admiration. He had been worried that his living might not be secure had Peter told his uncle of Lucy's rudeness, and after seventeen years he was reluctant to move. The squire's temper was known to be easily roused. The fop Peter bowed and smiled at the applause.

"I believe," he said to the parson, "that my manner of dealing with the wench is some indication of the quality in my nature. Was clever, eh? You are not forgiven, you are merely ignored. I think I shew'd proper disdain there. How say you?"

The parson laughed and clapped politely. "Oh, indeed, indeed. The disdain was splendid, splendid. As to the quality inherent in your disposition, why that was never in doubt, my dear young sir.

"Now then," he spoke briskly. "We will call my sister in here. For in questions relating to all things-er-female, she has often been my guide and indeed mentor." He crossed to the door, opened it, and called out, "Sister, Sister?"

Miss Parson Brown appeared, almost as soon as he had opened the door. Lucy suspected she had been there through the entire proceedings, eavesdropping at the keyhole. She looked at Lucy, pursed her lips, and turning to her brother said with a saintly smile, "You called me, dear?"

The parson took her arm. "We are in something of a dilemma here. Thrown into it, I must say, by that person of your own sex that you see seated before you." Lucy was in receipt of a very cold stare from the spinster. So cold, in fact, she could have sworn an icicle formed in the air between them.

"After great and urgent deliberation," continued the parson, "I have come to the conclusion that a person of the same sex as the person I have formerly alluded to might prove the best agent in this matter. Though I hasten to add, gentlemen, that my sister being of the same sex as the aforementioned person, is in the order of being a natural accident. There is as you can see, no similarity between them. For my sister, as you will have noticed from her demeanour, is a woman of good breeding without vice, or malice; a creature in totality virtuous. Yeh and verily, verily, I say unto you the the virtuous woman, when found, being rare," he droned, "is a jewel without price etc, etc. I could quote further, but . . ." He turned and looked at Peter Royalston and found the young gentleman, to his surprise, sound asleep, his head wilting like a jaded daisy above his lace jabot.

"We will not disturb him," the parson whispered to Roger and his sister. "The young man has found the weather singularly oppressive and we have spent an arduous afternoon construing Tacitus. Also," he went on, looking at Lucy, "there has been some rumpus here, some badinage, some unpleasantries expressed which sorely tried him."

The Miss Brown looked again at Lucy and again Lucy thought she saw ice. She ignored the look and turned her attention to Peter Royalston. She had never in all her life seen anyone fall asleep so abruptly. *I suppose*, she thought, *this suddenness and ease in sleeping is one of the qualities of a gentleman along with a taste for powder and feminine furbelows.*

Roger Emmett had retired with the parson and his sister into a corner of the study and was deep in conversation. Lucy was hard pressed to hear what they were saying, for they spoke in hushed whispers. She knew the conversation must centre on her, because the three of them would turn occasionally to stare perplexedly at her. Then they would turn away from her to whisper again. It was too tedious to try to bend an ear for long. The steady snoring from Peter Royalston, combined with the heat and her own exhaustion from being rolled by Barney, beaten by Elizabeth and insulted by what seemed to Lucy to be the entire world, sent her head nodding too. She curled up, making herself as comfortable as possible on the hard chair, and in a little while, was sound asleep.

During the following week, matters at Ridge Farm proceeded very quietly. Lucy didn't ask what had been decided between Roger and the parson and his sister, nor did Roger choose to tell her.

Between Elizabeth and Lucy there reigned an uneasy peace. Roger took care to remain at home, so that it should be kept, and Toby and John were posted sentinels, to watch in case Barney Cowper, or any other young blood, should set foot on Emmett territory to make a grab at Lucy's virginity.

As for Lucy, she spent the week working about the house and walking about the farmyard with Mr. Magpie. She was allowed only as far as the farm gate and for the first time in her life felt herself a prisoner. She did her best to cheer herself, feeling sure Roger would tire of having her watched and would grow sorry at seeing her sad and relent.

The days passed quickly enough but the summer evenings stretched out before her, seeming longer because she was confined and could not walk to Ragby to joke and flirt with the rest of the girls on the village green. She had heard that Barney had been soundly thrashed by his master and hardly dared venture from the wheelwright's house. Lucy marked him as a coward, for she felt if he cared anything for her he would surely have found a way to meet and enquire how things were with her.

On the Friday morning following her visit to the parsonage Lucy was treading the linen in a wooden tub, with Mr. Magpie close by. When she was surprised to see Miss Parson Brown, coming in at the farm gate dressed in her best summer bonnet. Lucy frowned. The bonnet was of the type usually worn only at important events. The parson's sister looked gleeful, Lucy thought, even secretive and she wondered what the little woman could be calling about.

"Good day, Miss Brown," shouted Lucy in a loud voice, causing Miss Parson Brown to jump almost out of her wrinkled skin with surprise. "What are you a-visiting for, eh?"

"Pull your skirts down, Miss," the woman called back. "It is not proper for a wench of your age to carry your skirts so high."

111

Lucy jumped out of the tub and pulled down her skirts. "How, pray," she asked Miss Parson Brown, "am I to tread washing with my skirts about my ankles?"

"If you must tread the linen, tread it when you are not seen then, Miss Sinful," she replied.

Lucy grinned. "Until you came, I was not seen," she said as they walked to the door. "Anyway, surely it is not sinful for one woman to look on another's ankles. Or if it is, I never heard that it was."

"You are a wretch," said *The* Miss Parson Brown, wagging her finger at Lucy. "Lewd, wicked and naughty. If left to yourself, you would end in a bad way, of that I am certain, buried a pauper like your mother before you. Thank God fasting, girl, that you fell among people who care for your future."

By the time they reached the door of the farm, Lucy was a good deal more miserable than she had been since her beating. It was not much joy to a girl to be told that she would end in a bad way before she felt she had truly started on her life. "Well," she sighed, as *The* Miss Parson Brown tapped on the door, "if I am to end in a bad way, I may as well enjoy going to it, dammit, for weeping and worrying will not prevent it."

When she tried to follow the parson's sister inside, she was told sharply by Roger to stay without.

"Why so?" she hissed back at him. "How long am I to stay out here, in God's name? And am I to be spoken of in there, Sir? Is my business to be chewed over? For if that's the case I demand to hear what is said."

Roger appeared at the door, looking full of business. "Now see here, Lucy Emmett," he said gravely. "You have been the cause of enough trouble. You are to remain outside here while I talk to that pious lady. When I call on you, *then*, you may come." He pointed to the ground directly before the door, turned on his heel and disappeared inside.

Lucy knew it was no good to argue. She sank down on the ground and leant her back against the wall of the house. She waited a very long time. To Lucy it seemed an age before she heard Roger call her.

She turned and ran to him, her heart in her mouth. "Oh my," she whispered to herself, "what have I done now? He looks so stern and determined."

Roger stood in the door with his hands in his pockets and his clay pipe clenched hard between his teeth. "Wash yourself, bind up the hair and on with the bonnet," he commanded. "We are off out."

Lucy raised her brows. "Out where?"

"Never mind," Roger replied. "You'll arrive at the answer soon enough."

In less than half an hour she was seated beside Roger and Miss Parson Brown on Roger's cart. He drove it out through the gate, and turned the horse's head towards Ragby.

The horse was pulled up outside the smithy and was tethered by the door. Miss Parson Brown was helped down by Roger, then he lifted Lucy from the cart. "Keep the mouth shut and behave," he told her. "Up till now I have been too soft with you." He set her down on her feet and walked about her, making sure her bodice was tight-laced and that she was tidy and neat, in very much the same manner as the recruiting sergeants used when inspecting the country boys who had taken the shilling at Melton Fair.

He seemed to be satisfied that her appearance would not disgrace him and, turning to Miss Parson Brown, he said quietly, "You go in and say we are here. When you call, I shall come in. I don't want to seem too hasty in this matter."

She nodded, seeming a little flushed and flustered. "Quite right, and when you do come in, appear easy and uncertain as to whether you have made up your mind or no." She tucked a few wispy hairs back under the best bonnet, and smacked Lucy's hand. "And you, behave. Be meek, be silent and sweet. This is all in your best interest," she said. Then she scuttled away into the smithy.

Lucy stood by Roger and waited. She could hear the sound of Boost the blacksmith's hammer beating against the anvil. From the yard behind the forge came the screams and shouts of his several children who fought constantly among themselves. Roger leant against the cart and waved the flies away from the old horse's head. The day was hot again—the sun high in the sky. Even Lucy's wide-brimmed bonnet gave little protection. She could feel her skin reddening under its glare and the flies that left the horse's ears set about biting her, so that soon she was covered with small red bumps. *All this waiting*, she moaned to herself. *I am not one to wait. I was made for action, dammit*.

Roger was called into the smithy by Miss Parson Brown, and Lucy was left to wait alone. She sat down on the ground in the shade of the cart. In a moment, though, the blacksmith's children appeared. There were ten of them, all dusty, dirty-nosed brats, and they set about teasing her, jeering at her and tweaking her bonnet. She felt it best to ignore them. When they saw they would get no response they turned their attention on the horse, worrying it, and pinching and prodding it, just like the spiteful flies that bit at its ears and nostrils. Lucy grew angry at this, and jumping to her feet, she beat at them, shouting, "Lay off, you rudesby brats or I'll have the tripes from your bellies."

The children ran a short way off, giggling and shrieking. Then they picked up small stones from the roadside and threw them in showers at Lucy and the poor old horse.

"In God's name," Lucy yelled. "I've warned you. Be off, you ruffians."

In reply she got another shower of stones full in the face. She narrowed her eyes. "Right ho," she said, then picked up a handful of much bigger stones from under the cart.

When Roger stepped out of the smithy, he was greeted by a hail-storm of stones and the sight of a previously tidy Lucy, now hot and furious, doing battle with what appeared to be a thousand rug-headed children.

"Come off," he yelled, catching her arm and shaking more stones from her clenched fist. She dropped the stones. "What are you thinking of?" he asked, straightening her bonnet and beating the dust from her skirts. Roger sighed. "You cannot be left for a moment without finding yourself in some mischief, can you?" he asked, spitting on his handkerchief and wiping the dirt from Lucy's cheeks.

"I was about stopping those brats from abusing your horse, Sir," she said. "They may abuse me, for I can hurl back at them but the poor beast is tethered and cannot even run away."

"Well, well. They are gone now," said Roger. "If they return they may expect a leathering from me. Now calm yourself." He kissed the tip of her nose. "When you come inside, just smile and stand. No more is required." He hugged her hard. "As God is my witness, little wench," he said taking her hand in his, "I believe we have just the solution we have looked for."

It took Lucy some time to adapt to the change of light. The forge was dark after the bright sunlit day outside. But it was as hot as hell itself. Miss Parson Brown was sitting in the corner a little way from the huge forge fire, fanning herself with her bonnet and dodging sparks from the smith's hammer. The sparks flew hither and thither above their heads, bright pinheads of light falling into cascades at their feet. Lucy felt her hair and skin begin to run with moisture. Boost, the blacksmith, was a massive brawny man of about the same age as Roger Emmett. He was muscled about the neck and shoulders like a bull, *Needing only a ring through his nose to resemble one completely*, thought Lucy.

She stood next to her father, and watched the man lay aside his hammer to blow the flames in the fire with a great pair of bellows. He was stripped to the waist; his whole solid torso dripped with sweat. His body seemed to be covered with tiny, black wiry curls similar to the thicker ones that grew over his low-browed head. His legs and thighs were thick as the trunks of trees. In fact he was so solid and stolid that he seemed rooted.

He pumped the bellows, and flames of many colours shot roaring high into the stone chimney. The heat grew worse, painful, unbearable. Lucy was sure she would melt with it at any moment. Boost removed a piece of filthy linen he kept tucked into his leather apron and wiped the back of his neck.

Roger coughed to draw his attention. "Well, Boost," he called above the roar of the fire. "Here is the wench to be looked on."

The smith didn't turn. He just grunted and puffed, took up a pair of tongs, drawing another piece of metal from the fire. He laid it, white hot, upon the anvil, beating and shaping it into a rim for a cartwheel, sending more sparks showering down on everyone. When he had finished the beating of the rim, he turned it on the anvil sending his eye along its edge to make sure it was straight and true. Seeming satisfied with his work, he plunged it into a pail of water. The water boiled furiously and spilled sizzling over the sides, then fanned out into pools over the floor. At last he laid his work aside and sat down on an upturned pail. He looked at Lucy for the first time since she had arrived, nodded and grunted. She nodded back. Then he lifted an earthenware jug to his mouth and swilled down a gallon of ale at one gulp, or so it seemed to the round-eyed Lucy. Wiping his hand across his fat lips, he raised his eyes to meet hers. They were raw from the heat, the lashes burnt from them, and they were narrow and piglike, under the tight, thick, knotted brows.

He waved a hand, huge and flat as a harvest ham, and nodded again. Lucy felt the eyes gobbling her up. She looked quickly at Roger. He was smiling, looking mighty pleased about something. Then she looked at the parson's sister whose expression was positively smug. She turned back to Boost, who was hauling himself onto his feet and moving slowly in her direction.

As he advanced she felt herself growing smaller, as though someone beneath her was digging a trench. When he arrived, and faced her, she realised with a shock that her nose reached only to his hairy navel. Miles of him remained, towering above her like a mountain. She cricked her neck trying to look up at his face. His great tangled head glowered down at her, the loose mouth spreading into a smile. She felt the huge, flat, hamlike hand swing through the air to land heavily on her shoulder. It struck her in very much the same manner as his hammer struck the anvil, her knees bent beneath the blow.

"Ah. That's it." The voice rumbled up from somewhere about his belly, growling out of his mouth like thunder on a calm night. "Ah've seen her an looked at her before today, Rogert Emmett," he said. "Don't think because Ah've not said nothin' that Ah've not liked what Ah've seen."

Roger's dear old face was transformed with delight and pride. "I thought as much," he said, slipping his arm around Lucy's shoulders. "There's never been a man who's seen her and not been taken with her. Now what do you say man, eh?" He punched the blacksmith playfully in the chest with his clenched fist. "Come on. Don't be bashful in God's name. Say out. She's handsome, is she not? Come on. Let me hear it?"

Boost went shy for a moment. Then his body was suddenly taken by what Lucy thought was a fit or a spasm of some kind. It trembled and shook so hard she feared for a minute that the roof of the smithy would tumble around her ears. Then a roar of laughter escaped from him and the shaking stopped. She gritted her teeth as she felt a stubby, rough finger tilt her chin. Her eyes gazed into his. She saw with horror that his look was tender.

"Ah'll say it then, to please yew. It's a real handsome wench."

There was a shrill cry of triumph from Miss Parson Brown. Then, much to Lucy's surprise, both Roger and the smith fell to slapping one another on the back, laughing, shaking hands, spitting on palms and rubbing them together as though some sort of bargain had been struck. The jug of ale was passed. There was a deal of gulping, wiping of mouths, and more back-slapping and much more laughter. Lucy wondered what could have occasioned such glee. She was going to ask but was lifted in Roger's arms and carried back to the cart. On the way he covered her in kisses.

"Call when you will, old friend," Roger shouted, as he whipped the tired horse into a slow easy trot.

The smith didn't waste time. The next afternoon he appeared, wearing a large blue and white spotted handkerchief on his head, the four corners knotted into a cap. In his great right hand he clutched a bunch of pink dog-roses, picked on the way to Ridge Farm. He offered the roses to Lucy. She took them from him. They were much crushed and wilted. Then she looked into his face, and all at one moment she came to the full, terrible realisation of the nature of the bargain struck between the smith and Roger the previous day.

"Ah'm come a-courtin' Lucy Emmett," growled the smith. She tried to speak but no words would come. Her mouth would only open and close, in a sort of awed imitation of a small fish beached on the river bank.

"Ah'm not one," the smith continued, "to waste time on such matters as courtin'. Since my last wife died, I've not had time to think on such things, what with the brats to see to and my work an' all." Lucy's blood ran cold. He hitched up his breeches. "The thing is, I'll not court longer than a week. The sooner we are wed, and Ah've got yew homed up, the better for all I say."

Roger came across the yard from the barn, striding out, fit to burst. The smith was a good man, hard-working, rough but honest.

"What ho," he shouted. "Courting her so soon?" He slapped Boost's back and smiled at Lucy. Then seeing the flowers he winked at Boost. "Well, well, what a swain. Flowers and all. Well, maid, you are the lucky one. When is the wedding then, eh?"

Lucy threw down the flowers, and trampled on them, bursting into hysterical tears. She swung round on Roger, crying; "Oh, you cruel, behind-the-back beast. How could you strike this bargain without asking my leave? There is no wedding. I will never marry this hairy giant. You may see me dead first."

Two astonished men watched her run across the farmyard, leap over the hedge like a young deer, and make off up the fields towards the Charnwood.

CHAPTER IV

The Great Metropolis

In which Lucy makes off for London.

Lucy was sobbing as she ran, her feet flying across the fields. Her instinct to run had been overpowering, like the instinct of fox or hare when pursued by a pack of baying hounds. She was desperate to put as much distance as possible between herself and the odious smith. All she was aware of as she ran was that single thought, accompanied by the pounding of her heart and the gasping of her breath.

She reached cover at last, entering the thick summer undergrowth of the Charnwood through a break in the hedge, and stumbled along, parting the high clumps of white cow parsley before her, the sharp aroma of wild onion pricking her nostrils. Above her head, stout oak branches, heavy with glossy, frilly-edged leaves, formed a cool dark canopy. She didn't stop until she reached the tallest oak of all. As soon as she did, she clambered up it, feeling for secure footholds in its ancient, gnarled trunk. Arriving breathless at the top of the tree, she found herself, as she had hoped, well hidden by a curtain of foliage, safe from the eyes of the smith or anyone else who might search for her.

She couldn't stop crying. The tears poured from her eyes and great gulping sobs wracked her. In her most desperate moments she couldn't have imagined a fate worse for herself than to have to couple with a man like Boost.

"Oh, horrible, horrible!" she cried, beating her fists against the thick bough. "Oh, I would rather die than marry that monster and play mother to all those brats. Oh, and have more brats to come."

This last was the worst of all. She held her breath in an effort to stop crying and compose herself. Looking down at her legs dangling on either side of the bough, she saw to her surprise that they were badly torn, scratched and bleeding. She must at some point have run through brambles and briars.

At last the sobbing stopped. She wiped her eyes and blew her nose on the hem of her petticoats. *Now what am I to do?* she thought. *Where do I run now? For I'm damned if I will find myself married to a man I find so repulsive in every degree. To be not yet seventeen and to find myself betrothed to such a walking horror. What sort of fate is that in God's name?* She blew her nose again and lifted her chin. There was a good deal of cool thinking to be done if she was going to discover a way to escape the smith's embraces.

It was pleasant in the tree. The branches stirred and murmured softly around her, sighing in the gentle breeze like a thing that breathed and had a soul. It was a long time since she had climbed a tree. Not since she was quite small, when she joined Toby and John in search of bird's nests. *Nor have I ever perched so high*, she thought, as she parted the branches and looked out over what seemed to be the whole land. It was a magnificent sight to see the rolling hills and fields laid out before her under the cloudless azure blue sky.

There was Ridge Farm, tucked snugly away below her. A thin wisp of smoke from the ever-burning fire in the hearth curled idly away through the chimney in the neat thatched roof. She could see the chickens and geese pick their way about the yard, appearing like tiny white and russet brown dots. The old carthorse grazed peacefully in the field. But there was no sign of the smith or Roger Emmett. She suspected they must be inside the house, taking some ale and chewing over what was to be done about her. She could see Ragby village to the right of her. The close huddle of low houses, the church and its tower were easily made out. So was the churchyard, the tombstones like blunt white teeth jutting out of the verdant green of the long grass. In the near distance, she could see the roof of Ragby Hall standing above tall elm and yew trees. There lived the squire, Billy Royalston, his wife Jemima, and that stupid fop she had met at the parsonage the week before.

By standing on tiptoe and parting the higher branches, Lucy extended her view over the ridge and away across the valley. She could see a wide ribbon of shimmering silver river, winding its way through a vast parkland where the trees turned to blue as they met the sky on the distant horizon. In the midst of the parkland she could just make out a group of what appeared to be very grand buildings, constructed of gleaming white stone and surrounded by gardens and avenues of dark green poplars. The sun shone on many windows, and twinkled where its light caught the panes, like rosy pink stars.

"I wonder," she whispered with awe, "if that far-off beautiful place could be London?" She let the leaves fall across her view again, and sat back on the broad bough. Through her life she had heard of London. It was said to be a place of amazing wealth and stupendous iniquity. She had heard of people "Going to London" or "Coming from London," of people "falling into bad ways in London," and even that "people sometimes disappear in London." But she had never been able to find out exactly what or where it was. A shiver of excitement rushed through her on thinking that she might, by accident, have at last discovered the exact location of this profoundly mysterious place.

"London," she whispered, her rapture growing. "London, London, London," she shouted, throwing her arms wide, and almost falling from the tree. "The great metropolis," Peter Royalston had called it. "Oh," sighed Lucy, "that *would* be a place to go." She stood carefully again, raising herself on her toes, and peeped out of the tree. There it was, that magical place. How it shone in the sunlight, how the windows twinkled. "Dammit! I'll wager that's London," she said, seating herself again.

"I must go to London or take the blacksmith and his ten runny-nosed brats, with more to grow from my belly." Lucy knew she could not hope to hold out against marrying Boost if she stayed at Ridge Farm. She was strong-willed, but so was Roger and things between herself and Elizabeth had reached such a pass she was certain she would be driven to marry the loathsome fellow out of sheer desperation. "No," she said after more thought. "I cannot remain in Ragby. I am for London." She was jubilant now, determined to forge her own future. But oh! There was Mr. Magpie. How could she go anywhere without Mr. Magpie? She fell sad again.

"He would fall to a-whimpering and a-pining for me, dear creature. It may be that he would die without me, his poor heart broken by my wanton selfishness." A big tear dropped into her lap. "Why, imagine, you cruel wench," she snapped, "thinking of running off to London and forgetting poor, sweet Magpie?" She could see the dog's face in her mind's eye. His expression was sad, mournful, bereaved. "That's it," she said suddenly, clenching her fists. "Fall to it, Lucy Emmett. Think of a way to rescue the hound without being discovered. Then off, after your fortune, to London."

Now, Lucy did not know it but she had not, of course, been looking at London at all from her nest in that high Charnwood oak. The mysterious great place that had so fired her spirit was in fact Landsdun House, the country seat of the eleventh Earl of Landsdun, one of the wealthiest men in the whole country. It stood eight miles from the ridge and about ten in distance from the forest. There had always been a house of some sort on the site. It had been started, long before the Conquest, as a small wooden fortress, surrounded by a deep ditch and through the centuries had grown to its present splendour. It stood now, a fine palatial mansion in the classic Italian manner, among ornamental gardens of immense grandeur and several hundred acres of grass and parkland. A wide poplar-lined drive led to the front of the house, curving around lawns, smooth and green as the baize on a new card table and sweeping up to a flight of marble steps that climbed to the double front doors.

Above the doors was a carved portico of the same marble, embellished with masks of the two-faced Roman god, Janus, keeper of the door. The portico was supported on each side by three elegant Roman pillars. Directly in front of the steps, in the middle of the lawns a round lily pool had been sunk. At its centre stood a marble statue of Amphitrite, andd the water deity who was Neptune's wife. In her rounded arms, the goddess held a conch-shell, pouring from it a stream of crystal clear water to freshen the upturned faces of the waxy, white blooms that covered the pool's still surface. Four majestic stone lions guarded the house, one at each corner, lying on high stone plinths, their paws crossed before them, their large wavy-maned heads and blind eyes staring out over the surrounding countryside.

The bloodline of the Landsduns was ancient and noble. It could be traced back with ease to Saxon times, when the old tribal kings had divided the land among their most loyal and powerful friends. Since that time, each earl had served his country gallantly in war and with distinction in the civil services. They had all travelled widely, carrying back with them from the furthest corners of the known world furniture, paintings, statuary and all manner of costly and gracious finery for the improvement and decoration of Landsdun House.

Landsdun was big enough to house a multitude of guests. At the present time, however, there were none, for the earl had spent some two months in London. On the previous day, a message had been delivered to the house by courier, telling the servants that their master had been taken ill and wished to return to Landsdun on the following day so that the peace of the countryside might help him to recover. The earl would travel with his physician, Sir James Robertson—and with his only child, Charles, heir to the estate and known as Lord Melton, after his father's viscountcy.

This message had sent the staff of Landsdun into a veritable frenzy of activity. Now the earl and his son were on the road from London in a coach bound for Landsdun, and all the servants had been up since before dawn to complete their preparations. Brown, the earl's bailiff, had been striding around all day through the grounds and stables, supervising estate workers, grooms and farriers. He made sure that wood, produce from the farm and gardens were forthcoming, that the coaches and livery were spanking smart and that the animals' quarters were clean, with fresh straw laid and water provided. That the animals themselves had been groomed and curried until their coats, tails and manes shone glossy as silk. Brown paid particular attention to Lord Melton's black Arab stallion Jupiter. The proud high-stepping beast was led around the stable yard by a groom while Brown and the stable staff stood by, their eyes filled with admiration, for Jupiter was a magnificent specimen of horseflesh.

In the kitchens, the cooks and scullions were also busy at preparations for the earl's return. Mounds of fresh vegetables were carried in by gardeners, sides of meat were chopped, cut and tied by butchers. Bread had been made, and laid on racks to cool. Copper pans full of gravies, sauces and purees were being stirred over the big fire. There could never be too much food prepared at Landsdun for, apart from the earl, and his heir and any guests who might arrive with them, an army of staff was employed in the house. Any food left after the most menial had been fed would be given to the poor who lived on the periphery of the estate, people whose very lives depended on the scraps from the rich man's table.

The rest of the house was a hive of activity. Footmen and upstairs servants ran about, opening up windows in rooms locked since the earl's last visit. They drew back heavy drapes to let in the sun. Feather mattresses that had been taken out to air were being dragged back onto the big canopied fourposters. Chambermaids with warming pans stood by to make sure no damp remained in them, and laundresses hurried upstairs with armfuls of newly washed and ironed linen so that the beds might smell sweet and clean.

All through the house rugs and carpets had been lifted and beaten until the dust flew. Silver and furniture had been polished. In short, every corner was as clean and dust free as it could be considering the short notice. The butler had seen that new candles were put into gilt candelabra and crystal chandeliers, then his sharp eye had lit on the earl's two deerhounds, Rex and Regina. He had called in a groom and directed that they be searched for fleas, bathed, brushed and that their nails be cut and polished. Both dogs were then sent to lie in the grand entrance hall to await their master's reutrn, so that the sight of them looking so handsome and spruce would cheer him after his long and tiring journey.

The earl's coach was upon the London road, still about four hours distant from Landsdun. It was one of the grandest in the country; not even the King could boast of a superior vehicle. Its panels were of polished walnut. The doors bore the family crest and were edged with gilt, as were the windows. There were gilt lamps at front and rear. The coachman sat upon the box at the front, resplendent in scarlet livery, with a black tricorn edged with gold braid covering his snow white wig. He held a long whip in one gloved hand while the other held the reins and a stout leather crop. Two more coachmen, similarly smart in scarlet, travelled up on the rear of the coach. At a distance behind the earl's coach another, carrying personal servants and luggage, followed. This was not so fine as the earl's but was drawn like the first by greys, their red leather harnesses stamped in gold with the Landsdun crest.

The interior of the first coach was opulent. The upholstery was of red-buttoned leather, soft almost as velvet. There was a rich Persian carpet on the floor and red brocade curtains at the windows. Edward, the eleventh earl, a man in his sixty-eighth year, lay sleeping peacefully, his head and back supported by silk cushions on the seat opposite his son and Sir James Robertson. He wore a silver-grey silk gown, tied loosely around his waist with a silk tasselled cord. His long white hair hung loose around a face that continued noble in spite of his age and displayed all the best features of good breeding. It was marred in repose only by the deep etched lines that ran from his nose to his mouth, betraying something of the suffering his illness had caused him. Indeed, he was at peace only because Sir James had administered a sedative at the journey's start and was ready to administer more, should it be required. Sir James had been against the journey to Leicestershire, but the earl had been determined.

"Well. I take no responsibility for you," Sir James had told him. "I have advised you to remain in London, at least until your strength improves. It's ridiculous. You employ me to advise you, then you ignore my advice."

The earl had smiled up from his sick bed at his old friend and physician. "Ah," he replied. "But consider this. I should not have felt confident of living through the journey had I not followed your advice to the letter in the past, sir. But I feel that I cannot continue in this world for long and since I must be buried at Landsdun, it will be much more congenial for both yourself and my son if you travel with my live, rather than my dead, body. Especially in this heat."

Sir James Robertson was a kindly, genial man, though at times he was given to a certain gruffness of temper that could become explosive. His nature provided a perfect foil for the dry wit shared by the earl and his son, who also bore a marked physical resemblance to his father, though of course there was more than a forty-year age difference between them.

Lord Melton sat beside Sir James. Both of them had removed their coats, for the air in the coach was stifling in spite of the open curtains. Sir James had also removed his hat and wig. He fanned himself with his wide-brimmed hat and glanced at Charles, whose eyes had scarcely left his father's face for the entire journey. He was deeply moved by the young man's anxiety. The earl and his son had never been demonstrably fond of one another. The earl had married late in life and his wife had died when Charles was little more than seven years of age. From that time the boy's education had been in the care of tutors at Landsdun and the earl had taken to travelling. This separation from his parents had caused Charles to grow into a self-sufficient young man who, like his father, was not given to show affection. But it was obvious to anyone who knew them both that there was affection and even love between them.

Sir James knew this better than anyone. He had always been aware that their natures were too similar. They were both very private people and at heart, shy. Charles was now twenty-six years, tall and powerfully built. He had been carefully reared and educated to his estate and was in every degree a gentleman. His clothes also bore witness to his station in life. His broad shoulders were covered by a linen shirt of simple cut, fastening at the throat and wrists with small mother-of-pearl buttons. He had untied his silk cravat, reclining in only his shirt, buckskin breeches, silk stockings and black, silver-buckled shoes. His buff coat lay beside him. His forehead was wide and intelligent, his eyes grey, his nose aquiline, high-bridged and, in profile, Sir James thought very fine. These haughty, well-bred good looks had been his inheritance from his father. But from his mother he had inherited thick, dark chestnut hair, which he wore long and tied at the nape of his neck with a black satin ribbon.

Yes, indeed, thought Sir James as he studied the young man. *Wealth, good looks and impeccable ancestry combine to make Lord Melton the most eligible bachelor in the country, if not in Europe.* But in spite of this Charles had remained unmarried and there was every sign he would continue to do so.

Charles drew back the curtain from the window on his side of the coach and looked out at the passing countryside, through the dust raised by the coach wheels. He could see the river Stour and realised that they had entered Leicestershire at last. He let the curtain fall across the window again and reached across to his father, touching his hand gently. The old man opened his eyes. They were clouded with pain but still retained a little of his usual amused expression.

"We have just come into Leicestershire," said Charles

softly. "Would you prefer we stop so that you may rest and take refreshment, or shall we continue on to Landsdun?"

"Will the horses last, or do they need to be changed again?" his father asked in reply.

"My word," exclaimed Sir James. "I should think the damn things could trot till Christmastide at this rate."

"It was your idea that they should move so slowly," replied the earl.

"I did consider it better for your health, sir. But if you demand a gallop, pray ignore my caution and call out to the coachman. Or perhaps you would prefer to ride upon the box yourself?"

The earl laughed. "Come, come, Sir James," he exclaimed. "Let us have no more sulking from you. I shall do as I am told from now on, I promise. What is your opinion on this matter? Should I be hauled out into an inn somewhere and then hauled back into this vehicle like a sack of oats? Or should I continue directly to Landsdun and my own bed?"

"It is my opinion, as you well know, that you should never have embarked on this madcap journey," said the physician. "But, since you ask, I believe you would do better to have the coach stopped, not for the sake of the horses, sir, but for the sake of your health."

The earl nodded. "I'm very much obliged for your opinion," he said. Then, looking again at Charles, he asked, "How do the horses? Will they need to be changed do you think?"

Charles shook his head. "I believe Jack would have told us before now had he thought it necessary."

The earl shut his eyes for a moment, then opening them met his physician's gaze. "Oh," he said, his eyes twinkling. "I think we will continue to Landsdun."

"Blast you for a fool!" shouted Sir James, his Cumberland accent becoming very pronounced in his rage. "Do not blame me, sir, if you find yourself in a relapse within the hour. The consequences of this are upon your own head." He threw his hat on the floor of the coach.

Charles tried not to laugh, but it was impossible. Although his father was weak and very fatigued, he still found strength to bait his grouchy old doctor and was chuckling quietly to himself. But soon his eyes closed and he slept again and as soon as he was seen to be peaceful, Sir James leaned across and tenderly put a hand upon his head. He sat back in his seat beside Charles and shook his head.

"Do I imagine it?" asked Charles. "Or is my father weaker since we left London? He seems to become more frail by the minute."

The physician did not reply immediately. He found his medical bag from under his seat and pulled it onto his lap. Opening it, he removed a small silver brandy flask and unscrewed the cap from the top.

"Your father may be weak, young Sir," he replied filling the cup with spirit. "But I swear that I am weaker through worry." He drained the cup himself, then refilled it for Charles.

"My father always makes light of illness," he said after a little while. "It is difficult to judge quite what his condition is. From what you say, it appears grave." He had dropped his voice to a whisper so that the earl might not be disturbed.

Replacing the flask in his bag, Sir James frowned and turned to the earl's son. It was difficult to know how to say what he had to say. Though he had been charged by his patient to tell Charles the truth, it was no simple matter to do it. "Your father believes that he cannot live long," said Sir James quietly. He could not look at the young man. There was a pause.

Then Charles lifted his eyes and looked across at his sleeping father. "Do you share that opinion?" His voice had fallen so low Sir James had difficulty hearing the question.

"You know, my dear young man, that I would never worry you unnecessarily," he replied, his voice breaking with emotion. Charles nodded and fell quiet, his eyes still on his father's pale face. "I feel too," went on the doctor, "that it is my duty to tell you that my old friend there"—he gestured towards Edward Landsdun—"has for some time voiced to me a concern for your future. He has tried not to press you with his worries but . . ."

"He should not concern himself about me at this time,"

129

Charles said. "He should think only on his health."

Sir James found it difficult to pursue the task the earl had set him.

"I suppose," said Charles, "that he requires me to marry?"

"Well, if he should decline further, there is the question of the line," said Sir James respectfully. Charles looked angry, so he said no more. Perhaps it would be better to leave well enough alone for the moment. He could not understand the young man's reaction to talk of marriage; at the very hint of it, his face would contort with fury. Surely he understood his father's motive. The earl wished to see his only son married and the line secure before he died. It was natural, after all.

It was not that Charles was not interested in women. On the contrary, he had recently returned from his grand tour, visiting every major city in Europe, among them Paris, Rome, and Vienna. It had been reported to the earl that his son had shown an interest in many of the beautiful women he had met there but when it came to matchmaking, Charles had rebuffed every attempt. Sir James was present when the earl had questioned his son about the ladies who had found Charles very pleasing to them, ladies of quality who would have been delighted to find themselves given to the young man in marriage. When the earl had asked him if he had not found in all Europe a lady whom he could love, his reply was, "I loved most for a week." When his father attempted to press him further, the young man had left the room.

"Do you not think, Sir James," Charles asked, after some time spent staring out of the window, "that I am only too aware of my duty with regard to the line?"

Sir James smiled. "I'm sure you are."

"And," the young man went on, "my father was many years older than I before he took my mother."

"That is certainly true," replied the doctor, "but your father had a younger brother living at that time who it was thought could provide an heir if your father did not marry. Of course sadly your uncle was killed in the Americas."

Charles laughed ironically. "Yes, with not a legitimate

130

child to take his name though I believe the colonies are peppered with his bastards. I often wonder if my father would have concerned himself to marry at all, had his brother not been so negligent."

Sir James smiled. "It is a fact that none of the Melton heirs have been led to marriage easily. But I have to be serious, my young friend. I'm sure your father would be a good deal more content and that his health would even improve, if you were at least betrothed. For then if he should die, he would die confident the line was secure."

Charles sighed. "I have been aware for some time, that he worries on that score, and I really have given the matter some thought, Sir James."

"But not serious thought?" the physician asked.

"No, not serious thought, for until this day, my father's health had not given such cause for concern. I suppose now, though, I should consider the question of my marrying a priority. Though for the life of me, I cannot think of a lady I could be content with."

Sir James tapped him on the knee and asked eagerly. "What of Georgiana Stowe?"

Charles groaned inwardly. The lady's name had been put forward frequently as a suitable match. "Ah, yes, Georgiana Stowe," he replied, letting the curtain fall across the window. "Every time this subject is brought up Georgiana Stowe springs as if by magic onto everyone's lips."

Sir James pressed on. "Well, she's a rare beauty and I know that she is much interested in you. I agree with your father, you could not find a wife from a better family in England." Charles did not look very enthusiastic. "I did not tell you, did I, that her father General Stowe called upon your father only the other evening? He took great pains to tell the earl that his daughter speaks of you constantly. Constantly." The physician searched Charles' face for any sign that this news gave him pleasure. But the young man's expression remained impassive.

"Yes, speaks of you constantly. I met the young lady that we speak of myself once. It was after a masque at Vauxhall. She was dressed as Diana and, I must say, she

131

was exceedingly charming. Milk white skin, such a cloud of golden hair ... and her eyes, my dear young Sir ..."

"So, Sir James. When do you intend to propose to this goddess?" he asked.

"Good lord. I am a confirmed bachelor," he exclaimed. "I was merely trying to point out that she is most acceptable in the physical sense as well as in the blood sense. I mean her family is distinguished—not as distinguished as your own, that is true, but then there are few families that are. And she is very comely, you must admit?"

"Yes, Georgiana Stowe is most comely," he sighed. "But I do not find her interesting at all. She talks of nothing but decorating herself. Apart from that, her conversation is nonexistent."

Sir James looked glum but then brightened again. "I hear that she is very accomplished," he said.

"In what way?" asked Charles.

"Well, er, she speaks French like a native," ventured the physician.

"Well, I do not," replied Charles. "So that is no consolation to me. To tell you the truth, I am bored rigid by no more than ten minutes in her company. I find myself transfixed by the pattern in the wall-covering behind her head while she smiles and simpers."

"Lord, lord," said Sir James, beginning to lose patience. "This is ever the way with you. Every young lady who is brought forward as a partner for you is immediately dismissed as 'boring.' Surely to God, they cannot *all* be boring?"

"Well, it is to be admitted, I suppose, that some are *more* boring than others." Charles smiled ruefully.

Sir James raised his eyebrows. "I see, Sir. Might I then enquire into which category Georgiana Stowe falls? I mean, is she simply boring, moderately boring or very boring?"

Charles laughed. "Oh, very, very, boring," he replied.

There was silence while Sir James changed his tactics. "You don't imagine," he said after a little while, "that you would find her marginally less boring, perhaps, in bed?"

Charles shrugged. "That might indeed be the case. But it's a risky thing to discover. I mean, presumably I should have to marry the lady to find out. Unless of course you are suggesting that I seduce her?"

Sir James coughed and glanced at the earl. He slept soundly, thank God. "I would not have used that word myself," he said.

"But you used the word bed." Like his father Charles amused himself sometimes at Sir James's expense.

"I meant after marriage of course. I did not mean you to tamper with the young lady's honour," said Sir James.

"Well you need fear nothing on that score, for I believe that the honourable Georgiana Stowe is mercenary enough to hold out for her honour. Especially if she thinks that by holding out she may catch a fortune," Charles said cynically.

Sir James was shocked. "Oh. Come, come. She may love you. Did you never think of that?" he asked.

Charles laughed. "Oh, I'm sure she could love me to distraction, especially if she found herself mistress of Landsdun and a countess into the bargain. However, if it will please my father, I will try and cultivate Georgiana Stowe."

Sir James sighed with pleasure, and reached again into his bag for the brandy flask. "The earl thought you might care to invite the young lady to Landsdun shortly," he said offering Charles the flask.

"What. You mean during this visit?" Charles asked sharply.

"Why not? I'm sure a little feminine company will not come amiss. Think on your father. It would give him so much pleasure, my dear boy."

"Yes, but I have doubts that it will give me any pleasure at all," said Charles, gazing again out of the window. He had been called cold; he suspected it might be true. Georgiana Stowe was considered desirable by most of the young men in his circle, but she did not appeal to him at all. She was like most society girls. *Full of empty prattle, dishonest,* he thought, *and her beauty is largely the result of paint, cunningly applied.* He smiled to himself. *If ever I*

133

were to find a lady prepared to entertain me without having first daubed her face for two hours, I believe that I would fall in love as a direct consequence of severe shock.

"Why do you not send to her to come shortly?" Sir James piped up, disturbing his thoughts.

"I do not know where the lady is," replied Charles immediately finding an excuse not to contact Georgiana Stowe. "You see, she may be in London or in Hampshire or with her brother's family in Sussex."

"That is no great problem," said the earl, who had, to the surprise of his son, opened his eyes, and regained some colour. "We will send an invitation to all three places. I'm sure one will reach her."

Charles frowned. "I believed you to be asleep," he said sharply.

"So did I," said the earl, "until I found that I was awake and now that I am awake, why, I believe that my physician will not deny me a sip from his flask," he said, extending his hand.

It was already growing dark when Lucy climbed down from the tree. She had waited until the sun began to sink before attempting to rescue Mr. Magpie. She knew Roger and the rest of the family would be at their evening meal and that the dog would be in the yard, banned from the table so that the Emmetts might eat in peace.

When she arrived at the gate she found Magpie hunched in a doleful fashion outside the door, his nose resting on his paws, and his floppy ears draped over his eyes. He pricked them slightly when he heard Lucy's low whistle.

"Magpie," she called in a low voice. "Magpie. Come here to me." The dog twitched his nose, but remained in a heap. She did not dare dash forward and collect him for the door of the house was open. Nor did she dare call louder, for Roger might hear her and drag her back inside. Her adventure to London would then be well and truly over before it had begun.

"Magpie," she tried again. "Here," she called. But the

dog simply yawned, stretched and rolled onto its back, waving its paws in the air. *Well, that's it. I shall just have to leave the foolish hound,* said Lucy to herself. She turned away, but turned back again directly. She could not leave him. "He does not understand, the sweet apple, that he must come, or we shall never meet again."

Kneeling on all fours beside the hedgerow, she cupped her hands about her lips, and imitated the squeak of a field shrew, which was one of the dog's favourite dishes. At once he was at her side, his tongue lolling from his panting mouth and his plump rear wriggling in hope of food. He was surprised to find his mistress and not a juicy mouse and struggled when she lifted him in her arms. But he fell still when she kissed his nose and lay content against her breast as she carried him off towards the Charnwood and along the road which she believed would lead her to London, freedom, and a new life.

The smith had remained to eat with the Emmetts. Roger had thought it the least he could do to invite him to stay, since the poor fellow had arrived with heart and other parts high in expectation of a bride and bed companion, only to have his flowers trampled underfoot and the bride fly from him, as though he were a carrier of the plague.

Both of them had stamped about the fields calling for Lucy until they were quite hoarse. When she had not responded, they had decided to return to the farm and wait for her.

"Cease worry, old friend," Roger said cheerfully, slapping his hand across the doleful Boost's massive shoulders. "As soon as the sun sets, that wench will return like a swallow to the nest, for she cannot abide to be out alone in the dark, and fears witches and ghosties above everything. Take it as certain. For I know her ways."

But here they both were, back at Ridge Farm and tucking into their second trencher of potatoes and buttermilk; the sun was setting, and still no sign of Lucy Emmett. Roger was growing worried. He looked across the table at John and Toby and narrowed his eyes.

"Your sister did not hint to you where she might be

discovered, did she?" he asked suspiciously. He was still having the devil of a job keeping the rips off their sister, and he wouldn't have put it past either of them to arrange a hiding place for her. Both young men shook their heads and glared at the smith.

"I haven't seen her since this morning," Toby replied.

"Poor little wench," said John. "I did not know that you had betrothed her to him."

"Well, now she is betrothed," Roger said, scowling at his sons, "you two had better watch your tails. You know what I mean."

Toby and John lowered their eyes. "Perhaps she ran off because she wanted some small say in who she was to marry," John mumbled.

"It is not for her to choose," snapped Elizabeth. "That is her father's business. Nor should she have run off so rude from a decent man come to court in such a civil manner." She threw another log upon the fire. The sun going down made the evening chill. "She does not know her luck, that one," she continued, sitting upon the settle and warming herself. "To be betrothed to a man with a trade in his fingers, who will keep her for life in a manner comfortable, secure and proper before God."

The smith beamed at these words and wiped away the snail's trail of buttermilk that had dribbled down his stubby chin.

"Ah don't know, Ah'm sure, what took her to run off so, and at such speed. For Ah came here in all good faith," he growled, shaking his huge head. "Ah believed her keen, I really did."

Roger laughed and poured the man more ale. "And so she will be, old Boost," he cried. "You know how these young wenches are. Silly, wayward things until they are tamed. Do not expect them to know their own minds, nor what's good for 'em."

"No, 'tis true," the smith mused, "the woman never knows her own mind, for 'tis empty they say, 'till a man comes and fills it for her."

Roger filled his tankard until the ale frothed over the table. "Now hear this, old friend," he said. "I'll lay you a wager here and now, that she will enter that door at any moment. When she does, she will be beside herself with shame, desperate for forgiveness and hot with affection for you."

The smith smiled. "Do you say so?" he asked Roger.

"Listen, man. She's over the moon about you. Did you not see the way she looked on you at the forge? I tell you she ran because she plays 'hard to have,' that is all," Roger said earnestly. He prodded the smith in the ribs. "She will be back. Here's my hand on it."

He spat on his palm and held out his hand to Boost, who grinned.

"That pleases me to learn," he said, spitting on his own palm, and shaking Emmett's hand. "You know what Ah felt?" Roger shook his head. "Ah felt that the wench might be shy of me in some degree, her being young and green. Ah mean, she might be scared to have a proper man upon her," he said somewhat bashfully.

Roger looked thoughtful. "Yes," he said. "She is on the shy side, that little maid." He ignored the hollow laugh from Elizabeth.

"Aye that's it," he continued, winking at Boost. "The wench flew because she was shy." Both he and the smith laughed long and loud. "By God, she was sent into a tizz and no mistake. She fears the wedding night, I'll be bound. But after that, I wager, you will not find her shy at all, eh?" He prodded the mirthful Boost again with the sharp end of his elbow.

"That's what Ah believe," he replied. "All my wives were somewhat shy, though I soon eased them of that. Just deliver the wench to me. For after a week of marriage, I'll have her as soft and dutiful as the sacrificial lamb. But shy? Not a whit."

"Well," Sir James said cheerfully. "We shall soon be at Landsdun, thank God. Only about one more hour left of our travels and travails, I imagine." He put the gold fob watch back into the pocket of his waistcoat, and smiled hopefully at Charles. The young man did not acknowledge what he had said. Sir James sighed and folded his arms. There had been a dull and uncomfortable silence in the coach for a long time. The earl slept again and his son was incommunicado. Charles was deep in thought, trying to invent some way to avoid inviting Georgiana Stowe to Landsdun without offending his father. For it seemed the earl had his heart set on her becoming mistress of Landsdun in the not too distant future. Charles had even toyed with leaving the country. A friend of his at D'Aubignys Club was trying to set up an expedition to the unexplored South America. He already had a ship hired; all he needed was a full force of expeditionaries, willing to put up some money.

Charles groaned and looked at his father. *I am over a barrel*, he thought. *How can I embark on a trip to unknown lands? He is ill, and I am the only heir. That would kill him for certain, leaving me months away from England.*

Sir James roused him by tapping his shoulder. "You are out of sorts," the old man said.

"Not at all," he replied curtly.

"Come, come. I have known you since your infancy, young sir, and I know when you are out of sorts. You brood, like your father. He is deaf, dumb and blind to all who approach him. The same deep line appears between his brows, as I see so marked now between yours. I have known him to continue weeks in such a state. Now come," he said, trying to break the young man's melancholy. "I know your father's illness troubles you deeply, but it will not cheer him if he wakes to see you in such a black mood. Come, have some brandy," he continued, groping for his bag beneath the seat.

Suddenly they felt the horses pulled up abruptly. "Wo, wo, ho," It was Jack the coachman's voice.

"What in God's name?" asked a surprised Sir James, who had been sent almost out of his seat as the coach had pulled up. Charles reached quickly for his pistols. He kept a pair, primed ready, on the seat beside him whenever he travelled the roads, as a protection against highwaymen. He was a remarkable shot with any sort of firearm.

"What is it?" asked the earl, roused from his sleep.

"Ssh," Charles whispered. He grasped a pistol in each hand and pulled the curtain back from the window. It was pitch dark outside, the light from the moon was hidden by clouds and the lamps on the coaches did not give much illumination. He could make out the shape of the horses, though, and when he looked towards the lead horse's head, he could just see a dim shape standing in the roadway in front of the coach.

"What is it, Jack?" he shouted.

The figure was not on horseback so it seemed unlikely that it was a highwayman. They always employed fast horses so that they could make a swift getaway.

"It's all right, my lord," came the shouted reply from Jack. "It's a wench, my lord, that's all. Lost."

Charles sighed. "Well, tell her to lose herself somewhere else," he shouted. "My father needs his bed and Sir James and I are gasping for our supper." He was just about to pull his head back into the coach when one of the men who travelled on the rear, appeared at the window. He held his gun at the ready.

"You don't think, my lord, that the wench might be a decoy?" he whispered.

Charles raised his eyebrows. "A decoy?"

The man nodded. "This it seems is a new way of robbing, I have heard. A gang will send in a girl to stop a coach, so that they may discover how many firearms there are on board before they move in. I am worried about the coach that follows. I cannot hear it behind us, and fear that it may too have been held up."

The other servant from the rear of the coach had now joined the first. "I don't like it," hissed the second man. "The road here is well-lined with spinneys and there's good thick cover. There may be a dozen or more of them hidden at this moment with pistols pointed at our heads."

Charles opened the door and quickly jumped out into the road. Sir James leant forward and caught his arm.

"He is right," the physician hissed. "We have no way of knowing how many there are. Leave me a weapon. Your head may be blasted at any moment from your shoulders and I will feel a good deal happier if I can protect my own and your father's."

Charles smiled and handed him one of the pistols. Sir James took it and leaned out of the window to cover him. The young man was in his element when there was a whiff of danger in the air.

"Take care," Sir James called after him softly.

"Do not concern yourself with me," replied Charles, "and pull your head in or it will be shot off. Point the pistol down, or you will have shot it off yourself."

Sir James laughed. "I am concerned only for the ten guineas you owe me," he shouted.

"It's in my will for you," Charles called back in reply.

"Nonsense," he heard his father call. "He has no will."

Sir James roared with laughter. The earl had bucked up too. Like his son, he loved excitement.

"Had I known that," his physician said to him. "I should have demanded that a will be drawn up before he got out."

As Charles approached, the girl was questioning the coachman. "All I asked," she was saying in a country burr, "was if you are bound for London. Why cannot you carry me with you?"

It was taking all Jack's strength to hold the horses still. They were whinnying, stamping and rearing, their eyes whitening in the darkness. They could smell their warm stables at Landsdun and were anxious to be on their way. The girl took hold of the lead horse's bridle and held onto it.

"Leave go of that horse," Jack shouted. "I have told you time and time again that we are not bound for London. Now move off. What are you, wench, mad or something, jumping out in front of my team like that?"

Lucy was just about to shout again when she looked up and saw the barrel of a pistol pointing right at the spot between her eyes.

"Oh, sweet Jesus!" she screamed, letting go of the horse's bridle. "Lay down the gun, dammit." The next thing she knew was that the cold metal of the pistol was touching her forehead.

"Right," said a sharp voice. "Speak. How many of you are there?"

Lucy's heart fluttered like a butterfly in her breast. "Just myself and Magpie." she whispered.

"Who in the hell is Magpie?" the voice asked again.

"My dog," replied Lucy, gulping back tears of terror.

The gun was lowered. She looked up and her eyes met those of the young man holding the pistol. The eyes were grey and the expression in them was curious and somewhat bemused.

Charles found himself disturbed by the girl standing before him. Her dress was dirty, ragged, and tattered. Her hair was tangled and unkempt. But the dust and poor quality of her clothes could not disguise her dark, seductive beauty. He looked down at the fat dog who slept against the full round breasts and thought that he would have no difficulty sleeping as soundly, if only his head could lie on such a pillow.

"What. This *thing* is Magpie?" he asked, prodding the somnolent dog with the point of his pistol.

The girl's reaction was instant. Her eyes blazed, much to his amusement. She stepped back from him. "Leave off my dog with that gun, you bullying varmint," she snapped. "He is gun shy, so have a care."

Charles laughed. He was unused to such spirit in a female and such language was usually heard only from sailors, or soldiers for that matter. Her ferocity amused him. He prodded at it again.

"Nonsense. Gun shy? Why the stupid thing sleeps like a log."

"Hold off, I said," the girl snapped again. "I tell you, the dog is gun shy and can be fierce, even wild. Poke him again, and he will set on you and bite you. Look at these teeth he has." She drew back the dog's upper lip to show the silly creature's teeth.

Charles nodded. "I see the teeth and they are no problem to me. For if I am bitten, I shall shoot the brute and then it will be gun shy no more. Thus solving his problem and my own with one shot." He raised the pistol and held it to the girl's temple.

Good God, he thought. *I had almost forgotten my mission. We could at any moment find ourselves surrounded by highway villains. No, they are not fools to*

141

send such a very attractive decoy. His eyes narrowed. "Now," he said grimly, trying not to notice the girl's full lips and the fluttering of her eyelashes. "Why did you stop my coach and who is with you? Answer, for I warn you that I shall shoot without compunction and blow your brains out through your ears, unless I am satisfied by your reply."

Lucy winced and shut her eyes. She could feel the ice-cold metal against her temple and she did not have to use too much imagination to see only too clearly what would happen to her brains if the young man's finger should tighten on the trigger. Her knees trembled though she did her best to still them and her hands, wrapped around Magpie, were damp in the palms. Perspiration beaded her upper lip.

"Answer." The young man's voice was impatient and full of threat.

Lucy started, but her tongue was thick and her lips paralysed with fear.

"Come on quick," he said, pressing the gun harder to her head. "Who is behind this business and what has happened to my luggage coach?"

"Your luggage coach?" Lucy managed. "Who accompanies me? Dammit, I told you I am alone apart from this very fierce dog here, who will..."

Suddenly there was a yell from one of the liveried men. "I hear the luggage coach," he yelled. "It's approaching us at some speed, my lord." She felt the pistol lowered.

"Stop it," shouted the young man. "Stop it, or there will be a collision." Lucy could hear the sound of thundering hooves in the distance and the sound of coach wheels careering towards them over bumpy, uneven roads. The man who had shouted quickly snatched one of the lamps from the front of the stationary coach and ran off into the darkness to try to halt the vehicle hurtling towards them.

Escape. That word darted into her mind. If she could get into the cover of the trees at the roadside she could easily disappear. Nobody could find her in the darkness. She turned to run.

"Not so quick," said the young man. She felt his hand tighten about her arm. He tucked the pistol into the waist of his breeches and drew her towards him. His strong arm was around her shoulder. Lucy shivered at his closeness. Although generally she could not abide to be a prisoner in any sense, it did occur to her at that moment that it might be pleasant to be held by the handsome young man in different circumstances.

"I am still not satisfied that you are alone," he said, holding her even closer to him.

From the near distance the sound of horses, whinnying, was carried to them. Then came the sound of the coach juddering to a halt to the accompaniment of shouts and more nervous snorting from the horses. In a second, the liveried man who had been sent to stop it came running back again, holding the coach lamp high. He arrived painting, breathless beside Lucy and her young captor.

"It's all right, my lord. They are not harmed at all. They fell behind because they had trouble with the harnesses and had to stop to tighten them."

Charles looked down at the girl he held to him. She had been telling the truth.

"That is good news," he said to his servant. "Now back up on the rear box with you. Tell Jack we shall soon be on our way and tell the earl and Sir James that there is nothing here to concern them. Leave me the lamp, fellow." The man handed him the lamp and ran back to the coach. Charles held the lamp up and was able at last to see his prisoner really clearly.

"Can I go now?" she asked.

Her eyes met his. Never in all his travels at home or abroad had he looked into such captivating eyes. They were wide set, blue, fringed with thick glossy lashes. Very decorative, but more, they were bright, intelligent and sharp.

"Will you not tell me why you stopped the coach?" he asked softly.

"Well, I am bound for London."

Charles nodded. "I see."

"And I thought that if the coach was going there I might be carried on it. I have money to pay. I hoped that . . ." She was stumbling over her words.

"Money to pay?" Charles frowned. The girl was

143

dressed virtually in rags. She could not have much money about her. "How much?" he asked. The girl lifted her chin. "Two pennies," she said defiantly.

"Ha!" laughed Charles. "Two pennies would not carry you to London on a hay cart, Miss. Besides, you are going in the wrong direction. London is behind us."

Lucy's heart sank. "The wrong direction?" But she had been walking she had thought in exactly the right direction. "Oh," she gulped. "London is *that* way?"

The young man nodded. "That's right." She felt him put a finger under her chin and she lifted her eyes to his again. His expression was kind and a little amused.

"I believe you are lost," he murmured. "What is your name, girl?"

Lucy was going to answer. She was going to say that her name was Lucy Emmett; that she was running away from a fate that to her was worse than death—that she was lost and in truth beside herself with terror at the prospect of a night spent on the road. But she said none of these things. She dared not tell the young man she was a runaway for he might carry her back to Ridge Farm and straight into the waiting arms of the awful smith. Then there would be no escape for the rest of her life. Her eyes filled with tears, but she pressed her lips together.

"Will you not tell me?" she heard him ask. She shook her head. "I see." He seemed disappointed. "What will you do now?" he asked.

"I will continue. At least now I know the right direction." She wiped her eyes with her hand and tried to smile, though it proved diffucult.

She heard him sigh. He let go of her and looked down at her torn bare feet. "There is a physician in my coach who will have something to soothe those wounds," he said.

Lucy shook her head, "No, thank you. I will be on my way. They do not hurt me really."

He caught hold of her and shook her. She was surprised that his anger did not frighten her. Rather she thrilled at it. It was a sign of concern. Although she must go and never see him again, she wanted him to be concerned for her.

"Now listen," he said. "You do not seem to be a fool or

144

an imbecile, so I can only suppose that you are naive in the extreme. I do not exaggerate, I promise you, when I say that the roads are dangerous for anyone alone. Riffraff and murderers abound. I myself would not travel alone unarmed during the daytime, let alone in the night. I can only think that your family must be ignorant of this, if you have a family. Have you a family? No, I suppose that you will not answer."

There it is, thought Lucy. *He enquires after my family.* "It is to my family that I go. They are in London," she lied.

"I see." She felt him loosen his hold and push her away from him in a rough fashion. "Be off with you, then," he said. "The roads are littered with beggars and itinerants. If I concerned myself with everyone I had seen, my house would bulge with them. I was going to offer you some assistance, and suggest that you be carried back to Landsdun House in the luggage coach. A bed could be found, at least for the night, in the servants' quarters. But since you seem determined to continue upon the road, I realise that I would be wasting both my time and my breath." He turned away from her, cold and distant. This dismissive attitude rankled with Lucy—and to be called a beggar.

"I am not a beggar," she shouted after him. "I have never begged nor will I ever. Do not imagine because I am poor and alone that I am to be insulted."

Charles raised his eyebrows and turned to look at her again. She really was devilish pretty. She put him in mind of some of the Spanish women he had met at noble gatherings in Madrid and Seville. She had the same sultry looks, the same exquisite carriage, the same proud tilt of the chin. Had she not been dressed in such rags, she could easily have been mistaken for a person of superior breeding. He smiled. *I am quite captivated by her*, he thought.

"Now listen," he said softly. "The weather is turning and the wind is rising. Why do you not follow along in the coach behind? You will be well fed and tucked up for the night on my orders. If you are determined to continue to London, then I daresay it can all be arranged tomorrow. I could see that you are carried in the mail coach."

But the girl tossed her head again. "I am much obliged to you, sir," she said. "But I will not travel with a person who has insulted me and what is more, I question your motives in this."

Charles gasped. "You what?" he asked. "You—you question my motives?" Lord Melton was not used to having people question him.

"I do indeed," continued the girl. "How am I to know you are not hellbent to do me some injury?"

Charles's eyes narrowed. "Now you have insulted me, Miss. If you do not recognise a gentleman of quality and honour then that is your misfortune. I withdraw my offer and bid you goodnight." He turned on his heel and walked quickly back to the coach. "We will move off, Jack," he shouted, jumping in to join Sir James and the earl.

He was furious with the girl. Had she been a man he would certainly have struck the impertinent fellow full on the jaw. He heard the crack of the long whip and the coach moved forward. He slammed the door shut. He did not look at the girl again.

"What was the girl?" asked Sir James. "A beggar?"

"Probably," snapped Charles. "Though she denied it. That is the last time I hold out my hand in charity. She may rot for all I care." He was fuming and this amused both Sir James and the earl.

"Where was she bound for?" Sir James asked.

"London," replied Charles. "Walking with only a mangy dog for company."

The physician sighed. "The roads are thick with beggars and paupers."

"Not such pretty ones, though, I think," said Charles.

The earl smiled. "Aha, a pretty beggar girl. I wondered why you were so long in sending her packing. Had it been a crone, I doubt you would have tarried so long."

"You mistake me," Charles retorted. "I believe I should have been charitable no matter how old she had been. I should still have been concerned that she was unprotected and still would have offered her some assistance."

"Well," said Sir James. "If she is pretty, she will not remain alone for long."

'No, I suppose not,' said Charles fiercely. "I daresay some filthy knave will be upon her in no time and no doubt she will prefer his dishonourable intentions to my honourable ones. Do you know, when I offered to have her cared for at Landsdun, she said she suspected my motives?"

"Dear, dear," said the earl shaking his head. "I wonder what she imagined you were about?" He and Sir James exchanged smiles.

"Did you see her?" asked Charles. Both older men shook their heads. "She was in rags. Dressed like a scarecrow, covered in dust, and, well, damned rude. And I felt sorry for her." He sat back in the seat and folded his arms, falling once more into deep brooding.

"Ah well," said Sir James. "I daresay your concern was unfounded anyway, for she will survive. They are shrewd, the poor. You cannot be moved by every pauper you see. No, the girl will take her chance upon the road with the rest of her breed." He began to put on his wig and hat. They were not far now from Landsdun.

Charles remained quiet, the deep frown showing between his eyes. The earl looked keenly at his son. This was more than just charity spurned surely.

"Why has this pauper had such an effect?" he asked his son.

"I don't know," Charles replied. "I suppose she seemed naive and vulnerable. I felt she needed help. But was too proud to accept it."

"And she was pretty," said Sir James, beaming widely. "I should have felt the same, my boy. I am old but not immune to a pretty face, especially when it is in distress. Still, if she arrives in London, she will not keep her pretty looks for long. In a while, she will weary of sleeping on the streets. Her pride will desert her. Some foul harpy will collect her, recruit her to a bawdy house and then, my friend, you will not snap your fingers for her looks or anything else, for she will be riddled with the pox."

Lucy's temper soon left her and she felt disconsolate as she watched the coaches disappear. As the horses' hooves

147

became fainter so did her spirit. She bowed her head and tears spilled onto Magpie's sleeping face. Her pride had stopped her accepting help from the young man and she feared hers would be a case of pride coming directly before a fall. It was her pride that had caused her to run away. It was pride that refused to believe that she had been born merely to fill Boost's bed. The thought of the smith stiffened her resolve. The thing to do was to get as far as possible from Ragby, for at that moment he and Roger might be searching for her. Hoisting Magpie into a more comfortable position in her arms, she started once more upon her lonely way.

The road continued straight for a while but at last she arrived at a place where it forked. *Which is the London road?* she wondered, pushing her wet hair back from her forehead. Rain had begun to fall and the wind was rising. The road to the right of her seemed the most promising but, on looking up, she saw the chill dark shape of a wooden gallows standing out against the sky. The noose swung from it in the freshening wind. She shivered. Nothing would allow her to walk under the gallows. What if it proved an omen? What if she came to a bad end as a consequence, for it had been predicted by Miss Parson Brown. So she took the left way, taking care to walk on the grass that grew thick between the ruts left by carts in the winter when the ground was water-logged. But she found to her despair that the track became narrower and more bumpy as she progressed. In places the hedgerows almost touched on either side of her.

It had become so dark now that the entire countryside seemed wrapped in a shroud. Stars twinkled above her but the moon moved behind clouds, giving little light. It was so quiet she could hear herself breathe—so quiet her feet sounded heavy on the dew-wet grass. A mist was gathering low over the ground, swirling like thick smoke at the height of the verges and climbing higher by the second. She was tired and Magpie was heavy in her arms. But it comforted her to hold him close and his warm fur, though damp, stopped her hands becoming as numb and bloodless as her feet.

Back at Ragby, the entire custom of the Hare and Hounds was in a panic. Roger Emmett and the blacksmith had arrived pell-mell on Roger's cart in a state of high agitation. They had already combed the Charnwood with Toby and John but no sign of Lucy Emmett. When it was found that Mr. Magpie was missing too they feared the worst.

"As God is my witness," Roger said, "if that girl has run away, she is bound to fall foul of the countryside. 'Tis black as hell with the mist rising and she knows nothing of the further roads. The place changes at night, landmarks disappear. She will lose her bearings."

There was nothing to be done but to repair to Ragby and call out the men of the village to assist in a proper search. There were now assembled on the village green, about thirty Englishmen in all, every man jack of them fit to walk all night if need be. They carried lanterns and stout sticks ready to beat about the hedgerows of the whole county, to bring Roger Emmett back his daughter, and deliver to the smith his bride-to-be.

Boost stood beside Roger on the cart and addressed the men. "There's two casks of strong ale to any man among yew who brings Lucy Emmett to me in one whole piece, for she is promised as my wife," he roared. "Now in one whole piece Ah say, and yew all know my meaning," he said darkly. "Ah require her as she was when Ah last saw her or those same casks will be broken over the head of the man who makes mischief in her. Do Ah make myself clear?"

There was much shuffling, muttering and coughing from the assembly. Men looked down at their boots and pretended that the thought of tampering with the runaway was miles from their minds. A squeeze to comfort her, well, yes, but tampering, no. That was a different matter. Roger scrutinised the upturned faces and his eyes met the eyes of Barney Cowper, the wheelwright's apprentice. The boy looked too hot and eager by far to be after Lucy. *There's one randy young buck who can be relied upon to meddle with the parcel*, thought Roger. He raised his voice and pointed at Barney.

149

"You Barney Cowper," he called. Barney's eyes lit up. "You make off to the parsonage and see if they have any news there of my daughter."

"That is no mission to send me on," Barney said. "I wish to go off on the search. My eyes are young, sharp."

Roger nodded. "Yes. Not only your eyes are young and sharp neither," he said. "Now then. Off to the parsonage. If they have no news, then their prayers will not come amiss. Oh, and ask the parson if the sexton may be called out to toll the bell to signal Lucy the way home across the land."

"Well, when I have been to the parsonage, might I then join the hunt?" asked Barney.

"No," shouted Roger. "You may not. I am not forgotten your tussling with the girl before. Run off with you." Poor Barney turned tail for the parsonage. He was never going to be allowed to forget that romp in the hay.

"Now then," continued Roger Emmett as he watched Barney's lantern disappear up the road. "The rest of you sturdies make up teams. Take every road from Ragby, every track, every path. Look everywhere, no matter how unlikely. Scour about. Boost and myself will take the roads around the Charnwood, then move off towards the London way in case she has wandered ever further than we thought, or has been carried off by kidnaps to that heathen city. Now, if anyone should discover her, carry her back to the inn and send to the sexton to toll the bell three times, with a pause, then another three times with a pause. Am I clear?" he asked, looking hard at the men. "Must I repeat the signal that should be used if she is found so that we may be called back?"

There was more shuffling and murmuring and cries of "No. We are clear on that score."

"Fair enough," he said. "If you are clear, that's well and good. But by God, mark the words of the smith here." His voice grew gruff. "For not only will he kill any man who meddles with her to ruin her, but I myself will remove his giblets, and hang them about his neck." Having uttered this stern warning, Roger slapped the reins over the old horse's back and set off briskly through the mists towards the Charnwood and from there to the London road. Boost stood beside him, his face grim, his narrow red-rimmed eyes skinned for a sight of his runaway love.

It was as though a troop of giant glow-worms had invaded the district, for soon all the roads, fields, tracks, coppices, spinneys and woodland around Ragby were dotted with bobbing lanterns. Men called out for Lucy Emmett, their urgent voices echoing through the night. Never before in the whole history of the village had there been a search like it.

Word was carried to the parsonage by Barney. "Lucy Emmett has taken off," he said. This curtly delivered information was received by Miss Parson Brown who stood on the step in her nightgown with a shawl about her shoulders, blinking short-sightedly in the light from Barney's lantern.

"She has what?" shrieked Miss Parson Brown.

"Taken off," repeated Barney. "Run away. Bolted."

Miss Parson Brown drew her lips into a thin disapproving line. "The jade," she exclaimed. "The good for nothing strumpet. She is into bad ways or worse, I'll be bound. This business does not surprise me one jot. The girl was conceived in iniquity and will die steeped in it." She pulled her shawl tight about her shoulders to save herself from the rain and shook her head.

Barney asked if the sexton might be called out to ring the bell, so that Lucy could hear it and follow the sound home if she had a mind. Miss Parson Brown replied that she was not at all sure it was proper to summon such an abominable ingrate home by tolling a church bell. But she would enquire of her brother, "and learn his opinion on the matter." She crossed the hall and climbed the rickety stairs towards the parson's bedroom. She tapped timidly on her brother's door in case she distrubed him at his prayers, for she knew him to be the most devout man on the earth.

"Are you there, dear?" she called.

Had it been possible for Miss Parson Brown to look through wood, she would have observed her brother in a most curious position. He was sitting up in his narrow celibate bed with his nose pushed to its entire length,

151

jammed in fact, deep into a wide bottle of thick green mixture.

This he had purchased from the quack, Fitzmaurice, at some expense. The quack had informed him the mixture was rare, since the secret of its prescription had been discovered in the tomb of an Egyptian Pharaoh, the great Hotempetah, who, when he had lived, had suffered in common with the parson from a dripping nose. This wondrous liquid was a certain cure for that unfortunate malady and was brewed only upon the banks of the river sacred to those ancient, wise Pharaohs. It could be got only by the quack himself, being, as he was, an intrepid man of science.

The parson had taken to inhaling this strange concoction in secret for, although it had not cured his nose, it had proved to have a most pleasureable and beneficial effect upon another extremity of his body, not to mention his mind. For while sniffing the mixture, he would conjure up visions of the most exotic and divinely enjoyable nature and that part of him that had been fashioned for procreation, but had been neglected because of his calling, would be startlingly resurrected to continue uplifted, sometimes for an entire night. The visions conjured up by the Hotempetah mixture were always young, always attractive, always scantily clothed and, more important, always willing.

On hearing his sister's knock, he quickly withdrew his nose, corked the bottle, hid it under the pillow, adjusted his nightgown, took his black Bible into his trembling hands and called, "Yes dear, I am finished with my devotions. Enter, do."

Miss Parson Brown was surprised to observe that her brother's nose seemed coloured a gaudy green, but she ignored it, believing it due to a trick of the candlelight coupled with the fact that she did not have her spectacles upon her own.

"I am sorry to disturb you while you commune with . . ." she raised her eyes towards the ceiling. "But, my dear, there is a scandal of the worst kind. Barney Cowper is

152

without and asks if the sexton may toll the bell? For Lucy Emmett is taken off."

The parson's eyes rounded. Guilt attacked him. He had been thinking of Lucy Emmett just as he had heard his sister's knock. She had in fact disturbed his imaginary dallying with the girl.

"Yes, taken off," sniffed his sister. "Run away from her father, from a good man who she was promised to in marriage, all through my effort as you know, and is doomed now with no hope of salvation. It is as I predicted, she is come to a bad, bad end."

"Do not judge unless you are judged. Nor cast the first stone."

Miss Parson Brown was surprised. Had she not known they had run out of Communion wine, she would have sworn her brother had been imbibing again, for his face was flushed and genial.

"I am not afeared to cast a stone," she sniffed. "For I remain pure, as you well know." She was quite put out by her brother's reaction to news of the bastard girl's escapade. "Well, shall the bell be rung? Is it proper, is it nice, think you, that God's voice should call across the country to such a flaunter?"

The parson was all for the bell being rung at once to summon the flaunter home. As for himself, he would fall to praying at once for Lucy Emmett's safe return. As soon as his sister had gone he was as good as his word. While the sleepy sexton staggered across the churchyard to ring the big bell that hung silent in the church tower, Parson Brown slipped his nose once more into the bottle and found that a parson can as easily pray with his nose in a bottle as without. Yes, he prayed for Lucy Emmett with more fervour than he had ever mustered before, and lo, she came dancing towards him—there were the voluptuous breasts, the rounded hips, the sublime thighs, and lo, the whole glorious accumulation of spheres were undulating suggestively to strange, erotic Eastern music.

"Ah," sighed the parson as she moved, smiling, towards him, her eyes full of promise. "There is hope of a

153

resurrection, after all," Her soft hand caressed him. "Oh, Lucy Emmett," he groaned as that sorely neglected extremity towered to life. "Bong" went the Ragby bell. "Oh," moaned the parson, as the resurrection was achieved and the promise fulfilled.

"Bong." Lucy turned and cocked her head. So did Magpie. "It's the Ragby bell," she whispered to the dog. Lucy knew the sound well. The bell had a crack in it and its tone was eerie. But it was not a bad sound to hear when one was a girl alone on such a bleak night. She put Magpie down and considered what to do. Should she return to Ridge Farm and try to argue her case for not marrying the smith with Roger or should she continue on her way and take whatever fate held in store for her upon the highways and byways? This was indeed a dilemma.

I am afraid to return and afraid not to return, dammit. Though I wonder if anything that could befall me on the roads is as bad as what will befall me if I end in Boost's bed?

She knelt down to pick up Magpie again but became aware of strange sounds. Her heartbeat quickened. Night sounds they were, sounds she could not put a shape to. Vague rustling and whispering sounds from the hedgerows. Suddenly a swift, dark shape darted out of the ditch beside the overgrown track and before she could stop him, Magpie was after it, barking fit to wake the dead.

"Magpie," she called after him. But in a second he had vanished into the mist. "Oh, Magpie," wailed Lucy. "My one and only friend and comfort gone." She ran after the dog, stumbling over the sharp flint stones that were hidden in the deep grass. "Magpie?" she shouted, tears pouring down her cheeks. The dog was hungry and the creature it chased was perhaps a rabbit. The thought of food was the only thing that could whip the dog into action. "Magpie?" called Lucy. "Magpie?" Now as she ran the track grew ever narrower. The mist closed in and turned to fog.

Branches caught at her hair, and beat at her cheeks until they were sore.

She stopped running. It was useless. The fog was as thick as porridge. She must be near a river or stream. She dared not continue in case she found herself precipitated into even deeper water. Her heart was about to break. She felt if she had lost Magpie, she had indeed lost everything. Then a high-pitched shriek pierced the still night. Lucy froze. What if the dark shape had been a stoat or weasel? What if the predator had caught sweet Magpie by the throat?

"Oh, no," wailed Lucy, flinging herself full length into the grass, and covering her ears as the shrieks became shriller, "it is certainly my little Magpie in his death throes. And it is all my fault," she sobbed.

Lord Melton and Sir James Robertson were disturbed at their late supper by the tolling of the Ragby bell. Charles was still out of sorts. The pretty minx who had halted his coach was still on his mind. He kept thinking about her and it was something of a nuisance to him. He was not given to pining in any way after females, especially not insolent females and especially not ragged, beggarly, insolent females, no matter how damned pretty.

"What in heaven's name is happening in that village at this time of the night?" he asked, slamming down his glass of port and striding over to the window.

"What bell is that?" asked Sir James. "What an appalling noise."

Charles drew the velvet curtain back from the window and looked out. "It's the blasted Ragby bell," he replied, "I'd know that noise anywhere. It has a crack in it. I have often toyed with the idea of creeping into the village church, under cover of darkness, and cutting the damned thing down so that I am saved forever from its jangling."

"Perhaps they have a hayfield or rick fire," said Sir James. "Can you see anything?"

"No," replied Charles. "The ridge hides Ragby from Landsdun and the mist is very thick now. One can only just see the very tips of the trees in the park and along the drive." He let the curtain fall across the window again and returned to his deep winged chair opposite Sir James near the fireplace. "I wonder where that girl is now?" he asked. "Probably perishing somewhere from exposure." He took up his port again and watched the old physician light his long churchwarden's pipe.

"I wish you would cease worrying about her," said Sir James. "You have done nothing but rattle on about the pert little ha-porth since we arrived."

"Ha," laughed Charles mirthlessly. "I am not worrying about her. I was merely making an observation." A frown grew deep between his brows again. "The rain is quite heavy now," he said, "and the mist is worsening by the minute. One could catch a pneumonia out there."

"Bong" went the bell again. "Well, we are not out in it," said Sir James, "so let us relax and finish our port and then retire to our beds." He stretched out his legs to the fire and puffed contentedly on his pipe.

The earl had been taken to his bed immediately upon their arrival at Landsdun and supper had been served for Sir James and the heir in the library. This had been Charles's choice, for he preferred to eat if possible in a less formal manner than was usually the custom at Landsdun House.

Although the library was a large room with high moulded ceilings, its decor of dark green Chinese silk and book-lined walls gave it a closed-in and intimate atmosphere, very different from the reception and entertaining rooms which were opulent to a degree. Supper had been wheeled in and served by a butler and footman and a very welcome and nourishing repast it had been. The beef cut from a rib had proved to have been well hung and was tender. There were vegetables beside it and gravies and sauces to enhance the flavour. A Musselborough pie had been prepared for Charles, since it had been one of his favourite dishes since childhood. There were also brawns of pig, salads, custards and small

156

cakes, claret to accompany and port or French brandy to follow.

Sir James had sampled everything and was left a comfortable and replete man. His wig was upon his lap; his waistcoat buttons were undone to allow his bulging belly greater freedom and his long churchwarden's pipe had been lit. But Charles had only picked at his supper, and even the usually well-loved Musselborough pie lay virtually untouched by him.

"Bong." The Ragby bell reverberated once more across the ridge. When its echo had ceased, both men sat in silence, preoccupied. There was nothing to disturb them at this late hour but the gentle tick of the ormolu clock upon the mantle, the hiss of sap from the logs in the fire, the patter of rain upon the windows and the low whine of the wind in the chimney. Sir James watched his young companion through eyes narrowed, behind a blue wreath of pipesmoke.

Charles was still brooding. His mood, ever since his meeting with the girl on the road, had alternated violently between this morose brooding and a restless pacing of the room like a captain in a sea squall. He was displaying all the signs of a man racked with desire. Sir James thought it a pity the young fellow did not show such interest in Georgiana Stowe. Here he was in an agony about a pauper met on the road that he would never see again.

"You know that it is not proper, this concern over the girl."

Charles looked up. "I have told you, I am no more concerned about her than I would be for any other person so obviously distressed and out in the open on such a foul night," he said. "If my concern seems to you excessive, then I must apologise."

Sir James laughed. "Do not apologise to me," he replied. "You are not the first man to be stirred by a pretty face. It is natural that you should feel moved in your manly parts. You are young, after all, and have youth's sudden appetites."

Charles looked angry. "Sudden appetitites?" he exclaimed. "You mistake me, Sir."

"I think not. I have seen men moved like this before. I have been moved thus myself. There is no ache worse, my boy, than the ache of a lust that cannot be satiated," said the old man. "I have felt it often, and in my youth thought I would die of it. But I never did."

Charles looked into the fire. "I have told you, sir," he replied, "that you mistake me. You mistake chivalry and concern for dishonourable intentions."

"I do not indeed," retorted Sir James. "Where do you suppose chivalry and concern spring from? Why, from the well of lustful desire. We cannot accept our animality and so we have invented chivalry, concern, honour."

"What of love?" asked Charles.

"That, too," said Sir James.

"Do you suppose that when Jupiter is taken to a mare, he will suffer the pangs of love?" Charles smiled. "Ah, but even animals have preferences. I may lead Jupiter to a mare but if she does not appeal, he will have none of her. Would you deny me what I would not deny my horse? All right, I will admit I was captivated by the girl. Call the attraction what you will—lust, plain desire—I have never in my life felt such an overpowering . . ." he broke off and shook his head. "I agree that it is ridiculous. I cannot explain it, nor can I rationalise it, so I will not try. I am surprised myself. You know that I do not normally fall into this sort of thing. I mean, I have never waxed lyrical over a woman's eyes or any other part of her. By God, I have been able to take them or leave them."

"Perhaps you only allow yourself these emotions because you know that they will never be tested," replied Sir James thoughtfully.

Charles looked surprised. "What do you mean?" he asked.

"Well, it is often the case when a man fears deep contact with a woman, that he will become enamoured of one he can never have. A woman who remains always out of reach, for whatever reason. I myself carried a flaming torch for a happily married lady for ten years, forsaking thoughts of all others. I dreamt of her constantly. And I never saw her from one year to the next. But had she come to me one day, her eyes full of love, saying: 'James Robertson, I am yours,' I should have taken the next packet out of Plymouth and absconded to the Indies, I promise you."

Charles laughed heartily at this. "So that is how you managed to remain a bachelor. You made it your business only to fall in love with women who could not, or would not, be able to reciprocate it?" Sir James nodded. Charles looked thoughtful again and sipped his port.

"What do you suppose you would do if the girl were here now, begging you to take her?" asked Sir James. "Do you suppose you would?"

Charles remembered the heart-shaped face, the proud tilt of the girl's chin. "I think I should be the one to fall begging," he said, smiling to himself.

"Then what sort of a man would you be?" asked Sir James. "You would be turned to a beggar. The son of an earl turned to a beggar for a rough girl's favours? Come, I lose patience with you. Put her out of your mind. If your lust is urgent, console yourself by all means. Command your manservant to have a chambermaid brought to you; that will remove the ache." He pointed at the Musselborough pie and laughed. "Satiate yourself with a chambermaid, my boy, and you will sleep as snug and easy as that pie was in the oven."

"You are an incorrigible old devil," said Charles, pouring the old man more port. "But in all probability you are right. I daresay that if I had that girl in my bed at this minute, well, I should be thinking of ways to rid myself of her."

Sir James nodded. "This is one reason why I urge a marriage for you," he said eagerly. "I mean, if you could bring yourself to marry Georgiana Stowe, you would not have to spend time with her. I mean, providing the question of children is taken care of and her material comforts are catered for, you need not speak to her, except in the course of your social duty. So my dear boy, the line will be secured, you will have done your duty, your father will be a happy man and you? Well, you will have met your obligations to society, and nobody will blame you if

159

you take a mistress to enjoy. You would be freer by far married than you are unmarried."

Lord Melton roared with laughter. "Sir James," he said, "If I did not know for certain that you were born and bred in Cumbria, I would swear you were an Irishman. How in God's name would I be freer married than I am now, for then, by your plans, I should have a wife and a mistress whereas now I have neither?"

Sir James laughed and shrugged. "You cannot blame me for looking after your interests," he said. "For mine are tied up with them. Just think if you have a wife and a legion of legitimate children and a mistress with a brood of bastards, it will make me a richer man, for I shall have a fee for each of them. I presume of course that you will engage me to care for their health?"

"Oh, of course," replied Charles with mock gravity. "I just hope I do not prove sterile or you are going to be a deeply disappointed man."

The physician bowed his head and winked. "I do not think we need worry overmuch about that," he said. "Will you write to Georgiana Stowe tomorrow?"

Charles sighed. "Yes," he said, "I shall write to Miss Stowe." He filled his glass and stared into the fire. The face of the girl met so briefly on the London road looked back at him, her eyes flashing as bright as the leaping flames. He turned away from the fire, leant his head against the back of his chair and closed his eyes to shut out the memory. The face faded but the inexplicable ache remained.

"Bong." Lucy had stayed awake as long as she could. But now she felt that she could keep her eyes open no longer. She had called and called to Magpie but there was no sight nor sound of the little dog and she was resigned to the fact that he must be dead. She had curled up under a flowering elder for shelter, but there was none. The rain poured down, the wind blew and the fog was full of imagined horrors that became more real as her fatigue grew. She looked up at the sky with heavy eyes. She could just see a cold moon sailing along behind ragged clouds

160

which engulfed its light, sending eerie light patterns moving about her. A witches' moon. All the phantasmagoria of her childhood nightmares came to haunt her and a shiver ran down her spine. There was the witch, Anna of the Charnwood, whose restless wraith haunted the countryside. Her cape was made of the skins of babies, flailed from them while they lived. There was the warlock "Sam of the Hill" who ate the hearts of maidens before his victims' staring eyes.

Lucy was shaking from cold and terror. She shut her fantasy-filled eyes and gave herself up for dead on the spot. She could do nothing now to escape whatever foul emissary the great reaper would choose to collect her foolish wayward soul. All that she could be certain of was an imminent, probably painful death.

"Woof." She opened her eyes. Again. "Woof, woof." It was closer. It was Magpie. Her heart lifted. "Magpie," she called, struggling to her feet, crying with joy. She could hear the dog bounding towards her, hear its excited panting. She strained her eyes through the darkness, and yes, she could make out the dark shape racing towards her. Nothing could be so bad now. Magpie had returned. In an instant he was in her arms, licking her face and nuzzling her with his nose.

But then she was aware of another movement in the near distance. She looked up. There was a light approaching. The light swung from side to side and then a huge figure appeared, looming out of the misty enveloping darkness. Magpie began to whine. Lucy thought she would scream. But she did not. She tried to run, but she could not. She was nailed to the spot, transfixed by that awful ominous thing bearing down on her. Paralysed. "Oh, sweet Jesus, have mercy, save me," she whispered, shutting her eyes fast. She felt a huge cold hand grip her, iron hard, about about her arm.

"Ah've got yew," rumbled a voice from above her.

Lucy looked up. It was Boost the blacksmith. "Oh," gasped Lucy, and fainted clean away.

161

CHAPTER V

Rescue at Ragby

In which Charles and Lucy meet again.

"Oh, how I wish I had perished," wept Lucy, "to think that I was so near escape, and that I am so far from it now."

Roger Emmett and his two sons were in a turmoil to know what to do with the distraught girl. She had been weeping for hours. The blacksmith had carried her back with them to Ridge Farm after finding her in a state of collapse. They had tucked her up on her mattress before the fire, then Boost had left, promising to call back on the next day.

Just when everyone else was about to take to their beds, Lucy had woken and, realising that she was caught, had started sobbing again. Elizabeth managed to crawl away to her bed behind the curtain but the three Emmett men, weak with fatigue, were engaged in keeping something like a wake, though instead of a silent corpse, they watched over an angry and hysterical Lucy.

Dawn was breaking but her fury had not abated. "Oh, cruel, cruel, cruel," she wailed, shaking her fist at heaven. "I rail at fate, I rail at God."

"Hush," said Roger. "You must not say that." He watched the door anxiously in case at any moment a bolt of lightning sent from a much-abused God would enter through it and strike them all dead.

"It is not fair," cried Lucy. "Not fair, that I should have to marry a person I hate."

"Oh, cannot you quiet her?" asked a hollow-eyed Toby, who was seated at the farmhouse table with his head sunk onto his hands.

"No," replied Roger Emmett firmly. "She is just trying to wear us down, boys, and I'll not give in, even for her tears. She may cry till doomsday for, as God is my witness, I gave my word the smith shall have her. We spat on palms and shook our hands and that is a countryman's bargain that is not to be broken. When she has finished these dramatics, she will come to see that this marriage is the best thing for her."

"No, I shall not!" shouted Lucy. "I know well enough what is good for me and to marry that hairy monster is not. Why, my flesh crawls when I see him. 'Tis not fair, I say again, that a man may choose who he is to marry but a maid, dammit, must obey the whim of her father. It's not fair, you hear me? This whole world is run by men; fathers and husbands—and as far as I can tell the lot of them are damned imbeciles and should not be trusted with the care of a pease pudding, never mind the fate of a human creature. Wouldn't you say that I have more wit in my tiny finger than the smith has in his whole body?" she demanded. No reply came. The men were too worn out by her to argue.

"Well, I have," she snapped answering her own question, "and yet I have willingly to give my whole life into his care, to do with what he will, before I have even had the chance to see what my life might be. Well, it's not fair and if you were in a state such as I find myself in on this night, you would be shouting unfair too. But hear this, sirrahs. Because you are men you would not be ignored. It seems to me that you have no rights in this world if you are female—and if you are female and poor, then you are thought less of than a stone. A maid has no value except for breeding. Oh, when I think how I could so easily have been saved from this. I could dash my brains out against that wall. I had the offer of shelter for the night and to be carried tomorrow to London. But I refused. Why? Because of pride, pride, pride."

She thought of the young man she had met on the road, of how he had held her in his arms, of how gently he had spoken to her at first, until she had spoilt it all by being froward. She covered her face with her hands and wept bitterly. Her first real chance to escape and see more of life, and she had ruined it by her hot-headedness.

"Well," said Roger, rising wearily and crossing to the window. "Other girls accept their father's will; I do not see how you can find it so hard. For I, in all honesty, do my best for you and a marriage with the blacksmith, who is a man of skill and has property, is the best marriage you can hope for in Ragby."

"Aye, in Ragby," shouted Lucy. "But outside the window there is a whole world somewhere that I have not seen nor will ever see if I marry the smith. In a short while I shall be with child, one every year of my life, like the other wives of his who had died under his passions."

Roger looked out on the new day bleakly. This hatred of being kept in one place, this lust for new experience must spring from her gypsy blood. He left the window, murmuring that there was work to be done and went behind the curtain to rouse Elizabeth so that she could rekindle the fire and prepare breakfast.

"I have learned something further about my condition," continued Lucy to Toby and John. "I have realised how little I know. How ignorant I am." She sniffed and dried her eyes. "That is something that you do not realise until you have travelled and seen a little of the world."

"Seen a little of the world?" exclaimed John, grinning at Toby. "Why you only moved about four miles from home. It seemed further because you were wandering about in circles." He tickled her under the arms which was usually a good way to cheer her and it did, for in spite of her former misery, she started to giggle and soon was begging him to stop.

"She is an ignoramus, it's true," said Toby, winking at John. "Mistaking Landsdun for London."

"Well, what do you expect when I have never gone further than Melton in my life and then with my father to watch over me?" said Lucy.

"I hand it to you for nerve, though, stopping the Earl's coach upon the road, and asking for a lift." John was laughing at her, so was Toby; they thought her night's adventures the most amusing they had heard in their lives.

"'Twas not nerve, I tell you, 'twas ignorance. I did not know it was the Earl's coach. I do not properly know what an Earl is, nor an heir, come to that. Mind you, the young man was passing handsome, just about the best set up I have seen. Such smart breeches, oh the cut of him was grand. If I met him again and was made the same offer, I should go with him like a shot." She smiled to herself, remembering the way he had put his arm around her, the way he had looked at her.

"Tell me," she asked after a time. "I have been wondering. Is an Earl gentry, like the Squire Billy and his nephew?"

Both her brothers were amused by this. "No. The Earl is quality, dunderhead. Only the King is more quality than an Earl. So you can stop smiling and mooning in that silly way," said Toby. "For it is not likely you will meet with him again. Quality cannot abide the common folk."

"Quality?" mused Lucy, remembering the quack's sign: "Corncutter to the quality. Well, damn. Had I known then what I know now, I could have called out to the Earl that I knew the man who cared for his feet. I must tell the quack Fitzmaurice when I see him again that I have hobnobbed with his quality clients."

"Isn't it a wonder that the quality are cursed with corns, though, when they travel everywhere by coach?" cried John, tickling her until the tears ran down her face. Although she laughed and seemed more cheerful, Lucy was sad that the young man was a quality person. Had he not been she might have been able to speak to him again, but as he was quality and the son of an Earl, he was as far from her as the North star is from the earth.

On that same morning across the ridge at Landsdun House, Charles was woken as usual by his manservant, Culpepper, who carried a bowl of chocolate into his room. The servant could not help observing as he opened the curtains that his young master was in something of a gloom. The servant naturally put this sluggishness of spirit down to too much port at supper and a late night. Culpepper, though, was wrong. Charles was loath to rise on two counts. Firstly he had enjoyed through the night some startlingly vivid dreams of the pretty girl who had stopped his coach. She had appeared to him as Amphitrite the goddess who stood at the centre of the lily pool outside Landsdun and had put out her arms, calling him to join her there among the tender white blooms. He had been about to do that when Culpepper had woken him and he was reluctant to open his eyes and lose her.

It was not surprising that these dreams seemed so much more pleasant than the reality of his life on that day, for he remembered that he had promised to write to Georgiana Stowe and invite her to Landsdun. It loomed before him as he bathed and dressed, and as the morning progressed, the letter assumed Herculean proportions. Even a brisk canter through the park on the incomparable Jupiter did nothing to buck him up. The prospect of writing to Georgiana, the whole idea of courting, wooing and finally marrying her, filled him with an emotion that could only be described as panic.

"That is what it is, panic," he muttered to himself as he sat at his desk in the library later. "Panic. I feel the burden of my duty to the line, my position in society, weighing me down. If I were other than I am, a simple man and not an Earl's son, then I could wait until I had found someone to love, and not marry merely for reasons of propriety." He gazed out of the window at the statue of the goddess of the lily pond. How he wished that the smooth marble would melt into the enchanting flesh of the girl who had last night become the girl of his dreams. He sighed and picked up a sharpened quill. Sir James had been right. It was an easy matter to love a woman you could never have. But could you grow to love a woman that you *must* have? On the other hand, *must* you grow to love her? Many other men of his station married for convenience and the arrangement was often very successful. Once they had laid in their heirs, they did not bother with their wives. They made mistresses of women more to their taste and, after all, why should he spurn what so many others had embraced? He dipped the quill in the silver inkwell, and wrote. "My dear Miss Stowe." Then he paused and frowned. This letter had to be approached with proper decorum. He was about to embark on a social contract.

"You will have heard no doubt that the Earl's health gives his physician and myself some grave cause for concern. At present he is at Landsdun and it is my intention to remain at his side through the remainder of the summer, in the hope that he will improve which is what we pray for." He bit the tip of his quill thoughtfully.

"I have recently become aware of a desire to see you again and it would give me great pleasure and satisfaction if you would do me the honour of visiting Landsdun in the near future with your gracious mother." *I had better invite the mother*, thought Charles, shuddering at the prospect of Mrs. Stowe's arrival, *for they would think it odd if I did not suggest a chaperone. I do not know which is worse for nonsensical cant, the mother or the daughter. Both together is more than I can bear to contemplate. But there. What a man must suffer for duty.*

"I would be obliged," wrote Charles, "If you would reply to this my enquiry at your earliest convenience. My father sends his salutations to your family along with the hope that their health continues robust. Please convey my regards to your mother and the general. I remain, Miss Stowe, your obedient servant. Melton."

He laid aside the quill, blotted the letter with a sprinkling of sand and thought that he had better read what he had written. He was anxious not to sound too formal but on the other hand he must not sound too eager.

"In truth, I am not a bit eager," he murmured, as his eyes travelled over the creamy monogrammed vellum. "But I must appear *suitably* eager.... Oh what a business this is. I have recently become aware of a desire," he muttered . . . "it would give me great pleasure and satisfaction. Now does that sound too flowery and emotional? My dear Miss Stowe? Should I perhaps have addressed her as My dear Georgiana? No. No. That would be far too familiar. I must start this as I mean to continue. I mean, we are approaching a formal marriage here; it is not as though we were friends or lovers."

He read through the note once more. It would have to do. He had promised Sir James a game of cards at two o'clock and it was almost that time now. He made two more copies so that three could be despatched, one to the Stowe House in Hampshire; one to their house in Pall Mall; and one to the home of Georgiana's brother in Sussex, in case she should be visiting there. He folded all three, dropped hot wax on them and pressed in the Landsdun seal. Then handing them to a footman with orders they should be despatched at once, he went to join Sir James at cards, glad that his task was over.

A week later a reply arrived from the Stowe House in Hampshire. Charles opened the letter with a certain amount of trepidation.

"Dearest Melton," gushed Georgiana. "I cannot say how thrilled I was to get your letter and such a charming letter too." Charles turned white with embarrassment. "Thrilled, charming . . . *dearest*?" The words jumped out at him. What could he possibly have written to lead the lady to call him . . . dearest? He read on, mesmerised. "Of course I shall come to Landsdun if you desire so much to see me." *That's it*, Charles thought, remembering his letter. "I have recently become aware of a desire to see you again."

Oh, why did I write desire? he groaned. "But do not be too disappointed, dear, dear Charles, for I cannot possibly come until mid-September at least." *Thank God*, breathed Charles. He had thought for a moment that she was already on her way. "For I have to be measured and fitted for the new gowns that I will wear at Court through the next season. But as soon as I am done with that, I shall come to you with my mother. My family wish me to thank both yourself and the Earl for your kind enquiries after their health and they all send their hopes that the Earl's will soon improve. Until that day when I shall see you, I remain, your very affectionate Georgiana."

Charles folded the letter. Sir James had been right. Georgiana was keen on him, or rather, he suspected, keen on the idea of one day becoming a Countess. The words "dearest" and "thrilled" and "very affectionate" swam around in his head. The letter stank of scent and was covered in kisses and love-knots. How like Georgiana the letter was. He might have known she would not have the sense to conduct this business between them with a proper degree of well-bred detachment. All he had done was to write and ask her if she would visit Landsdun. He had not offered love or passion. He had extended a tentative finger and she had replied with a letter that threatened to engulf him in the worst sort of sentimental rubbish.

"She is too eager," cried Charles. "Far too eager." He felt like a man who had unwittingly conjured up an uncontrollable monster. Georgiana Stowe was affectionate, she was eager, she was coming.

Back at Ragby, Lucy had, by the skin of her teeth, managed to contrive a sort of stay of execution. Boost had been ready to have the banns nailed to the church door at once but by a good deal of haggling, wrangling and heated argument Lucy had the day put off until after her seventeenth birthday in September. She needed, she said, time to prepare herself *spiritually* for the nuptials.

She had received a few crooked looks when she had asked Roger to call in the parson so that she and her suitor could consult him on the subject. Her instinct, though, had proved right, for the parson was very much on her side. He agreed that a period of courtship was most proper. Lucy was young and needed time to come to the right frame of mind for such a solemn contract; who better to lead her to the right frame of mind than the parson himself?

"Mm. Yes," he said gleefully, rubbing furiously at his nose, his eyes drinking in Lucy's resplendent charms. "Lucy Emmett shall come to the parsonage every day to take spiritual instruction from me so that she might at last be led, a God-fearing dutiful wench, to the altar on her wedding day."

Boost was not sure about this at all. He did not like the way the parson looked at Lucy, nor did he approve the way Lucy smiled so dazzlingly at the parson all of a sudden.

"Ah'm not with this at all," he rumbled morosely. "Ah mean, Ah never had none o' this business with my other wives. Ah mean, there it was just a matter of yew saying the word, parson, and me getting down to my side of it. There was no talk of spiritual preparation then. Ah mean, Ah don't see as what a blacksmith's wife has to do with matters spiritual. Ah don't care if she's not prepared so long as she can mash up a pan of swedes for me, draw my ale and warm me at night. Ah mean, there's ten brats at the forge waiting to be washed and wiped. Ah thought that Ah'd have her all sewn up within the week."

You'll not have me sewn up at all, thought Lucy, *if I have my way*.

"Mm. Well your other wives were not so young, so naughty, nor so, er, pulchritudinous," observed the parson, his gaze fixed on the rim of Lucy's bodice.

"Aye, she is young," replied the smith, watching the parson watching Lucy's bosom. "But as for being pulchie whatsit, Ah would not know. All Ah want is a wife and it seems she's being kept from me by a lot of high-falutin' ideas and big words Ah do not understand." Boost was very suspicious of this waiting idea. The parson was now sweating and fiddling with his Geneva bands.

"Oh, Obediah," pouted Lucy. "Do not be such an impatient old thing. It is only a little longer to wait until you have me and rest assured that through the good parson's ministrations, I shall be brought to you a better person and at last a proper Christian wife." She gazed up at the parson, her eyes bright and promising. "When shall I call on you, parson—tomorrow?" she asked.

"Oh, Aphrodite," whispered the ecstatic parson.

Only a few days after he had received the first letter from Georgiana, Lord Melton was the wary recipient of

171

another which came with the mail coach from London, this time along with a three-day-old copy of *The Spectator*, for Sir James Robertson.

Charles walked into the library and handed the paper to the old man who grabbed it with as much excitement as though it had just fallen hot from the press. While Sir James fell to devouring the news from France, Charles took the letter over to the desk by the window and turned it over in his hands.

"Oh, God," he groaned. Georgiana had drawn a heart upon it, with the letters M and G above it surrounded by intertwining ivy leaves. "I, er, I seem to have another letter here from Georgiana Stowe," said Charles.

"That damned madman, the Marquis Hurugue, is demanding that the French King be forced from Versailles to live in Paris. He has tried to march on Versailles to remove him. The fellow should be locked up—was locked up in a lunatic asylum until he was released by the Revolutionaries. These people, my boy, will throw the crown in the dirt." Sir James' worry over the grave situation in France would not normally have been lost on Charles, but there was this letter from Georgiana Stowe. "I hope it is not a love-letter," he said, though it did look like a love-letter. "It's all well and good her writing love-letters but it's a bit damned stiff I think, so early in the proceedings. I hope, in sincerity, that she does not expect me to reply in the same vein as she writes. I am, after all, an Englishman, not some deuced foreign Lothario full of empty phrases." He broke the seal on the letter. There was Georgiana's flourishing scrawl. "She might at least have waited until I had replied to her last letter," said Charles.

"Dearest, dearest Melton. I still hear nothing from you and am beside myself with worry for you, dear creature." Charles became aware of a constricting feeling in his throat. It sounded very like a love-letter so far, though somewhat tortured. "Do not torture me with silence." He was right, it was tortured. "For I cannot bear not to know how you are. Write to me and assure me you are well and that no evil thing has befallen you. Tell me that you long to see me as much as I long to see you, for I count the weeks, the days, the hours, the minutes, the seconds . . ." The letter ranted on for a distance about love and feelings, then turned abruptly to Georgiana's favorite topic—decoration. The decoration of her precious self.

"Dearest, I am in a spin here, as you can imagine, of fittings for gowns. You know what a whirl it all is for a lady and you will see a great change in me when I visit." *Why?* thought Charles, *has she grown another head?* "For my mother has at last engaged a dresser for my hair and I am very much in fashion now, wearing it powered and high, though not too high since my father will not approve it owing to the expense of having it opened and cleaned. It will not go longer than three weeks without being opened in the summer." Charles winced and wrinkled his nose. To his mind there was no stink worse than the stench of rancid fat and stale powder that came from a lady's head in high summer.

"I am allowed one patch *enjouée!*" He frowned and puzzled over this for a while then turned to Sir James.

"What is a patch *enjouée?*" he enquired.

The physician looked up from *The Spectator*, where he had been reading about the terrible starvation among the French and their request for English flour to be exported to them.

"I think that it is a patch which covers a dimple," he replied.

"Good Lord," exclaimed Charles. "What next?"

Georgiana's letter continued. . . . "I have wondered if you would prefer that I wore a patch *l' Assissine* or perhaps one *l'Friponne* to one *enjouée?* Do tell me your preference and I shall take care to wear it for you. Oh, my new gowns are gay. One I think you will like in particular is of a rose pink Paduasoy silk with a fichu in the same shade and yet another I have which is a Polonaise over a jupe pannier, this in Celestial blue with Amarinth, and a Caracao behind."

"And what, pray, is a caracao behind?" asked Charles. "It sounds like some manner of physical disability."

"I suppose that it must be some new fashion, my dear boy. You know these ladies, there is always some pretty geegaw or other to take their fancy."

Charles could not bear to read any more. It continued

babbling about gowns then at the bottom there was a rash of kisses and love knots penned by the effusive Miss Stowe.

"God, what a mawkish letter," groaned Charles. "The trivia of her life astounds me. I hate anyway to see women decked out like puppets, all powdered and painted until they resemble ancient Picts or street whores." All his old antipathy to Georgiana came flooding back. He stood up and paced the room.

"You know, I am damned if I will entertain thoughts of Georgiana as my wife if she insists on pursuing these heinous habits. Why, for God's sake, must she powder her hair, apply red to her lips and cheeks, and cover herself in patches? I do not understand these so-called fashionable women. I do not know a man who does not find natural looks in a woman more appealing. I mean, for instance, the pretty country girl I met on the road needed no paint or artfice to tempt a man to look at her, to desire her even. Put a girl like that among these fashionable women and she would shine out, sweet and fresh, like a wild rose among a bunch of artificial flowers."

He sat down at his desk. "I suppose I must reply to this nonsense," he sighed, picking up his quill. "Dear Miss Stowe," he wrote. "Do not concern yourself after my health. I am quite well, though the earl continues to grow weaker by the day." He paused, wishing that there was a woman close to him with whom he could share his anxieties about his father, a woman who could penetrate his guarded exterior and teach him to speak what he felt in his heart. No, Georgiana Stowe was not that woman. As he wrote he spoke the letter out loud so that Sir James could hear. "I am happy to hear that you are pleased with your gowns, but in reply to your enquiry as to which type of patch I should like to see upon your face, I must quote from 'Smith's Invective Against Patching':

'Hellgate is open day and night,
to such as in black spots delight.
If pride their faces spotted make,
for pride then hell their soul shall take.

'If folly be the cause of it,
let simple fools then learn more wit.
Black spots and patches on the face,
to sober ladies bring disgrace
Lewd Harlots by such spots are known,
Let Harlots, then, enjoy their own.'

"You may gather from this that my answer is none. I despise all patching and all leading of the face, preferring to see a lady's countenance in as natural a state as possible. In that way a gentleman might see more exactly what is being offered to him. I remain, Miss Stowe, your most . . ."

"I agree about the lead," said Sir James. "It is a frightful hazard to health. So many ladies die from it and so many men die paupers from the expense incurred by it. I remember Lady Coventry died from an excess of lead, leaving it on so long that it had in the end to be scraped off her. There was more lead on the lady's face than had been used to line her coffin. You know, her husband would for years cry out against it and chase her around the dinner table so that he might remove the obnoxious stuff with a napkin. He is dead now too, poor fellow."

"What did he die from?" asked Charles, sealing his letter to Georgiana.

"Why, from chasing around dinner tables," replied Sir James. "You might think on that through your courtship with Miss Stowe, for you will find that it is as useless to try and prevent a lady painting herself as it is to look for snow in July."

Although Lucy's idea of visiting Ragby Parsonage to take religious instruction from the parson had started as a ploy to put off for as long as possible her marriage to the blacksmith she found, as the weeks passed, that she was learning more about the wider world than she had ever imagined possible.

She thought the parson's instruction both interesting and informative—she learned quickly, remembering the letters she had so slowly pieced together in Melton, and the parson proved he was in truth a clever teacher—although he of course was interested in something other than knowledge. To have the luscious Lucy Emmett close to him in the privacy of his study was a pleasure that he had dreamed of and would not have missed, even if it did mean hell and damnation at a later date.

He was too fearful of transgressing against his calling, of course, to carry his desires to their ultimate conclusion but he would take every opportunity to press himself against Lucy's body while he tutored her or he would knead at her pretty arms, even snatch a kiss in passing. But only in the solitary confinement of his bed at night, with the aid of the magical "Hotempetah mixture," was he bold enough to allow his passions full rein.

Because Lucy was eager to improve herself from ignorance she prevailed upon the parson to teach her to read from the Bible and from the other learned books he kept about him. This he did willingly for, sitting close to her at the desk, he was able to titillate his sensuality by rubbing his foot against her leg. In this way he got pleasure and Lucy got knowledge. He taught her to read the entire contents of a book entitled *The Great Duty of Frequenting the Christian Sacrifice* in just this way. Then they both turned their attention to the globe of the world and, with the parson's hand firmly planted upon her left buttock, she saw how England lay in a vast ocean and, although small when compared with other continents, held a position of huge import in the known world. Mr. Carey's recently prepared atlas was brought out, and with the parson's hands having wandered a little further, she saw at last where London lay in relation to Ragby. Then she learnt to write her name, with the parson's face close to hers. Oh, what satisfaction it gave him to see his pretty, clever pupil bent over her writing tablet, that little pink tongue working so hard in concentration against her full lower lip.

Progressing further by the day, the parson grew in boldness and she was soon able to copy from the Bible, with a little close physical attention from him.

"Wisdom is the principal thing. Therefore get wisdom and with all thy getting get understanding."

The parson having presumably got understanding in his youth was ready, in his dotage, to get some other experience under his wig and under Lucy's skirts.

But Lucy longed for wisdom and longed for understanding. Sitting in the parson's study gazing around at the shelves of dusty books, she realised what a legion of knowledge and literature had been denied to her because of her lowly station. All through those summer weeks, Lucy held out a hope that she would be spared in some way from marrying the blacksmith, but on the day of her seventeenth birthday, in spite of her cries that she was not ready, the banns were at last nailed to the church door. The date announced there was the tenth day of September. *Only three days of freedom left*, thought Lucy, as she turned away from the church door in tears.

Boost had been loitering outside the parsonage every morning while Lucy was inside. For the entire time she was in there, he would keep his eyes glued on the study window. He would not look away until Lucy appeared at the door, then he would escort her back to Ridge Farm. The blacksmith appeared simply to be an attentive swain, but beneath the surface of his bull-like, low-browed exterior, dark and jealous, even violent emotions were raging. Obediah Boost had his suspicions.

As soon as Lucy tripped down the parsonage steps looking smug, and tying her bonnet he would catch her arm and ask, "What did yew and the parson do today?"

Lucy would smile and say that he was teaching her to write out a verse or read a psalm.

"What's he teaching yew to read for? Ah cannot read nor do Ah know any normal person as can. Reading's for parsons, gentry and quality folk, not for common simple folk the like of yew and me."

"Call yourself simple, dimwit. I wish to learn as much as I can in life," Lucy would reply. "I do not know why you question me in this way, I am safe enough with the parson, I should think."

"Ah do not know about that," said Obediah. "Ah have my suspicions. This is a head that yew see upon my shoulders, yew know. Not a turnip."

177

There were but two days now to go to their wedding and the lustful bridegroom-to-be did not want another man to snatch from him what he had waited so long to enjoy.

"Ah've never liked the look of that parson," he said to Roger later that night over a drink in the Hare and Hounds. "He looks to me like a man who abuses himself. Well as far as Ah'm concerned he may abuse himself till he turns inside out and vanishes up his own backside. But just let me catch him abusing my Lucy and Ah'll abuse him with this." He thumped a massive knotted fist up and down on the oak table, sending Roger's ale spilling upon the floor.

"Oh, I tell you," sighed Roger Emmett. "I'll be a happy man when that wench becomes a wife and you have the care of her. These last few years while she has been growing to a woman have been the very devil, as God is my witness. Naught but worry for me, I can tell you, man." He hoped that once Lucy was married, her brothers would remove their affections from her and look seriously for wives for themselves. *It is not too much,* thought Roger, *for a man to ask to be left alone with his wife, to enjoy a little peace in his old age.*

On Lucy's wedding day he planned to give her the gold earrings Margaret had removed from Esmeralda's ears on her death. They had been hidden away in the linen chest at Ridge Farm. They would look well on Lucy, Roger thought, for she had grown into the living image of her gypsy mother. He sighed. It seemed such a long time ago, that day when he had walked up the snow-covered field and seen the Romany wagons against the Charnwood oaks. So long ago and yet Esmeralda Lee was still vivid in his mind. He still remembered the heat of lust she had roused in him, to his eternal shame. It was no wonder Lucy, being that sultry gypsy's daughter, would cause men to lose their heads.

⁕

On the morning of the ninth of September, at Landsdun House, Jupiter was brought forth from the stables to the mounting-block in the yard for Charles as usual. But this morning's ride was to be no ordinary one, for he was setting out to meet Georgiana Stowe and her mother who were en route from London. Sir James had offered to accompany him on the expedition and a bay gelding had been saddled for him, since a quiet horse was more suitable for an elderly gentleman like the physician.

The idea of riding out to meet the Stowes' coach had certainly not been Charles'; it had been the Earl's idea. It was a matter of courtesy that his son should meet Georgiana and her mother on the road and escort them back to Landsdun. It would, after all, be the lady's first visit to the house and, besides, General Stowe had written to the Earl to say the coachman was a new fellow and could not altogether be trusted to take the right road, once out of Bedfordshire.

The day was blessedly a warm one, summer still not having quite grown into autumn and there was a bright sun as Charles and Sir James rode out through Landsdun's gilded gates. Its rays gleamed on the horses' carefully curried coats so that they rippled like silk as they sped through the trees that lay outside the walls of the estate. All around, the forests were changing colour and the whole countryside was a picture in bronze, gold and yellow tints.

It was a good hour of hard riding before they achieved the top of the ridge. They reined up the horses beside the Charnwood to rest for a minute for it was hard work riding uphill all the way. They stopped side by side and looked down at the magnificence of Landsdun lying below them in the valley.

"You must bring Georgiana out of her coach to let her see this view," said Sir James, puffing slightly because he was unused to exercise. "I swear there is no other so beautiful in the world as this panorama. She will thrill to her soul, my boy, to think that she will be mistress there one day."

"Yes. But will she thrill at the beauty, or will she thrill simply because it will make her one of the wealthiest women in England?" said Charles.

He was frowning now as he fondled Jupiter's ears and watched a flight of birds that were migrating early swoop low over the house as though in a last goodbye before

179

flying south to warmer climes. Would Georgiana love Landsdun as he loved it? Would she see it as he saw it, as a home and not simply as a symbol of wealth and power? He thought of his children running and playing in the parkland as he had when he was a boy. Would he love those children, from the womb of a woman that he did not, could not love? These thoughts disturbed him. Until now he had never really thought of his children, except as an idea, and a vague one at that. But now, from the ridge, seeing the house from this distance, he fancied himself returning on some day in the distant future and finding in that place he loved so well, a wife that was a trial to him and children who were strangers. He felt chilled and sad.

Perhaps the thought of his father lying so frail and ill in his canopied bed is what disturbs him, thought Sir James, studying the heir's handsome, brooding face.

"You may find Miss Stowe is a comfort at this time. Did you never think that you may do her an injustice to think her a mere light-headed creature? She may have depths you have not yet discovered. You must not judge too soon or too hasty."

"I pray with all my heart you are right, Sir James," Charles whispered, digging his heels hard into Jupiter's flanks and turning the animal's head towards the forest. Seeing when he looked back that the old man's face was red with exertion, he said, "You are hot and thirsty I think, my old friend?"

Sir James nodded and laughed. "I am indeed and I am without my trusty brandy flask. I did not think it quite proper to bring it to sup on the way lest the ladies should smell it upon my breath and be offended."

Charles laughed. "What a gallant you are, to be sure. I will tell you what we will do to slake your thirst. We will ride to Ragby and visit the inn, for Culpepper, my man, tells me that the landlord at the Hare and Hounds pulls the coolest draught of ale in the whole county. We will take some, you and I, and while we do, these beasts can be left to water." He spurred Jupiter on towards the village with Sir James in pursuit, shouting, "But ho, what if we miss the coach?"

"We will not," shouted Charles back to him, "for while we are at the inn, I will post someone at the Ragby toll. The coach will have to halt there to pay." He was galloping away from Sir James at speed and it was all that the older man could do to keep him in sight. The gelding was no match for Jupiter's excellence.

"Slow down," yelled Sir James after him. "Miss Stowe will not thank me if you are delivered to her with a broken neck." But it was no good. Jupiter had felt his power and was in his stride and Charles was raised in the stirrups, giving him his head, his worries lost in the exhilaration of a fine day and a superlative steed.

Boost was waiting outside the parsonage as usual for Lucy. It was to be her last day there, for on the next morning she would become his wife and he would snatch from her that treasured virginity. The thought sent the blood rushing to his loins. His sharp eyes were on the study window but his hands were in his pockets. At a little distance from him, his ten motherless children were rolling about among the graves, scraping and arguing, wrestling and fighting as they were wont to do on any and every occasion. It would not be long now before he had an energetic young wife to manage them for him. Boost leant on the parsonage gatepost and allowed his thoughts to wander around the delights and comforts a married man might enjoy and he felt quite pleased with his lot, all in all.

"Aye say. You there," he heard a high-pitched lah-di-dah voice call out. "What are you about, you scurvy fellow? Burglarization, eh?"

Boost turned his glowering face away from the window for a moment and saw the most extraordinary figure approaching him through the churchyard. This figure was dressed in vibrant red pantaloons, a scarlet and yellow wide-skirted coat, red and yellow striped silk stockings and red high-heeled shoes. It teetered along the bumpy ground, stumbling over molehills and graves avoiding these and the tumbling children with the aid of a long cane surmounted by a floppy scarlet bow. On the very pinnacle of all this frenzied regalia there wagged a silly-looking head, with curled gingery hair dressed to a foot high, above a pallid haughty face, and perched on top of the hair, like a wren on a steeple, there sat a tiny black hat. It was Peter Royalston, and the hat was his latest fashionable acquisition. He would have told anyone who enquired that it was a *Nivernois Chapeau Bras*. But no one would have enquired, for the hat looked as though it had arrived there by accident and was kept there by an act of will.

"Well?" he called querulously pushing the children from his path with the tip of his cane and holding a lavender-filled pomander to his nose to save him from any smell of country animal or country human. "Reply, you imbecile. Why do you stare? Have you never viewed a representative of the gentry before? Mm? Have you no task in life but to loll about there? Reply," he commanded poking the awestruck Boost with his cane but keeping a good distance from him. He did not care for the look of him. "Lard," he sighed. "The fool has no tongue, I suppose, gawp-faced goon that it is."

Boost was gawping for he was astounded by the dizzy spectacle presented by the squire's nephew. He had seen the fop before but he had never imagined such a curiosity would actually approach him and speak.

"Ah'm waitin' for someone, sir, if it pleases yew," he managed when he had recovered himself. "Ah'm not about anything untoward, Ah will assure your honour."

Peter Royalston preened himself and looked up at the massive man with imperious disdain, if that is possible for a person who is towered over by a human mountain. Peter did his best for it was rare for him to meet anyone who was stupider than himself.

"For whom do you wait them, mm, you predacious mooch, you?" he enquired, raising a thin, plucked brow and burying his nose in the pomander. Lard, how the fellow stank of sweat and smoke.

"Why, Ah'm waiting upon Lucy Emmett, who is to be my bride. She is within, your worship, taking spiritual instruction from the parson."

A bright light lit up in Peter Royalston's head. He was

182

aware of the parson's dalliance with the bastard chit for he had come across them both about this spiritual instruction when he had arrived for his Latin lesson on a morning in the previous week. So this grim, blank-visaged bumpkin was the hoyden's suitor? Oh, this was sport indeed. Here was a scandal, such as he had hoped for. What a distraction!

"Haw, haw, haw," he giggled. "You mean the ditch-bred wench, La Belle Tournure of this fraytfull, bestial locale? And, lard, what did you say she was about, spiritual instruction? Oh, yes, I'll wager she is. Oh I say, spiritual instruction! Oh, I do believe that he is instructing her but on what subject must be left to the wild imagination. Oh Lard, I delight in this, I really do. You wait outside like patience upon a monument, dullard, while inside the parson meddles with your minxy sonsy. Oh. Lard," he gasped, adjusting his minute hat. "I am quite fatigued with the drollery of it."

Peter's amusement knew no bounds and he giggled so shrilly that he did not hear the bellow that left the blacksmith's lungs. "Meddles?" bawled Boost, his jaw dropping to meet his chest. "Meddles?" he gasped. Peter stopped giggling and fell to simpering. "Did Ah hear yew say . . . meddles?" asked Boost slyly.

"Aye, meddles, fingers, tickles, twiddles," trilled Peter Royalston merrily. "Lard, booby, tweaks and filches, nibbles and pinches, don't ye know?"

"Ah did not know," growled Boost ominously. "But Ah tell yew sirree, Ah've had my suspicions."

"Haw, yaw, haw. Oh, what a priceless fool. Here is a man who loiters outside while inside his wench is banjaxed. Oh, is it possible? Oh Lard, I am weak with hilarity. Just peep in at the window, sluggard, and you will see what you had suspected being executed. Oh, Oh," he shrieked, for the man's hand had suddenly darted forward and fastened itself to his throat. "Oh Lard, hands off you fraytfull thing, you. I am a gentleman. Attack me and the ultimate penalty shall be paid."

Boost was not at all impressed. He simply shook Royalston in the air like a feather duster and then dragged the whey-faced fop towards the window, growling, "Ah shall see for myself what goes on and if yew lie, Ah tell yew, gentleman or no gentleman Ah shall skewer you and chew your giblets and spit them over the moon."

"Oh Dowsabel, oh sweeting, oh honeysuckle treasure," cooed the parson, sitting close to Lucy while she was carefully engaged in writing out a proverb. "Oh my callipygian pippin, my divine Hebe, let me taste the nectar that drips from those two rubificatious lips." He had his arm twined about her waist and his cheek very close to hers, observing her tongue, poking out from her mouth as usual as she tried to form perfect script. Neither the parson nor Lucy noticed the dark shadow that fell across the window, so engrossed were they both they did not even hear the bellow that Boost roared out when he saw the parson bend his head to take the kiss he had asked for. But they both looked up when they heard a pane of glass shatter and they both leapt to their feet when they saw two brawny fists grab the window frame and wrench the window from the wall.

The appearance of young Lord Melton and Sir James before the inn at Ragby caused something of a stir, since it was not often that the hostelry entertained such distinguished visitors. Quite a small crowd gathered to see them dismount, and as the word spread, more people hurried to the scene.

The landlord arranged for the horses to be watered and a hoary old local wearing a rough smock and gaiters, and with a face bedecked with cinereous side whiskers, was commandeered for the price of a penny to hobble off and stand sentinel at the Ragby toll, so that Georgiana and her mother might be told the heir was in the vicinity and would shortly be on his way to meet them, should the coach by chance arrive early on the road.

Cool ale was drawn into tankards by the landlord, who refused all payment saying that the honour of having the earl's son at his premises was payment enough for him.

Soon Charles and Sir James were seated at a stout table chatting amiably with their host, while he told them of country matters, of the common man's view of the revolution in France, and made them laugh heartily when he regaled them with tales of the Squire Billy's eccentricities, of his escapades and his protest against Pitt's horse tax, when he had set out to ride to Parliament on a cow to show how hard the tax hit the gentry, only to have the beast die under him before he got even as far as Market Harborough.

It was pleasant, thought Charles, to converse with folk from a different station in life, for heaven knows he had little enough opportunity to learn how their thoughts ran. He was sorry when Sir James drew out his fob watch and said it was time that they were upon their way. They had just mounted and were about to depart when they became aware of a commotion among the crowd of villagers, and then suddenly they were startled by loud cries of "Oh, Lard, help, help, murder, murder," which came from the direction of Ragby church. When they turned their alarmed faces in that direction, they saw a fantastical sight approaching.

"It is Peter Royalston, the squire's nephew," laughed Charles, pointing at the curious figure that dithered towards them across the village green.

"By God, what a demented poppinjay," exclaimed an astounded Sir James.

"Yes," said Charles. "I believe he fancies himself a Macaroni."

'Oh Lard, I say, it is fraytfull, don't ye know," cried the fop to the people who were now surrounding him. Men were running out of the fields, alerted by his shrieks; even the ducks from the pond waddled busily forward from the water, bright-eyed, blunt-beaked spectators. "The parson," shrilled Peter, "is being pugilized by a maniac monster of adamantine proportions, Lard, scrambled, you flaccid rustic ruminants; mangled, you ragamuffins; pulverized, done to death. Lard, am I not clear?" he appealed of the folk who stood by openmouthed. "Rescue, rescue, rescue."

"Royalston," shouted Charles riding Jupiter into the

throng. "What's this? Did you scream murder?"

"Oh Lard, my Lard," gasped Peter, seeing the Landsdun heir looking down at him. "You will, my Lard, excuse my perturbation but I sweah it is the most fraytfull scene of mayhem that it was evah my misfortune to witness in my life." He tried to execute a flourishing bow but failed. "See, I am all of a pother with it," he quavered. "I shake, I tremble, I dwindle."

Charles did not dally. He turned Jupiter towards the parsonage with all haste. "Everyone follow the heir," cried the landlord of the Hare and Hounds, sensing a chance for excitement. The populace of Ragby swarmed after him—men, women and children. The women armed with their dish mops, rolling pins and ladles, the men waving reaping-hooks and pitchforks, while the children ran alongside, bowling hoops and whipping tops. At the rear of this motley army came the fop, pursued by about a dozen curious ducks.

When Charles rode in through the gates of the churchyard, mounted on his handsome black horse, he was greeted by a sight that he was never to forget. Miss Parson Brown and the ancient sexton were running around in circles wringing their hands and howling that the parson was being murdered. One of the front windows of the house had been wrenched entirely from the wall and was lying in the churchyard as though thrown there by a freak wind. Swarms of dirty, fighting children were climbing in and out of the gap left by the window-frame, passing out piles of books to smaller children who sat around on graves and made paper darts from the torn pages.

From the bowels of the house came a terrible roaring, as though some huge, powerful Leviathan was smashing every part of the parsonage with its massive tail. As Charles leapt from Jupiter's back he caught a glimpse of a blurred white face at an upstairs window. Catching Miss Parson Brown by the arm, he asked. "What goes on here, mistress?"

"Oh," wailed the distraught spinster. "Oh, my Lord Melton, help me, help me. My brother and that bastard

186

Emmett jade are inside under siege and the blacksmith is hellbent on blood. Oh rescue my brother, sir—protect him, for he has done no wrong." She fell to weeping on the ground at Charles's feet and grabbed his boots so tenaciously, that he was unable to move. The people of Ragby were now flooding in through the gates, brandishing their weaponry.

"Oh I saw it, I saw it. My prediction is come true. That girl is bad. She has brought a sword of wrath down upon our heads but save my brother, my lord, save him," whimpered Miss Parson Brown. "He still has God's work to do."

Charles was by now surrounded by his army who were all ready for a war, or worse, by the look of them. They shouted, "Are you going in, my lord?" and "Take care, my lord," and "Someone send out for the magistrate," and "Someone fetch a rope. We'll hang the blacksmith."

"Should we send for arms, do you think?" asked Sir James, who had arrived very short of breath at his side.

"No. I have a pistol on me and will use it if necessary," Charles replied. "Does anyone care to tell me this fellow's name?" he asked, raising his voice above the uproar.

"Obediah Boost," said Barney Cowper, stepping forward and touching his forelock. "If you are going to venture in there, my lord, well, I'll come in with you. I'm not feared of him." There was a bloodcurdling howl from inside, followed by the sound of splintering wood.

"Oh," wailed Miss Parson Brown, "he is ripping up the floorboards."

"As long as he is not ripping up the parson," said Charles dryly. "Will some kindly person please take this lady off my boots so that I might move forward?" The sexton obliged Charles and dragged the parson's sister away from him, though she still stuck out her arms trying to clutch at him like a sea squid.

Free at last, Charles walked towards the door, stopped, cupped his hands about his mouth and shouted, "Boost. Obediah Boost? This is the Landsdun heir speaking, and in the absence of the magistrate I must assume responsibility for the law here. Now, I warn you, there is talk of a hanging. So are you going to be a good fellow and come out or must I come in and get you?"

There was no reply. Merely the sound of more wood being sundered. Charles frowned. This was not his idea of a way to spend a pleasant autumn morning.

"Where is the damned magistrate anyway?" he asked Sir James.

"I understand that Squire Billy is magistrate here and the fop tells me that he is in London, at the tables," replied Sir James.

Charles sighed. "Well, that fellow in there is obviously too maddened to hear reason so I suppose that I must go in."

There was a loud cheer from the villagers as their hero walked up the steps.

"I'll come in with you," said Sir James.

"No, stay here," said Charles. "If I have my head broken I shall need a physician. You, what's-your-name, the volunteer?" He beckoned to Barney, who was also cheered as he moved stealthily towards the heir with a chisel in his hand.

"Good old Barney," everyone shouted. Barney grinned back at them and waved a casual hand.

They walked into the hallway and heard a bellow from above.

"Ah'll get yew, yew wench-kisser, yew damned meddling, tickling filcher yew."

Charles stood at the foot of the stairs and smiled. So *that* was the cause of the disturbance.

"It sounds as if the parson has been up to no good with the girl," said Charles to Barney.

Barney grinned. "There's no man in the village who'd miss that chance if it presented itself, I'll vow."

"Pretty?" asked Charles.

"Oh," said Barney, clenching his fist and lifting his arm.

"That as well? No wonder the poor fellow has gone berserk. Boost?" called Charles, thinking to give the man another chance since his crime seemed to have been caused by jealous passion. "Come on down here and talk

188

with me like a sensible fellow. This rage will do nobody any good."

"Ah will not," came the reply, "and yew can buzz off, or Ah'll bust yewr guts and all."

Charles dodged several pieces of shattered floorboard that came raining down from above. Some of it though caught Barney on his head.

"Ouch," cried Barney clutching his skull. Are you mad, Boost? This is Lord Melton down here talking to you."

"Ah do not care if it's German King Georgie himself. Ah'm going to kill that parson and Ah'll kill Lord Melton too if he don't watch hisself and Ah don't care if Ah swing for it."

"He bluffs," said Charles.

"He don't," gasped Barney as two china chamber pots, mercifully empty, came crashing down, to miss them both by a hair's breadth.

"Right," snapped Charles, his face very grim. "Can you fight, Barney?"

"Like a spring stag, my lord," said Barney, stabbing the stair rail several times with his chisel to show that he was a killer at heart.

"Good man," said Charles. "Follow me," He took the stairs two at a time, finding when he arrived with Barney behind him upon the landing, that the smith had torn up most of the floorboards and was now using a stout oak floor joist as a battering ram against a bedroom door.

It took Charles a little while to completely digest the scene for he had not been prepared for a man of such immense size. True, the fop had said that the fellow was of adamantine proportions, but here was a veritable Samson. He wielded the floor-joist as though it were the merest twig and the solid door was already beginning to splinter under his powerful blows. Yes, it was going to take two men to tackle this stout fellow.

He nodded at Barney and they both leapt forward with great gusto. Charles threw both his arms around Boost's bulging chest and Barney grabbed him about the knees to try to bring him down.

"Come along. That's enough destruction for one day,"

said Charles only to feel the man's hand swat him on the head and the blow sent him flying backwards to land with a thud against the bannisters. Just as he fell to the floor he happened to look up and saw poor Barney caught up into the air by the smith's arm and then, after wriggling and yelling for a while, he was tossed ever so casually, as though he weighed no more than the merest shuttlecock, over Charles's head, landing in the hall below among the shattered pieces of the chamber pots. "Barney?" called Charles. There was no reply.

He looked at the smith who was now smashing the door again. He was winded but admiring. Had the circumstances of their meeting been more sociable, he would have signed up the man on the spot as a fist fighter. He was just the sort of fellow that a boxing buff might search for all his life.

"Well," pondered Charles looking at Boost's rippling muscles. "I like a fight myself but I am not a fool. This looks like a matter of superior wit against superior strength. How am I to tackle this brave fellow?"

Just at that moment he heard a girl's voice call out from the bedroom, "Obediah Boost." She sounded stern and no nonsense. "You stop all this banging and frothing, do you hear me? You have the parson stiff with fear in here." That, thought Charles, is presumably the "bastard jade."

"Stiff with fear, is he?" bawled Boost. "When Ah saw him a little while since he was stiff with something else."

"You damned slanderer," the girl yelled back. "You stop this, do you hear me? Act decent for once in your life."

"Yew wait, Lucy Emmett. Ah'm nearly through this door now and when Ah am, Ah'm going to flatten the parson and then Ah'm going to set about yew," shouted the blacksmith.

"You and whose army, pray?" Charles smiled at this. "Who knitted you that you think yourself so tough, you stupid great boar? You believe that I am going to stand here shaking when you enter and wait for you to beat me, I suppose? Well, you better watch out for I have an implement here and if you enter, you are going to find yourself crawling about the floor, searching for the

190

meagre brains that lived in your head before I cracked your thick skull for you."

Charles looked around him. The girl had the right idea. There on a chest near the bannisters was a copper warming-pan. He stood up and lifted it. It was heavy, still full of coals. Swinging it through the air, he hit the blacksmith a forceful blow just at the base of his skull. There was a grunt, then an exhalation of air. *Splendid,* thought Charles. *That was a blow to fell an ox.* He waited for the man to crumple but to his amazement he did not. He turned round, faced Charles and dropped the floor joist.

He stood suspended with surprise for a moment, his eyes round and rolling like alley marbles, then he blew through his nose, bared his teeth and slowly stretched out his hand.

"I am going to have to hit you again," shouted Charles swinging the warming-pan once more. Wham, he hit Boost dead on the chin.

"Ooff," gasped the smith. Charles waited. He saw the eyes glaze over. Was he going to fall? He tottered for a while, his expression now soft almost benevolent. The knees buckled, the hands clutched at thin air and then he crashed to the floor like a felled Colossus. Charles breathed a deep sigh of satisfaction and dropped the now bent and mangled warming-pan.

"It's all right in there," he called at the bedroom. "You may come out. It's all right, unlock the door."

"Did you kill him?" the girl's voice was eager.

"I doubt it," Charles replied, looking down at the recumbent Boost. "It would take more than a mere mortal to kill this character."

He heard the key being turned in the lock and the door started to open.

"All right up there?" It was Sir James calling up from the foot of the stairs.

"All right," called Charles, turning and looking down at Sir James from over the bannisters. He was administering to Barney who was also surrounded by giggling village girls, only too eager to nurse him.

Suddenly he felt a hand fasten itself to his ankle and a

terrible growl rose from behind him. Charles froze, then turned to see the smith rousing himself. It was impossible. The man was indestructible. Then the door opened and in a flash something white whizzed down through the air and met the smith's head full on. Charles winced. The sound was of splintering china or perhaps bone. Boost's eyes crossed, then he dropped back onto the floor.

"Oh good shot," cried Charles, looking down at the smith.

Then he looked up and his eyes grew wide with disbelief. There, framed in the doorway, stood the girl who had stopped his coach on the London road all those weeks before. The girl that he had thought about and dreamed about so often since. The girl he thought never to see again and she was even more vibrantly beautiful than he had even remembered her to be. Was that possible? Could a girl be more desirable in reality than she appeared in a lonely man's dreams?

Oh, it was more than possible. Here was the palpable proof of that possibility. Her translucent skin had been turned a honey gold by the summer's sun, setting off the midnight gloss of her hair and the sapphire blue of her eyes. His glance travelled from those bewitching eyes to the full ruby lips, then down her soft throat to the swelling sublimity of the breasts that rounded above her tight bodice. She seemed innocent of her beauty, wearing it easily, even carelessly. Oh, how he wanted her.

"Now at last I have your name," he whispered. "Lucy Emmett."

Lucy dropped the handle of the water pitcher that she had broken over Boost's head, and bobbed a hurried curtsey.

"Good day, sir," said Lucy Emmett.

CHAPTER VI

Cupid's Sweet Arrows and Ambition's Cruel Snares

In which Lucy dares to dream, and Georgiana triumphs.

Charles quickly stretched out his hand and caught hers, raising her from her curtsey. As their flesh met, he became aware of a sudden quickening of his heart. The desire to embrace her was almost overwhelming. With that instinct born in a man when he meets with a powerful attraction, he felt certain that if he should embrace her, she would not resist but would reciprocate with a passion as fiery as that which he fought so hard to suppress. He found his hand tightening around hers. He wanted to pull her to him. To feel her soft breasts yielding against him. Her lips parting under his.

But with that admirable restraint which comes from an early education in strict discipline, he let go of her hand, and found the strength to return to the everyday pleasantries of *social* intercourse.

"I take it you live here in Ragby?"

Lucy nodded. Her face still flushed from the surge of emotion she too had felt at his touch. Her eyes were clouded, melting.

"I see." He avoided those eyes. "What happened to the London excursion?"

"I was caught, and carried back here by him."

He watched Lucy prod at the felled smith with her foot.

"Oh. Bad luck," murmured Charles, deducing from her voice that the last thing on earth she had wanted was to be caught and returned to Ragby, especially by Boost the blacksmith.

Now her eyes were blazing. Gone was the former soft, yielding look. *I do not know which expression in those eyes excites me most*, thought Charles.

"I wish he had been killed," said Lucy. "I really wish it, though I know it wrong and a sin. But I must marry him tomorrow, in spite of praying with all my heart that it could be avoided. 'Tis not fair, is it? That I should be forced to marry a person that I find so insufferable? Is it fair, I ask you?"

Charles looked down at the smith. He was a big, lusty fellow. But his wits were no match for Lucy, that was certain.

"Who says that you *must* marry him?"

"Why, my father."

"Mm. Well then. There is no question of fairness in this. Duty to your father must prevail." *What am I saying?* Thought Charles. *I sound like a parson myself.*

"But you have my deep sympathy," he went on. "For I am in about the same spot."

"But I hate him. Hate him," cried Lucy, much distressed.

Charles' pity was roused. More than pity. He did not want her taken by the brute that lay at his feet. He did not want her taken by anyone except....

He moved away from her slightly, not trusting himself to stand close to her any longer. Now a deep sense of disappointment filled him, along with the fierce desire. His joy and surprise at seeing her again, the wild thrill that had so moved him when he had touched her, had blinded him to the wide difference in their social positions. He had learned that, more than being a common-born girl, Lucy was a bastard. Now she had told him that she was betrothed to the blacksmith. While he was the heir to a great estate and an honourable title. He could not help but smile. It was ironic the way this unlikely, low-born girl had moved him, when so many fine ladies had failed. One would have thought that "never the twain shall meet," let alone touch each other, let alone.... But accident had thrown them together, and here he was having to move away from her, because he could not trust himself not to kiss her, and more, wanting her to return his kiss, and more desperately, wanting her. More still desperately, wanting her to want him. No, the flame she had kindled in him was not something that could be extinguished by a casual flirtation. He must ignore it, or be burnt by it.

"I have heard that you were at the very bottom of this fracas," he said sternly.

"In a way," retorted Lucy. "Though I would not say that the whole blame is on me. 'Twas not all my fault the parson turned to explorer. Nor that Boost here went berserk."

Charles tried hard not to smile. "Where is the parson now?"

"Inside on his bed. In a daze of terror."

"I see. Well, I had better send for some sturdies to move this fellow here, and parson's sister to tend to her brother. As for you, you must count yourself lucky indeed that I arrived in the nick of time. For the mind reels at what mischief this fellow might have done you, had he succeeded in breaking down that door."

Lucy squared herself and lifted her chin. "He would not have damn well taken me without a fight, I can tell you," she said angrily. "I am no shrinking violet. But I wonder what a mess he might have made of you. If I had not appeared in the very nick of time and saved you from his temper."

"Saved *me*?" laughed Charles dismissively. "Oh, I think you may content yourself that I had the matter well under control. I am not a man who cannot handle his own fights. I do not need a slip of a girl to save me."

"Oh," said Lucy. "That is strange indeed. For when I emerged with the water jug I could have sworn your face was as white as a fish's belly with fright."

"Fright?" said Charles coldly. "Fright, miss? I think that you mistook my grim determination to finish the fellow. I often grow pale when I am fierce." *My God, this girl has the devil of a cheek!*

"Why did you not finish him then?" asked Lucy, just as though she were engaged in a squabble with her brothers.

"Because," shouted Charles, "you marched out with your damned jug, and deprived me of the pleasure." His heart was pounding now with fury.

"There is no need to shout," said Lucy placatingly. "But all I can say is. . . ." She got no further. He caught her arm. Pulled her to him, and glared down into her face.

"Silence," he commanded. "Utter one more word and I shall not answer for the consequences. I do not know what it is with you. But it was the same when first we met. You have such an awkward, and contrary way that you would send the mildest man in the whole universe, screaming mad for blood. I tell you, I am not one jot surprised that this blacksmith went on the rampage. I just hope he has the sense to beat you soundly when he has married you. For I suspect that is the only way to keep you in order."

Her lips had begun to quiver. Now two tears dropped onto the front of his riding coat.

"'Tis no good to weep. Tears will not help. I am impervious to them. Now, come on, compose yourself, and follow me."

"I cannot," sniffed Lucy.

"Why not?"

"I do not know what has become of my dog," she wailed.

Charles watched her fold up and sink to the floor at his feet, in such a state of dejection that one would have thought her whole world was grinding to a bitter end.

"Oh, Magpie," she wept. "Are you lost to me forever? Oh, I would not put it past that beastly Boost to have found him and wrung his neck, as easy as one would wring out a dishcloth."

"Oh, come," said Charles softly, feeling awkward because of the tears. "I am sure the man would not take his wrath out on a dog. Surely the hound is here somewhere. Come. Stop the tears. I know how you feel. I am an animal lover myself."

"You are?" Lucy stopped crying for an instant and looked up at him adoringly. Charles could not resist that look. "Of course," he said curtly. "What Englishman is not? Magpie?" he called, stepping over the recumbent blacksmith to stick his head around the bedroom door. He could see the parson collapsed on his bed, but no sign of a canine inhabitant.

"Drat the little fiend," said Charles out loud. Lucy was weeping again. "Magpie," called Charles, walking around the bedroom.

"Wherever you are, show yourself. Damn your eyes."

"Do not swear," cried Lucy from the landing. "He cannot abide oaths, you will frighten him all the more."

"What ails you, you minx?" asked Sir James, who had arrived panting at the top of the stairs.

"I have lost my dear dog," wailed Lucy.

"Thank yourself lucky indeed that you did not lose every one of your limbs. You naughty girl," said Sir James. "Where is the heir?"

Lucy nodded towards the bedroom. "Inside."

"Charles?" called the old man entering the bedroom and finding, to his surprise, the Landsdun heir crawling about on all fours, whistling and calling, "Magpie. Magpie."

"Charles," exclaimed Sir James. The heir jumped to his feet. "Good heavens, my boy. Cannot you hear the commotion outside? The Stowe coach has just driven up to the gates out there. The ladies must have got impatient. Come along now. I do not relish feeling the edge of Mrs. Stowe's tongue if we are not out there to greet them."

"You have not seen a small dog about the place, I suppose?" asked Charles.

"Good God, sir," snapped the physician grabbing his arm and pulling him out of the room.

"Maybe he bolted," Charles said to Lucy when he was on the landing again. "Perhaps he ran home?"

She shook her head. "No, he cannot run. He is too fat, and half blind besides."

"I take it the hound is the same fellow who is gun shy?" asked Charles.

She nodded.

"Mercy. The animal is so riddled with afflictions, 'tis a wonder that it lives at all," observed Charles. He helped Lucy up from the floor and, using his good cambric kerchief to dry her eyes, said kindly. "Now. Do not be down-hearted. He will be found I am sure."

Sir James did not comment on this display of affection. But he did note it and thought it very strange. Most unusual for the heir.

When they arrived out in the sunshine a few moments later it was to see that all the villagers had rushed towards the gates to see the unaccustomed sight of a quality coach in Ragby, and there was indeed a commotion.

Lucy trailed off among the graves, calling so disconsolately to her lost dog that it wrung the very strings of Sir James' heart. "That little wench seems to dote on her dog," he said to the heir, brushing the dust off the young man's coat, for it was marred and dirty from crawling about the floors.

"She's a pretty creature." He looked keenly at Charles who was watching Lucy.

"Sir James, you remember some weeks ago, our coach was stopped on the London road by a girl?" Sir James nodded.

"Well. That is she."

"The deuce it is," gasped the old man.

"Try the church," called Charles after Lucy. "He may have sought sanctuary if he is siege shy as well as gun shy." He had thought to make Sir James smile, but the quip was lost on him.

"I hope you are not planning to pursue her. You know she is to be married." Sir James was worried remembering how obsessed the heir had been with the girl who had stopped their coach. "I mean, it would be most unfitting." He had no reply from Charles who was tieing the long auburn hair that had come loose back into the black

198

ribbon. He composed his appearance just in time. For there was an audible gasp of awe from the crowd that had run to the gates. It parted, and Georgiana Stowe and her mother swept through the populace of Ragby towards Charles and Sir James.

"Melton!" cried Georgiana, extending a kid-gloved hand for him to kiss. "Oh, where have you been hiding? We waited what seemed like hours at the toll. How could you have been so neglectful, and after we had suffered such a long and tedious journey too. My mother is quite hurt, and so am I."

"Magpie?"

Charles looked 'round. Lucy was searching through the long grass. He took Georgiana's hand and bent to kiss it. "You have my sincere apologies and so has your mother. I was detained as you can see by a disturbance which is now happily concluded." What Georgiana made of the scene around her may only be guessed at. The churchyard was full of torn books and fighting children. One young man lay in the grass, wounded, tended to by a cluster of girls. Another man, big as St. Paul's, was staggering out of the parsonage holding his head. He was supported by two village men.

A lady appeared at a bedroom window, and shrieked, "My brother is in a catalepsy. A catalepsy!"

The rest of the villagers pressed against Georgiana, tweaking at her dress, and murmuring. "Did you ever see anything so grand, so rich, so fine?" and a fop dithered around on the periphery trilling, "May ward. May ward. Such quality. Such breeding. How correct. How very *comme il faut*." While above all the babble a high plaintive voice cried, "Magpie. Magpie?" like a wraith in a crypt.

"You know Sir James, of course," said Charles. Georgiana was too well bred by far to allow such an extraordinary scene to draw a comment from her. Besides she always ignored what she did not immediately understand. So she smiled, and put out her hand to Sir James, who said, "My pleasure," bowing very low. First to her, and then to her mother, who looked very cross, very hot, and ready to do battle.

199

"Oh, madam," Sir James continued hurriedly, "what a pleasure it is to be sure for an old man to find himself in such beauteous company. It does my heart good to gaze on you."

Mrs. Stowe was quite taken back by this scuppering of her ill humour. She had been about to berate the heir and Sir James for their tardiness. But now, her expression turned to simpering flirtatiousness. "Oh, enough, you rogue," she giggled, poking Sir James shapely with her finger just beneath the last button on his waistcoat. "You don't mean it. You know you don't."

"Indeed I do," insisted the physician. "For when I first saw your face, why, I could have sworn that Autumn had retreated and Spring had burst forth again in all its promising profusion. And as for your lovely daughter, why I need not enquire either as to how she continues for I see, just by glancing at her countenance, that she rivals the sun in its brilliance."

Georgiana smiled and turned away from Sir James, leaving him to flatter her mother further. "Must I rely entirely upon old men for my compliments?" she asked Charles archly. "You have not even expressed pleasure at seeing me. Which is a trifle ungallant, don't you think, under the circumstances?"

She was not immediately answered, for Charles' eyes were transfixed by the sight of Lucy Emmett climbing on top of the high stone wall that surrounded the churchyard calling, "Magpie? Magpie?" and displaying an expanse of sharpely brown leg as she did so. "Oh, dammit, Magpie. You ungrateful lousy cur. Come here in God's name or I shall abandon you to the stoats. As God is my witness, I will."

"Er. You did not glimpse a dog as you arrived, I suppose?" asked Charles. Georgiana's lips tightened, and her hands clutched her reticule with such savagery that she appeared determined to tear it apart. "Oh! How can you talk of dogs when you have not even said that you are pleased to see me?"

"Oh, I thought I had said that," murmured Charles absently. He was still watching Lucy. She was trying to scramble down off the high wall. He wondered if he should go and help her.

"Well, you have not," said Georgiana plucking at his sleeve to draw his attention.

Ah, thought Charles. *That's good, she has managed to get down safely.* "Well, of course I am pleased to see you," he said to Georgiana. Oh, but Lucy had hurt herself. She was bending down, spitting on her finger and wiping little beads of blood off her kneecap. "Are you alright?" Charles called.

"Alright," Lucy shouted back. "It's only a graze." She took the injury in her stride and in a moment was off again in search of her dog. *What a girl*, thought the heir.

Georgiana Stowe was not a little put out by Charles' interest in a common girl. "You did not notice that I left off patching to please you?"

Charles tore his eyes away from Lucy and looked at Georgiana properly for the first time since she had joined him. "Oh. So my letter had some effect after all."

Georgiana slipped her arm through his and whispered in his ear, "I have wanted so much to please you, Charles. My whole life is to that end."

They walked slowly through the long churchyard grass towards the gates and her coach. Georgiana was radiant, delighted at last to be upon the Landsdun heir's arm, basking in the admiring looks from the inhabitants of Ragby.

Georgiana's grandeur had not been ignored by Lucy, either, and it came to her, as her wondering eyes drank in every detail of the lady's finery, that for the first time in her life she was looking at a lady of quality. Georgiana's complexion was milk white, her lips pink as rosebuds. To Lucy, whose complexion owed its colour to the sun, and who was ignorant of the cosmetic arts, this seemed a miracle. The lady's hair was powdered, and it was arranged in cascades of ringlets at the nape of her swanlike neck. She wore a pretty leghorn straw, decked with forget-me-nots. Her dress was of a fine, pale blue silk, with a darker blue velvet redingote over it. This was trimmed about the wrists and caped shoulders with the softest white fur. To Lucy she looked like an angel who had sailed down from heaven for a visit, as transient as a rainbow. It was all Lucy could do not to run away out of sheer shame and mortification. How could she ever have imagined that Lord Melton could have looked on her, Lucy Emmett, bastard of this parish, with anything more than pity, or worse, ridicule, when such a creature as that was so obviously enamoured of him? How she clung to his arm, and smiled, and pouted, and flirted, whispered in his ear and laughed. A high tinkling laugh like a silver bell.

"So," whispered Lucy to herself, "*that* is what it is, to be quality, and rich and favoured."

"You like my dress?" asked Georgiana. "'Tis a new one."

"You look fine," said Charles.

"Oh heavens. Must I be content with that?" begged Miss Stowe, who needed compliments as any other human needs air. "Shall I not have a kiss to prove how fine you think me?"

They were at the gates now, waiting for her mother and Sir James and they were surrounded by a group of curious, grinning villagers. Charles was not about to put on a show for their benefit.

"Not here."

"Oh come," coaxed Georgiana. "I shall suffer awfully for lack of a kiss."

"I do not kiss in public."

"Not even a peck?" Georgiana should have been warned by Charles' deepening frown. "I do not *peck* in public either, and I may say that if you ever expect to be pecked by me, you are to be mightily disappointed. If you long to be pecked, well, find yourself a rooster."

Georgiana was furious. Three hours had been devoted to her toilette, before setting out on the journey that morning. All to impress Charles, and he was as stuffy and cold as he had always been with her.

"Perhaps I shall have a kiss later, then. When we are not so public, sir." Her voice was bright but her face was sullen.

"Woof!"

The bark came from the direction of the parsonage. Charles turned to see a small black and white shape tumble down the steps, then waddle forward. Peering around, shortsightedly, from under a pair of huge floppy ears.

"Oh, Magpie. *There* you are" cried Lucy, who ran forward to collect him. But at that precise moment, Jupiter and the bay were being led away from the house by one of the grooms who had traveled from London on the rear of the Stowe coach, and Magpie, hearing Lucy's voice but uncertain which direction to take to get to her, decided to remain where he was and sat down plum under Jupiter's aristocratic nose. "Whoof," he barked for good measure. It was this, along with the unexpected sight of an animal in his path, that sent Jupiter into a frenzy. He reared into the air above Magpie, snorting and whinnying, his powerful front feet beating at the tiny dog.

"Stop," yelled Charles running forward, for Lucy had dashed under the horse's flailing hoofs to resuce her pet. Charles stopped in his tracks and shut his eyes. It was impossible that she could escape being maimed. But when he allowed himself to look again, Lucy was sitting on the parsonage steps with Magpie in her arms, kissing his twitching wet nose. "You know, I suppose, that you might have been trampled." Charles looked down at her. She was carefully examining Magpie for bruises, cuts, bites or hoof marks. "Anyway, you are alright," sighed Charles, "thank God."

"I've a good mind to tie a stone round that flea-ridden cur and toss it into the nearest deep water," said the groom angrily, "frightening a highbreed horse."

"Lay a hand on the hound and you'll reckon with me," snapped Lucy. "Much good a horse is to anyone, no matter how highbred, if it shies at the sight of a dog."

"Perhaps he ain't seen an oddity dog like that before," observed the groom sneeringly.

"Where are you from, pray?" Lucy asked.

"London," replied the groom.

"Well I *ain't* seen nothing like you before either. So about your business lest I tie a stone 'round *your* neck, and drown you for an oddity, too."

Charles laughed loud and long. "You know you have a deuced straight tongue for a female," Charles told Lucy.

"Some people say 'tis too straight, even rude," said Lucy. She was blushing, mistaking his admiration for censure.

"Oh, not rude. Forthright, perhaps, but not rude," said Charles. He looked down at her and smiled. He was tormented by her beauty, and amazed at her spirit. Even when she argued with him.

"Your lady waits for you."

Charles glanced back at Georgiana, impatiently tapping her foot and muttering to Sir James and her mother.

"Oh yes. So she does."

"She's a very grand lady."

"Yes. I suppose she must seem so to you," said Charles. "Well, er . . . well, I suppose that I must sat goodbye." His voice sounded empty. He extended his hand. Lucy did not take it. But buried her blushes in Magpie's fur, and mumbled. "Goodbye, sir."

"Well. Good luck anyway. I hope all goes well for you," said Charles brightly, hoping she would look up. She did not. "Oh, come. Be kind. At least say goodbye. We may never meet again, and we have cut quite a dash together, today. One way and another."

"Don't mock me," said Lucy raising her eyes to his.

Gently he touched her cheek with his finger. "I would never mock you, Lucy. Never forget that. Others may mock you, but I? Never. For you have spirit, and that is a rare thing."

"How long will it last, if I marry the smith? Not long." She blurted this out.

"Nonsense. You will run rings around him," said Charles.

"You do not know what it is like. You can have no idea. I will be with child every year. You do not know how it kills women." Tears had filled her eyes again. She looked desperate.

204

Charles looked away from her, towards Georgiana, then back to Lucy. "You are really afraid?"

She nodded.

"I cannot promise anything," said Charles, and then he bowed and walked away.

"Whoever is that strange girl?" asked Georgiana with a laugh, as he joined her and her mother and Sir James.

"May Lady," cried Peter Royalston, who was nearly mad with impatience trying to introduce himself. "If you require any intelligence on that score you may rely on me." He stepped forward making a deep bow, and the tip of his nose touched the hem of Georgiana's gown.

"I am, most devine and noble lady, your sarvant Peter Royalston, heir and nephew to Squire William Royalston at this district, and am, as you may deduce from my mode," he swept an explanatory hand over his outrageous apparel, "one of the rare elite here. The rest being a nefarious, ramshackle and dilapidated band of hee haws, don't y'know. Lard, churls and chawbacons. Look about you. You must agree. Positively neolithic." He shuddered. "The wench there," he went on, pointing his long beribboned stick in Lucy's direction, "is of the same stuff. But worse, of an indeterminate breed. 'Tis a bastard, although I'm strapped if its name doesn't escape me for the minute."

"Lucy Emmett is her name," said Charles coldly.

"Oh, Lard. Haw, haw. That's it."

"I am not surprised that you know her name. I could not help noticing that you fraternized with her quite comfortably," said Georgiana. "I am in wonder as to what you found so consuming in her. You stayed so long. Still, I suppose she has a sort of tawdry grace, for one so *low*."

Charles was about to defend Lucy, but Sir James coughed and dug him in the ribs.

Charles turned briefly and looked back at Lucy. She stood watching him depart, the sun sending dazzling lights through her long black hair. She smiled, then turning away from him, walked towards the blacksmith sitting on the grass. Her hips swayed rhythmically.

"Come. I think we have loitered long enough here."

Mrs. Stowe's voice was sharp, her eye on Charles sharper. She laughed. "I knew that the heir was a keen judge of horse flesh. I did not imagine for a moment though that he indulged in that other sort of judging. *Hardly* a sport for a gentleman."

Sir James was quick to Charles' rescue. "Oh, good grief, ma'm, I think that you exaggerate the interest. Doesn't she, Charles?"

"I am sorry," said the heir. "I seem to have lost the gist of the conversation. Be so kind as to escort the ladies to the coach, Sir James. I will follow along in just one moment." He ignored the old man's frown and took Peter Royalston by the sleeve. "I have a few words to address to Royalston here. Come, Royalston," he said, pulling him to one side. Charles waited until Sir James and the ladies were out of earshot, and then said to Peter, "Well. This has been a regular rattle, all this." He nodded about him.

"Oh Lard, absolutely fraytfull," replied the fop. "For the parsonage is wrecked like the Hesperus, and the parson's mind sent as silly as the grin on a bedlam cat."

"He's a devilish dangerous fellow," said Charles.

"Who, the parson?" asked Peter.

"No. The blacksmith."

"Oh, quite," agreed Peter. "Horrid great hairy bogey. I was near strangled by it myself, don't ye know."

"Should be locked up for it," said Charles grimly, "restrained. I dislike to worry you, Royalston. But I feel it only fair to warn you, that while he was bellowing that he would kill the parson, and make a hash of the girl, I heard your name mentioned."

"My name?" Royalston was clearly horrified.

Charles nodded. "'Royalston is next,' he said. He may not have meant it, of course. But you should be forewarned."

"Lard!" squeaked Peter Royalston. "You feel I should incarcerate him with alacrity?"

Charles patted him on the shoulder. "I think you would be wise to arrange it. I mean if you do not, there is the chance you may wake one morning with your throat cut."

"My throat cut?" shrieked the appalled fop. "Oh, how

can I evah thank you, my Lard, for informing me on that foul, murdering miscreant's murky intent. I shall have him incarcerated immediately. Oh, when I think that I may have been slain. Slain! Oh were I not at this moment in the very glass of fashion, I should be upon my knees in the very dust to you, giving thanks. I am your slave, upon my ward I am. If evah I may be of sarvice to your lardship, why your lardship has only to ask and...."

"Well, on my word, 'tis a very curious thing you should offer, Royalston," replied the heir. "for you may indeed be of service to me, if it would please you."

"Please me?" shrilled the fop. "To serve a person such as yourself who is in the very cream of society...oh, I am yours to command."

"Perhaps you will see that the Emmett girl is saved from marrying the scurvy fellow, then," said Charles. "If you manage that, you will have my undying gratitude."

"Your undying gratitude," murmured Royalston. Then a look of cunning entered his usually vacant eyes, for Peter Royalston, though stupid, was not quite so stupid when he caught a hint of scandal. Charles caught the knowing look cast him by the fop and realised that if he was not very careful, his interest in Lucy would soon become a subject for gossip throughout the county, that it might even arrive at Landsdun to be whispered among the staff, and nothing was whispered at Landsdun without coming eventually to the ears of the earl. Charles knew that gossip of that sort could only distress his father, especially in his present state of health. And Charles did not relish the idea of having his supposedly amorous adventures with a country bastard girl laughed over and discussed in every club and coffee house in London.

"Not at all," he snapped. "My interest in the girl is purely altruistic. I do not care whether she is wed or no. But I think 'twould be wrong for her to be forced to marry that crude jack against her will. What if he murders her? I should not like her death at my door. That is all, and if you, Royalston, start twittering abroad any scandal about me, I promise you the very devil of a reckoning." With that ominous warning he turned on his heel and walked away.

But the heir's stern warning was lost on Peter Royalston, for the fop was in a reverie. "His undying gratitude," whispered Peter, turning his attention to Lucy Emmett. So, she had caught the eye of Lord Melton himself, a gentleman of the very highest order. Peter Royalston had long dreamed of moving in real Society circles, perhaps of even being presented at court? Until this moment, that longed-for presentation at court had remained a dream. He was, after all, merely the heir to a county squire, and had no influential and powerful friend to introduce him into that wonderful glittering world. But what if he could be of service to the heir, and earn his undying gratitude? Lord Melton was frequently at court. He was intimate with people who were intimate with the King. "Oh, Lard," gasped Peter, as he conjured up a picture of himself in a suit of the most exquisite gold cloth, bending his knee to the King himself. "Vhat ho, Royalston," said the German King. "Vee are zo very pleased to zee you. Tell us. Vere did you haf that splendid suit made? I svear that you are the *Nonpareil*."

Lucy had just watched the smith led away to a cell in the village where he would be kept secure until Squire Billy returned from London to hold an Assize Court, and decide what was to be done with the destructive fellow, when Peter Royalston sidled up to her and with much nudging, nodding and winking informed her that he was privy to what was going on, and that she should not hesitate to take him into her confidence.

"What do you mean, what is going on?"

Peter Royalston merely giggled and winked again, "Oh, you most fortunate thing you," he said, squeezing her hand, "you may play the innocent with me. But I see the way things wag. I have the jist of the thing and am in his confidence. You may be straight with me. It will go no further."

"What will go no further, dammit, man?" asked Lucy. "I really cannot know what you are chunnering about."

"Oh, do not pretend, most favoured of creatures," Peter

called after her as she walked through the churchyard gates to go home to Ridge Farm, and the reckoning with Roger and his wife. "There is no other person in the wide world, I do assure you, better acquainted with the curious ways of the nobility. I know Quality when it is smitten, upon my ward I do." Then the fop rushed back to Ragby Hall, to write a note to Landsdun.

It is done. Charles stood alone in the library that same evening and read the note that had just been delivered from Peter Royalston with a good deal of angry disquiet. *The smith is a prisoner, and when my uncle returns will be dealt with. Have no fear. She whom your heart has seized on will be safe. My sword is drawn to guard her virtue. Only utter, and I shall be of service. Were the winged god himself flown from the realms above 'tis not possible that he were a more eager and willing servant to yourself and your fille de joie. I am yours forever to command, and am mum. My lips are sealed, my eyes blind, my ears are shut in your service. In short. I am the most secret of lovers' agents. But name the trysting place, and I shall whisper to her. Yrs. Cupid.*

"My *fille de joie?*" roared Charles. He screwed up the note and threw it on the fire. "Cupid?" he hissed pacing the floor. "How could I have been so indiscreet? What possessed me? Good God. I must have been mad."

Peter Royalston had put two and two together and made twenty-two. It was impossible now that he should ever see Lucy again. Impossible. If this nonsense got out he would be a laughing stock in Society. The Landsdun name coupled with the name of a country bastard?

"Oh, there you are my boy," said Sir James, looking around the library door. "The ladies are waiting to be taken in to dine. By the way," said the old man, catching him by the arm and whispering to him, "Mrs. Stowe is still very tight-lipped about what passed this morning. You know she has an idea the girl is at the bottom of it. I know you have an itch for the pretty creature, but be a sensible fellow and control it. For in my view it would be a very ungentlemanly way of behaving to call Georgiana to Landsdun, and then to neglect her in order to pursue an obsession for such a girl. For if it got to General Stowe's ears, you would have the censure of all decent Society on you."

Lord Melton straightened his lace jabot, and looked at Sir James with steely grey eyes. "There is one thing, sir, that you may always be certain of. I am a gentleman and will conduct myself as such," he said. "Upon that honour that I hold dear, Georgiana shall not be neglected. But her mother had better hold her mischievous tongue, or I may be tempted to loosen mine and *order* her to hold it. Now, shall we join the ladies?"

While Charles was dining in magnificence at Landsdun House, Lucy was chewing on a piece of green salt bacon at Ridge Farm, and was lucky to have it, for she was in disgrace again. Elizabeth had called her a "No good." Roger had called her a "demon of destruction" and Toby and John had not said anything, for the moment they opened their mouths to defend her, Roger had ordered them out of the house. Magpie had been banished to the yard and Lucy to her bed, with the wretched piece of bacon. And as she sat on her bed, trying to make a meal of it, her worries threatened to make a meal of her.

She was mostly worried about what would become of her when Boost was finally free. For he blamed his imprisonment on her. So did everyone else. Miss Parson Brown had even said that she would petition the squire to have Lucy deported for causing the parson's loss of wit and all the damage to the parsonage. Lucy had been slightly relieved when Boost had been locked up because it left the question of their marriage in the air. But while she gnawed on the unpalatable piece of bacon she began to wish that things were as they had been prior to the siege. The worry of marrying the smith seemed nothing to the worry about deportation. Deportation really was a bad end. In fact deportation was the *very* end.

Although the day had brought its share of trouble, it had brought Lord Melton to her again, and as she curled up on her mattress, her eyes closed with his face in her memory to comfort her and his last words to her to sustain her. "You have spirit and that is a rare thing."

She shivered with pleasure when she remembered the look in his eyes when he had touched her. The feeling that had raced through her when his hand had closed around hers. She had thought he meant to kiss her. Had wished that he would. But he had drawn away. Lucy opened her eyes and listened to the sounds of the night birds. There were owls after field mice, and voles. Night jars called. The distant coo of pigeons disturbed at their rest echoed around the house, and she ran through the day's events in her mind. She almost laughed out loud when she thought of Peter Royalston. *What had the silly fellow meant saying that I was most fortunate? What did he mean, "goings on"? What proceedings was he "privy to"? Why did he look so knowingly at me? Why was he suddenly so friendly?* She sat bolt upright, her eyes wide. *What had he meant . . . he was "acquainted with the curious ways of the nobility"?* She frowned trying to remember what he had called after her.

"I know Quality when it is smitten." That is what he had said. Lucy's mouth fell open. *Was it possible? Oh no it couldn't be. There was that beautiful, beautiful quality lady. But wait, What had Charles said? "Come, be kind. Say goodbye. We may never meet again." He had not said. "We will never meet again."* "Oh," whispered Lucy, hugging herself in the darkness. "Perhaps it is possible. Dare I think it is?"

In the week that followed Georgiana's arrival at Landsdun, Charles did his utmost to banish Lucy from his mind. His nights, though, were full of dreams of her, and during the day, although he did his best to entertain Georgiana he found himself hard pressed to resist the temptation to ride out to Ragby. This urge was almost overwhelming, for his dreams had shown him what he would do if he were ever to find himself close to her again.

211

But he did fight the urge, hoping that the infatuation would pass and that Georgiana Stowe would become more acceptable to his affection.

By the end of that week his attitude towards Georgiana was somewhat changed. He did not find her conversation more interesting, but he had begun to view her considerable physical charms with a sort of detached interest. Since arriving at Landsdun with his father some weeks earlier, he had missed the company of those London ladies who were delighted to entertain him in their beds, when he felt the need for that sort of distraction. And thoughts of Lucy, and the desire those thoughts roused in him, made his continuing celibacy even harder to support.

True, Georgiana painted herself. True, her beauty was rather too full blown and opulent for his taste. But Charles was too honest with himself not to admit that a taste for opulence was one that a man *might* under certain circumstances easily acquire.

By this time, too, the earl's health had improved. This was partly due to his extended rest in the country, but it was due more to the presence of Miss Stowe at Landsdun. Unlike Charles, the earl was not irritated by her constant chattering.

Being an older man he enjoyed indulging her with compliments, as did Sir James. For Georgiana's way with men was to wheedle for compliments and then to appear broken-hearted if they were not immediately forthcoming. And it is after all a rare man who can resist feeling flattered by appearing to have so much power over a pretty young woman's happiness.

Indeed so much was the earl's health recovered in the company of Miss Stowe that he felt well enough one night to join his son, Sir James, Georgiana and Mrs. Stowe for dinner in the great dining room. The earl did not neglect to toast his "fair visitor" as he called Georgiana, declaring to the extreme delight of that lady and her mother, that he thought of her almost as his own daughter.

Charles was pleased to see his father seated again at the

head of the long polished table, appearing strong and in good spirits.

Georgiana, in a dress of silver brocade cut low in the bodice, showing off her full white breasts to perfection, sat on his right. The diamond ornaments in her hair sparkled in the light of the many candles that flickered in the crystal chandeliers.

Charles sat opposite her and found her a feast for his eyes. If only he could shut his ears to Georgiana's prattle, he would certainly enjoy exploring the other undoubted delights that lay covered by that oh so cunningly seductive silver gown.

Georgiana was not unaware that Charles had warmed towards her, and she allowed her eyes to meet his often across the dinner table. She had always found him attractive. The strong-jawed face, the cool grey eyes, the heavy glossy fall of chestnut hair. That almost cynical curve to his mouth.

Lord Melton was a handsome, virile young man. But he might have been the ugliest man in christendom as far as Georgiana Stowe and her mother were concerned, and he would still have been the best catch in the country. To marry a title, as well as enormous wealth and good looks—well, that really was something to strive for. And Miss Stowe and her mother were certainly striving. But more than a week had passed and Charles still had not asked for Georgiana's hand. However, earlier that evening the earl had suggested that a ball might be thrown at Landsdun in the next month for the ladies' entertainment. It was also the start of the hunting season if any other excuse was needed. Mrs. Stowe was well aware the earl was on her side for a match between Charles and Georgiana and had whispered to her daughter that the ball might be the perfect occasion for an engagement to be announced. If only Georgiana could find some way to get Charles actually to ask her. It was high time her daughter secured her position once and for all. Charles was not impervious to women, although he had a reputation for being impervious to their wiles. She reminded Georgiana

213

that he had obviously found a common girl in Ragby very pleasing, and if a common girl could set his blood on fire, there was no known reason why Georgiana might not do the same.

It was imperative that Geogiana get a proposal from Lord Melton as quickly as possible. There would be other young women of beauty and quality at the ball. Did Georgiana want to lose her chance of such a very illustrious marriage? Their engagement *must* be announced at the ball, before all the members of Society who would flock to it. Then her elevation to the nobility would be certain. Mrs. Stowe was not tardy in observing that Charles' eyes had been upon her daughter throughout the evening. Charles must be caught while his mood was right. So when they rose from dinner, she suggested that Georgiana might benefit from a walk outside to take the air. When Charles said that he would accompany her, she wasted no time in sending a footman to request that Georgiana's maid carry a wrap to her daughter, and instead of preparing herself to chaperone them, she turned to the earl and asked him if he would care to hear her play upon the harpsichord? And in this way, Charles and Georgiana found themselves as if by magic alone beside the lily pool.

The evening was still and peaceful; only the sweet tinkling music of the harpsichord disturbed the deep quiet. The moon was a full circle above the dark trees of the ridge, and the sky shimmered with a million glimmering silver stars.

Charles watched Georgiana for a while as she leaned over the pool, and gazed down into the water, and found her closer proximity even more disturbing. The sight of her breasts spilling out over her low decolletage as she skimmed the still surface of the pool with her finger tips aroused his passion. Georgiana knew very well what stirred a man, and feeling him watching her with a look that spoke of desire, she leant further forward to try and pluck one of the year's last lilies. But of course the flower lay too far from her grasp, and her vain effort brought Charles to her side.

"Here," he said, handing her the white flower. "I am

afraid that it is a sad specimen. Had you been here earlier in the year, you would have found them at their best."

Georgiana raised the waxy bloom to her cheek, then brushed the cool petals with her lips. Charles smiled. The moonlight softened her painted face. She lay her hand upon his chest. "Why have you been so cold to me since I came?" she whispered. *Poor creature*, thought Charles. *She could not help being vain and empty headed. It was not her fault she had been raised to be a mere ornament.* "I am sorry if I have seemed cold," said Charles gently. "It is my way. You must not let it distress you. If you knew me better you would know that I am far from cold. On the contrary."

"Oh but it does distress me," said Georgiana. "I am of such a warm and affectionate disposition myself, and am used to being treated in the same manner. It quite destroys me when I am not."

Charles felt terribly guilty at this. For looking down at her, he saw her lower lip was trembling, and her eyes had filled with tears. "Oh, Georgiana," he said, quickly taking her hand, "I apologise. I know that I can be short sometimes, even rude."

"Yes," she replied. "Yes, you can be short, and cruel, and cutting. But I shall forgive you. If I can have a kiss to pay me for all your unkindness. You cannot say that we are too public now, after all."

Charles laughed. "It is true, we are not." He looked down at her. She had closed her eyes, her lips were parting to receive his kiss.

"Oh, Melton!" she sighed. "I have waited so long for some sign of affection."

Charles felt his long-suppressed passion overwhelm him. He caught her fiercely to him, holding her so tight in his arms that he heard the breath rush from her. He pressed his lips against hers, but instead of giving herself up to his urgent kiss, she stiffened and struggled to free herself, crying, "Sir, have a care. Do not be so rough." He pushed her from him and at once she shook open her fan, and peered into the small mirror hidden in its back. "Oh, see. You have quite disturbed my face," she moaned.

"Good God. How is a man to kiss you *without* disturbing your face when you insist upon caking it with that rubbish?" said Charles, seeing that the lead on her face had cracked.

"Well I certainly did not expect to be so roughly fallen upon," laughed Georgiana. "A lady does not expect that—especially not before marriage."

"Oh, I see," snapped Charles. "There are premarital kisses and post-marital kisses, are there? I was ignorant of that, and so you must excuse me. Perhaps, madam, you would do me the honour of explaining the difference?"

Georgiana giggled coyly. "A kiss before marriage should be affectionate but *never* passionate. After marriage—well, a lady would expect to endure an embrace that is more . . . robust?"

"Endure," said Charles dryly. "I see. I am greatly comforted by that. For a moment I had imagined that a gentleman would have to beget his heirs by a process of thought transference." He turned and walked away from her up the steps, but Georgiana ran after him and caught his arm. His anger, when she had repulsed him, his mention of heirs had convinced her that with only a little more manipulation she might bring him finally to a proposal.

"Oh, Charles. You have not understood. How can I allow the more intimate embraces when I am not totally sure of what you intend? Cannot you understand I might be terribly compromised?" She took his hand, and cast down her eyes. "What I endeavour to say is that my reaction would be quite different if I had some indication of my future position."

Charles' expression was as stony as the faces of the four lions that stood on each corner of the great house. "Do I understand you correctly," he asked. "May I take it that you are prepared to offer yourself to me at a price?"

Georgiana paled. Though this was precisely what she had meant, she did not approve of hearing it described so bluntly. "How dare you, sir?" she gasped.

Charles caught her arm, and turned her roughly to face him.

"No, madam," he said through clenched teeth. "How dare *you*?" Did it never occur to you that I might not want you at all? At *any* price?" He felt her recoil.

"You mean we are not to be married?" she asked. Her eyes were hard and bright. "You understand that everyone expects it, do you not? *Everyone*?"

Charles let go of her arm and bowed very low. "All that I wish to communicate is that I have doubts that I am prepared to continue to oblige everyone *except* myself. Now, if you will excuse me?" He bowed again with sardonic courtesy, and walked quickly away from her up the long flight of steps.

When Georgiana entered the music room alone a few minutes later, she had outwardly at least composed herself. But the bright and overgay manner with which she answered the earl's enquiry as to why his son was not with her alerted her mother.

"He simply expressed a wish to retire early," said Georgiana with a shrill little laugh. "Heavens, that is all." Mrs. Stowe, certain her daughter was distressed, excused them both, saying that she and Georgiana were also feeling fatigued. As soon as they were alone together in Georgiana's bedroom, Mrs. Stowe demanded an explanation. Georgiana at last let her temper rip, and marched up and down the room in a fury. Charles had misused her, she said. He did not want to make her his wife. Her whole life was in ruins. She was shamed—dared never go near her society friends again because she had told them all that a marriage between herself and the heir was certain.

Now, Mrs. Stowe was not a woman to give up easily. She had set her mind on her daughter's becoming a countess, and when she had calmed Georgiana sufficiently, they set about devising a plan to ensure that Charles would have to marry her. Like it or not.

Charles was sitting in a deep chair in his dressing room sipping a glass of brandy and smouldering as hot as the fire in the grate when Culpepper his manservant went to answer the knock on the door.

He was astounded when he opened it to find Miss Stowe, wearing only the flimsiest of lace gowns to cover her otherwise naked body. Before he could enquire politely if she had come to the wrong door, and offer to show her to her mother's, she had pushed past him into the room and fallen on the floor at Charles' feet. Her hair had been brushed out and hung loose about her shoulders, and her face, puffy from crying, was innocent of paint. She caught hold of Charles' hand and started sobbing.

"Shall I leave you, my lord?" asked the embarrassed Culpepper.

Charles nodded. "Wait outside." The servant left, shutting the door behind him.

"Now, madam. What do you mean by bursting into my room and appearing so scantily clad before my servant?"

"Oh, I could not help myself," wept Georgiana, her shoulders heaving. "I am so distraught that I have displeased you that I have come to beg forgiveness." Charles tried to stand, but was prevented by her laying her head upon his knee. "Oh, if only you knew how I longed to let you have your way with me, you would not censure me, I promise," she moaned. "Have a care for a foolish creature who would give herself to you gladly and extort no price of any kind, and has not, only because she feared that you would think her loose, as well as stupid."

"Really," said Charles coldly. "This change is very curious. You must forgive me if I seem suspicious, but only a short while ago, you feared being compromised by a kiss. I find it hard to believe that you are so soon prepared to throw caution to the winds, by appearing here in my dressing room wearing little more than your skin. Also I think I should tell you that I do not desire to 'have my way with you' as you so coyly put it, and I think that must be the end of this ridiculous conversation." Saying that, he took her arm and pulled her to her feet. As she stood up she let the gown fall from her and stood naked before him. Catching both his hands she pressed them against her breasts and cried out imploringly, "Oh God, surely you will not be so cruel as to reject me when I have thrown

218

aside my pride and come to you upon my knees. Do not break my heart, when I would do anything. Anything to gain your love."

"I did not ask you to discard your pride," said Charles. "That is the last thing in the world that I would ask any woman to do. As for gaining my love? I realise now that it can never be yours." He was about to lift her gown and put it about her shoulders. But she flung her arms around his neck pressing her body against his and searching for his mouth with hers. "Oh kiss me, now," she whispered desperately, "and I will show how willingly, how joyfully I will accommodate you."

Charles felt himself weaken at feeling a woman's warm, vibrant flesh against him after so long a time. Her mouth was hot and demanding against his. Allowing his hand to travel down the smooth contours of her back, over the curve of her rounded buttocks, he felt her tremble under his touch. His tongue moved over her lips.

"Oh, you want me," she whispered. "Oh, I know you want me."

Lifting her into his arms Charles laid her down upon the Aubusson carpet before the fire, then crushed her mouth with his, fiercely, hungrily. While all the time a voice inside him cried out. *Not you. Not you. Lucy. It is Lucy I love.* But under the bruising onslaught of his kisses, Georgiana was unaware of the voice. Her face was triumphant.

"Georgiana?" It was Mrs. Stowe's voice. Charles drew back. Caught the light of triumph that shone in Georgiana's eyes. At last he understood. He stood up, stared down at the naked woman, and smiled. "It seems, Miss Stowe, that I am the one who has been compromised," he said dryly. He could hear Mrs. Stowe outside the dressing room door now, questioning Culpepper. He could hear the man trying loyally to elude the questions. He threw Georgiana her gown. "Cover yourself and then get out," he commanded. Crossing to the door he threw it open, and said to Mrs. Stowe, "I cannot allow my man to answer for me, madam. Your daughter is inside." He watched the woman's eyes widen with shock, as though she had no idea that Georgiana was with him. "My heavens, sir," she gasped. "How dare you compromise her in this way?"

Charles laughed and shook his head. "Madam, tonight has convinced me, if ever I needed convincing, that compared to yourself and your daughter I am a mere amateur at the devious arts." He watched Georgiana rush into her mother's waiting arms and burst into tears again.

"There, there," said Mrs. Stowe. "Come. I will not blame you two young people for this. I remember youth's sudden appetites only too well. Your father, when I tell him, I am sure will understand. And the earl," she looked at Charles, "will expect his son to do the honourable thing."

The following morning when Charles returned from exercising Jupiter, he went to the library to join his father and Sir James. The earl was lying on one of the leather chesterfields when he entered, with a bemused expression on his face. Mrs. Stowe was there. So was Georgiana. They were sitting at the desk in the window discussing the guest list for the ball.

Charles sat down next to Sir James, who seemed very amused. "Did you enjoy the ride?" asked the earl, in a rather pointed manner.

"Very much," replied Charles. "The *horse* is in excellent condition."

"Well, I am pleased to hear that," said the earl. "Oh Georgiana," he went on, turning to Miss Stowe, "You had better include Squire Royalston, his wife and his nephew in the list." "Oh," pouted Georgiana. "Must we invite locals?" The earl laughed. "Of course the squire must come. He's the very salt of the earth. I should hate the old fellow to feel snubbed. He is a rough diamond, but hugely amusing. Oh, by the way, Charles, talking of diamonds, I have sent to London for a jeweler to travel here. I thought you and Georgiana would want to discuss the design of a betrothal ring with him. Georgiana tells me she prefers emeralds, though. Don't you, Georgiana?"

So it is fixed, thought Charles. *So simply.* He looked over at Georgiana and the smile he received was smug. "I do," she said. He inclined his head and smiled. She *deserved* his congratulations after all. She had been victorious where so many other women had failed. Sir James whispered in his ear. "Your father and Mrs. Stowe thought the matter had better be settled with as much speed as possible. Particularly after last night's escapade. They have fears that I may have to perform a delivery before the wedding if not."

Charles stood up and pushed away his chair. "The only thing that will be delivered before the wedding is the betrothal ring," he said loudly. "Of that, my good Sir, I can assure you. No matter what is said to the contrary, and no matter by whom it is said."

He noticed as he left the room that Georgiana did not even have the grace to blush.

CHAPTER VII

Love Will Always Find Out
the Way

*In which Cupid intervenes, but Charles and Lucy find
their own way to love.*

"Psst."

"Oh!" screamed Peter Royalston.

"Psst!" It was Lucy Emmett tapping on the sitting room window at Ragby Hall. She crooked her finger and beckoned to him. "Open up," she mouthed silently against the window pane. It took the fop a little while to recover himself enough to raise himself from the couch on which he had been reclining all morning. He had been reading a novelette entitled *Love Will Always Find Out the Way*, and at the same time, planning what he would wear at the Landsdun ball.

The invitation had been received that morning by his aunt Jemima, who had immediately gone into a decline because she had no suitable gown to wear, and because she believed that the squire would never agree to provide money for a properly magnificent creation.

Peter tottered over to the window holding hard to his thumping heart. He lived in terror of a visit from Boost, although the fellow was secure behind bars. Peter imagined the maniac snapping those bars like twigs and raging off towards Ragby Hall to perform the throat cutting operation Lord Melton had envisaged as not only possible but probable. How he wished the squire his uncle would hurry back from London and do his duty as a magistrate so that he could be rid of the ever-present threat.

"Oh Lard, what a start you gave me," he said to Lucy when he'd pushed open the window. "Fraytfull."

"Sorry. But I had to talk with you," said Lucy, raising her skirts and climbing over the window sill into the room.

Peter Royalston viewed this eccentric entrance with some trepidation; after all, one never *quite* knew what the chit would do next.

"In private," she whispered, looking furtively around as she pulled Magpie in after her and closed the window. "'Tis a matter of the utmost importance."

The fop's heart fluttered. "A matter of the utmost importance?" he asked breathlessly. "Might it, this matter of the utmost importance, concern a certain noble gentleman of our acquaintance?" Lucy nodded. It did indeed. For a whole week she had been waiting for an opportunity to slip away from Ridge Farm, seek out the fop and question him about Lord Melton's feelings towards her.

"Just so," she said.

"Oh, Lard," trilled the fop, grasping her hand and pulling her after him towards the couch, "You intend to take me into your confidence at last. Come tell all, do." Peter Royalston still had not received a reply to his "Cupid" letter, but he was not dismayed by that. He had received an invitation to the ball at Landsdun, and regarded that invitation as a sign from Lord Melton that he was now a member of the heir's circle. The fact that the invitation had been addressed to his uncle and aunt made not a jot of difference to his certainty that he would soon be a close confidant to the heir, and an even more frequent visitor at the court of King George. All that remained to ensure his elevation was that he could be of real use to Charles in this *affaire de coeur,* and now here was *Amorette* herself, ready to pour out her heart. "I wait with breath bated," breathed Peter, as soon as they were both seated on the couch. "You may be explicit with me. I am the very monument to discretion, don't y'know. Lard, I am discretion itself."

"Well," Lucy started tentatively. "Well, this noble gentleman of our acquaintance," she pulled Magpie up on her knee where he straight fell into a deep sleep.

"Yes, yes," said the fop eagerly. "Do not tell me. Let me guess. I have it—you wish me to carry a *billet doux*? Oh, this is all too too enthralling." His hand flew to his heart.

Lucy frowned, took a deep breath and continued, "Well, if you remember, you said that he was smitten."

"Oh, he is," said Peter.

"And I have imagined that he might care for me, although I am half afraid to think it, in case it is not true. Every night, every day since you told me he favoured me, I have thought of little else. Oh, how I have dreamed of him coming to me, of having some sign that it were true, and not merely a silly girl's idle fancy. But oh," she sighed, "through all my dreams, I think I must be mistaken. I am just a common creature, and he is such a very great gentleman."

"Lard, have no doubts, briar rose," Peter exclaimed. "For love is blind I do assure you. Nevah have I seen quality so moonstruck. Nevah have I seen a gentleman so infatuated."

"He told you that he loves me?" asked Lucy, anxiously searching Peter's face for some sign he was teasing her. Oh, surely he would not be so cruel.

"Told me. Told me? What need had he to tell me? His looks, his manner, his every movement conspired to verify my opinion. He is love's captive, passion's slave. You are the queen of delight, and I? I am Cupid," said Peter raising himself on one toe, and posing holding an imaginary bow and arrow.

"I thought that you were Peter Royalston?" said a

225

puzzled Lucy. She had always had grave doubts about the fop's sanity.

"So I am," trilled Peter. "But I have fallen under love's thrall, and am transformed, transmogrified. You see before you the incarnation of that blind winged God. Soft—listen," he whispered, shutting his eyes and cupping his hand around his ear. "You will hear, if you are silent, the zing of arrows, the twang of lutes." Lucy listened very hard, but heard nothing except the sound of pigeons cooing outside, Magpie's gentle snoring, and scampering rats racing within the decaying wainscotting of Ragby Hall. But, oh, what did it matter if she did not hear Cupid's music? Charles loved her, and they would make music of their own. "Oh this is more wonderful than I ever hoped for. Charles is to my mind the finest, the most perfect, and well set-up young man that I did ever look on, and he loves me, does not care that I am poor and a bastard. Does not care that I am ignorant, and wayward. Does not care that I am not Quality." Her eyes were shining. "Oh I am smiled on by fate, blessed by fortune." She burst into tears.

Peter had not bargained for such a show of genuine emotion from her. He wondered if he ought to tell her about the invitation to the Landsdun ball, and the fact that Lord Melton's engagement to Georgiana Stowe was to be announced on that occasion. After all, Lucy ought to understand that although the heir desired her, she could never be more than a diversion for him. Quality gentlemen often dallied with females from the lower orders. But no, perhaps the heir would not want Lucy to know of his forthcoming marriage, for the chit might not be so readily eager to be dallied with. Females, especially very young ones, were unpredictable creatures, and Peter was not prepared to risk Lucy coming between him and his own glorious future. "I have told you that love is blind, makes no distinction between class and commoner. It is indiscriminate. You may take it as certain that the heir desires you, or why should he prevail upon me to lock up the smith, and use my influence with my uncle so that you should not marry him?" Lucy looked up, her eyes wide with astonishment. "He did that?" she asked.

Peter nodded. "Oh Lard, he *did* so. He would have that maidenly part of you for his own. His arms alone shall crush you, he alone shall enter your perfumed garden. You are still a virgin, are you? Or did you lie?" Peter was suddenly worried that some other person might have entered the perfumed garden already, for he remembered the ructions at the parsonage when Roger Emmett had brought Lucy before the parson for being caught in the hay with a village 'prentice boy.

"But, of course I am," said Lucy tossing her head.

The fop sighed with relief, "Make sure you guard that part with your life," he said. "Remember that the heir honours us both. You will enjoy his interest, and his passion, perhaps even a little—" He rubbed his thumb and forefinger together, signifying money.

Lucy jumped up. "Do not imagine that I would sell myself," she cried. "If I give what I have, I shall give it freely."

"Oh, and so do I give my sarvice free," said Peter. "Although of course I am sure he will insist on rewarding me for being so stalwart a soldier in his sarvice. I evah believed I was destined for the Royal presence," he said, examining his fingernails haughtily.

"When will we meet, he and I?" asked Lucy. "Did he say?"

Peter smiled like a sphinx. "You long to face him, and faint to feel his arms I suppose?" he asked.

"Oh, I do," breathed Lucy joyfully. "There is so much that I would say to him."

The fop pulled her down beside him upon the couch, and giggled. "Hark to me," he whispered. "There are certain tiny obstacles that must be overcome, I think, that have prevented our illustrious gentleman from clasping you to his heart. But once he knows that you are passion's plaything, why, I believe an assignation might be easily arranged." He picked up the novelette and pointed to the title.

Lucy looked closely at it *Ll-ove*, *W-ill*, *Al-ways . . . Find*

Out—the Way," she read, then her eyes met those of the fop. "The zing of arrows? The twang of lutes?" he asked gleefully.

Lucy nodded, her expression filled with rapture.

Mrs. Stowe had just descended the wide staircase at Landsdun and, as she crossed the hall towards the library, she met a footman at the door. He was bearing a letter on a silver salver. It was late in the day for a letter to be delivered at Landsdun, and Mrs. Stowe was curious. "Is that for me?" she asked, thinking suddenly that it might be from her husband the General. She was waiting for a reply from him to a letter she had sent, telling him that Georgiana was to be Charles' wife and asking him to come to Leicestershire to discuss plans for the wedding, the date and such like, for the details would have to be announced at the ball.

"No, madam," said the footman bowing, "it's for Lord Melton, and has just been delivered by a servant from Ragby Hall."

"Oh, then its probably a reply from the squire to our invitation. Give it to me. I'll hand it to your young master," said Mrs. Stowe. She tried to take the letter off the salver but to her surprise the footman quickly prevented her.

"I am sorry," he said firmly, "the servant said that the letter was only to be given to Lord Melton, and he himself gave strict instructions, that if there were any more letters sent here from Ragby Hall they were to be given immediately into his hand."

Any more letters, thought Mrs. Stowe. Then she wondered why the footman looked so uncomfortable. If the letter was simply a reply to the invitation to the ball, what harm could there be in her giving it to Charles? But it was obviously more than that, or why had Charles thought it necessary to instruct the servants in the way he had, and why was this wretched footman looking so embarrassed? She snatched the letter off the salver. If there was anything going on that concerned Charles she would know about it.

"But, madam," protested the footman.

"Do not be so impertinent," hissed Mrs. Stowe, "and be off about your business, or I shall prevail upon the earl to remove you from your position." Instead of going into the library to join Charles and Sir James she hurried across the hall and opened the door of one of the drawing rooms. It was empty. She closed the door behind her and crossed to a sofa table. There was a candelabrum there, and she could examine the letter more clearly. She frowned. It had been sealed several times. Whoever had written it had taken great care to render it as difficult to open as possible. She held it up to the light. It was useless, she could not make out any of the writing through the thick vellum. Then she paced up and down the room. Her instinct told her something was afoot. Charles had been far from warm towards Georgiana or herself since the night she had sent her daughter into his dressing room. Mrs. Stowe had not been surprised, but she had not let it worry her. The important thing to that title was neither here nor there. In Mrs. Stowe's opinion the end always justified the means. Some people might think her unscrupulous but few would deny she was a devoted mother, with her daughter's best interest close to her heart.

But Charles had been curiously resigned. He had not protested at all. Why not? What if he were planning to wriggle out of the engagement? No, he wouldn't. The heir was a man of honour. He would always do the right thing. But this letter from Ragby. Ragby? She stopped pacing. That day when she and Georgiana had arrived ... "That girl!" she gasped. Charles had not stopped looking at her, and in such a way! Was it possible that the heir was pursuing some sort of *affaire* with the creature, while at the same time preparing to marry her daughter? Surely he would never dare. To dishonour General Stowe's daughter? To prefer the embraces of a common village girl to those of a young lady of quality and breeding? On the other hand, how many members of the aristocracy had she heard of who had indulged perverse appetites. ... If Charles were behaving in an improper manner *before* marriage, how would he behave after? Not that that would be a reason to prevent the marriage. But it would be as well to know, so that her daughter might be prepared. How her fingers itched to open the letter. She was disturbed by a knock on the door, and she put it quickly into her reticule. "Come in," she called. It was the footman.

"Dinner is served," he said bowing.

Mrs. Stowe got the distinct impression that the footman disliked her. It was the first time in her life that she had ever contemplated that a mere servant might have human emotions.

"But of course we must open it," cried Georgiana. "If it is just an innocent letter, no harm will have been done, for it will have been sealed again and Charles will never know." They had eaten, spent a short time in conversation with the gentlemen, and then retired to Mrs. Stowe's sitting room, where she had wasted no time in showing Georgiana the letter and telling her of her suspicions.

"I have to know if what you suspect is true. I don't care what he does after the marriage. He may have as many mistresses as he likes, providing he is discreet. It will signify nothing when we have been married for a reasonable time, for then I may have my own *amours*. But *now*, before we are married, only just betrothed? Perhaps the whole world knows about it except me? For all I know, he may have been visiting Ragby often to satiate himself with the little bitch, and what if the servants are in cahoots? How am I to be mistress here in the future and have any respect if they know that I am being made a laughing stock behind my back even before I am married?"

Mrs. Stowe knew that Georgiana was quite right. She looked down at the letter. Surely it would not be so difficult to open it, read it and then reseal it. She crossed to a bureau, sat down and picked up a small tortoiseshell paper knife.

Most honoured, most exalted Sir. I have spoken to the enchantress and she has poured her honeyed passions forth. How she palpitates to see you. How her heart, her

230

soul, her very life are yours. I know well that the path of
true love never did run smooth, but Venus herself bids me
to render it less stony, and I must obey, and conspire to
bring you together, tomorrow, under cover of darkness. I
shall bring her to the gates of Landsdun. Come at eight
o'clock, and you may sip the sweet ardour that pours forth
like nectar, from her trembling expectant lips. Come and
be requited. Yrs. Cupid.

"So. Cupid lives at Ragby Hall," said Mrs. Stowe coldly.
"How dare he!" cried Georgiana. "How dare he?"

Lord Melton sank into his chair before the fire in his
dressing room with a weary sigh. It was late. He was tired,
but he doubted he would sleep. It was a very long time
since he had passed a restful night, torn as he was by
thoughts of Lucy and his duty to the line. He sighed. He
had watched the dawn break every morning. Every
morning he was tempted to ride to Ragby, find Lucy and
carry her away. He laughed. Mad. He was mad. Mad and
infatuated. Every morning he told himself he was mad,
and talked himself out of it. He marveled that any man
could be so adept at resisting what he wanted to do more
than anything, and he hated himself for not being more
volatile, more spontaneous, less careful of convention.
Many young men in his position would not have hesitated,
but those same young men would not have felt so deeply.
They would have taken Lucy, pleasured themselves with
her and then discarded her, leaving her ruined. She was
too young, too trusting for that. "Pour me a drink, will you,
Culpepper?" he asked as his man entered the room. "A
letter for you, my lord," said Culpepper, closing the door
behind him. Charles looked up at the clock on the mantel.
It was nearly midnight. He took the letter. "When did this
come?" He recognised the writing at once. It was from
Peter Royalston. Culpepper handed him a glass of
Cognac. "I do not know, my lord. Mrs. Stowe's maid
handed it to me, and sent her mistress's apologies. She said
that the lady had forgotten it." Charles put the glass of
Cognac down on a side table. "I thought that I told you

that you were to instruct the footmen that all letters from Ragby were to be handed directly to me?"

"But I did, my lord," said Culpepper.

Charles smashed his fist down upon the side table sending the glass flying. "When I give an order, I expect that order to be obeyed." He shouted, "Good God. It's like talking to that wall."

Culpepper was not used to being shouted at. He had served the heir for many years and they were more like friends than master and servant. "I am sorry, my lord, but I must insist that I did carry your instructions to the footmen," he said calmly, bending to pick up the glass from the floor.

"Well, perhaps they did not understand you," shouted Charles. "Get downstairs and question the footmen. Ask them which of them received this letter, and when it was delivered. Go on. Hurry, forget the glass."

"But you may cut yourself, my lord," said Culpepper.

"Good God. I'm not a child that I cannot be left with a little shattered glass for five minutes," said Charles through clenched teeth. "Go downstairs and find out who disobeyed me."

Culpepper left, very much in a huff, almost slamming the door.

As soon as he was alone Charles undid the fop's letter. *I have spoken to the enchantress.* The fool had spoken to Lucy, and if the fellow was to be believed, she... "She loves me," Charles spoke out loud. Then sat suddenly down in his chair and read the letter again. Yes—that was what the fop was trying to say, *cut through all the flowery exaggerated nonsense, and it says that she loves you.* He closed his eyes. "I could see her tomorrow. Why not? why not?" He felt excited, then he groaned and clenched his fists. "I *long* to see her. No, I *ache* to see her. Oh Lucy, Lucy, Lucy," cried Charles to nobody, or so he thought, for Culpepper was just turning the knob and entering the room, as the last "Lucy" burst from Charles' breast. Behind Culpepper was the unfortunate footman who had started to panic when he heard Charles shout "Lucy" for his name was Lacey and he feared the worst.

"Well, Lacey," said the heir sternly, "it seems that you have disobeyed my orders." He stood up and clasped his hands behind his back. He hated to scold the servants, but really this was too much.

"Oh, no, my lord. I was on my way to give it to you, but Mrs. Stowe, my lord, she..." The footman's voice faltered.

"What about Mrs. Stowe?" snapped Charles.

Poor Lacey started to stutter. "Wwwell my lord."

Culpepper helped him. "Lacey explained your orders to Mrs. Stowe, but she snatched the letter from him, and made off with it into the red drawing room."

"Tttold me I'd be dismissed if—" Lacey went on.

"Snatched it?" shouted Charles.

"Yyes, my lord," said Lacey.

"What time was this?" asked the heir. "Jjust before dd dinner, my lord."

"I see." said Charles. "You may go, Lacey, and I apologise for misjudging you." Lacey bowed and left the room with a sigh of relief. Culpepper followed him and shut the door. When he turned to look at Charles he saw the young man's face had turned as black as the night outside. "Why didn't she simply bring it straight to me, I was in the library with Sir James, or hand it to me during dinner?" Charles said out loud.

"Quite," said Culpepper pouring his master another drink. He suspected that Mrs. Stowe had read the heir's letter. The lady was ruthless in any matter that might concern her daughter. She had, after all, tricked a proposal out of Charles. He handed him the Cognac. Their eyes met.

"Are you thinking what I am thinking?" Charles asked.

Culpepper nodded. "Look at the wax," he said.

Charles turned the letter in his hand. "It has been resealed?"

Culpepper nodded. "Two different coloured waxes." Culpepper was quite right. The fop had used a common red wax to seal the letter. But Mrs. Stowe had melted the wax that was used at Landsdun to reseal it. The difference in colour was so slight not everybody would have noticed

233

it. But at Landsdun only the best quality wax was used, and this was darker, browner in colour.

Charles felt a surge of anger race through him. "I could kill her for this." In a second he was at the door.

Culpepper caught his arm. "No, my lord. Your father—"

Charles stopped, his hand on the door knob. His servant was right. It would do no good, anyway, to drag the lady from her bed and accuse her of opening his letter. She would deny it, and it couldn't be proved, it would cause bad feeling and injure the earl's state of health. But there was no question of meeting Lucy now, not outside Landsdun.

"If there's anything that I can do, my lord?" Culpepper ventured.

For a moment Charles hesitated to confide in him, then he said, "You are a good, loyal fellow. Come, have a drink with me."

Culpepper set out for Ragby early the next morning, the day still chill from the night and the dew. His first call was to be at Ragby Hall. He had a letter for Peter Royalston in the leather pouch that hung from his side. After he had delivered this message, he was to find out where a girl called Lucy Emmett lived, and ask her if she would name a place where Lord Melton could speak with her in private.

By the time he got to Ragby, the village had been about its business for a good three hours, the sun was warming the day, and he found the little community a hive of activity. But when he rode through the rusting gates of Ragby Hall he found a pall of quiet hanging over the dilapidated pile. The curtains were still drawn, there was no smoke from the chimneys, and his horse's hoofs sounded loud on the cobblestones of the yard. After hammering on the front door for ten minutes, he repaired to the door of the kitchen and hammered on that. At last it was opened by a fat slattern of a girl with greasy lank hair, and a frowsty gown, who rubbed her sleepy eyes, informed him that her name was Betsy, that the squire was not back from London and that her mistress was in a decline and not to be disturbed.

"'Tis Peter Royalston I have come to see," said Culpepper. Betsy informed him the fop was in his bed and was not to be woken before midday.

"Tell him to make an exception for once," replied Culpepper, pushing past the slattern, and finding his own route to the sitting room. *Dear Cupid*, the heir had written, *you are a meddling fool. On no account come to Landsdun tonight, and on no account write to me again. You are on your honour to save the girl from marriage, and from any other harm, and to hold your foolish tongue. Neglect to do any of these things at your peril, for I shall come personally to do you a serious and painful mischief. I wish you to inform my man as to where Lucy may be found, and do nothing more. Melton.*

"Oh, Lard," gulped the fop when he had read Charles' terse message. "Serious and painful mischief."

A little while later Culpepper arrived at Ridge Farm, he had been told he must make every effort not to be seen by anyone but Lucy, so he hid behind the high hedge. His master had regaled him with a very comprehensive description of the girl's looks, and he had no difficulty recognising the alluring, dark-haired, blue-eyed creature who appeared presently carrying a pail of seed with which to feed the poultry. And he noticed, as she leaned forward to throw them their food that nature had provided her with two other eminently seductive spheres apart from those glorious blue eyes.

Since her meeting with the fop the previous day Lucy had been dreaming of Charles. That night she was going to meet him again and she thought of nothing else. Would he take her in his arms? Would he kiss her at last? Would he tell her he loved her? Would he be strong, passionate?

"Lucy Emmett?"

Lucy turned as somebody called to her from behind the hedge. She put down her pail, and saw a face peeping out at her. The man put his finger to his lips. *Who could it be?* She turned and looked at Magpie, afraid he would run at the stranger, but he was fast asleep by the door.

"Who are you?" she asked when she had joined the man behind the hedge. He didn't answer at once but took her hand and pulled her into the ditch. Suddenly she was afraid and started to struggle and tried to cry out. She felt a hand cover her mouth, and heard the man whisper.

"Do not be alarmed. I am come from Lord Melton with a message."

Lucy immediately stopped struggling and turned to the man, her face eager. "From him?"

The man nodded. "I am to tell you that there are good reasons why he cannot meet you tonight, and I am to tell you that on no account must you come to Landsdun."

Lucy felt her heart sink and her throat tighten, tears sprang into her eyes. "You mean, he doesn't want to see me after all?" Her voice came in a whisper from between her trembling lips.

Culpepper put his arm around Lucy's shoulders and said, "Don't cry, little wench. Lord Melton fears that if you come to the gates of Landsdun, you will not be left alone with him, and he does want to be alone with you."

Lucy looked up, "He does?"

Culpepper nodded. "So cheer yourself," he said. "And name a place that he might meet you tomorrow morning, a place where you may be alone with him, safe from prying eyes, where he may properly declare his affection."

Lucy was transformed by a wild thrill of excitement. "His affection," she cried throwing her arms around Culpepper's neck. "Oh, there is nothing in the world I hold so dear as his affection."

Culpepper tried to extricate himself. To have Lucy's body so closely pressed against him was delightful, but on the other hand . . . "Say where he shall meet you," said Culpepper hoarsely.

Lucy asked him if he knew the biggest oak in the Charnwood and when he said he did, it was decided that Charles should meet her there at nine o'clock on the following morning.

"Will you give him a message from me?" asked an elated Lucy. Culpepper nodded, and before he could

236

draw breath he felt each of her hands on either side of his head, and her lips against his. So prolonged and full of fervour was that kiss that Culpepper was afraid his breeches would burst.

"Tell him that," said Lucy.

Culpepper nodded, numbly, as he watched Lucy lift her skirts, climb out of the ditch, and skip off out of sight.

The river flowed, wide and slow along the bottom of the big field that sloped up to the Charnwood. The water was deep and clear, and small silver trout shimmered through its rippling frondy weeds, weak sunlight catching at the rainbows in their scales. Lucy stood naked at its edge, her silky, honey-gold skin kissed by the gentle whispering Autumn breeze. She dipped her toe in the water. It was cold, but would be invigourating. She was going to bathe herself, wash the dust of Ridge Farm away before she went to the great oak to meet Charles. "My lover," she whispered. As she waded into the river, an otter's sleek black head broke the surface and then vanished when its brown button eyes saw her. It was colder than she had expected and she submerged quickly, swimming under the water for a while, to emerge seconds later gasping and shivering, her hair glossy and sleek as the otter's had been. She had a small cake of rough soap in her hand, and rubbed it into her hair, lathering it into bubbles and then dipping her head into the water so that her hair fanned out on the surface of the river, washing away the soap until the dark tresses squeaked when she tugged them through her fingers. She soaped her body in the shallower water, and thought of Charles, conjuring up images of him, images of him smiling at her, whispering to her, touching her, loving her, dreaming those dreams common to every young girl who has been kissed, but has never been loved.

"Oh, to be loved," breathed Lucy, running her hands over her rounded breasts and curving hips as she imagined Charles would do, caressing the full contours, stroking her thighs, the hard places, the soft places, the light mounds, the dark warm places, that she knew so well and that he was yet to discover. Then with a sigh and a secret smile, she lay down in the crystal water, turning slowly onto her back, spreading her arms, sailing easily with the current, watching the white feathery clouds scud across the blue sky above her, the birds dance on air, feeling the world turning and her body turning with it, giving herself to the day, and praying that it would make her a woman, and that Charles would be *the* man.

The leaves were falling from the trees in the Charnwood, carpeting the forest with millions of curling fluted shapes from palest yellow to the darkest amber, from copper to bronze and mahogany, so that the floor and canopy that surrounded Charles was a splendour of russet and aureate hues. Jupiter trotted through the deep crispy leaves snorting and tossing his long black mane, sniffing the scented air, arching his neck gracefully, as though he appreciated what a smart sight he made against such a vivid backcloth. And Charles in a coat of cerulean blue, white buckskin breeches and black boots so polished they rivaled Jupiter's glossy flanks, searched for the big oak where Lucy would come to him. He found it at last. It was unmistakable—a fortress of a tree, with vast gnarled branches spreading wide as though to keep all other trees at bay. He felt a sharp stab of anxiety when he saw Lucy had not arrived; but then he was early, having galloped all the way from Landsdun, only slowing to a trot when he had entered the Charnwood.

He dismounted and tied Jupiter's reins to a low branch, letting the horse nuzzle at the thick fallen leaves and nibble at the bits of greenery that could be found there. The sun sent long shafts of light cutting through the vaulted branches to the earth at his feet. It was the most perfect day, but he felt restless, and cursed with a multitude of anxieties, his features set in a frown. What if she didn't come? What if she'd been prevented? Was she really as anxious to see him as he was to see her? Obviously not, or she would have been there. Oh, how he ached for her, and had ached for her through the weeks that had now turned to months since he had first seen her. And still he hardly knew her, had hardly spoken to her, and here he was waiting for a girl who was almost a stranger, and yet in a way so well, so totally known. Now he knew what the poet meant: "I did but see her passing by, and yet I will love her til I die."

How he had scoffed at his friends' tales of agonies suffered when love was unrequited. Now he knew well the misery and torment he would suffer if Lucy... He heard Jupiter whinny nervously. Somebody was approaching through the trees. He turned, feeling his heart start to pound, his temples throb, his legs weaken, his mouth turn dry, and then he saw her, running towards him through the golden forest, her raven hair rising on the breeze, her lips warm, her cheeks flushed, her eyes alight, her body lithe and yet supremely feminine, rounded and yet strong, burgeoning with life—and natural as the day. She was magnificent.

"Lucy," he cried joyfully, and ran towards her catching her in his arms and sweeping her off her feet. "Lucy, Lucy, Lucy," shouting her name loudly, exultantly, feeling her soft arms around his neck, her sweet breath against his cheek, and then her mouth coupling with his, and the whole world slipping away, in the heat, the sublime melting of that most yielding kiss.

"Oh," whispered Lucy when they had drawn apart. "Oh, how I have dreamt of this."

"And so have I," murmured Charles, planting tiny, quick kisses on her nose, her chin, her cheeks, her forehead, her ears. "I have been so impatient, and I am so angry with myself," he groaned. "So angry." He took her hands and drew them to his lips, kissing the palms and then the backs of them, and then the tips of her fingers.

Lucy offered her mouth again, and as his lips closed on hers she felt his arms moving around her waist, pulling her closer, so close she hardly knew where her body ended and his began. His lips left her mouth and moved to her throat, his tongue traced the full curve of it, gently, delicately sending tremors through every nerve in her body.

"Why are you angry?" she whispered.

239

"Because I waited so long to hold you," murmured Charles. "Because I hesitated like a fool, because I should have gathered you up in my arms that night when I first met you on the London Road, and forced you to come to Landsdun with me."

Lucy smiled, trembling as his lips brushed the tips of her breasts. "Ah, but then I was a fool, and would have struggled," she said quietly.

"And now?" asked Charles, lifting her into his arms, and looking down at her radiant face against his shoulder.

"Now, I will not struggle at all," she sighed.

They lay side by side under the harbouring oak, she cradled in his arms, both naked in the leaves, her blue eyes looking deep into his grey eyes, seeing her own image mirrored there. He caressed her as she had imagined he would in her dreams, slowly, intensively, reverently, as though she were some supremely precious being, while she moved her hands along the tautness of his powerfully muscled arms, feeling a proper man close to her, intimate with her for the first time.

"You are lovely," he whispered, pressing his face into the roundness of her stomach.

"And you," whispered Lucy. "You are so fine, and so loving."

As he ran his fingers through the glossy down between her thighs, she groaned and closed her eyes.

"You are a virgin?"

She whispered, "Yes," in reply, glad that she was, but half wishing she were more experienced. Then perhaps she would not tremble so, and perhaps she would not be so overwhelmed. She opened her eyes and he was looking down into her face.

"I will not take that from you," he said gently.

Lucy cried out and pressed his hand to the moist place between her thighs. "Take it," she whispered pleadingly, "oh, take it."

He gave a cry almost of anguish, and buried his face in her hair. He was trembling now, shaking, and when his lips

240

met hers again they were almost brutal, hungry, demanding lips, and Lucy's returned kisses were as fierce as ravenous as his, then he moaned and covered her. Her nails bit into his shoulders, her body rearing, her legs sprawling, widening, beckoning him in. He entered her, and as he did so she cried out, transported to a plane somewhere between joy and sharp terror. He was moving in her, and moving her so deeply that she feared complete obliteration. Tears, bitter and sweet, ran from her fluttering eyes, bitter tears for her lost maidenhood, and sweet tears to welcome her miraculous blossoming. All was lost and found. He poured into her and she into him. One creature lived and breathed on the bed of coppery leaves.

"Oh, my dear lover," cried Lucy as she felt his maleness shudder from him in a hot molten river. "Oh, my darling," she cried again as she reached completeness and looked with rapture at her lover's face, seeing in his answering smile every delight that has ever been dreamt of in the whole history of woman and man. True lovers do not part, or speak, but hold each other, and for a long time Charles and Lucy lay entwined, naked and vulnerable upon the earth, blessed with that profound silence that follows deep completion.

"Do men dream of perfect love?" asked Lucy after a while.

Charles smiled and looked at her face that lay cradled in the crook of his arm. "Yes," he said softly, "men do dream of it, but often are too fearful to admit they do."

"But a man may talk to a woman about his dreams, may he not, and not be scoffed at?"

"Only to the woman of his dreams," whispered Charles, brushing her lips with his. "Any more questions, Miss Emmett?"

"Oh, an eternity of questions. I have always been curious about men," Lucy replied.

"Have you indeed? Well it's to be hoped that your curiosity has now been satiated," said Charles.

"Oh, it has not, for I am a very, very curious person," said Lucy vehemently.

"Then I hope you will confine your questioning to me, for I should not like to think of another man providing you with the answers," said the heir.

Lucy looked up at him and saw he was frowning. She sat up and put her arms around his neck. "Shall I whisper a secret?" she asked.

He nodded.

"You are the only man in the world that I have the slightest bit of curiosity about," she said. Charles laughed and kissed her, for she had slipped her hand between his legs, and was caressing him there, and rubbing her body against him and nuzzling his face with hers. "I'm afraid that I shall have to disappoint you for a while," Charles said. "You see, a gentleman must have time to recover himself."

"What about ladies?" asked Lucy.

"Mm. Well, ladies have a reputation for recovering rather more quickly," replied Charles, watching her lie back against the leaves and spread her legs wide. She sighed and closed her eyes, shielding her face with her arm from the sun. He leant across and placed the palm of his hand upon her rounded belly, feeling a shudder run through her, as he did so.

"Oh, I ache," she whispered, moving sensuously under his touch. "I ache." He felt himself stir with hunger for her. "I want you again," he said, pulling her to him and entering her for a second time. "I want you again, and again, and again. . . ."

Luncheon was served at Landsdun each day at one o'clock sharp. Always had been. "Luncheon is served," said a weary Lacey, entering at the library door.

"Yes. Yes, yes," said Sir James exploding into truculence. "We *know* that it's served, man." He had to be careful not to swear before the ladies. "That's the fourth time you've popped in and said 'luncheon is served' like a cuckoo from a clock." The footman shrugged and popped out again, closing the door. Sir James looked at his heavy gold watch. It was almost thirty minutes past the hour. Where was the heir? He should have returned from his morning ride ages ago.

"You'd think he would have made an effort to get back in time for lunch," said Georgiana.

"Oh no, it is obvious that he is upon some jaunt or other," said Mrs. Stowe.

"Yes, but surely he knew that Papa would be here."

"Lord Melton knew that the general was coming, but he did not know that he was coming today," said Sir James, casting a bleak eye on General Stowe, who stood near the window, stern, straight backed, tight-corseted.

"One must wonder at his rudeness, though, you must admit, and wonder, too, what could have kept him out for such a very long time," said Mrs. Stowe, catching her daughter's eye, and nodding her head.

"Exactly," said Georgiana coldly. She had a feeling that Charles had made a fool of both herself and her mother. He had not left Landsdun on the previous night, as they had thought he would; in fact he had lounged around all through the evening, with a smug smile on his face, reading of all things a book of sonnets. She was sure that he was in Ragby now, with *that* girl.

"Perhaps Jupiter cast a shoe," ventured Sir James.

"Somewhere around Ragby?" asked Mrs. Stowe.

Sir James was beginning to grow a little tired of Mrs. Stowe and her daughter. It was as though they were sharing a secret of some sort—they kept nodding at one another and pursing their lips disapprovingly.

"Oh, I'm sure it would be quite convenient if Jupiter did cast his shoe in Ragby," said Georgiana. Her mother's reply to this was a mirthless laugh. *Ragby?* thought Sir James, and then he flushed. So that was what all this nodding and tightening of lips between the ladies was about—they thought the heir was in Ragby taking his leisure with that pretty bastard chit. But surely the young fellow had sworn off her?

"Ooh," groaned the general.

"What ails you, Bunty?" asked Mrs. Stowe.

"Pip in the gut," snapped the general tersely.

"There," said Mrs. Stowe, "now he has turmoil in his stomach, and it is all the heir's fault."

"Oh!" cried Georgiana, bursting into tears and rushing towards the door.

"Come, to your room and repair," whispered Mrs. Stowe, leading her daughter out of the library.

"Fancy a brandy, Bunty?" asked Sir James when the ladies had gone.

"I wouldn't say no to one, Jamie, old fellow," said a relieved General Stowe.

A light patter of rain had begun to fall. "We had better dress," murmured Charles languidly. "Oh, no," whispered Lucy. "I love it here."

"And so do I," said Charles. "But I love you more, and if you catch a fever what shall I do? So come. On with your clothes." He pulled her to her feet after rising himself, and smiled at her sleepy expression. She was heavy with love, her limbs relaxed, her lips and body bruised. She grumbled but did as she was told and dressed, and then helped Charles to pull on his boots. The sky had grown more overcast by the time they had finished and the rain was much heavier, so Charles carefully wrapped his blue coat around Lucy's shoulders, feeling sad that her dress was so threadbare, that she had not even a chemise under it, that she wore no covering on her feet, and had not a cloak to keep her warm.

"This is all wrong," he muttered.

She looked at him surprised, and caught hold of his hand. "What do you mean? How can it be wrong when it has been so wonderful?"

Charles shook his head and pulled her to him, holding her close in his arms. "I love you, Lucy Emmett," he said gravely.

"And I love you," said Lucy in return.

"And because I love you I must *do* something," shouted Charles angrily, shaking his fists at the sky. Lucy laughed. She had often seen Roger do that, railing at heaven.

"We will do something," said Lucy. "We will be together always, always, just like today."

Charles looked down into her radiant young face. "Lucy, I must tell you something."

She smiled up at him, droplets of rain clinging to her ebony curls and to the thick lashes around the wide blue eyes. With a shock he realised that she was little more than a child, although in many ways she was so much the woman. "I must tell you the truth, because I owe you the truth, and it is my duty, do you understand?"

She nodded and kissed him. "Do not be so serious, we are going to be so happy," she said.

His heart froze, he dreaded hurting her, but she must understand how things were. "Today, I have taken something from you that should properly have belonged to your husband." He felt her recoil. For a moment he thought that she might strike him.

"Belong to whom?" she cried. "That which you took belonged to me; and was mine to give, freely, and I have given it freely. You need not feel guilty, for I do not, nor need you speak to me of duty."

"But I am thinking of you," said Charles. "Do you understand?" He took her by the shoulders and shook her. The rain was pouring down, soaking them, but they were oblivious to it.

"Well, I am obliged to you for thinking of me, but you need not, I have a mind of my own."

"Will you wait and let me finish?" shouted Charles.

"Finish then," said Lucy.

"I am to be married soon."

It was as if he had struck her. She lowered her head. *Of course he could never have married me*, she thought, but still, in her heart she had longed for it. "To the Quality lady?" she asked, almost inaudibly. She knew what his answer would be.

"Yes," said Charles softly. "Her name is Georgiana Stowe."

She raised her eyes and looked into his, with a pang he saw that her expression had clouded; she had lost the childish, trusting look. When she spoke, her voice sounded mature. "You promised that you would tell me the truth, Charles."

He nodded, and taking her hand kissed it. "Always," he said.

"Do you love her?"

His eyes met hers again. "No. I do not love her."

"Then why are you intending to marry her?"

It was some time before he answered. "Because she is *suitable*." He was filled with self-hate.

Lucy nodded. "I see." Then she smiled, and put her hand on his shoulder. "Duty?" she asked.

How quickly she had understood, Charles thought. "But we will be together often," he said, taking her in his arms again, for he could see she was fighting back tears. Her eyes were brimming.

"But you will be married," whispered Lucy.

"Yes, of course, but I will arrange a place where we can meet in comfort. I know what I will do, I shall buy you a fine house—you would like that—and pretty things to wear, and you will have money and jewels, and ride in a carriage."

Lucy remembered the fop, rubbing his thumb and forefinger together.

She turned away and wiped her eyes. "I must go home."

Charles caught her arm. "If you will be patient for a while..."

"What of your wife?" asked Lucy.

"You do not understand, things are different, not so simple, in my circle. There is a code of behaviour, there are certain conventions to be observed, a wife is a wife, and a mistress is a mistress."

"What is a wife in your circle?" asked Lucy.

"Why she is honoured with my name, my position, my children."

"And a mistress?"

His arms closed about her. "A mistress is to love and enjoy."

"Tell me why it would not be possible for a Quality gentleman to have a wife that he loved and enjoyed too?"

"It is possible, and some gentleman are fortunate in that respect, but I am pledged to a marriage of convenience, and I must find love elsewhere," said Charles. His shirt clung to him.

"Because I am not *suitable*?" said Lucy.

Charles had promised to be truthful, and he was. "No, you are not suitable to be my wife; I have a title, and I must have an heir."

"And you would not have an heir from a bastard," said Lucy bitterly. "But you would have a bastard from a bastard."

He tried to touch her, but she shook herself free and handed his coat to him.

"If anything happens, if you quicken, I promise the child will want for nothing," said Charles.

"Except a name," replied Lucy.

"But a name is nothing," said Charles.

"Nothing?" cried Lucy. "Nothing?" She walked away from him and then swung round. "Bastard is a name, and that is nothing?" She was crying again, this time angrily, and Charles felt that her anger covered a well of hurt and misery that had been hidden from him until this moment. "Take my coat, and I will carry you home," he said.

She shook her head. "No."

"But you cannot walk through this rain with no cover?"

The sky was black, there was a roll of thunder from over the ridge. A storm was brewing. Lucy drew herself up and lifted her chin. "I will go home alone," she said, and then she ran to him, and kissed his cheek.

"Why?" asked Charles.

She smiled, and shrugged. "Pride," she said, and then she ran away from him through the trees.

The sky over Landsdun House was rent with lightning, bright forks of it threatening the high chimneys and the parkland trees, traveling over the ridge towards the oaks, blackening their gnarled topmost branches, striking at their ancient trunks. But the oaks of Charnwood had

247

withstood many a lightning storm, and would send sap into the wounds, and would bear leaves again in the following spring.

Charles did not go down to dinner that night. He stayed in his dressing room. The day had been a revelation to him. He had traveled out that morning to meet a girl—a simple, sweet, spirited young creature—to find himself confronted by a person of great depth, of many facets and complexites. When their time together had drawn to an end, in a day, Lucy had grown up, shaped herself before his eyes. She was formidable. He smiled, remembering her curiosity, she was fascinating, and he would not let her go, not now that he had really found her.

Lucy had been questioned by Roger and Elizabeth when she got back to Ridge Farm, and she told them that she'd been walking in the Charnwood, felt tired and fallen asleep. She was not believed, but neither Roger nor her step-mother persisted because Lucy seemed changed. She did not fly into her usual tantrum. She answered them quietly, civilly, almost solemnly, and then sat in the inglenook letting the heat from the logs dry her clothes and hair. Roger sat close to her and lit his pipe, and when Elizabeth had gone to bed, and Toby and John had braved the foul night, for a visit to the Hare and Hounds, it was just like the old days, when she was a child, and was content to be just that.

"Tell me about my mother," she said, after a while.

Roger looked down at her, and stroked her hair. *Why had she to grow up, and why had his Margaret to die?* He had needed her to guide his hasty ways, her cool head to quench his hot stubborn temper. "What can I tell you about your mother, wench? I loved her, as well you know, and since she went, everything has gone wrong for me."

"Not my Margaret mother," said Lucy. "The mother who bore me."

Esmeralda Lee, thought Roger, and a tear trickled down his weatherbeaten cheek. *Sweet gypsy Esmeralda, walking across the whole country to bring my child to me.*

He wiped the tear away. "You heard everything that was to be said about her when you were a little thing, from Margaret."

"But I do not even know her name," sighed Lucy. "I only know that she was beautiful, and that she died giving me my life. I used to pray that her ghost would visit me in my dreams, and whisper to me who I really am."

She turned and looked up at Roger. "I am not going to marry the blacksmith ever," she said defiantly. He smiled. "As God is my witness, Lucy Emmett, you are grown into the very devil of a woman," he said.

She laughed, and jumped up, spat on her hand and extended it to Roger. "Is it a bargain then?" she asked.

"It's a bargain," he replied, spitting on his own hand, and shaking hers. "Have you given any thought as to what you'll do with yourself in your life, if you're not to marry the smith?" asked Roger.

"I have," replied Lucy. "I intend to better myself."

"You'll have to marry for that," said Roger.

Lucy shook her head. "Now that I am a good deal wiser than I was, I see that nothing is so simple as I thought it, nor yet so difficult. There are ways, and there are means, and I intend to find out what they are."

Roger stood up. "Well, you are a good deal wiser than I. For I've lived many years, and as God is my witness I'm about as wise today as I was when they cut my cord, and I'm not abashed to say it." He had crossed to Margaret's linen chest, and opened the lid, put in his hand, took out a leather pouch, opened it, dropped the pouch back into the chest, and closed the lid. "But there's one thing that even a fool such as me can see. You are grown to a proper woman, Lucy Emmett, and you must have what is yours." He opened his hand, and Lucy saw something gleaming in his rough palm. She ran to him, and looked. Two golden earrings lay there.

"Mine?" she gasped. "For me?"

He nodded. "They belonged to the mother that brought you to the world, and they have been kept for you, until this day."

Lucy took the earrings and closed her hands around them. "So I have something of her, after all," she whispered. "But you should have sold them, there have been so many times when the money would have been so useful." She watched him draw himself up, and saw the pride shining from his eyes. "They were not mine to sell," said Roger Emmett. "I would die before I took something that was not mine." Lucy lowered her eyes, remembering Margaret's death—the earrings might have saved her. "But you may sell them if you wish," said Roger.

"Never," said Lucy. "Never."

Squire Billy had received the note from his nephew several days previously. It had been a garbled account of the events at the parsonage and had said that he must repair to Ragby to hold an Assize Court. Then as a postscript Peter Royalston had added, "Hurry back. My life in your hands, my murder, most imminent." If there was any message less likely to call the squire posthaste back from London, it was that. The thought that his nephew might be murdered if he delayed his return was too, too tantalizing. So he stayed in the metropolis while his money lasted, played the tables, and partook of all the entertainment that city could offer gentry on the loose.

What finally brought him back to Ragby was a suspicion that his gout would soon attack him as a penance for his hard drinking, and what was worse, he received a visit from "Signor Gonorrhoea," a singularly unpleasant Italian fellow who did dastardly things to a gentleman's private parts. This condition he had got from a six-penny whore, in St. James's park. As soon as the visitor had made himself known, the squire had quickly dosed himself with "Keyser's pills" brought from an apothecary in Orange Street, and when these had wrought no improvement, he had taken a seat on the next stage to Leicestershire, observing as the coach started on its bumpy way that the popular advertisement was so true.

"Happy is the man who in his pocket keeps whether

with green or scarlet ribbon bound A well made C."

The squire would make sure that he was well protected by such a condom before he searched out another "Midnight Moll." "Or before entering a Chop House, by all that's holy," he told the poor passengers whose fate it was to be travelling in the same direction at the same time. "Yer cannot be too careful," said the squire sagely, after regaling all those unfortunate occupants with the gory details of his malady. "For a whore will always give it to yer, whether it cost yer six pence or half a guinea." The squire was a gentleman midway between fifty and sixty, round as a rum tub, with a florid, heavy-jowled face. Under his wig, he had no hair, and he wore a "Ravenhuller hat." His coat was blue, his buttons brass, his breeches brown. "Goin' to be a pig of a journey," said squire Royalston, looking out of the window; and it was. The rain fell, the wind roared, thunder beat the air like a gong. Trees were felled by lightning along all the mud-engulfed roads, and it took a very long time—two days and two nights, and another day beside—before the squire achieved his own territory, and by the time he walked through the door of Ragby Hall there was quite a small lake contained in the rim of his hat. It was after midnight, his temper was bad, Signor Gonorrhoea was playing silly devils in his breeches, and the largest toe on his left foot was throbbing so hot it was a miracle it had not burnt a hole through his boot.

"Hell and damnation! I am in purgatory," he screamed, stubbing the offending toe against the front doorstep. As usual he hit out with his stick at his servant Wilchup, yelling that he was to call the quack Fitzmaurice to come and bleed him. When Wilchup replied that the quack could not be found so late, he received another blow from his master's stick, and was told he was discharged, and was to pack his bundle and leave at once. Wilchup ignored this, for he could rely on nothing at Ragby Hall except being sacked on a regular basis.

"Well, rouse Betsy, and tell the foul baggage to bring me a bowl of hot water, for me toe. 'Tis an infernal scourge, I say," shouted Billy, limping into his sitting room, where, to add to his torments, he found the fop still alive, with his nose pushed into a novelette.

"I thought yer'd be murdered," he growled disappointedly, easing himself into a chair.

"Lard, no," piped the fop from his reclining position upon the couch. "Nearly was though, 'pon my life."

"Pity," grumbled Billy. "Where's me wife?"

"In a decline," said Peter.

"Pernickity old bitch," said the squire. "What's that?" His rheumy old eyes had settled on a letter propped on the mantelpiece.

Peter's face fell. He had meant to hide the letter. It was from Miss Parson Brown, and he suspected it had something to do with the damage to the parsonage. He suspected, too, that she required the squire to have it repaired. Money would be mentioned, and any mention of money to be spent on repairs to his property always sent the squire on the rampage.

The fop gulped. "Lard, I do not know," he said weakly.

"Fetch it to me," said Squire Billy darkly.

Peter handed him the letter and then said quickly, "Bed I think." He yawned several times to convey to his uncle that he was off to it, but Billy said, "Sit down," in a voice that contained such a degree of threat Peter thought that he better do as he was told. *Dear Squire, In your absence there has been the most violent and dire deed perpetrated against your property, and against the Parson my dear brother,* wrote Miss Parson Brown. *The Parsonage has been torn asunder, floors gape, doors hang off hinges, and my brother has been sent out of his senses. He walks like a man in a mystery, not knowing who he is or where he is. Boost the blacksmith did the heinous deed, but Lucy Emmett the bastard of Ridge Farm is behind it. She tempted my brother, Sir, to do the Devil's business with her, and drove the blacksmith mad with lust for blood. The damage to the Parsonage will cost twenty-five whole guineas to repair, but my brother cannot be repaired, and I therefore beg you to deport the Emmett girl and the maddened smith, from out this country, lest more misery and perturbation be caused by them. Yrs etc.*

"Hell and damnation," roared the squire. "Twenty-five guineas, twenty-five guineas? By all that's holy I'll call an Assize for the morning and deport the culprits."

"Lard. Don't you mean culprit?" said Peter. "'Twas the smith that did the damage. 'Tis he who is a danger to life and limb, don't y'know."

"Driven to it, by the Emmett gel," shouted the squire. "There's never a skirmish without there's a female somewhere at the bottom of it. She has cost me twenty-five whole guineas, and for that I shall deport her to the Antipodes."

Peter Royalston suddenly saw his whole future disappear—all his hopes fly out of the window—if Lucy were sent from the country. Charles would do Peter a serious and grave mischief; worse, he would never mingle with the nobility, never be a fashion plate in London, never hob nob with the king. He jumped to his feet. "But you can't," he shrieked.

"Oh, can't I then," said Squire Billy. "You wait, you will see what I can do."

"Lard, no, you will *not* send Lucy Emmett away," shouted Peter, throwing his novelette at the squire's head and scoring a direct hit.

"What?" gasped the squire. He had never seen the fop so taken before.

"I shall not allow you to spifflicate my hopes in this manner, I shall not allow you to deport the hoyden."

The squire's mouth hung agape. "Oh, yer won't, won't yer? Well why not, pray?"

The fop stamped his foot. "Because," he cried hysterically. "Because, because, because..."

"Because what?" asked the squire.

"Because," said the fop weakly, "Because I *love* her."

"*You! You* love her?" roared the squire.

"To distraction," whimpered Peter, and collapsed in a faint upon the floor.

CHAPTER VIII

That Girl

*In which Lucy is taken under Cupid's wing and emerges
a swan.*

Wilchup was summoned to bring a pail of water and
toss it over Peter Royalston; then he hauled the bedraggled
creature to his feet and propped him up in a chair, where
he sat, looking for all the world as though he had been
marched over by an entire battalion of The King's
Dragoons and then dropped in a river. Wilchup's method
of revival had been quite unnecessary, for Peter had not
fainted at all, but had merely feigned to faint, in order to
escape further questioning from his uncle. It was a ruse he
had used to his advantage since childhood. But on this
occasion it failed to save him.

"Alright," said the squire. "What's all this balderdash
about love, and distraction, about spifflication of hopes,
and what I can or cannot do?"

"May health is not good," wheedled Peter. "Aye am
frail, and have evah been so."

"When yer were born," said the squire sternly, "yer
father, God rest his soul, was so beside himself with
exaltation when told he had a son, that he had to be

restrained from vaulting over the moon. But when you were brought to him, and he saw what he had been sent, then he had to be restrained from shooting yer. It is my opinion that those who restrained him did the world a great disservice. Now speak, or I shall settle the world's score and shoot yer meself."

Peter had no option but to continue with his bluff. He told his uncle he had been captivated by the charms of Lucy Emmett, and that if his uncle sent her from the country it was certain he would languish, perhaps die. The squire might have ignored his nephew's protestations of passion, except that Mrs. Jemima Royalston, a person more sympathetic to Peter's fantastical notions than her husband, was roused from her sleep and entered the room at that moment to enquire what kept her husband and her nephew conversing so late. When the squire told her of their nephew's extraordinary declaration, Mrs. Royalston threw up her hands with delight, rushed to Peter, hugged him to her bosom, and cried "Oh, you treasure, does this mean that I am to have a daughter at last?"

"Daughter be damned," shouted the squire. "He don't mean to marry. Imagine how rum a touch it is, that that apology for a man should manage to cover anything more than a well stuffed couch?"

"We are talking of love here, Mr. Rude, not of copulation," snapped Mrs. Royalston.

"Love without copulation?" roared the squire. "Why, that is like saying the girl if she be starving should be satisfied with a sniff at her supper."

"Take no heed of him," said the roly-poly Mrs. Royalston to her nephew. "He knows nothing of the finer things. When are we to meet this sweet sunbeam?" Mrs. Jemima Royalston, though barren, was a lady of stupendous maternal feeling, and all her solicitous love had been showered upon Peter. She it had been who had fostered his love for romantic literature, for frills and furbelows, for crimping and capering. Her chief desire had been for a daughter of her own, and having none, she had used Peter as surrogate.

When Lucy Emmett arrived at Ragby Hall on the next

morning after being summoned by the squire and his wife, the lady was quite thrilled by the picture presented. "Oh. What a pretty creature," she cried, throwing her arms around Lucy, who was still ignorant as to why she had been sent for. "Why, she is perfection itself, is she not, husband?"

The squire, who had been bled that morning and was feeling weak, had to agree. He had been going to scold the girl for her part in the damage to the Parsonage, but he had not been expecting a creature so comely. He felt new blood being made where old blood had been removed. His gout and venereal embarrassments seemed mere trifles, he rallied and his temper improved. "She's no beanpole," grunted the squire, not wanting to appear too enthusiastic. "But she has cost me twenty-five guineas, remember."

"Oh. You shan't deport me, shall you, sir?" gasped Lucy, remembering Miss Parson Brown's warning.

"Poo. Of course he shan't," said Mrs. Royalston. "What is twenty-five guineas?"

"Twenty-five guineas is twenty-five guineas," said the squire grimly, "and if I told yer the trouble I had got for six pence, yer would fully comprehend why I am suspicious of all females."

"Now come and tell me all about yourself, chick," said Mrs. Royalston.

Lucy gave her as comprehensive an account of her life as she could, and Mrs. Royalston listened intently, rolling her eyes, throwing up her hands, weeping when she heard of Lucy's birth and motherless state. All this confirmed Mrs. Royalston in what she had first suspected: the "sunbeam" needed caring for, and she, Jemima Royalston, was the lady to do it. It was only after Lucy had been subjected to a huge amount of cuddling and kissing from Mrs. Royalston, that she at last was told the reason why she had been called to Ragby Hall.

"Loves me?" she laughed with disbelief.

"There yer are," said the squire. "She don't believe it either."

"Oh, hush, Billy," said Mrs. Royalston, then she turned

257

again to Lucy. "My nephew is a tender creature..."

"Girlish," cried the squire.

Mrs. Royalston glared at him. "Sensitive, and reared to be gentle, but he loves you indubitably, and I shall say this here and now before my husband. I shall not let a paltry twenty-five guineas, nor the unfortunate circumstances of your birth nor a bully's bellowing come between my nephew and the creature he adores."

"Balderdash," cried the squire. "The fellow's a pansy."

"Hold your tongue," said Mrs. Royalston.

"Fool," said the squire.

"Tyrant," said Mrs. Royalston.

"If he adores her so much, where *is* he then?" asked the squire.

"In his bed, where you have put him with a fever from a pail of water," replied Mrs. Royalston.

The fop was sitting up in bed with his hair in curl papers when Mrs. Royalston ushered Lucy into his chamber. The room stank of camphor and cloves. He was wrapped in a shirt made of a large amount of red flannel, and he coughed continuously.

"Here is sunbeam come to see you, Treasure," cooed Mrs. Royalston. "I shall leave you both alone, but just for the space of a wink. We should not want passion to overcome propriety, should we?" She sent a rapturous smile in Lucy's direction, and then left the room.

"Whatever possessed you to say that you loved me?" asked Lucy, as soon as the lady had departed.

Peter ceased coughing at once, and patted the bed beside him.

Lucy sat down.

"Oh, Lard," he said, "I was quate beside myself with panic. My uncle had threatened to send you to the Antipodes and I blurted out the first thing I could think of to prevent it. I didn't dare tell him of my promise to the heir. But nevah in may life have I regretted anything so megriminously, Aye do assure you, for now that I have

258

said that I love you, Aye fear that I may be constrained to act upon it."

For a while they both looked bleakly at one another. Lucy certainly did not want to be sent to the Antipodes, wherever that place was, nor was she keen to enter into this fiasco with Peter. Then there was Charles. She was beginning to regret her hasty refusal of his offer to make her his mistress. Much as she hated the idea of sharing him with Georgiana Stowe, much as she balked at the knowledge she could never bear him legitimate children, the thought that she might have driven him away, and might never see him again, nearly broke her heart.

She confided her fears to Peter, who was delighted to hear that the heir and Lucy had come together, and that he had made her such a splendid offer. But he could hardly believe his ears when she told him she had refused. He wondered where the chit got "the sauce" from, a low bred bastard, "cocking a snook" at the heir of Landsdun, what next? Had the hoyden no conception of the machinations of society? Though the more he considered the present circumstances the more he came to realise they might be used to his advantage if only Lucy would cooperate.

"You say that you have begun to regret refusing the heir?" asked Peter.

Lucy nodded. "I feel that perhaps I was hasty. Oh! I don't know, I suppose I just want him all to myself, and..."

"No," said Peter imperiously, holding up his hand. "Pray silence, Aye am thinking." So Lucy waited meekly.

Yes, thought Peter, *the heir might actually prefer to have a mistress who was legitmately married. The nobility often did, and their wives certainly did; it was a secure and discreet arrangement that was quite in keeping with "the mode." In fact Peter would have enormous power as Lucy's husband if he complied with the heir's desires, and he would share in all her good fortune. He could see himself well set up in a fine London house, with a yearly stipend at his disposal. Of course the marriage with Lucy would be in name only, and that would certainly comfort*

259

*the heir. But would the girl agree? No matter—that was
something that he and Melton could discuss together. But
what if the heir had lost interest. Perhaps after the
"peccadillo" in the forest, his appetite had decreased, and
all was lost. There was only one way to know, he must
bring Lucy and the heir together again, dangle her charms
before his eyes, and then...*

Lucy was bursting to speak. "You see I love him so, that
when he told me that he loved me too but had to marry
Georgiana Stowe out of duty, I felt so hurt, so mortified,
that I quite lost my head."

*Oh, if the heir had declared his love, all was certainly
not lost.* "Ah, but don't you see?" said Peter. "The nobility
is evah concerned with duty. But once duty is cared for,
then they are concerned with enjoyment. Duty must
always be *seen* to be done, but enjoyment, nevah. In
society," continued Peter, now well into his pompous
stride, "appearance is all, Aye do assure you. Society
requires only that one *appear* to behave in a manner
complicit with its accepted mode of conduct."

"You mean," asked Lucy, "that one must be a
hypocrite?"

Peter winced. The girl really must be cured of this plain
speaking. "The word," said Peter, "is discreet."

"Well, I should not do well in this so-called discreet
society," said Lucy. "If I am not suitable to be the heir's
wife, I am damned if I see how I should be suitable to be
his mistress."

"There is a vast difference between the two states," said
Peter. He was getting quite irritated; he had never in his
life known a person so given to questioning.

"Whatever the difference," Lucy went on, "I have not
the manners, and I am so lowly born."

"Oh piffle," said Peter. "I repeat, appearance is all. One
might be a toad, but if one appeared in society attired as a
swan, a swan one should be. But with one proviso..."
Here Peter leapt out of his bed. "One should *swim*—and
not hop. *Compris*?" he asked.

"You mean that I could be a swan if I were taught?" she

asked eagerly. "Oh, emphatically," replied Peter. "Like Georgiana Stowe?" asked Lucy.

"Oh, Georgiana Stowe," said Peter dismissively. "She is very fine, I suppose, and quality without doubt, but even Georgiana Stowe might be improved, and she has nevah, after all, had the advantage of may tuition in the finer points of *bienseance*. I am in the vogue, don't y'know? Aye am the most punctilious punonder of propriety and decorum. Oh, two days with me, is warth a yeah with another master. I promise you."

It occurred to Lucy that if she allowed herself to be guided by Peter Royalston and digested the finer points of etiquette, she might at last be considered "suitable" by the heir. Peter told her they should continue with his bluff for the present, so that he might take her under his wing. She agreed, for by following her own instincts she had done nothing to improve her condition.

When Mrs. Royalston entered the room a second later, she fully expected to find the young couple locked in an embrace, but no such thing. Lucy Emmett was standing in the centre of the room, and her nephew was sitting on his bed, poking at her with his long cane, calling, "Deportment, deportment. Lift the shoulders, straighten the back, raise the head. Oh *mon Dieu*. Eyes front. Now, move. No, do not swing the arms, curve the arms forward. Oh, Lard, stupid, stop and start again." The tuition had begun.

Peter prevailed upon his aunt to allow Lucy to move into Ragby Hall. The lady was delighted to agree, and so was the squire, for as he said he "liked the cut of the filly," and he had solved the problem of the twenty-five guineas by fining the blacksmith that amount at the Assize Court.

Lucy was both sad and sorry to leave Ridge Farm. Sad to leave Roger, Toby, and John, but glad to leave Elizabeth, and to feel herself at last on her way into the wider world. Magpie, of course, accompanied her to Ragby Hall, and the appearance of the dog there sent the squire into a fret. But Lucy and Mrs. Royalston between them managed to calm him down, and soon the squire became quite attached to the animal who took to following the old man around. "He is devoted to you," said Lucy, "and that hound is a very choosy mutt, I can tell you. It doesn't keep company with rogues or scoundrels."

The squire was much flattered, and soon Magpie did not have to walk anywhere, for the squire carried him and fed him better than he had ever been fed before.

Part of Peter Royalston's plan for his own advancement was that Lucy should accompany him to the Landsdun Ball, and he prevailed upon his aunt to write to the earl and ask if he might bring a young companion with him. The reply came from Landsdun written in the earl's own hand that of course Peter Royalston might bring a young companion to the ball, and at once the entire company at Ragby Hall was thrown into a flurry of preparation. The ladies and Peter were anxious to plan what they should wear, and the squire in a panic about how much he would have to spend.

One day a Madame Millicent arrived at the hall with her assistant, a colourless girl who looked all the time as though she were on the point of tears. Madame, a woman with a formidable chin and chest, was a dressmaker, and her assistant was weighed down by a huge mound of material samples, all of which looked to Squire Billy to be far too expensive.

The Madame and her girl were followed by two gentlemen, if one could describe them as such. The first, known as Monsieur, looked more like an Italian than a Frenchman to the squire, who distrusted all foreigners deeply, but Italians most of all. "That fellah's an Italian," he said to his wife.

"Nonsense," said Mrs. Royalston. "How could he be an Italian?"

"Well, he looks like an Italian," replied the squire darkly, "and only an Italian would have the nerve to look like an Italian." This Monsieur, it seemed, was an "artistic advisor" to the other gentleman, also known as Monsieur, who was a tailor. They also carried a vast amount of silks, brocades, velvets and taffetas between them. Mrs. Royalston and Lucy went to ground with Madame and her assistant, and Betsy the slattern was kept busy running errands for pins, needles, chalks, and tapes. Peter was tended to by the Monsieurs in his chamber, from which room there came shrill sounds of hysteria and cries of "Aye have nevah worn purple in may life and shall die first," and "But eet eez *the* colour, sir. Eet eze *the* Mode."

Squire Billy removed himself to his sitting room with Magpie and locked the door. But to his horror he discovered there was a plot to transform him, and at last, having been bullied mercilessly by his wife and cajoled through the keyhole by Lucy, he submitted and found himself being pinned up in brown paper, with the two foreigners flying about him with tape measures, making derogatory remarks about his figure.

"What's wrong with me figure, damn yer?" asked the squire, studying his portly reflection in a long glass.

"But eet eez so fet," said Monsieur one.

"End zo theek," said Monsieur two.

"This figure," said the squire, determined to fly the Union Jack, "is an Englishman's figure, and it is not to be cast aspersions at. It comes from eating good beef from infancy. Good grub? Understanday Vous? Good liquor. Comprehend what I am do you? *Le gentilhomme Angleterre Manifique?* Not *Le froggie fragile*, nor no *Italian swathey. Non. Je suis a Primo English Gentleman. Primo. Comprehendo?*" shouted the squire.

Both foreigners looked at one another and shook their heads.

"You must vere a corset."

"Never," said the squire emphatically.

"Billy. You must wear a corset," said Mrs. Royalston. "Mustn't he, Lucy?"

"Oh, you must," said Lucy sitting on the squire's knee and kissing his cheek.

"Must I?" asked the squire.

"Yes, you must, you naughty thing, don't you want to look the smartest man at Landsdun?"

Mrs. Royalston watched this picture with some pleasure. Her husband had become a good deal less crusty since Lucy had arrived at the Hall.

"Yes, but I don't much want to be tortured," said the squire.

"You shan't be," said Lucy, "for I shall see to the stays

myself, and if those Monsieurs lace you too tight, well, I shall box their ears."

"Oh, alright," grinned the squire, and he got a kiss on the nose from her for being so accommodating.

"I just wish to make one thing clear," said the squire. "If I die when I am shown the bill for all this nonsense, do not bury me in the corsets, or I shall return to haunt the lot of yer."

While the inhabitants of Ragby Hall were preparing themselves for the ball, Landsdun House was filling with guests. Grand carriages full of quality ladies and gentlemen swept through the countryside, and further carriages full of manservants and maidservants, and wig boxes and hat boxes, and trunks of gowns, and trunks of finery followed after them. An orchestra from London arrived in three coaches and their instruments followed in three more. Another coach arrived with six men in it, experts to look over the ballroom floor, which had not been used for some years, and another arrived with a gentleman to chalk out the steps of the latest fashionable dances on that floor once it had been properly prepared.

Georgiana Stowe's brother, Dolph, arrived with his wife, Emma, and their four children. His manservant came, her maidservant came, so did two nursery maids, a governess, a tutor, and a children's cook, and a wet nurse for the baby. "Oh Dolphi," cried Georgiana, clapping her hands. "Oh, Melton. See—here come Dolphi and Emma and the children."

"Yes," said Charles dryly, "so they do." He had joined the general, Mrs. Stowe, Georgiana, Sir James, and several guests in the great hall to welcome Adolphus Stowe and his family.

"How de do, Melton. You look sprite," said Dolph; then he pumped Charles' arm up and down as though he wished to remove it from his shoulder.

"Hello there, Dolph," said Charles.

"How de do, Ma," said Dolph.

"Oh, Dolph dearest," said Mrs. Stowe, kissing her ebullient son.

"How de do, Pa," and so he went on.

"How de do, Melton?" simpered Emma his wife.

"Oh hello there, Emma," said Charles. The children were still to come.

Charles shuddered when he saw the "Dolphi Baby" at the end of the line in the arms of its wet nurse, its Stowe face surrounded by lacy bonnet, its chubby Stowe hand clutching a silver rattle, and its pouty Stowe lips drooling a trail of regurgitated milk.

Charles hoped he would not be expected to do more than smile at the baby. The child looked as though it were quite capable of doing a man an injury with its rattle. It was an obvious candidate for its grandfather's Cavalry Regiment.

Charles was beginning to envy the earl his ill health. All this greeting of people was too tedious, that and the prospect of the ball in two days' time had his temper sorely tried. None of his own circle of younger friends had yet arrived, wisely waiting until the very last moment so that they might escape most of the more boring formalities. Still it was his duty to bear it all with a fixed smile. But as soon as it was all over he was determined to see Lucy again. When the ball was over, Georgiana planned to return home to prepare for the wedding, and Charles would be free to go to London. He was going to try and persuade Lucy to go with him, in secret of course, and he had high hopes she would agree to become his mistress once she fully comprehended the glorious bounty that would be hers if she did.

"Kiss the baby," said Georgiana.

Mrs. Jemima Royalston's ball gown was of bright yellow satin, and when it was off her it looked very fine. But when it was on her it looked disastrous. It was the sort of gown that did very well on its own own without a body in it, but when a body was in it, it started to droop off the shoulders, and hitch up its hem and generally misbehave. "What do you think, Puss?" asked Mrs. Royalston, parading before Lucy in her huge unruly yellow gown.

"Oh, my. Very becoming," lied Lucy. Mrs. Royalston

looked like a large mobile egg custard, but Lucy was too fond of the lady to dash her happiness. "This with a pink lace fichu, don't you think, Puss, and my garnets and my pearls?"

"Oh my," said Lucy. "I should say so."

"And imagine my hair, dressed high, and powdered with the ship upon the top?"

Madame had made an ornament for Mrs. Royalston to wear on top of her head. It represented a ship, of black velvet with yellow sails. Peter was to wear purple, after much pressure from the Messieurs, and when he saw himself in his suit he could scarcely bear to remove it. He kept saying, "'Tis the colour worn by the ancient emperors, don't y'know, and 'tis the king's colour, too."

Lucy knew the tailors had bought too much purple cloth from a merchant and were anxious to be rid of it, but she was too fond of Peter Royalston to tell him so. Lucy and Peter did very well together for the most part. True, he was silly, opinionated, and effeminate, but he had spent so much time and effort in teaching her deportment and how to conduct herself in polite company that she would be forever in his debt.

The squire, well, the squire looked very well. Lucy had advised him on the choice of cloth for his suit: cinnamon coloured velvet which he would wear with a green brocade, embroidered waistcoat. With his corset under this finery he cut a robust figure, and was most proud of himself.

"*Voilà!*" shouted the tailors.

"Mercy!" said the squire. "Hell and damnation!" he howled when he saw their bill. But he was soon calmed down.

Lucy had been worried about her gown, for Madame and Mrs. Royalston had tried to press vivid colours on her, and so had the fop, anxious that his protégée should catch as many eyes as possible. But the squire had said, "The hussy may please herself," and she had. Lucy's gown was of pure white satin, with a white brocade Polonaise over it, a white lace fichu, and no other trim. She had chosen well, for the white of her gown offset her dramatic colouring to perfection, and when she donned it complete for the first time, the squire had been very complimentary.

"First class," he said, "deuced pretty. I'm damned if I shan't dance yer off yer feet meself, if me gout holds off."

"But you cannot wear those earrings," said Mrs. Royalston, pointing to Lucy's gold rings.

"Why not?" asked Lucy.

"Why not!" said the fop. "We are invited to a quality melee, don't y'know. Not to a village dance."

On the afternoon of the day prior to the ball, Georgiana Stowe rushed into the red drawing room crying, "Oh, this is too bad, *too* bad! Mother, why did you not think of it? It's too bad, too bad." Then she threw herself on a chair and sobbed.

"Too bad?" asked Mrs. Stowe, looking up from her needlework.

"My gown," sobbed Georgiana. "It's too bad. It really is."

"What's too bad about it?" asked Charles wearily.

"It won't go with the ring. My engagement ring. Emerald."

Mrs. Stowe's hand shot to her mouth, and Emma Stowe's hand shot to her mouth. Both women leapt to their feet and rushed towards Georgiana.

"What are we to do?" cried Mrs. Stowe.

"I don't know," cried Emma. "I shall just have to have another gown made, that is all," said Georgiana. "By tomorrow night? Impossible," said Mrs. Stowe. "What's wrong with the dress?" asked Charles. "Perhaps if we all sit calmly and ..."

"Oh, my heavens. The most important night of my life is ruined. How can I wear a hyacinth silk and amethyst, with an emerald ring?"

"Well, of course you can," said Charles.

"Don't you understand?" sobbed Georgiana. "It's not just the colours, it's the pattern. It's wrong, wrong, all wrong."

"What colour is hyacinth, anyway?" asked Dolph.

"Er-a, hyacinth is, I believe, a flower, a very small flower," said the general solemnly, "which varies in colour, between a—"

There was a knock on the door.

"I have told you," wailed Georgiana, "that it's not just a question of colour!"

"Come in," called Charles. It was Lacey, the footman.

"Mr. Fred Plunkett. Mr. Bob Pinkerton. The honourable Giles Wentworth and—"

"Willie Caruthers," shouted Charles, jumping to his feet.

"The same, my lord," said Lacey smiling, and when he stood aside, four smart young bucks marched in.

"Thank God," breathed Charles, and meant it. At last here were kindred spirits. His "circle" had arrived.

"You have no idea," said Charles later to the four young men, now safely lodged in his dressing room with a game of cards going and a couple of flasks of Cognac at their sides, "how very relieved I am to see you."

"Been grim, eh?" asked Willie.

"Beyond description," said Charles. This statement brought murmurs of sympathy from his friends. "It's women's business, is it not?" said Giles Wentworth who was the handsomest and most rakish of the bloods. "When me sister was to be married, all us men flew the house for three months prior to the event, lived at the club, damned comfortable too. Let the ladies get on with it. Know what I mean? That way missed all the flaps, the panics and the pets. No wonder your nerve is shot."

"Poor old Melton," said Willie.

The night of the ball arrived, and suddenly Lucy was cold with trepidation. She had been so excited by the prospect before her, so involved in learning to deport herself correctly, to handle her fan with ease, to dance, to answer in a ladylike manner when asked a question. "Might I get you a cup of cordial, Miss Emmett?"

"Oh, why, thank you, sir" (shake out the fan, raise it slowly to your face, peep over the rim of the fan, flutter the lashes) "how very kind" (then lower the fan and snap it shut).

"Are you engaged for the Polonaise, Miss Emmett?"

"Oh, dear, there was the dance programme. What did one do with the fan, if one had a dance programme and a cup of cordial? Poor Lucy had been so concerned with being proper in all things, that she had quite forgotten her worry about Lord Melton's reaction when he saw her at the ball. Surely it would be a shock to him. Pleasant or unpleasant? What if he was outraged? She could hear his voice, cold, commanding, "Remove that ill-bred girl from this house immediately."

"Let me see you," cried Mrs. Royalston. Lucy turned from the long mirror where she had been examining herself for the million flaws she just knew she had. "A vision," cooed Mrs. Royalston, the ship bobbing on top of a veritable ocean of white hair. "A vision. Oh, Puss, you are a delight."

Soon all the Royalston party were in their carriage bumping along the country lanes on their way to Landsdun House. Lucy was getting more panic-stricken by the minute. "Oh heavens," she kept saying, "I am sure to make a complete fool of myself."

"Oh Lard, nonsense," said Peter. "You will do very nicely if you follow all may instructions." Peter had no doubts at all. Lord Melton would have to look to his laurels, or some other gentleman at the ball would snap up Lucy Emmett for his mistress.

"Oh, I do hope so," said Lucy, wringing her hands. "I mean, I feel so . . ." She was trembling like an aspen, all her usual spirit fled. *What if Charles were angry with her, what if after their lovemaking and her hasty departure, he had never wanted to see her again. What if he hated her?* "Weak," she whispered. "I feel so weak." *Oh, where was that former Lucy Emmett who could tilt her chin and say "Boo" to the world? Was she gone forever, and had this weak and waffling female taken her place?*

Georgiana Stowe wore the hyacinth gown, for another simply could not be made in time. "It will look terrible, terrible, terrible," she sobbed. "As soon as that emerald is upon my finger, everyone but *everyone* will say how *vulgar* I look."

Mrs. Stowe stepped back and looked at Georgiana. To the eye of the perfectionist, the colour and pattern of the gown was not exactly correct to wear with an emerald. It was just too flamboyant somehow. Perhaps it was the amethysts sewn into the bodice, or the ruches in the skirt. The engagement ring itself was a very flamboyant piece of jewelry. The gown should have been simpler, to set off the ring.

"I mean, it's not really hyacinth, is it?" said Georgiana. "When the light is on it, it looks more like puce. Green with this will be a disaster."

"Just get the ring on the finger," snapped Mrs. Stowe. "The colour of the gown or the ring is now immaterial."

The orchestra was tuning up and the guests who lived locally were arriving. The earl had to greet them from a chair, for he was too weak to stand. But frail though he was, he had been determined to be present at his heir's engagement ball. His physician, Sir James, stood by his side in case his services should be needed during the evening.

Charles had to wait in his dressing room until he was signaled to escort Georgiana downstairs. It was after all her evening, and she was determined to choose just the right moment for her entrance in spite of her misery about the dress.

Pinkerton, Plunkett, Wentworth, and Willie Caruthers were already below, looking over the ladies. Willie's mistress, Elizabeth Clive, had arrived earlier in the day with her husband, and Willie had not yet had a chance to converse with her. But since Clive himself had his eye on the wife of Colonel Hampton, there was a good chance Willie would be left alone with Elizabeth for a part of the evening at least.

Charles strode up and down his dressing room, very ill at ease. He wore a suit of silver brocade, and a fall of lace at his throat and wrists. His hair was powdered and pulled back into a velvet bow, and because he kept shaking his head, Culpepper had to trot after him, with a soft brush to sweep away the powder that fell onto the shoulders of his coat.

"Do stop that," said Charles. "Stop fussing around me, man."

"The powder, my lord," said Culpepper.

"*Damn* the powder," shouted Charles. "Where is that blessed woman?" He looked at the clock. It was almost nine-thirty. "Go to Miss Stowe's room and enquire of her maid if her mistress intends to emerge this evening, will you?" said Charles. "Let's get this charade over with."

Culpepper did as he was told, but returned almost at once with the message that Miss Stowe wasn't quite ready.

"I am not quite ready either," snapped Charles. "But I am prepared to look as though I am."

Men with lighted lanterns stood all along the drive to Landsdun house, and as the Royalston coach pulled up at the front of the house two more men ran forward to open the coach doors and help the occupants out. Lucy was so overawed by the sight of Landsdun close to, that she stood entranced. It seemed impossible that human hands could have built it or that a human mind could have conceived it. And to think people lived in such a place, and to think she was about to enter it! Now her knees really were shaking, her teeth actually were chattering, and it wasn't because the night was cold.

"Now, look here," whispered Peter, as they walked up what seemed an endless flight of marble steps towards the huge front doors.

"Glide, do not bounce, and no hitching of the skirts, remember?"

Lucy nodded.

"What are we?" asked Peter.

"A swan," said Lucy in a whisper. They arrived at the doors. Lucy could hear the sound of music, the hum of many voices. The air was perfumed with the scents of the quality people inside.

271

"Quate," said Peter. "And what do swans do when they wish to cough?"

"They lift their fans so," said Lucy, lifting her open fan to cover her mouth.

"And the sound they make?" persisted Peter.

"Hem," coughed Lucy delicately.

"Quate," said Peter Royalston with satisfaction. "Yes, I think you will do very nicely. But Lard, only remember, if in doubt, refer to me. For Aye can be relied upon to be correct in all matters appertaining to propriety and decorum." Saying this, he extended his arm, and Lucy was very glad of it, for she felt this ball was bound to be either the making or the breaking of her.

"Squire William Royalston, Mrs. Jemima Royalston," called Lacey in sonorous tones from the front doors. "Mr. Peter Royalston, and—" He looked at the card he'd been handed, and then he looked at Lucy. "Er, Miss Lucy Emmett," whispered Peter nervously, he had meant to write in Lucy's name on the invitation card, but he had forgotten "and Miss Lucy Emmett," called Lacey.

Lucy breathed a sigh of relief, there had been a moment's tension, and she had thought she might be sent away after all, but all was well. For the moment.

Lucy was as overwhelmed by the grandeur of the entrance hall as she had been with the exterior of the house. It was an effort for her to raise her eyes, there was such a riot of crystal and gilt, such a profusion of rich tapestry and portraiture—treasure everywhere, and before her a wide marble staircase swept away towards the loftier regions of the house. "Oh, it's magnificent," she breathed.

"Only one of the most superior establishments in the entire realm, that is all," whispered Peter, "and you refused the further attentions of the gentleman who will one day inherit it. Oh, and this is not the extent of his fortune, Lard, no, there is the London house, another in Scotland, one more in Ireland, and other wealth, both at home and abroad. More than anyone could fully comprehend." Maids appeared from nowhere and took her wrap and Mrs. Royalston's, and then another footman walked forward and ushered them to another pair of gilded double doors. Sounds of laughter and much gaiety came from the room beyond. "Squire William Royalston, Mrs. Jemima Royalston, Mr. Peter Royalston, and," called the second footman.

"Miss Lucy Emmett," whispered Peter. "'Tis not on the card, fellow, 'twas an error don't y'know."

"Miss Lucy Emmett," called the annoyed footman.

Everyone turned when the squire's party were announced. They were the last to arrive in the anteroom. This room was even grander than the hall if that were possible, and Lucy could see the ballroom beyond it. Everywhere there was a riot of colour, people, more vibrant looking than she had ever seen before, or had even imagined. There were dazzling lights everywhere, from crystal chandeliers, sending the jewels upon the ladies' throats, hands, arms, wrists, and ears flashing; blue turquoise, ruby red, rainbows of colour exploded from a sea of diamonds.

Lucy felt a thousand eyes on her as she entered in her simple white dress. She wore only a humble string of seed pearls about her neck. She felt almost naked, as though she had arrived in her shift. Her heart was pounding.

If it hadn't been for Peter Royalston's support, she would have turned and run, back to Ridge Farm and Roger and John and Toby. They were the people she belonged to.

"Ah, William, how are you?" she heard a voice say.

"I am very well, milord, consid'rin'. Sorry to hear about yer health, though I trust yer feelin' heartier now?" replied the squire.

Mrs. Royalston and Peter were both introduced to the earl, and then Jemima poked Lucy in the ribs. "Go on, Puss, curtsey to my lord."

Lucy moved forward in a daze, and dropped a curtsey. She raised her head before she rose and found herself looking into the eyes of a most charming old man. He was smiling at her, with just that quizzical expression she had seen on Lord Melton's face sometimes. So this was the earl, his father.

"Miss Lucy Emmett, milord," said the squire proudly.

The earl extended his hand and raised Lucy from her curtsey. "I am pleased to meet you, Miss Emmett," said the earl. "You, I believe, are our young last-minute guest, are you not?"

Lucy nodded.

"Well, had I known we had such a rare beauty living local to Landsdun, I should have taken care that we sent you an invitation and you should not have been a last minute guest, should she, Sir James?" The earl turned to look for his physician. But the old man had disappeared.

"That girl's here," said Sir James, bursting into Charles' dressing room without even knocking. "That girl, that girl!"

"What girl?" asked Charles tetchily. He was still waiting for Georgiana.

"That Emmett girl," puffed Sir James. Charles felt his heart stop beating for a fraction of a second. *Lucy at Landsdun?* It wasn't possible. As though to be convinced he asked, "Lucy?" in almost a whisper. Sir James nodded and then collapsed in a chair mopping his brow. "Brandy," he gasped to Culpepper, who filled two glasses. The full implication of Sir James' message had not yet struck the heir.

"Here?" asked Charles sinking into a chair opposite Sir James (without lifting the skirts of his coat Culpepper observed). Sir James nodded again. "With that fribble fellah from Ragby Hall." He took a glass of brandy from Culpepper and swallowed a huge gulp.

"But how?" asked Charles, taking his glass of brandy from the tight-lipped manservant (four hours with smooth-thing irons to remove any wrinkle from that coat, and now ruined).

"How?" repeated Charles.

Sir James shrugged. "By coach?" he volunteered lamely.

There was a long, thoughtful pause.

"Anyway," said Sir James, "she looked quite stunning, my boy, quite superb, all decked out, quite entrancing. The ladies—the looks—the envy! The gentlemen, my dear fellow, the admiration, upon my word. Your young circle, me boy, the bloods, all agog. Plunkett spellbound, Pinkerton boggling. Wentworth wide-eyed, and Willie getting nasty looks from Elizabeth Clive. Everyone's asking who she is, where she springs from, and why she's not been seen before, and . . ." here his voice trailed away. "It wasn't your scheme, this, was it? he asked anxiously. "Because if it was, it's going to cause a rumpus when the Stowes—."

Charles shook his head. "No," he said. "I have a feeling this is one of Cupid's naughty pranks."

Lucy could hardly move for young men, very well turned out and handsome young men they were, too. Her dance programme was already two thirds full, and there were still more coming. The four "bloods" had been the first forward. They were all single and eligible, and apart from Willie Caruthers, who was somewhat hindered now by the presence of Elizabeth Clive, a sulky looking lady in a black gown, they were free to flirt where they pleased.

The bloods were feared by the mamas of all the single young ladies present, for they were very eager and hot young men. Hot to have what they wanted from a girl, but not hot to marry. Quite the contrary. There was not one mama in the country with a gently reared young daughter, who would leave that child alone with any one of the bloods, for they were impossible to manage.

"Look," said Willie Caruthers, to Lucy. "You have a free Polonaise there, do be kind."

"Well," said Lucy, frowning, "I have begun to wonder if I am ever to be allowed to sit down during this evening."

"Oh, good gracious," said Willie. "If we find that you are fatigued by that time, I'm sure I shall find a place where you might get some relaxation with me."

Lucy smiled, for the other bloods were much amused by this.

"I doubt whether relaxation is what I should get," said Lucy.

"Right on the nail," laughed Pinkerton. "She reads you like a book, Caruthers."

"I think that I read you all," said Lucy.

"Oh, tell me I shall have that Polonaise?" begged Willie.

"You shall have the Polonaise," said Lucy. "But that is all you shall have."

Willie at once seized her hand and kissed it, to Elizabeth Clive's chagrin. "I shall hold you to that," he said, ignoring his mistress's daggerlike looks.

"I am terrified that I shall forget all you taught me," Lucy whispered to Peter. He had told her that all the different dance steps were marked out in different coloured chalks upon the ballroom floor, but she had quite forgotten which colour represented which dance, and after all, dancing with Peter around the sitting room at Ragby Hall was of a very different order from dancing among hundreds of accomplished people at Landsdun.

"Oh Lard," hissed Peter. "Just *follow* the rest, and if you should evah falter, just make a pained face, and the gentlemen will think that they have stepped upon your feet, and will have to halt and apologise. You may do that as often as you please, for no true gentleman would evah admit that a lady is clumsy or at fault, 'pon my ward. Even though he knows for certain she is. Oh, Aye say, come along, the heir and Miss Stowe are about to descend."

Everyone was moving out of the anteroom into the hall to see the heir and his young lady come down the stairs. There was a tremendous bustle, and Lucy and Peter joined the throng gathered in the great hall.

"Oh, heavens," whispered Lucy. "I am begining to wish that I had not come."

"Oh, piffle," replied Peter, craning his neck for a first glimpse of the heir.

"Here they come," was the muffled cry from the front of the crowd, and then an audible gasp from everyone surrounding Lucy. She looked up, and at the top of the marble staircase she saw Lord Melton looking every inch the heir to his vast fortune and title, and beside him, her hand resting lightly on his arm, was Georgiana Stowe. There was a ripple of applause as they started slowly to descend, followed by the General and Mrs. Stowe, and Dolph and Emma; and cries of approbation from all the

276

older ladies, who declared that they made a splendid pair.

Lucy could not deny it. Charles so tall, so elegant in his silver brocade, and Georgiana beside him in the most beautiful dress that Lucy had ever seen, nodding and smiling, accepting the adulation of the guests as though she were a young queen.

"Look at that dress," whispered Mrs. Royalston. "Look at the amethysts upon it. Did you ever see such wealth on one young lady?"

Charles was looking for Lucy, his eyes traveling over the upturned faces below him. Sir James had said she was wearing white.

"I feel wretched," whispered Georgiana with the fixed smile on her face. "This gown is quite wrong. See, in the lights it's puce, it's not hyacinth at all. This is the last time I deal with that dressmaker."

Charles couldn't see Lucy at all, there were so many people. "I see that Elizabeth Clive is in black again," hissed Georgiana. "I'm sure it's the same dress for every function, just with a new trim. Clive is very tight fisted." Her eyes were moving over the ladies present. Although she was far from satisfied with her own gown, she had the satisfaction of knowing it was the most expensive worn that night. And her mother was right, what *did* it matter, if the cattier ladies present might criticise her for being too showy. She had won the most eligible young man in the realm. They were almost at the bottom of the stairs, and Georgiana's triumphal entrance was almost over, when her eyes met a pair of very blue ones, and her mouth fell open.

"Oh, no," said Georgiana, in a voice audible to her mother.

"Whatever is wrong?" hissed Mrs. Stowe.

"It's that girl," wailed Georgiana.

CHAPTER IX

A Vain and Audacious Gentleman

In which Lucy discovers that hate may be as powerful a passion as love.

"So it is," murmured Charles.

Lucy looked wonderful. He wanted to take her in his arms and cover her with a million kisses—no, two million kisses—but he had to be content with just looking. He felt mightily frustrated.

As for Lucy, seeing the heir again had sent her weak at the knees.

"Lard, he has seen you," whispered Peter.

"I know," said Lucy.

"He's smiling at you," the fop whispered again.

"I know," replied Lucy softly, and she smiled back. She and Charles did not need words to communicate—his smile had sent a loving message to her, and her smile had sent one back to him across the milling throng of guests in the hall. All Lucy's fears that the heir might have been displeased to see her left her. There was no chance she could get near to him. People surrounded Georgiana and Charles, congratulating them, kissing her and shaking his hand. Georgiana was far too well schooled in the niceties of behaviour to allow her displeasure at seeing Lucy to show in her face. She greeted everyone with a fixed smile and answered them through clenched teeth. Nobody could have suspected she was seething with fury. "I suppose that girl being here had nothing to do with you?" she hissed at Charles.

"Georgiana?" Mrs. Stowe interrupted hurriedly. "Come along, the earl is waiting to make the formal announcement." Mrs. Stowe was very concerned that there be no scene between her daughter and the heir. When the world at large knew that Georgiana Stowe was certainly to be the bride of Lord Melton, then Georgiana would have the power to dictate to the heir. Then if she was displeased with him, she could make it known, but until the public announcement there was always the chance Charles might change his mind—and that was something that the lady was not prepared to risk.

Sir James helped the earl to his feet. All the guests had assembled in the anteroom to hear the announcement. Lucy, Peter Royalston, Mrs. Royalston and Squire Billy were right at the back of the crowd. They had to crane their heads to see.

"My Friends," said the earl, "I believe that none of you are in ignorance of the auspiciousness of this occasion."

"What is he going to say?" asked Lucy.

"Ssh," said Peter.

"The reason for this ball must be the worst kept secret in history, I think." There was much laughter at this, and some applause.

Lucy stood on tiptoe; she could see Charles standing on one side of his father, and Georgiana Stowe standing on the earl's other side, looking not a little pleased with herself.

"So it will be no surprise to you all, to hear that my son has asked Miss Georgiana Stowe to be his wife." The earl's eyes filled with tears, and so did Lucy's. She had not realised. Of course Charles had said that he was to marry Georgiana, but now she was to hear it said in public. It made it real, certain. The man she loved was to marry another. She watched the earl take Georgiana's hand.

"And I am pleased and proud to announce to you all that the lady has done him the honour of accepting." There was loud applause and cheers from everyone at this. The earl held up his hand and quieted the guests. "Most of you will know it is the custom in my family that the ring be presented in public, so that there may be no doubt of intent." Lucy was almost blinded with tears. She saw Charles step forward and take Georgiana's hand. There was an audible gasp as a huge emerald caught the light from the candelabra, and when the ring was upon her finger Georgiana smiled as the heir bent his head and kissed her cheek. Then the earl kissed Georgiana. "That emerald is the size of a duck egg," said Mrs. Royalston, wiping her brimming eyes. All the ladies were weeping; weddings and engagements were meat and drink to them. "The wedding date shall be announced later," said the earl. "And now, let the ball commence." Charles and Georgiana led the way into the ballroom.

"Oh, Puss, don't cry so," said Mrs. Royalston, taking Lucy in her arms. The girl was sobbing. "Soon it will be your turn."

"No it won't," sobbed Lucy. "I am not suitable."

"What ails the child?" asked the squire.

"Don't fuss, Billy," said Jemima.

"Now come, Puss, there is a minuet to start."

"I don't want to dance," said Lucy. "But Peter is waiting," said Mrs. Royalston.

Lucy looked at the fop. "You should have prepared me for this," she said. Peter looked embarrassed. A crying swan was not something he relished.

"Royalston?" The fop turned. It was Giles Wentworth, the Honourable, talking to him. "Me?" asked Peter. Wentworth, nodded, bowed, clicked his heels. "I wonder, sir, if you would permit me to partner Miss Emmett in the minuet? I understand that she is engaged to you for the first dance, but you look like an accommodating sort of fellow."

"Oh, I am, my honourable sir," said Peter. "I am always ready to accommodate the nobility."

"I do not wish to dance," said Lucy. The fop ignored this, and executed a flourishing bow. He was only too pleased to have Giles Wentworth partner Lucy in the minuet. He feared more tears, and besides, the sight of Lucy on the young blood's arm, would give the heir something to fret about.

"He's a strange fellow," said Giles to Lucy. She had managed to compose herself now.

"Who, Peter?" she asked.

"Very," said Giles. "Gave you up just like that." He clicked his fingers. "Damned if I should've if you'd arrived with me."

Lucy smiled. "What would you have done, if the tables had been turned?" she asked.

"Oh," said Giles, "I should have biffed the fellow's snook for him."

Lucy laughed. She liked Giles Wentworth best of all the bloods. He had an air of dashing gallantry about him. He was not so handsome as Charles, of course, but he was handsome. "There, that's better," said Giles. "It's good to see you smile, you looked quite stricken for a moment earlier." Wentworth had had his eye on Lucy since her arrival and was already to dance with her later in the evening. But he was an impulsive and highly impatient young man and was inclined to take what he wanted when he wanted it. The methods he used to achieve his ends were always bold and unconventional, and for that reason he usually got his way.

"You might have had your snook biffed," said Lucy.

"What, by that fellow?" asked an amazed Wentworth, pointing towards Peter Royalston, who was on his way into the ballroom with his aunt. "I doubt it." He turned and looked down at Lucy, then offered her his arm. Lucy took it. Suddenly she felt a good deal cheered up. "You know, of course," said Giles Wentworth, "that you are the most beautiful female here tonight?" He was leading her towards the ballroom, and now all eyes were upon them.

Lucy could hear the whispers as she passed. Who was she? Where did she come from? It looked as though the Honourable Giles Wentworth was taking up with the strange girl.

Lucy could not help but preen a little; she only wished it was Charles who was leading her to the dance. Charles who paid her the compliments. But Charles never would, not in public.

"Come," said Giles, "be straight with me. That Royalston fellow, you aren't stuck on him, are you? Now don't tell me that you are, for I shan't believe you."

Lucy laughed. "Why should I not be?" she asked.

"A beauty like you?" said Giles. "No, that fellow's not your style."

"You don't think so?" Lucy asked as they entered the magnificent ballroom.

"No, I don't," said Giles, leading her out onto the floor, so that they might take their places for the minuet.

Charles saw her enter. Their eyes met. For an instant he looked surprised.

"And what is my style, pray?" asked Lucy.

"I am your style," said Giles Wentworth. "And if you doubt it, try me, and see if you don't agree."

What the hell is Wentworth up to? Charles asked himself. *Why hadn't the fop led Lucy in for the first dance?* He could see Peter Royalston standing at the edge of the ballroom, simpering and beating time with his long cane. He looked back at Giles and Lucy. Giles was whispering to her as their bodies touched, intimate whispering it was, and she looked as though she did not mind at all.

"We are out of time," hissed Georgiana. Charles hurriedly righted matters. If one got out of time in a minuet, everything went to the dogs.

"I want to know how that girl comes to be here?" Georgiana went on. "How did a low-bred bastard like that get to Landsdun?"

"She's not the only bastard here tonight," said Charles. "Though she is probably the only one who would admit to it." He didn't look to see the effect of this remark on

Georgiana, for his eyes were on Lucy again. Wentworth was looking pretty damned comfortable for a fellow who had not long since lived in ignorance of her existence. That fop certainly had something to answer for.

"No, I have never been to London, although I have always dreamt of it," said Lucy. The dance was over. Giles bowed low to her, and she dropped a curtsey. "Oh, but you must come, we cannot allow you to bloom unseen," said Giles, leading her off the floor. "Are you engaged for the next dance?" Lucy raised her programme, remembering to slip her fan over her wrist first. *I am getting the knack*, she told herself. "Oh yes I am," she replied.

"Might I enquire to whom?" asked Giles.

"To me, Wentworth," said Plunkett. "I was the first in."

"Oh, how damned convenient," said Wentworth to Lucy. "I shall be engaged to you after all."

"Convenient?" gasped Plunkett.

"Very," said Giles. "You have just paid a debt."

"I have?" Plunkett looked puzzled.

"Indeed," said Giles. "I have an IOU from you in my toilette box for twenty guineas. Consider it discharged in exchange for this dance with the lady."

"You shall not have this dance," said Plunkett, bowing to Lucy and preparing to lead her to the Quadrille. "I shall pay the debt in kind. Twenty guineas, when you like."

"The money is of no interest to me," said Wentworth. "But the lady is of great interest." He took Lucy's hand and led her away.

Plunkett followed them. "Damn you for a cheeky hound," said Plunkett. "Now come along, Wentworth, play the game. This is my dance."

"Would you like to save this gentleman twenty guineas?" Wentworth asked.

Lucy looked at Plunkett. He was all hot and bothered, while Giles was quite cool, not ruffled in the slightest.

"There," said Giles before she could answer. "Thank Miss Emmett. She has left you a richer man." Poor Plunkett was left, his mouth gaping at Wentworth's audacity.

"That was naughty," said Lucy.

"Oh don't chide me," said Giles. "You would have been bored to death by him. He's a good fellow, a very good fellow, but slow. They hail from Yorkshire, his family you know, very wet, very dismal, very remote. Great distance from London to Yorkshire."

"Aren't we going to dance?" asked Lucy, for he was leading her out of the ballroom. "I hope not," said Giles, "for I am parched."

"So am I," said Lucy, "and I am no great dancer."

"I noticed," said Giles. "You trod on my feet."

"Are you supposed to say that?" asked Lucy.

"Well, you did it so often that I had begun to suspect you were intent on injuring me," Wentworth replied.

They entered the supper room laughing. Lucy thought that Giles had been right, he was very much her style. She found him exciting, as well as entertaining.

There were ten long tables laid out in the supper room, covered with white damask and lace cloths, and groaning with food and drink. When they had their drinks in their hands Giles said, "Come along," and led her out into the hall.

"Where to?" asked Lucy.

"We must find a bolt hole," said Giles, looking about like a cornered fox. Lucy followed him as he opened a door. She found herself in a huge drawing room, all red velvet, silks, and gilt. Giles shut the door behind them.

"I was determined to escape your chaperone," he said, leading her towards a couch by the fire.

"My chaperone?" asked Lucy, sitting beside him.

"That large lady in the mountainous yellow dress with the ship?" Giles pointed to the top of his head.

"Oh, you mean Mrs. Royalston," said Lucy.

"Whoever she is, she had her beady eye on me," said Giles.

"Nonsense. She is a sweet lady, and very kind," said Lucy.

"Ah, but would she be kind to me?" Giles asked. "I doubt it. I've had some damned tough skirmishes with chaperones in my time. And mamas. Desperate. Older ladies with young girls in their care are the very devil. I would rather tangle with a boarding party of Barbary pirates, I assure you."

Lucy laughed, and leant her head against the back of the couch. She suddenly felt quite weary—it must have been from all the excitement, the preparation for the ball, the worry of trying to remember how to conduct herself. And there was Charles and Georgiana. She closed her eyes. Though Giles Wentworth was a lively and welcome companion she wished with all her heart that Charles could be alone with her. She longed to feel his arms around her again, his lips on hers. She sighed as she remembered their lovemaking in the forest. *Oh, if only we could be together all the time*. She wanted to live an open life with him. A future full of furtive meetings and deceptions seemed hardly a future at all—and yet not to see him, not ever to have him close to her, was an unbearable thought. She knew that if he asked her to be his mistress a second time, she would not refuse.

"Lucy?" she opened her eyes, startled, she had been so lost in her thoughts that she had quite forgotten Giles.

"That's a fine thing, falling asleep on a fellow."

"I wasn't asleep," laughed Lucy. "I was thinking."

Giles took her hand. She raised her eyes and looked into his face. What a handsome, rakish face it was. "You are a strange girl," he said, lifting her hand to his lips.

"Strange?" Lucy asked.

"Very," said Giles. "You look like a princess from a fairy tale, but you dance like a carthorse."

Lucy burst out laughing. "Oh, worse, come, be honest," she said.

"Alright. Like two carthorses," laughed Giles.

"Oh, I love your insults," giggled Lucy. "Do continue." They both laughed heartily.

"There you are, you see," said Giles. "What other girl would take a jocular insult in such good part? Most girls would have been in fits of tears by now."

"Most girls," said Lucy with a smile, "would not have

been alone with you, Giles Wentworth. Would they?" He laughed.

"Most girls would be too scared to be alone with me."

"Oh dear," said Lucy, with mock terror. "Are you armed?"

Giles moved closer. "Only with charm," he said.

"Oh dear," said Lucy. "Vain, as well as audacious."

"There, you see what I mean, you are strange, you are very beautiful, but you have character too, and humour. That combination is most rare, believe me. Now one might find a plain girl with character and humour, those qualities will have developed to compensate for her lack of looks. As for most beauties, well they are damned boring—it's no use to hope for a decent exchange with them. You don't talk to 'em, you just look at 'em. Oh, you must come to London, the town would welcome you with open arms. You are *made* for London," said Giles.

Lucy sighed. "Even if I dance like two carthorses?" she asked. She felt Wentworth slip his arm around her shoulder. "Ah, but nobody would know that. For I shouldn't let you dance with anyone but me, and I should adore you so much I would beg you to trample on me regularly."

"Oh, I should hate to deprive you of pain," said Lucy.

"Good," said Giles. "Come tomorrow." Suddenly he was kissing her hand again and then her throat, and then her cheeks.

"Oh, don't," said Lucy. "Please stop." But it was too late. His lips met hers. For a moment she resisted but to her surprise, a tingle ran up her spine and forced her to submit. However, a second tingle told her that she must not, she belonged to the heir. She struggled, and Giles let her go. Her cheeks were hot. Wentworth was smiling. "Now that is the sort of pain that I really enjoy. I could come to bear that very easily, morning, noon, and night. Let me take you to London tomorrow. You will never regret it." He tried to kiss her again, but she jumped up. It had been a shock to her, that she could enjoy the embraces of a man other than Lord Melton.

"I must go," said Lucy, but Giles stood up and gripped her arm.

"I *shall* have you, you know," he said. "Make no mistake about that, and if you have another man in that pretty, pretty head, forget him for he is a non-starter."

"Aha!" cried a voice. The door had been flung open. They both turned. For one awful second, Lucy had thought it was Charles. But it was Plunkett, his honest Yorkshire face flushed with aggravation. Behind him stood Pinkerton and Willie Caruthers. "Your twenty guineas, sir," said Plunkett, throwing a bag of coins at Wentworth's feet.

"The debt is discharged, and the lady is mine." He bowed to Lucy. "Your servant, Miss Emmett," and he proffered his arm.

"Oh don't be an idiot, Plunkett," said Giles. "The dance must be over."

"But the next is mine," said Pinkerton, glaring at him.

"And then I am engaged to dance with the lady," said Willie Caruthers, "and we don't mean to be cheated, do we, Pinkers?"

"No, we damn well do not," said Pinkerton. Wentworth smiled, and adjusted the lace at his wrists, then said very civilly, "Miss Emmett's apologies that you are to be disappointed, gentlemen, but she is engaged to me for the rest of the evening," Lucy opened her mouth, but Giles held up his hand and silenced her. "No, no further apologies are called for, both these gentlemen understand that it is a lady's prerogative to change her mind."

"Shall I tell you what you are, Wentworth," said Plunkett, approaching Giles with what Lucy thought was a disturbingly hostile expression on his face. "You, sir," said Plunkett, his nose now only an inch from Wentworth's, "are an out and outer, sir."

"Repeat that, will you?" said Wentworth, still smiling.

"An out and out bounder, sir," said Plunkett very loudly.

"Am I indeed?" said Wentworth coldly. "Take that back, or you *won't* live to regret it."

"I shall not," snarled Plunkett. "I repeat, sir, that you are a bounder."

Giles nodded, solemnly. "And you, sir, are a dull pudding," he said. Plunkett's face turned the colour of a ripe plum. "Take that back," he said.

"A dull pudding," said Giles, "and what is worse, a dull *Yorkshire* pudding." There was a minute's stunned silence, then Plunkett pulled off his coat and threw it upon the floor and Giles undid two buttons on his waistcoat. "Put up your dukes," said Giles. "I was just about to," said Plunkett, raising his fists.

"A moment, gentlemen," called Willie Caruthers. "Play the game, shake hands."

"My dear old friend," said Giles to Plunkett. "You have my deepest apologies."

"And you have mine, Wentworth," said Plunkett. To Lucy's amazement the two bloods shook hands very warmly, wished each other the very best of luck, and then Giles Wentworth biffed Plunkett's snook so hard that Plunkett fell to the floor like a sack of oats.

A little while later, Lord Melton saw Lucy enter the supper room. She was not alone. The bloods were with her. Caruthers and Pinkerton looked alright, but Plunkett's nose was squashed to a pulp and there was an ominous swelling above Giles Wentworth's left eye. They were all in very good spirits. Charles had been looking for Lucy, or rather looking out for her, because the Stowes had all stuck to him like poultices, so that he couldn't move without finding one of the family at his elbow. He had spoken to Peter, who was tipsy and had mentioned something about marrying Lucy, which Charles had imagined to be a result of his inebriation. "In name only," Peter had said, "and this monumental sacrifice I make in your sarvice, may lard, and expect no reward for it. No, no, do not press riches upon me, do not elevate me to the aristocracy, and do not mention may existence to the king, for I shall die, Aye promise you, I could nevah appear at court, I am too humble."

Charles had asked him where Lucy was, but he didn't

seem to have the faintest idea. Charles had suspected she was with Wentworth, now those suspicions were confirmed. "Excuse me," said Charles to the Stowes. He wanted to talk to Lucy. She was not alone, so it would not look improper.

"Where are you going?" Georgiana asked. "To see the bloods, madam," said Charles, walking quickly away from her. Georgiana nudged Dolph.

"Oh, I'll come too," he called after Charles. "Say how de do to them."

The bloods' display of pugilism had left Lucy a bewildered girl; it had been in the end very very good-natured, very sporting—and they had, it seemed, enjoyed themselves vastly. Wentworth had of course won, and Lucy was now engaged to him for the evening. He and Plunkett had retired to clean off their faces and change their linen, and then joined her and Pinkerton and Willie in the hall. Then it was time for supper. It was as simple as that. They were as jovial as if there had been no fight at all, and what was more curious, not one person as they entered the supper room commented on Plunkett's pulverised nose or on Wentworth's eye now turning black. It was all very curious.

"Here comes Melton," said Willie. "Oh God, with Dolph Stowe, what shall we do, fellows, stand firm or stampede?"

"I don't envy Melton, having him for a brother-in-law," said Plunkett. "We could always do Landsdun a favour and arrange an accident for the booby," said Wentworth. "Something very fast, and very final, with a gun. Wait for it," he said as Dolph bore down on them.

"How de do, Wentworth," said Dolph, pumping Wentworth's arm.

"Ah, Dolph," said Wentworth, "hello, there."

Charles was looking at Lucy and she was blushing. "You haven't met Miss Emmett, have you, Melton?" asked Wentworth.

"How do you do, Miss Emmett?" said the heir. She curtsied; now she was blushing furiously, for his eyes were very penetrating. She felt as though he were looking right through her, that he knew what had transpired between her and Giles Wentworth, and that the guilt she felt was written all over her face.

"Actually, Miss Emmett and I have met before," said Charles looking first at Lucy, and then at Wentworth's eye, and then at Plunkett's nose. "She has quite a talent for setting men against one another." This was said with such a note of cold sarcasm Lucy could hardly believe that it was uttered by the same man who had held her in his arms and whispered such loving words to her.

"It is not my fault," Lucy said in retaliation. "If men must always be battling to prove themselves superior to another man. Why, I have seen cocks fight in the same way."

Giles laughed. "Melton would never fight for a lady, Miss Emmett, that's not his way; he is altogether too controlled. As to myself, I enjoy a dust up, and what I have for tonight's tussle was well worth it. Miss Emmett is engaged to me for the rest of the evening," he told Charles. The heir gave him a sharp look, and then his eyes met Lucy's. "Wentworth is a very impulsive fellow, as you have probably discovered," he said. Lucy lowered her eyes. "He is the sort of blood who would lay his life on the line for a speck of dust, if he suspected another fellow wanted it. It is not the *thing* itself that is important, it is the getting of it; once he has it he loses interest."

"Ah, but I do win," said Giles.

"But ultimately you are the loser," said Charles, "for you value nothing except your reputation as a winner." He bowed to Lucy, and as he did so he whispered in her ear, "I must speak with you."

"When?" Lucy whispered back.

"Be at the foot of the stairs in ten minutes," and then he bowed to all the bloods, and returned to Georgiana, with Dolph Stowe following hard on his heels.

"Oh my handkerchief," said Lucy. "It's in my reticule."

"Send a maid," said Giles, but Lucy said, "Excuse me," and walked quickly away from him into the hall.

Culpepper was by the stairs. "Quick," he said. Lucy followed him up the wide staircase and across the landing. He opened the door and Lucy found herself in a dressing room. There was a fire burning in the grate. Culpepper closed the door. "The heir said you are to wait here," he said. Lucy sat down by the fire, her heart beating. In a second the door opened. It was Charles. "Cover for me, will you?" he asked his man. Culpepper nodded and went out, shutting the door behind him. "I feel like a fugitive in my own house," said Charles. He and Lucy looked at each other for a while in silence, then he crossed to her, took her hand, pulled her up from the chair, their lips met, and at once Lucy was drowning in passion. For all his charm and audacity, Wentworth was no substitute for the heir. "We have not long together," said Charles.

"I know," Lucy answered breathlessly. "Oh, kiss me again." Again they kissed, and then their words poured from them in torrents.

"As soon as I saw you tonight, I wanted to love you, I almost went mad to see you so close so often, and not to be able to take you in my arms," said Charles.

"That is what I wished for, to have you hold me and love me. When I saw you kiss Georgiana Stowe on the cheek, oh, Charles, how I cried," said Lucy.

"Lucy, I have not stopped thinking of you since that day in the forest. Why, oh, why did you refuse my offer? Now you are here, and you see how things are, surely you will not do so again."

"I regretted it almost at once," said Lucy, kissing him fondly. "Oh, my darling, it is just that it is so hard to share you with another, to accept that we can never marry, nor that our children if we have them could have their father's name."

Charles held her tight. "I know, I know, but we are already more to each other than most legitimately married people, and as for sharing me, you will never have to do that. I love you, and I am all yours."

"And I yours," said Lucy. "Giles Wentworth, oh, Charles, it was nothing, a silly flirtation—"

"Promise?"

She nodded and kissed him again. "Oh, promise, promise, promise."

Charles frowned. "Wentworth is quite ruthless, you know, he cares for no one. Once he has a woman he discards her. You are so young, and so—God, I wanted to strike him when I saw him with you. 'Till now he has been my friend, but I could kill him."

"You were so cold to me," said Lucy.

"Cold?" Charles laughed. "My blood boiled." He sat down in a chair and pulled her onto his knee. "Anyway, perhaps I shall not have to kill him, for I have made up my mind to abduct you."

"When?" Lucy asked eagerly. Charles took her face in both his hands and kissed her again. "The day after tomorrow, unless you come willingly."

"Oh, I shall come willingly," said Lucy, "but if I didn't, you would abduct me, wouldn't you?"

Charles laughed. "I should have to, for unless I hide you away I shall have not only Wentworth, but a whole host of other fellows to kill. Now listen, I am going to have Peter Royalston bring you to London."

"Oh, Charles," whispered Lucy, her eyes shining.

"By the way," asked the heir, looking puzzled, "what is all this nonsense about your marrying the fellow?"

"Oh heavens, that was just a ruse," said Lucy, "to save me from being deported to the Antipodes. You know there is no truth in it, except that Mrs. Royalston and the squire, well, they seem to think that—"

Charles clicked his fingers. "That could serve us well. Perhaps Cupid is not such a fool after all. If people in general think you are promised to him." He thought for a minute. "I know what I shall do. I shall invite you all to my house in Pall Mall."

"What, the squire, Mrs. Royalston, and Peter?" asked Lucy. Charles nodded.

"Neither the earl nor anyone in the town will think it suspicious if all four of you are my guests. That will stop any gossip, and you can stay at Pall Mall until I can find a house for you. I shall feel better, if you have the Squire and Mrs. Royalston with you for a while. I mean the fop is all well and good but he is the most stupendous idiot. I shall work something out, at any rate, and then, Oh, Lucy . . ."

"Kiss me again," said Lucy, and Charles did. It was a long kiss, a very long kiss. They had to part at last to breathe.

"I wish I could marry you," said the heir.

"Oh, so do I," whispered Lucy, "but I see why you can't. I could never be mistress in this great house, so I shall be *your* mistress instead."

Charles held her tight in his arms. "And mistress of *our* house," he said. "It will be better than being married, I promise you, for a husband as a rule spends as little time as possible with his wife, whereas I will spend every possible minute I can in your company, and we will be as happy as—what?"

"Turtle doves," said Lucy.

"And love each other," said Charles.

"Forever and ever," whispered Lucy, "and make love forever and ever too, and never sleep. Kiss me again."

Charles kissed her again. "And never, never sleep," he said when she had rested her head against his shoulder, "except when we are so exhausted by love-making that we must."

"We will sleep in each other's arms, and wake and make love again," said Lucy, kissing his ear.

He laughed. "And be exhausted again, and fall asleep again. When shall I eat, or conduct my business?"

"We shall both be too tired to walk," said Lucy. "My legs will be so weak, you shall have to carry me out for air."

"My legs will be too weak," said Charles. "I know, I shall buy you a Phaeton and four, like Kitty Townshend, and you shall drive everywhere." "Who is Kitty Townshend?" asked Lucy.

"A Courtesan," replied Charles. "A very fast lady, and not only in a Phaeton. Still you shall not be fast, except with me. No Giles Wentworth, nor no other bloods are to visit."

"On my honour, I shall allow nobody but you through the door," said Lucy solemnly crossing her heart.

"I hope not, for once you are seen on the town, every buck and rake will be sniffing at that door," said Charles. "Still, I intend to advertise in *The Spectator* for a ten-foot eunuch to guard you, on the rare occasions when I am not in attendance."

"What is a eunuch?" asked Lucy.

"Do you know what a gelding is?" asked Charles.

Lucy looked shocked.

"You mean they do that to men?"

"Not to Englishmen," said Charles.

"My father does it with his teeth," said Lucy. Charles winced. "To the male lambs that he doesn't want to breed from, he bites them off. But anyway, you will not need a eunuch, for I shall be altogether yours; kiss me again." Charles kissed her, and then sighed.

"I must go soon." He lifted her off his knee, and stood up. "I hate to, especially since my bedroom is just through that door."

"Oh we daren't, dare we?" asked Lucy mischievously. "I mean if we were caught there'd be the devil of a scene."

"I could say I found you in a faint on the stairs," said Charles. They both looked towards the bedroom door, and then at each other.

"If we were quick?" said the heir.

"Yes, but could we be?" asked Lucy.

They both looked at the door again, then Charles swept her up into his arms strode across to the bedroom door, kicked it open with his foot and said, "Curious that you should faint like that?"

"Wasn't it," said Lucy.

"Ah, Culpepper" called Sir James, arriving in a breathless state at the top of the stairs. "Have you seen the heir? His father wishes to retire and wants to bid him goodnight; and Miss Stowe feels neglected."

"I think he's in the garden, sir," said Culpepper.

"But it's raining," said Sir James.

"He was hot," said Culpepper.

"But it's *pouring*," said Sir James.

"He was *very* hot," said Culpepper.

"We had better launch a lifeboat, if he's gone out on such a night," said Sir James, turning to go back down the stairs. At that moment, though, Charles appeared next to Culpepper. "I thought you were in the garden?" said Sir James.

"I was," said the heir.

"Well, how the hell did you get here?" asked Sir James.

"Servants' stairs," said Charles, following the old man.

"Have you seen Miss Emmett?" asked Giles Wentworth in the hall. Sir James looked at Charles, whose face betrayed nothing. "She's in the garden, I expect," Sir James said to Wentworth.

"But it's raining," said Giles.

"Pouring," said Sir James, "but she was probably very hot."

"You took a damned long time to collect a handkerchief," said Giles to Lucy when she eventually joined him in the anteroom.

"Well, I couldn't find my reticule," said Lucy. She had done her best to cover with white powder the marks the heir's passion had left on her breasts and arms, but she had been so transported by their love-making that she found it hard to be composed, and she was sure her face would reveal their secret to everyone she met.

"Well, it wasn't in the garden, was it?" said Giles.

"Of course it wasn't in the garden," said Lucy. "It's raining."

"And you're not wet," said Giles. Lucy sighed. She could see Charles standing by the door of the ballroom. He turned and looked at her; she sent him a dazzling smile, he sent one back, she had to restrain herself from running to him and hugging him. "Well, where was it?" asked Giles.

"In his bedroom," said Lucy her eyes still joined with the heir's, and then she cried "Oh!" and covered her mouth.

Through the rest of the evening her eyes kept meeting the heir's. Every opportunity that allowed them to brush against each other was seized by them both. When the ball was over Lucy left her thoughts in heaven, and her heart there, too. When she got to her bed, she slept like a baby, dreaming the sweetest dreams of her life.

Charles woke early on the next day. He bathed and dressed and was seated at his desk before seven, where he wrote two letters, one to Squire Billy, and one to Cupid.

Dear Squire Royalston,
Tomorrow I am going to London for a short visit, while Miss Stowe goes to Hampshire with her family to prepare for the nuptials. Last night, I spoke to your nephew, who told me that he desires to see a play at Covent Garden, which has its last performance on Thursday. Therefore I have arranged that I shall carry him and Miss Emmett there in my coach with me, and while in London they may stay with me at Pall Mall. Perhaps yourself and Mrs. Royalston would care to visit, too. If this is the case, then my invitation is extended to you both. No doubt this notice will be too short for yourself and your wife, and so I shall wait for a reply from you tomorrow. In haste, Melton.

Dear Cupid,
I shall arrive at Ragby Hall at ten tomorrow morning and shall expect Miss Emmett and yourself to be ready to enter my coach for a trip to London. This will be news to you, but she will explain all. You are to stay in my house in Pall Mall. I have extended the invitation to your Aunt and to your Uncle, who may follow at a later time convenient to them both if they wish. In haste, because of preps for departure, Yrs, Melton.

"Oh, may ward," cried an excited Peter when he had read the letter. He ran up the stairs to tell Lucy. "We are on our way," he said excitedly. Entering her bedroom he handed her the letter and sat down on the bed. "Pall Mall," he said. "May ward, what Quality."

297

Lucy read the letter and smiled. Charles had wasted no time. "At ten tomorrow," she said, and then she told Peter what Charles had in mind.

"Oh, what an honour, Billy," said Mrs. Royalston, "what an honour! What an impression Peter must have made on the heir. Well, I am not a jot surprised, that boy was made for high society."

"I shan't go," said the squire.

"What?" cried Mrs. Royalston, with anguish.

"I shan't go," said the squire.

"But Billy, if you don't go, I cannot go," said his wife.

"That's right," said Billy, "and then there shall be no money spent on frip fraps in Oxford Street, the Strand and Holborn Passages. Anyway, I have just come back from London, and am still paying for my last visit."

"But I have not been to London for three years," wailed Mrs. Royalston. Then she burst into tears, and waddled off upstairs to tell Lucy.

"Puss," she said, wiping her eyes and sniffling. Lucy patted her bed and Mrs. Royalston sat down next to her nephew. "Oh, Puss." Then her tears came in floods.

"I suppose the squire is digging in his heels," said Lucy, putting her arm around Mrs. Royalston's shoulders.

"Lard, I thought he would, the beast," said Peter.

"Did he say why?" asked Lucy.

"Oh, need you ask," wailed Mrs. Royalston.

"Money?" asked Lucy. The lady nodded her head. Lucy jumped out of bed. "You shall go," she said, pulling on the pretty sprigged cotton gown Mrs. Royalston had had made for her; then she ran out of the bedroom, down the stairs, into the breakfast room, sat on the squire's knee, and said, "Now then, what's this I hear about your not coming to London?"

"I shan't," said the squire. "Nor shall anyone else. I am not Croesus that I have guineas to hand out like blades of grass. That ball cost me a packet."

"The London trip shall not cost you a penny," said Lucy.

"Mm, I have heard that story before," said Billy, "that ball was not going to cost me more than a gown each, for

298

yer and me wife, and a suit of clothes for meself and me nephew. What transpired? Three gowns each, for me wife and yerself, I learned afterwards, not to speak of a bonnet each, and that damned ship for her head. Then a new wig for me, and another for Peter, not to mention a corset that near strangled me all night."

"Oh, you looked so handsome, though," said Lucy.

"No," said Billy. "I shan't be budged. Off me knee with yer, I am unbudgeable."

Lucy stood up. "Oh cruel," she said.

"You shall not budge me though you call me cruel," said Billy. "The Royalston men are like the oaks of the Charnwood—stout fellows—nor storms nor lightning shall bend us or break us, nor a girl's cries of 'cruel' budge us."

Lucy circled around for a while, looking dejected. "We are to stay at the heir's house at Pall Mall," said Lucy. "It shall cost you nothing." She knew how much Mrs. Royalston wanted to go to London. "I shall miss you both terribly if Peter and I must go without you."

"Give up," said Squire Billy. "See, I am not budged." He caught Lucy's eye. "You'll pine I suppose?" he said. Lucy nodded. "So will Magpie." The squire looked at the dog, who was asleep at his feet. "You'll carry the hound with yer, will yer?" he asked. Lucy nodded. "It will cost me more than a penny for the stage, and then there's a night's stop at an inn, more if the weather grows worse."

"All of which the heir will reimburse," said Lucy.

"He did not say that in his letter," said the Squire.

"I don't suppose he mentioned gaming in his letter, did he?" asked Lucy. "That doesn't mean there won't be any."

"Gaming?" asked the Squire looking suddenly keen. "What sort of gaming? Card gaming or dice gaming?"

"Card *and* dice gaming," said Lucy. "You told me yourself he plays at the best tables. I'll wager there'll be a few games set up for the dark nights." The squire thought hard for a while. "I shouldn't want the hound here to worry for me," he said.

"Dice and cards," said Mrs. Royalston later. "Say those two words and that man will move a mountain to get to

299

them. Now, Puss, we had better start the packing. You and Peter shall go with the heir in the morning, and the squire and myself shall follow later on the stage." Mrs. Royalston clasped her hands together. "Oh, Bond Street," she cried, "Oh, Puss, wait until you see the shops."

"Wait until you see the theatres," said Peter. "'Tis a pity it's Winter, for there shan't be much to do about St. James's and Vauxhall. But, Lard, I sweah we shall not want for entertainment with the heir, may ward."

"I had better tell that slattern to get out the smoothing irons," said Mrs. Royalston, hurrying from the room. "There's pressing to be done."

"Oh, I am so excited, so happy," said Lucy, hugging the fop, and then dancing around the room. "Imagine, soon the heir and I shall be together in our own house."

"Oh, Lard, we must have our own establishment," said Peter haughtily. "We shall want to entertain and so forth. Lard, I shall settle for nothing less than Cavendish Square, St. James's Square or Portman Square. If he so much as mentions Fenchurch Street or Lombard Street you are to reply, no, indubitably."

"Why?" asked Lucy.

"Because," Peter replied haughtily, "Fenchurch Street and Lombard Street are not fashionable, and I should not be seen dead in a house in either of them."

Lucy frowned. Surely Peter did not mean to live with her. She was about to question him when there was a knock on the door. It was Wilchup, looking all agog. "It's a gentleman come to the front door," he said.

"It's the heir," cried the fop. "He couldn't wait."

"No, it ain't," said Wilchup. "It's someone of the same ilk."

"Did you not ask him for his name, you incredibly incogitable moron?" asked the fop shrilly.

"I did," said Wilchup.

"And Lard, did he reply?" cried Peter.

"He did," said Wilchup.

"What did he say?" shrieked the fop, almost tearing his hair.

"He said, 'The Honourable Giles Wentworth,' and asked if Miss Lucy Emmett were at home," said Wilchup.

"Good morning," said Lucy, entering the sitting room. Giles turned from looking out of the window and bowed. He looked very fine, in his dark green velvet riding coat and buckskin breeches. Mrs. Royalston was sitting in a chair by the fire looking very flustered, pretending to embroider, but casting so many wary looks in the gentleman's direction that she pricked her finger continuously.

"Good morning," said Giles to Lucy. "I did ask Mrs. Royalston if I might converse with you in private, but she seems to imagine some foul deed shall be perpetrated against you, if we are left alone."

"It's not proper," said Mrs. Royalston huffily. She mistrusted the Honourable Giles Wentworth, his rakishly handsome face betrayed him as an advantage-taker, and adventurer, a heartbreaker. Title or no title, Giles Wentworth was not a person to leave a young girl alone with.

"I think that Mrs. Royalston is quite right," said Lucy.

Giles looked irritated. "We were alone last night and you are still in one piece," he replied.

"Just," said Lucy.

Mrs. Royalston looked horrified. "Puss," she cried.

"Do not be alarmed, dear," said Lucy, patting her hand, "the gentleman's weaponry was no match for my armour."

Giles laughed. "Oh I wouldn't say that, if I remember right, I scored several hits, one of them palpable upon the lips."

Lucy blushed. Mrs. Royalston gasped. "Without much difficulty, too," said Wentworth.

Lucy felt her temper rise. "Why have you come here?" she asked.

"To see you," said Wentworth with a wicked grin.

"Well now that you have seen me, perhaps you will leave," said Lucy.

301

"You have forgotten my offer," said Giles. "To take you to London."

"I have not," said Lucy. "My reply is the same as the one that I gave last night. And now will you go?"

"I don't think so," said Giles, parting the skirts of his coat and taking up a comfortable position on the window seat.

"Then I shall," said Lucy, turning towards the door.

"I don't think so," said Giles mockingly.

Lucy turned and looked at him. She sensed something threatening in his voice. "Why should I not?" she asked warily.

He flicked some imaginary dust off his breeches. "I had an opportunity to speak with Georgiana Stowe this morning," he said.

Lucy stiffened. "Really? What has Georgiana Stowe to do with me?" she asked.

"Just what I asked myself," said Giles. "For when I mentioned your name, she said, 'What has that girl to do with me?' in just such a tone of voice as you have used. Curious, isn't it? Actually, she said, 'What has that *bastard* girl to do with me?'"

Mrs. Royalston jumped to her feet and threw down her sewing, all ready to attack Giles Wentworth, but Lucy restrained her. She sat down, but she looked furious.

"Yes, Miss Stowe was very put out by the mention of your name, as put out as you were when I mentioned hers. I have had a lot of experience of feuds between ladies," Giles went on.

"I am sure," said Lucy.

"Feuds?" cried Mrs. Royalston. "What does he mean, feuds? I shall get the squire my husband to heave him from the house." Giles ignored this second outburst.

"It is alright," said Lucy soothingly, for the lady's maternal and protective instincts were roused. "Just leave us to talk for a moment."

"Oh, Puss, alone with him?" Mrs. Royalston said. "Oh, no, dear, he is a fiend, and a rude one, gentleman or no gentleman."

"Please," begged Lucy, "you may trust me."

"I'm afraid it would be useless if I gave the same guarantee for I should not be believed by you, ma'm," said Giles. "But I am sure Miss Emmett is buckling on her armour, and so my weaponry will be as useless against that, as it was last night."

"Please," begged Lucy again, and at last Mrs. Royalston pottered from the room shaking her head.

Lucy shut the door, and as soon as she had she rounded on Giles Wentworth, her eyes flashing. "Dammit, what do you mean by coming here, with your evil insinuations?" She marched towards him. "You have upset Mrs. Royalston, a kind lady whom I love dearly. You have said shameful things before her, you have—"

Giles caught her wrist. She tried to free herself but he held her hard. "What evil insinuations?" he asked. "Have I insinuated anything? Everything that I have said is true, it is in pursuit of the truth that I have come."

"The truth?" Lucy asked.

Giles nodded. "Georgiana Stowe seems to know a good deal about you. Strange that a quality lady should concern herself with a poor bastard girl."

"How she could know a good deal about me, I cannot imagine," said Lucy, "for I have never spoken to the lady."

"Is there need for a lady to speak to another to know her?" Giles asked. "In my experience two women can sum each other up in an instant. And they do, especially if one is a threat to the other." His grip on her wrist tightened. "This chat I had with Miss Stowe was over breakfast, you understand. All the Stowes were there, a few other house guests and Sir James Robertson—very embarrassed by the mention of your name—the earl was not present nor were the bloods. They are late risers."

"And the heir?" Lucy blurted out. She regretted her question at once.

Wentworth's eyes narrowed. "No," he said, "Melton was not present, and you see, now there is another curious thing: why should you worry whether he was present or not, unless what I suspect is true?"

Lucy flushed. Giles pulled her towards him. He gripped

303

her wrist so tight she felt the blood to her hand stopped. There was something in his present mood that terrified her.

"I do not know what you suspect," she said trying to sound unconcerned.

He drew her down beside him on the window seat, and taking her face in his other hand, he forced her to look at him. Her eyes met his. She tried to look away, but he stopped her.

"Last night, the matter of the missing handkerchief, remember?" Lucy nodded. "While you were conducting your very extended search, Georgiana Stowe had scouts out looking for Melton. None of the footmen could find him. She was very agitated, so agitated that she let slip she suspected the staff of being in cahoots with Melton."

Lucy laughed. "Good heavens, what did she mean?"

"That the staff in the house knew well enough where Melton was, but were taking care he should not be discovered. And curiously enough," said Wentworth, "and you must admit that this has some significance, she then sent servants out to look for you. And you could not be found either."

Lucy's heart missed a beat. Wentworth was searching her face for signs.

"You are mad or drunk, or both," she said, "so early in the morning, too."

"Do you deny it?" asked Giles, his face contorted.

"Deny what?" asked Lucy, pulling herself loose from Wentworth and standing. She was trembling so much she had to grip her hands together to stop herself from crying. Wentworth seemed in a state bordering on obsession. He stood and faced her. "You deny it, then?" he asked. "That you are Melton's whore." He was not prepared for the strength of the blow across the face that he received from Lucy Emmett's hand. The mark on his cheek blazed.

"You forget that a girl may defend her honour. I am no whore," said Lucy.

Giles raised his hand to his face and smiled. "But you *are* a bastard," he said.

"That I cannot deny," Lucy replied. "Now that you have had a reaction from me, are you satisfied?"

Giles shook his head. "Last night I told you I would have you, Lucy Emmett, and I shall not be satisfied until I do."

Lucy's eyes leveled with his. "If I guess your meaning right, you are going to be a mightily frustrated man. For I shall never give you satisfaction," she said determinedly.

"You may not *give* it," said Giles, "but I shall have it all the same."

"Never," cried Lucy, but he caught her in his arms, and pressed his lips to hers, holding her so hard she could not move. A strange excitement filled her, she felt terrified, threatened, but elated. It was hate that filled her, and she feared for a moment that it might prove a more potent force than love. He pushed her away from him, he was smiling and shaking his head. She struggled to be composed, not to betray the thrill he had roused in her. "You are young, you are beautiful, you have humour and spirit. Now I find that you have strength. You are formidable," said Giles, "but I spy a chink in the armour."

"There are none," said Lucy, lifting her chin.

Giles lifted his forefinger. "One chink," he said.

"And what is that?" asked Lucy.

He walked away from her towards the door. "I shall not tell you," he said, but he paused when he got to the door. "You know," he said matter-of-factly, "Miss Stowe is off to Hampshire today."

"I did not," said Lucy.

"Wedding preparations," said Giles. "You ladies, and your preparations."

Lucy felt the blood drain from her face. Surely Giles could not know she was going to London with Charles. But perhaps Lord Melton had told him; he was his friend after all. She felt very confused.

"There is talk of a Christmas wedding, because of the earl's health. His heart is set on this match, has always been. He wishes to see the line secured before he dies, and Melton will do everything to ensure his father's wishes are carried out to the letter," said Wentworth.

305

"As every dutiful son should," said Lucy.

"Oh, indeed," said Wentworth. "Melton is duty, itself."

"A servant shall see you out," said Lucy crossing to the bell by the fire and pulling it to summon Wilchup.

"So no hint of scandal, then, should reach the earl's ears, no whisper that is unpleasant, no hint of a," he paused, "of an undesirable alliance."

Lucy smiled. "Thank you for calling, sir," she said, for Wilchup had arrived and opened the door. Wentworth laughed.

"You are a strange girl, Miss Emmett," he said. "But I'm damned if I don't see the makings of an outstanding woman."

"See the gentleman out, will you?" said Lucy.

Wentworth crossed to her and took her arm. "Oh, alright," he said confidentially, "I shall tell you what the chink in your armour is, shall I? I feel so confident now that it can't hurt my plan."

"You may say what you like," said Lucy.

"You love him," whispered Wentworth. "*That* is why I shall win." And then he followed Wilchup from the room.

CHAPTER X

Pall Mall

*In which Charles makes "a cake" and Lucy causes
a hum.*

"It is like a dream," said Lucy, "like a wonderful dream.
I fear that at any moment I might wake and find that it is
one."

Charles smiled and pulled her close to him. They were
in his bed at the house in Pall Mall, lying between silken
sheets, properly together at last, tired from the long
journey from Leicestershire—but not too tired to make
love.

"All that you have to remember," said the heir, "is that
this is the reality, our love for each other. The rest, the
world outside this room, is the dream." He kissed her
gently and stroked the dark curls back from her forehead.

"Oh, I wish it were so simple," she sighed, snuggling
against him. "It is easy for you to feel confident, but I
am a stranger to this world"—she pointed around the
richly furnished bedroom—"and a stranger to its ways.
Only a short while ago, I lay in rags upon a straw mattress;
now I lie naked in silken sheets, and you tell me it is not a
dream?"

"Feel me," whispered Charles. "I am real enough, am I not?"

"Oh, you are," breathed Lucy, "you are." She closed her eyes and thought of all that had happened over the last three days—the ball, then the plans laid for London, her goodbyes to Roger, Toby and John at Ridge Farm, the tears—for there had been tears. That poor place had been her childhood home, Roger Emmett the only man she could call father, Toby and John her dear brothers, all her memories were with them—memories that she could not share with anyone else. Not even Charles, close though he was to her, could fully comprehend the strong ties she felt with that lowly farmhouse, with the land around it and with the three men who worked that land.

Then there was Giles Wentworth. She had not mentioned his visit to the heir. Charles had seemed so happy, so carefree on the journey, so delighted to have her with him, that she had hesitated to cloud his high spirits. And anyway, it had all been so exciting, so different. The journey in the grand coach. The stop at an inn by the road for the night. And then London at last. Oh the noise and bustle of so many carriages and chairs. Street vendors crying their wares, nosegays and fish, buns and fruit, ballads and pamphlets, and singing birds. There were beggars, some with a leg or arm missing, some with frightful sores or ulcers, sitting on heaps of straw with mournful faces, their hands stretched out and their voices plaintive above the hurley burley throng crying out for alms. Then there were strollers, posture masters, puppet show men, fiddlers, tumblers and toy women, tallow chandlers and other merchants. Cattle were driven through the narrow streets, as were geese and other fowl. The stench was powerful; the cries of the beasts added to the tumult. Ladies and gentlemen of Quality rubbed shoulders with the most wretched people Lucy had ever seen. Pigsties stood next to palatial mansions, squalor and immense wealth lived hand in hand. They had been late arriving at Pall Mall, and it was quite dark. Lucy and Charles had climbed the stairs ostensibly to change their clothes, for they were both very dusty from the journey. But bed had beckoned. They had not eaten; sleep and lovemaking had caused them to forget that other appetite.

"Hungry?" asked the heir. Lucy nodded. She was still thinking of Giles Wentworth, it seemed she could not put him from her mind. "Then we must eat. I shall have supper brought to us."

"In bed?" asked Lucy.

"Absolutely," said the heir, ringing the bell by his bed, and pulling her towards him again. "We must remind each other to eat sometimes, or we will perish from severe malnutrition and exhaustion before you have properly enjoyed the metropolis." They fell to embracing again, and Culpepper had to knock several times before he was heard. "Supper," said Charles as soon as the man was in. Culpepper bowed. "For two, sir?" he asked, peering, to see if he could see a dark curly head in the bed.

"Of course," said the heir. "For three," said a voice from under the covers, and then Lucy emerged smiling. "Hello, Culpepper."

Culpepper bowed and smiled. "Good evening, Miss Emmett." He could see why the lady had remained hidden. Her shoulders were bare and he had reason to believe the rest of her was too. All the staff at the house knew of the heir's attachment and could be relied upon to be discreet as were the staff at Landsdun. Culpepper had seen to that.

"Supper for three," he said looking at Magpie who was sitting by the bed licking his chops. "Very well, I'll send orders to the kitchen." Then he bowed and left them.

"Charles?" said Lucy when the man had gone. "How long have you know Giles Wentworth?"

"Why do you ask?"

"Oh, nothing. I am curious, that is all."

"Yes, I remember that insatiable curiosity about men," said Charles.

Lucy laughed, "No, silly," she said, "I am just interested to know."

Charles put his arm around her. "I have know Giles for

years. The earl and his father are friends. Their seat is in Berkshire, and ever since I can remember Wentworth has been the devil himself."

Lucy shuddered. "Why do you say that about him?" she asked.

"I have already told you that he treats women abominably," said the heir. "One lady even killed herself as a direct result of his advances."

"What did she do?" Lucy was horrified.

"Drowned herself," said the heir.

Lucy grew cold to think that a woman had been driven to self-destruction because of Giles Wentworth.

"Did he spurn her affection?" asked Lucy.

"Ruined her," replied Charles. "Promised to marry her, and when she was with child, backed down."

"That is disgraceful," said Lucy.

"Well, I'm not sure that all the fault lay on Giles' side. The lady was something of an hysteric. I don't know the full story, but Giles has always been a bit of a 'chancer'; he loves excitement and he must have action—how he gets it, he doesn't care. The normality of life bores him—he and I are alike in that respect—but our circumstances are different. Giles is the youngest of three brothers, and it's quite in order for him to act the rake, whereas I am the heir, and must act more responsibly—well, up to a point," he finished, grinning and tickling Lucy's chin.

"Does he know about you and me?" asked Lucy. Had the heir told him about their hopes of a future together?

"I hope not," said Charles.

"I thought that you might have confided in the bloods," said Lucy. "They are, after all, your friends."

"The bloods are the last people I should confide in," said Charles. "If they knew you were here with me, it would be all over the town by now, every club should hum with it. They'd not tell to make mischief, you understand, they'd just think it an almighty jape. Melton caught by a pretty country girl," he kissed her fondly. "By a magically lovely, lively country girl. Melton who was such a blood himself that his heart, never truly stirred by a woman

310

before, was trapped by a pair of blue eyes. A prisoner, and such a very willing one."

"But it is bound to come out," said Lucy.

"Of course," said Charles, "but after the wedding, then it will hurt only one. Even the earl will turn a blind eye once I have done my duty. And you, Lucy Emmett, will be a lady, and such a grand one with your own fine house, and such a lot of gowns and jewels, that all will envy you. You should like to be envied, I think." "I should prefer to be respectable," said Lucy.

Charles laughed. "With your looks, my darling, you might be as celibate and respectable as a nun, but nobody would believe it."

"I suppose not," said Lucy. "Well, better to be an unrespectable woman and happy, than a miserable woman and respectable, I suppose."

"True," said Charles solemnly. "And now I'll tell you what we are going to do. We shall do something very, very unrespectable again that will make us both very, very happy." He lay down and pulled her down with him.

"But the supper," whispered Lucy.

"To hell with it," said the heir, cupping her breasts in his hands.

"Charles," asked Lucy.

"Yes?" said the heir, softly brushing her cheek with his lips. "Remember you told me about Kitty Townshend with the phaeton, and you said she was fast."

"Yes," whispered the heir, parting her legs.

"Well, how *fast* is she?" asked Lucy.

"Well," he replied thoughtfully, "she could probably pip you to the post in a phaeton, but you definitely get there faster in a bed."

The next morning both of them luxuriated in bed while their baths were prepared, their arms locked around one another, whispering plans for their future. They had eaten supper, but at two o'clock in the morning, so they had slept until midday. Lucy could hear a great bustle of activity in the next room. Maids were carrying coppers of hot water from below stairs.

"There are two priorities this morning," said Charles firmly.

Lucy kissed him again.

"No, I must be strong-willed," he said. "We must engage a maid for you, and we must search for a house for you, for soon I shall have to return to Landsdun."

"Oh, don't talk of that now," murmured Lucy, searching for his lips.

"No," said the heir, turning his face away. "I really must be strong-willed or we shall get nothing done." There was a tap on the door. "Enter," called Charles, sitting up and trying to look businesslike.

"The baths are ready, sir," said Culpepper.

"Two?"

Culpepper nodded. "Side by side, sir," he said dryly.

"Right," said the heir. "Now listen here, Culpepper, we shall need to engage a maid for Miss Emmett. See to that will you, and we must find a house. Oh, and the squire and Mrs. Royalston will arrive sometime today—see that rooms are made ready for them, will you?"

Culpepper nodded. "Very good. Oh, and, sir, that other party."

Charles frowned. "What other party?"

"Mr. Royalston, sir."

"Oh, Good heavens, the fop," said Charles. "Why, the fellow had quite gone from my head."

"He is complaining, sir."

"Complaining?"

"Of neglect, sir."

"Neglect?"

"It seems, sir, that he requests a servant, sir." Culpepper made a grimace of distaste. "A body servant, sir, since he has no man of his own."

"Well, you attend to him for the time being," said Charles.

"I am sorry, sir, that is not my place, sir," said Culpepper firmly. "I could not bring myself to care for his, er body, sir. It's his dress, sir, it is too, well, unusual."

"Perhaps you could persuade him to be less outrageous?" said Charles.

"I think not, sir," said Culpepper. "I imagine the gentleman is past all *human* influence. I believe, in short, sir, that it would take an act of God, and since God has allowed him to continue so bizzare, sir, I must conclude that God himself believes him to be past redemption."

"Is there nobody?" asked the heir.

"There's a boot boy," said Culpepper.

"Elevate him," said Charles. "Oh, and, Culpepper, carry Miss Emmett's dog out will you. I believe it requires some attention." Culpepper approached Magpie in a very gingerly fashion. "Very good, sir," he said, taking the dog into his hands as though he were lifting a keg of gunpowder with a lighted fuse. "I am sure that a suitable tree will be found somewhere."

Charles and Lucy sat side by side in slipper shaped baths full of steaming water, perfumed with rich-smelling oils. They were so close they could soap each other, and they did. It was delightful, especially for Lucy who was unused to such comfortable bathing. Seeing the Heir naked always brought cries of admiration from Lucy. She told him how superb she thought him over and over again. His body was strong, firm, and straight, broad shouldered and narrow hipped.

"Oh, you are a fine figure of a fellow," she said as she watched him climb from his bath. He put out his hand to help her from hers. "You must be careful not to pay me too many compliments," he said, "or I shall become as vain as you."

"I am not vain," protested Lucy.

"You are," said Charles. "I have seen you looking at yourself in the mirrors. When I first knew you, you were hardly aware of your charms at all. I think that I am going to lose my country girl, and shall have a lady of the town on my hands." He was joking with her, Lucy knew. She joined him by the fire, and they patted each other dry with towels that were warming there. "Still you have more cause to be vain than most," said Charles standing back to admire her nakedness. Her breasts were high, full, and firm, her waist narrow, and her hips curved outwards in what Charles regarded as the most sublime manner. Her skin glowed

313

and shimmered when wet, and there was a shine all over her. Her heavy dark hair was damp from the steam and clung around her face and shoulders like strands of thick black silk. "When Mrs. Royalston comes, you must shop for some suitable frills and fancies to wear, but if I had my way I should cover you in a sack from head to toe, so that no one but myself could see you. I should unwrap you several times a day, and when I had finished with you, tie you up again with strings." His hands were moving over her body again.

"Top priorities," she whispered, as she felt him reach the moist parting of her thighs. She moved closer to him, her soft roundness against his firm hardness, sighed and closed her eyes. He drew her down onto the carpet before the fire, his lips searching for hers. "I think that I shall be strong-willed later," he murmured.

"So much for strong will," said Lucy, looking smugly at him across the breakfast table later. It was already early afternoon.

"Who is Strong Will, by the way?" asked the heir, eating some ham and slices of beef.

"Oh. Just a fellow who takes baths with me," said Lucy.

"Well, if I catch him, I shall trounce him," said the heir.

"Too late," laughed Lucy. "I trounced him myself."

"I suppose he sleeps with you, too?" asked the heir.

"He never sleeps," replied Lucy.

"An insomniac?" the heir suggested.

"An insatiable," she replied.

"Will won't be strong for long," said the heir, slipping his arm around her shoulders. "In fact," he whispered in her ear, "I doubt that Will will find the strength to throw his leg over a horse for the rest of today." They were interrupted in their laughter by Peter Royalston dashing into the breakfast room crying, "I am destroyed."

"Oh, surely not," said Charles. The fellow sank down on a chair and fanned himself with his hand. He was only half dressed.

"Look at me," the fop pleaded. Charles looked, so did Lucy. "May waistcoat has been buttoned in the direction, have you seen what has been provided to care for me?" Charles shook his head.

"A dwarf," said the fop. "There, you don't believe me, I read your disbelief, your eyes betray you, very well, I demonstrate." He rose from his chair, teetered over to the door, and beckoned. "*Voilà*," he cried. A boy stood in the doorway, a very small boy. A very thin small boy, with a very large coat on, and too-big shoes stuffed with straw at the ends of his stick-like legs. "How high is this?" asked Peter, pointing imperiously at the miserable looking child.

"Three feet?" suggested Charles.

"Quate," said the fop. "A dwarf."

"He will grow," said the heir.

"I doubt it," replied the fop. "It is stubborn."

"What is your name, boy?" asked Charles.

"Sam, milord," whispered the boy in a terrified voice.

"And are you stubborn, Sam?" asked the heir of the child recently elevated from the care of boots to the care of the fop's clothes.

"Sometimes," replied Sam. "Milord," he whispered as an afterthought.

Lucy's heart flew out to the poor little fellow; she beckoned to him. "How old are you, Sam?" she asked, taking his hand.

"Oight," replied Sam. "I fink."

"Eight," said Lucy with great show of surprise. "He is tall for eight, why, an absolute giant for eight, I do declare."

Sam grinned, and shuffled his feet.

"That may be so, but you must agree that it is quate unsuitable to dress a gentleman. Aye am used to better sarvice."

"Oh, rubbish," cried Lucy much annoyed at Peter's pomposity, "better service indeed. Why you have never had your own dresser. You have shared Wilchup with Squire Billy. Now just because you are at Pall Mall and the heir's guest, you imagine he should furnish you with a dresser as well as food and lodging. Now sit down and stop fussing."

Peter sat at once but looked mighty petulant.

"'Tis a pity to send such a smart, tall boy back to the boots," Lucy whispered to Charles imploringly. Charles took her point. She wanted to engage the boy to her. "Perhaps Sam likes dogs," suggested Charles.

Lucy's eyes lit up. "Do you like dogs, Sam?" she asked.

"Oh, yus," said Sam enthusiastically, "like anyfink."

"Very well," said Charles. "If Miss Emmett agrees you may take charge of her dog for her, and run errands and such like."

"Oh, I do agree," said Lucy. "I should like nothing better."

Charles pulled the bell rope and summoned the butler. "This young fellow," he ordered, "requires a suit of red livery, with silver buckles, silk stockings, and a pair of well fitting shoes. See to it, at once." The butler bowed and made his way out followed by an amazed Sam saying "Cor" over and over again.

A maid for Lucy was soon engaged, a young woman with large brown eyes and red hair called Cassie. Cassie was Irish, and came, Culpepper told Lucy, "highly recommended." And Lucy saw why as soon as they had been introduced; the maid raced about her closets pulling at the few articles of clothing she had, and ran off below stairs with them, "to get them in order," she said. "And when your wardrobe arrives from the country I shall get that in order too." Lucy didn't dare admit that Cassie had her entire wardrobe in her arms. One white ball gown, one day dress, and one morning gown, did not a wardrobe make, thought Lucy, as Cassie vanished on her mission.

That same night Squire and Mrs. Royalston arrived, both complaining bitterly of the jolting they had got on the journey. Lucy took Mrs. Royalston up to sit by the fire in her salon upstairs, where she could revive herself with tea, while Charles and Squire Billy kept company in the blue drawing room, where a stronger beverage was served. Gentlemen abhorred tea, Lucy had learnt.

Peter Royalston had been locked in his chamber for the afternoon in a pet because of having no dresser, which worsened when he found that Lucy had a maid. And no amount of cajoling from Lucy, conducted through the locked door of his chamber, would persuade him out to greet his aunt and uncle.

"Bah, the fellow's a daisy," the squire told Charles over their brandy. "Yer haven't sucked up this bosh about his marrying Lucy I hope."

Charles was quite surprised to hear this remark from the squire.

"Don't you believe it?" he asked.

"I don't," replied the squire. "If yer want my opinion it's a blind."

"A blind?" asked Charles. The squire nodded and looked cunning.

"The chit has set her cap at another, in my view."

"Oh, you think so," said Charles trying to sound casual. "Any ideas?"

Billy tapped the side of his nose with his forefinger, and winked. "I have, but I await further developments," he said. "But rest assured, as soon as I know the identity of the man, you shall be the first to know."

"Much obliged to you, sir," said the heir with relief.

"Don't mention it, sir," replied the squire.

"Oh, Puss," sighed Mrs. Royalston. "What a grand establishment this is. The very 'tip of the top' I vow. Had anyone told me that I should one day be couched in a house at Pall Mall, I should have told them they were mad. But here I am, and here are you." Lucy smiled and looked around her salon. It was both smart and cosy. "But you know we are both quite out of touch here, don't you, Puss?" Mrs. Royalston went on. "I was watching the fashions in the streets as I passed, and my, it has all changed since I was last in the metropolis. What is in vogue in Leicestershire is quite out here, I am afraid." She viewed her scuttle-shaped bonnet with some distress, and then pointed to her gown. "I shall not dare to move about for shame, persons will think me a shriek on feet."

"I do not much mind being thought out of fashion," said Lucy, "since I have never been in it. But I must admit I am not immune to a pretty gown when I see one."

There was a knock on the door and Lucy called "enter" just like the heir did. Sam opened the door, a transformed Sam, a spick and span Sam in a red suit, white stockings, and black shoes, with smart silver buckles on them. He had been scrubbed and wore a small white powdered wig upon his head.

"Dammit, Sam," cried Lucy, forgetting her ladylike ways with the shock of seeing him so changed, "You are a swell, and no mistake!"

Sam, however, had not forgotten his manners. "Fank you, Miss," he said, bowing stiffly. "Now hiff I may, I have come to take chawge of the dawg." Lucy had to fight not to laugh, as she watched Sam lift Magpie from the floor to her feet. "Anyfink else, miss?" he asked. "No, Sam," said Lucy almost crying with mirth. "Nufink else, fanks."

All through supper Mrs. Royalston complained of being out of touch with the London mode. She and Lucy had both changed for supper with the invaluable assistance of Cassie who had put up their hair in most becoming style. Mrs. Royalston's had been drawn over horsehair pads and powdered. But Lucy, who knew the heir's hatred of powder either on the hair or on the face, wore hers in a knot on top of her head, with a few stray tendrils pulled loose to curl about her cheeks. She wore the white dress that had been made for the Landsdun ball, and Mrs. Royalston wore her yellow (without the ship).

"Puss and I must both shop," said she firmly to the squire, "or we shall be disgraced."

"That's what I feared about coming," the squire told Charles. "Shopping. Why is it that women *must* shop, and men don't give a hang whether they shop or not?"

"I love to shop," crowed the fop hopefully.

The squire sent him a withering look across the table. "I said *men*, not daisies," he said.

"Do you like to shop, Miss Emmett?" Charles asked of Lucy. "I never have shopped in my life, sir," she replied. "But I am sure I should not hate it." This formality was kept up between them all through supper, for Mrs. Royalston's sake. Unlike her husband this lady was firmly convinced that her nephew meant to marry Lucy, since Lucy had not told her otherwise because the heir thought it better to leave things as they were at least for a while. Neither she nor Charles wanted to do a thing to shock the dear lady. That was why Charles had to wait for what seemed hours before he could venture across the landing to Lucy's bedroom like a thief in the night. Lucy had told him that Mrs. Royalston would insist on tucking her up, then returning to make sure her shift was pulled down, and wouldn't work up and strangle her. Such was Jemima's devotion to her Puss, that all dangers were taken into account. If she could have slept for her she would have done.

"What the he—," cried Charles, tripping over an obstacle in the dark just when, at long last, he had achieved Lucy's door.

He looked to the floor, and saw a sleep-eyed Sam, curled up like a cat there. "What are you doing here?" whispered the heir harshly.

"Me duty, milord," Sam said. "Watchin' out for Miss Emmett and the dawg." The heir's temper quickly left him; he was quite moved by this display of loyalty from the urchin. "Well done, Sam," he said, bending to pat the boy's head. "Duty first. I shall give you six pence tomorrow." Then he stepped over the child and slipped into Lucy's room.

"I have decided that the ladies shall shop at my expense," he said when he joined his guests for breakfast on the next morning.

"Oh never, sir," cried Mrs. Royalston, "we are already in your debt."

"Not at all, ma'm," replied Charles. "I am in *your* debt, I assure you, for were it not for the charming company of you two ladies, I should be a dull fellow at the present."

"What do you think, Billy?" Mrs. Royalston asked the squire, who was halfway through a second plate of kidneys. Billy looked at the heir, and then at Lucy, who was purring like a kitten who had just bathed in cream.

"Come," said Charles to the squire, "let me treat the ladies, sir."

"Looks as though one has already been treated," said the squire, "with or without my leave."

So at eleven o'clock, Lucy, Mrs. Jemima Royalston,

Cassie, and Sam with Magpie set off in Charles' carriage for the shops, with a letter, signed and sealed by him that directed all purchases made by the ladies be credited to him. Lucy had asked how much they should spend, and he replied, "What you please."

The shops in Bond Street, The Strand, and Holborn Passages, and Leicester Square were full to overflowing at that time of day with ladies, so well turned out, that Lucy and Mrs. Royalston felt like absolute country mice. The haughty, turned-up noses of the shopgirls confirmed their sense of being dowdies. But the moment the heir's letter was produced, the noses twitched, and those same girls were turned to models of helpful politeness. In every shop, Lucy and Jemima were sat on chairs, while the very latest in gloves, shoes, pelisses, tippets, reticules, and bonnets were brought for their close perusal.

Lucy swore off stockings at twelve shillings a pair, but Cassie said "*Only* twelve shillings, a bargain," so Lucy forced herself to order six pairs. She and Jemima bought, and bought, and bought, sending Sam and the coachman back and forth to the carriage laden with band boxes and parcels from every shop.

"Oh," said Jemima, "I am quite spun, with all that. Where now?" They were back in the coach.

"Oh, home," said Lucy. "Gowns," said Cassie.

"Gowns?" Lucy cried. Of course they had been buying "oddments."

"But where?" she asked Cassie. The maid looked gleeful. "Well, if money is no object," she said, "there is only one place in town, and that is at the house of the most renowned *modiste* in London."

"Who's that?" asked Lucy, quite awe struck by this lofty sounding description. "Madame Blanche," cried Cassie, squeezing Lucy's hands. Lucy looked at Mrs. Royalston. "Shall we?" she asked. Mrs. Royalston nodded. "No harm just to look," she said.

"Bruton Street," Cassie called to the coachman.

As it turned out they bought no gowns at all, for the price of the cheapest at Madame Blanche was one hundred guineas, and Lucy was quite put off. "What, a hundred guineas for a plain checked cotton half dress?" she asked Mme. Blanche, a lady whose fashionable appearance was somewhat married by a wall-eye. "Oyez," said Mme. Blanche, "but Modom won't faind another like it in the *ton*."

"I should think not," retorted Lucy. "For I should be the only one fool enough to pay a hundred guineas for it." Then in spite of Cassie's calls to stay and view some more, she said, "No, dammit, it's beyond all sense," and marched out.

"No gowns," asked the heir. "Didn't you see anything that caught your fancy?"

"Oh, we did, dozens," said Mrs. Royalston, "but Puss was quite right, we couldn't put you to such an expense."

"One hundred guineas," Lucy said to Charles. "One hundred guineas, talk about sauce."

"Well, from what I understand," said the heir, "that would generally not be regarded as expensive by a lady."

"That's what I told her, sir," said Cassie. "Three hundred for a simple ball gown should not be thought exorbitant."

"Did you think you were being taken for a flat?" Charles asked Lucy, with a twinkle in his eye. She nodded, thinking what Roger Emmett would do if someone handed him a hundred guineas—or handed him ten guineas for that matter.

"I couldn't wear anything so expensive," said Lucy. "I should just feel guilty and miserable." Charles smiled at this and left her salon, colliding as he did so with a string of footmen bearing that morning's purchases. For the next hour or so Lucy and Jemima Royalston were in transports trying on all the separate pieces of delightful frivolity. They were still in this orgy of trying on and taking off, when a footman came to the salon door and said, "Madame Blanche." Lucy's eyes nearly left their sockets; so did Cassie's, and Mrs. Royalston sat down so heavily on a tiny gold chair, that it creaked with protest. Madame Blanche swept in, all smiles, with a troop of girls after her carrying a huge collection of every sort of material imaginable. It seemed the heir had summoned the august lady to Pall Mall and that Lucy and Mrs. Royalston were to order three gowns each.

Lucy's head spun, spun, and spun, and then lost itself somewhere in the air as she poured over the rich array before her, all thoughts of expense and practicality lost with her head. Such cries of "Oh, lovely, and oh, look, and oh, my," had never been heard in Pall Mall before.

"Sam," she said, resplendent before her long mirror draped in a length of plum-coloured velvet, "go down to the heir, and ask him if he would venture an opinion on a gown." Sam was off at once like a hare, and in a minute Lord Melton a gentleman renowned for finding such matters as ladies' gowns boring beyond bearing, strode into Lucy's salon and took a bonnet off a chair to sit down.

"What do you say?" Lucy asked, turning a pirouette for his opinion.

"Turn again?" he requested, and she did so. "Quite the thing," said the heir. "The colour becomes you. Will there be a *thing* to wear with it?" he asked Madame Blanche. She looked perplexed. "A theeng?" He nodded. "You know, to er, cover the, er." He pointed vaguely in the direction of Lucy's chest. Madame Blanche smiled.

"Ah," she twittered, and signaled to one of her girls. "It's just that they all cut quite low," Charles explained to Lucy. "Shouldn't want you to get a chill."

Madame Blanche suggested a short round cape, to be made of the same colour velvet, lined with the same colour but in silk, and edged with sable. "That's it," said Charles. "That's the touch."

"And a sable muff, and a bonnet," said Madame Blanche, putting the bonnet on top of Lucy's abundant curls and handing her the sable muff. "Alright," said Charles, viewing the picture before him with great pride and satisfaction. "Throw the lot in."

"Oh, Charlie," cried Lucy, running to him and throwing her arms around his neck, "you are the kindest, dearest, most wonderful man on the earth." Then forgetting herself completely, she covered him with kisses. "And I love you," she said.

Charles was quite breathless and beaming when she had finished, and then to his gratification, Mrs. Royalston approached him, hugged him to her maternal bosom, and said, "You will excuse my familiarity, my lord, but you have made Puss and myself the happiest ladies in the world today."

Charles handed her his silk kerchief to wipe her eyes, and discovered to his amazement that his own were wet, too. "Think nothing of it, Ma'm," he said gruffly. "For what is a gentleman alive for, if it is not to pleasure ladies?" His eyes caught Lucy's, and he saw her fond smile. He took his kerchief back from the emotional Mrs. Royalston, patted her hand and coughed, then sat down and made himself comfortable.

"I'm blowed if I don't quite *like* this caper," said the heir to Sam. "It's the sort of thing a fellow might get used to without much difficulty." Charles felt quite drunk with the joy of giving. Unlike Georgiana Stowe and the other ladies of wealth who had surrounded him through his life, Lucy and Mrs. Royalston took nothing for granted, they did not regard his presents as their due. These were ladies capable of surprise and wonderment, and that fed his good spirits.

Lucy ordered another gown, this time of blue satin that exactly matched the colour of her eyes. "Oh, that's it," said the heir, jumping to his feet. "That's the colour, we shall have sapphires for you to wear with that."

"Sapphires?" gasped Lucy. "Sapphires for me?"

The heir nodded, and told Sam to run off and bring Mr. Culpepper to him. Culpepper arrived shortly to find his young master as merry as anything, surrounded by ladies and ladies' "articles." He said, "I want Jeffreys the king's jeweler brought here, he is to bring his case. Miss Emmett must have some sapphires to wear with that gown, don't you agree?"

"Oh, yes, my lord," said Culpepper, smiling at Lucy Emmett's glowing face. "I shall see to it at once." He left the room, pleased to see the heir lighthearted again. He had become too solemn and weighted down with problems over the last few months, far too serious for a young man. Lucy Emmett had broken through the heir's reserve, and for that alone Culpepper felt that she deserved all the sapphires in the world.

Lucy had sapphires and pearls in the end, for the necklace, earrings and bracelets she chose from Jeffreys' rich showcase contained both. She put the earrings in her ears, removing her plain gold hoops to do so, slipped the bracelet about her wrists, and then Charles himself fastened the necklace around her throat, taking advantage of their closeness to steal a kiss. "Now see how grand you look," he said, and Lucy, seeing in the mirror a person altogether transformed from a simple beautiful girl, into what looked remarkably like a singularly beautiful lady of quality, could only say, "Oh."

It had been impossible for Mrs. Royalston to ignore the fondness with which Lord Melton bestowed the jewelry, nor could she deny that there was an intimacy between Lucy and the heir that was unspoken, but demonstrated constantly. She knew well that a gentleman simply did not give jewelry to a lady unless there was an understanding between them. Later when she was alone with Lucy, she asked her if her suspicions were correct, and Lucy admitted that they were. Naturally Mrs. Royalston was upset that her nephew and her beloved Puss, were not, after all to be joined. But seeing Lucy so happy amply made up for her disappointment and Lucy's assurance that Mrs. Royalston should remain like a mother to her, no matter what the future held in store, quelled the lady's fears. Mrs. Royalston had thought Lucy would cease to need her once she had embarked on her new life in London, but she was wrong, for over the next few days she was Lucy's constant companion. The weather was cold but fine, and they were able to drive out to the parks and gardens of the metropolis and take the air, along with the other fashionables.

Peter Royalston, however, had been quite put out to hear that he was not to be allowed to make the ultimate sacrifice and marry Lucy for the heir's convenience but was only required to pretend he was betrothed to her for the present. And it was to placate the fop's disappointment that the heir announced a visit to the theatre at Covent Garden. Each day at five an officer keeper from the theatre was sent round to the houses of the quality and nobility, to inform them what was to be performed on the following evening, and when a pantomime was found to be on the bill, Charles said they should see it and have supper served in his box.

The theatre proved a revelation to Lucy, whose preconceived notion was that it would be a place of quiet dignity and solemnity. In fact she found quite the contrary when she entered the heir's box with the rest of the party, looked down into the pit, and saw it filled with ladies and gentlemen all shouting, whistling, and catcalling at the principals on the stage.

The whole house was in an uproar. "What is wrong?" she asked the heir as they took their seats. Charles looked at the programme, "Oh, lord, they have changed the bill," he said. "It's Shakespeare." He handed Lucy the programme.

"*Macbeth*," she read. "A tragedy in five acts."

Peter Royalston was hanging over the edge of the box trying to catch the attention of one of the outraged gentlemen in the pit. "Lard, what happened to the pantomime?" he called. "Don't know," yelled back a rip from the pit. "Return our money," shouted another from the gallery.

Lucy's eyes moved over the theatre; every pair of jaws there was fully employed, either with eating or with talking, or with bawling and hooting at the stage. The actors played on like a dumb show, for not a word could be heard from them.

"My, what a mob," said Lucy. "I'd rather face a devil's army."

"Oh they'll quiet down when we come to the porter," said Charles. "They came here tonight for a comedy show, and they'll not hush 'til they get one. Yes, I was right, they are going to cut to scene three." Lucy knew nothing of the play, but it seemed Charles was right, for the actors had had a conference in stage centre, with much serious head-shaking. This huddle had followed an attack on the principal actress, a lady of advanced years who had shouted bravely above the roar, "That which hath made them drunk hath made me bold."

At once a shower of fruit had been hurled at her head, and cries of, "Yes, ma'm, so bold you take our money under false pretenses. Get off and bring on the porter."

"Here comes the porter," whispered Charles, as the other actors moved off, and a hush fell upon the house. On came a man with a red nose and a lantern, to loud cries of "Hurrah."

"Here's a knocking indeed," said the man to the audience, and from that moment the house was content, apart from floods of laughter and applause at appropriate times. This scene was so successful that it was performed three times, and at the end of the third came an interval, when supper was brought to the box by servants from the house in Pall Mall. Charles sent Sam out to the piazza to buy some russet apples, which they munched with their meats. Lucy thought it all very grand. It was while they were engaged in their supper that an engraved card was brought in to the heir, who after reading it, frowned and said to Lucy, "This is from Giles Wentworth." Lucy's heart began to race and her cheeks grew quite hot.

"What does he want?" she asked. "Wants to join us. He's outside," said Charles, looking puzzled.

"Wentworth," cried the heir, when Giles entered. "I thought you went to Berkshire from Landsdun?"

"Did," said Giles. "But the hunting was off, bad weather. Miss Emmett, upon my life," he said, raising an eyebrow and passing a wicked glance over Lucy's low decolletage and then her sapphires. "I thought it was you, but I couldn't be certain, for you are so changed." Lucy blushed and tried to smile. "Thank you," murmured Lucy.

"Georgiana's still in Hampshire?" he asked Charles casually.

The heir nodded. "The Royalstons are my guests at Pall Mall for a while," he said. Lucy noticed Charles was looking uncomfortable and Giles Wentworth's searching looks were not the only reason. When she turned and looked at the house, she realised they were being peered at from all quarters. People were actually craning their necks to get a better view of their box, and some ladies, and more gentlemen, had their glasses trained on her. This close scrutiny, Lucy thought, was very bold, even rude; she was aware of a whispering and a murmuring running through the other boxes, and she realised with a shock that she was being discussed, and that some of the discussion was disapproving, certainly among ladies.

"Did you mean to make a complete cake of yourself, or are you quite mad?" Giles hissed in Charles' ear.

Charles looked around the theatre, he saw what Lucy had seen, but he better understood the significance. Giles was right, he shouldn't have brought the Royalstons to the theatre, he should have let them come alone. But he didn't want Giles to have the satisfaction of feeling that he'd caught him for a cake so he said, "You know that Miss Emmett is engaged to Mr. Peter Royalston, I suppose?" Lucy wished she could hear what Charles and Wentworth were saying, but they whispered close. She saw Wentworth look at the fop, saw Peter simper, and then Wentworth turned back to the heir and whispered something. "Don't be a damned 'flat,'" said Giles to Charles, "and don't take the *ton* for a herd of blockheads. That's been tried before, with savage consequences."

"The *ton* may think what they please," said Charles.

"Oh, they will," replied Wentworth, "and they do, my dear chap, for the hum is on, and you'll have to brazen it out; thing is, can Miss Emmett?" Charles looked across at Lucy. She was already wilting under the gaze of a thousand eyes, and more cutting tongues.

Giles handed him another card. "From Dolly Charrington," he said. "You and the party are invited to join her after at Berkeley Square." Charles looked across the theatre and saw Lady Charrington sitting in a box

327

opposite. She inclined her head when she caught his eye and smiled.

"You daren't turn Dolly down," said Wentworth, with what Charles thought was quite a gleeful tone of voice, "for that'll cause a riot."

Charles knew he was right; Lady Charrington was one of the foremost hostesses in London. Nobody turned Dolly down without falling foul of her spiteful tongue. "Better go and brazen it," whispered Giles, "or she'll really think there's something on."

"Did you bring her here?" asked Charles of Giles.

"What, Dolly?" asked Wentworth. "My dear fellow, Dolly brought me, you know how close she is to Mrs. Stowe, and if you would let the chit parade through St. James's in your carriage, you mustn't be surprised if the tongues wag. Dolly has spies through the length and breadth, my dear fellow, why she knows every stroke." Wentworth seemed so taken up with excitement, that Charles began to suspect that he might be to some extent responsible for Dolly Charrington knowing every stroke. Perhaps Giles had stirred the pot a little, just to add a dash of intrigue to what seemed like being rather a dull season. "Tell Lady Charrington that we'll be pleased to join her," he said. Giles stood up and smiled. "Oh, and Giles?" Wentworth looked down at him. "Do make it clear to Lady Charrington that Miss Emmett is spoken for."

Giles laughed. "Oh, my dear fellow," he said, spreading his hands in a pleading gesture, "would I do otherwise?"

Squire Billy swore off going to Berkeley Square in spite of his wife's protestations; he said he was tired and would return to Pall Mall. But unknown to anyone except Sam, who had given him the address, he took a chair to a bagnio in Star Court, where the whore-mistress wore the robes of an abbess, and kept the house well stocked with both nymphs and more mature strumpetry. The squire found the ladies there both fast and keen, and for three shillings he had his pick for the night.

Lucy and Charles had hardly entered Lady Charrington's before Lucy and Mrs. Royalston were separated from the heir and Peter by Giles Wentworth. "Come along and meet Lady Charrington," he said, hardly giving Charles, who had been collared by a group of ladies, a backward look. "Miss Emmett," he said to Lady Charrington. "Come along, Mrs. Royalston, I shall get you a drink." And then he wafted an irate Mrs. Royalston off into the crowd of guests before she could insist upon remaining at Lucy's side.

"Miss Emmett, my pleasure," murmured Lady Charrington through thin, painted lips. Lucy thought that she must be sixty under the paint, although the mask proclaimed a mere thirty-five. To Lucy that seemed like a hundred. The questions came fast and furious, with no time for considered replies. "You come from Leicestershire, don't you, moppet?"

"Er..."

"Yes, of course, weren't you at the ball at Landsdun?"

"Well..."

"You were, I didn't go myself—had a pip. It was a success, I hear?"

"It..."

"Pity I missed it, everyone went."

Lucy looked around. Most of the people in the room had been at the Landsdun ball; there was a lady in a black dress she recognised, and there were the other bloods, Willie Caruthers, Plunkett, and Pinkerton, now talking to the heir.

"How was dear Georgiana?"

"Well."

"Does she know you—wait, she doesn't, or does she, I think Giles said that she did, are you close or not?"

"With whom?"

"Why, moppet, Miss Stowe of course, though I think not, for she has never mentioned you, and if you were I should know absolutely, for her mother is my dear, dear friend from girlhood days. What a match she has made for her child, quite the touch. No more than everyone knew, though. Dear Melton, such a sprite and sturdy, and Georgiana has had a 'tendre' for years, what do you say?"

"Well," started Lucy, and at once she was gobbled up again, the thin lips hardly pausing for a lick. "I've never heard of the Emmetts, they aren't *known*, are they, what are they perhaps in trade?" This last word was uttered with such disgust Lucy thought nothing worse could be imagined.

"Farmers," she replied.

The lips curled with horror. "Farmers?" A high laugh followed.

"What manner of farmers?"

"Farming," replied Lucy like lightning. The lips paused for a second and then shrieked, "What? *Farming* farmers?"

Lucy nodded. Worse than tradespeople, she feared, and she was right.

"Good gracious," said Lady Charrington, recoiling, "I suppose Leicestershire must be swimming with 'em." Then her voice changed and she put her lips close to Lucy's ear. "Are you being pressed?" Lucy frowned.

"By whom?" she asked. Lady Charrington nodded over to where Mrs. Royalston was standing with Giles Wentworth, looking very distressed at being parted from her for a minute.

"I don't know what you mean," said Lucy.

"She does," said Lady Charrington. "You better warn her off, pushing you in from the periphery. I know her type, and she'll get short change from the *ton*, I can tell you. So be wise and go back to the country, we don't like pushers here."

Now it was Lucy's turn to recoil. She hadn't got the full meaning of Lady Charrington's words, but she understood the lady was telling her and Mrs. Royalston to leave the town, and she felt put out.

"Well," said Lucy. "This is the first time I have been invited to a place, only to be told to leave."

"Not at once," said Lady Charrington, patting her hand, "for I am sure you are not at fault, moppet. Certain ambitious persons have taken you in, I suspect. You've fallen flat, poor little thing. Never mind, I am sure there is a farmer for you somewhere, a *farming farmer*, on my word." This amused the lady and her cronies who had gathered around hugely, and they laughed, quite inelegantly. Lucy suddenly understood; this Lady Charrington was warning her off the heir—not only off the heir, but off any gentleman, thinking her fit only for a working farmer, which apparently was regarded in this elevated society as being the lowest of the low. The lady also thought that Mrs. Royalston was a person of the lowest sort too, and that really raised Lucy's ire; but she bit back her temper and smiled. She had already learnt enough from quality people to know that one should smile, even when one's intention was to kill. "Madam, the world has obviously grown much more evil since you entered it," she said to Lady Charrington. "Pray excuse me." With that she dropped a most graceful curtsey, and swanlike, glided away to join Jemima Royalston.

"Are you alright Puss?" Mrs. Royalston asked when she was joined by a very pale-faced Lucy.

"Perfectly, dear," said Lucy, planting a warm kiss on the lady's plump cheek.

"Been roasted?" asked Giles, with a smug grin.

"Tolerably well, thank you," said Lucy. "Are you pleased?"

"You know how I love pain," returned Giles.

"Especially other people's," said Lucy.

Giles laughed. "I have been keeping Mrs. Royalston entertained," he said.

"Painfully or otherwise?" Lucy asked, looking worriedly at the lady, who appeared very uncomfortable. "I suppose she has been roasted too?"

"Mrs. Royalston," asked Giles, taking Jemima's hand, "have I been anything but the most correct of gentlemen to you?"

"Oh Puss, do you think we could leave?" she asked.

It was no easy matter to leave Berkeley Square, for Charles was quite tied up in conversation, and Peter Royalston had become Lady Charrington's next target, and seemed quite unaware that he was one, preferring to believe that Lady Charrington's close questioning of him stemmed from a flattering interest. The fop was flying high, and short of beating him senseless there was no way to get him out, Lucy knew. She sat Mrs. Royalston down, and tried to catch the heir's eye. When she managed, she silently mouthed "Leave," but he shrugged his shoulders and was caught up again in conversation.

"Useless trying to make a dash," said Giles at her elbow. "Not the thing."

"Why don't *you* go away," Lucy hissed at him. "You damned mischief maker."

"Well, I'm damned," said Wentworth. "What have *I* done?"

"You know very well what you have done," said Lucy. "There is no need for me to tell you. The fox always sniffs his own stench first."

Far from being put out by this, Giles Wentworth seemed to enjoy it. He caught Lucy's arm. "Is the heir worried?"

"Not a bit," snapped Lucy, "why should he be?"

"Oh, quite," said Giles. "Then why are you?"

"Me?" laughed Lucy. "Worried?" She tried to move away from him, but he held her fast. "Listen, what did you say to make Dolly Charrington turn green?" he asked.

Lucy smiled. "I just told her she was an evil-minded old bat," said Lucy. She had not been prepared for the roar of the laughter from Giles Wentworth, nor had anyone else, for all faces turned in their direction.

"And so she is," wailed Giles, tears pouring down his face, "but I swear no one has ever had the nerve to tell her before, to her front."

"Hush," whispered Lucy, "everyone is looking at us."

"My word, so they are," said Giles, looking around at the ring of amazed faces that encircled them. "Oh, I say, let's get them really humming," he whispered to Lucy. "Let's really give 'em something to choke on." And then he caught her in his arms and kissed her full on the mouth, before the entire assembly. Before she could draw breath from the kiss the heir was at her side.

"You swine, Wentworth," he shouted above the shocked silence that filled the room. The eyes swung from Wentworth and settled on the heir's furious face. "I'm going to beat you for that," said Charles in a black voice.

"I dare you," Giles returned. "I dare you, Melton, for that'll really put the cat among the pigeons here." The heir took a step forward, but Lucy caught his arm.

"He's right," she said urgently. "Charles, don't, for it will spoil everything for us. Peter," She called shrilly. "Peter?" Peter Royalston teetered over to her side. "I have been insulted," she told him.

"Lard," exclaimed the fop, looking from the heir to Wentworth. "Oh, I say."

"We must go," said Lucy.

"Oh, may, very well," said Peter, offering his arm. He could see the heir's eyes were still locked with Wentworth's in a very ugly way. "Charles," begged Lucy in a whisper, "Mrs. Royalston."

"I shall expect satisfaction," said Charles to Wentworth.

"And I shall not deny you," said Wentworth to Charles. They both bowed coldly, and then the heir crossed to where Jemima sat, white as a sheet with worry and mortification for Charles and Lucy's embarrassment.

"I hate you, Giles Wentworth," said Lucy as soon as the heir was out of earshot, "and it will serve you right, if he runs you through."

Giles smiled and shook his head. "You don't, you know," he said. "You don't hate me, and I'll tell you another secret. If it did come to a pitch with points, you'd be hard pressed to know which of us to pray to have spared—I dare you to deny it."

"I deny it," said Lucy firmly.

"Liar," laughed Giles.

CHAPTER XI

Points Or Pistols?

In which Lucy discovers that resignation is not her style.

"Tell him that I require him to choose two seconds."
Lucy sat motionless, like something frozen in ice, as she
heard the heir command Culpepper to carry the message
to Giles Wentworth's house in Portman Square. "The time
shall be tomorrow morning at dawn, the place Parliament
Hill fields, the choice of weapons, shall be left to
him—points or pistols, it is immaterial to me."

"Very well, my Lord," said Culpepper, casting a glance
at Lucy whose face was a white mask of worry. On either
side of her sat Mrs. Royalston and Peter, both looked
almost as distressed as she.

The squire's whereabouts remained a mystery, for on
their return from Berkeley Square, he had been found
absent. Under normal circumstances Mrs. Royalston
would have made further enquiries, but worries for Billy
had been driven from her thoughts by this development in
Lucy's affairs. She took the girl's hands in hers and finding
them freezing cold, began to rub them to restore the

circulation. "Oh, he does not mean it, dear Puss," she whispered. "What, to shoot at another person or to brandish swords, in cold blood, never." Her voice did not carry much conviction, for Charles was pacing the blue drawing room looking mighty grim and determined.

"Charles," Lucy managed at last. "I beg you to reconsider. This is pure folly, to risk two lives over something as insignificant as a kiss. Why, it is madness."

"Not at all," said Charles in a very abrupt fashion. "Now that you have fully acquainted me of Wentworth's declared intentions, any doubts that I may have entertained over the necessity of fighting him have departed."

"Oh, Lard," gasped Peter, half thrilled and half terrified. "He talks of killing."

"I wish now that I had not told you of his visit to Ragby Hall," cried Lucy, "or that he had vowed to have me for himself. You talk merrily of fighting him, but what if he kills you?"

Charles smiled. "Lucy, a gentleman does not consider that eventuality. Would an army march to meet a foe, believing it had already lost the war? No. Doubts are destructive; positive thought alone triumphs. Off you go, Culpepper."

The manservant shook his head wearily and left.

Lucy threw up her hands in dismay. "Oh, dammit, Charlie, cannot you see this is just what Giles wants? A duel between you shall cause an even bigger scandal."

"Do not imagine that I am ignorant of that fact," the heir said coldly. "But tonight, by kissing you before the entire company at Dolly Charrington's, Giles brought me to your side, and the exact nature of our relationship is now common knowledge. By embracing you he also cast doubts on your honour, and for that he must pay. He has forced my hand."

Lucy ran to Charles and took his hand. "Oh, but my honour is nothing compared to your life."

The heir drew her into his arms. "On the contrary," he murmured, "to me your honour is everything, for it is coupled with mine; you are part of my life now.

Wentworth shall not besmirch either of us; you must know what the gossips will say."

Lucy drew away from him and sighed. "That you and I are passionately involved," she said wearily.

"Not just you and I." Charles was angry, he clenched his fists until his knuckles were white. "The deduction will be that Wentworth shares you with me."

"Oh monstrous, inflammatory lies," wailed the maternal Mrs. Royalston, throwing her arms around Lucy. "Oh, Puss, what a wicked place London is. Oh my dear young sir, you must know that Puss repulsed him, he might advance forever and she would retreat longer. Let them say what they please."

"Mrs. Royalston, I am quite resigned to their knowing that Lucy is my mistress, but I am damned if they shall say that my mistress is a whore."

"Perhaps the honourable Giles will apologise?" Peter ventured. Charles laughed. "Wentworth? Apologise? He would die first."

Lucy felt her heart flutter with panic. The words Giles Wentworth had spoken to her before she had left Dolly Charrington's were still ringing in her ears. *If it did come to a pitch with points, you'd be hard pressed to know which of us to pray to have spared.* She feared that Giles Wentworth might understand more of her deeper nature than she did herself.

"Come," said the heir. "It is almost two o'clock, and you look so weary. Go to your bed, I shall join you later."

Lucy shook her head. "No. I shall wait with you, until the message comes from Portman Square," she said. Her hope was that Giles would either apologise or refuse to be called.

Mrs. Royalston and Peter retired, and Lucy and Charles waited together before a dying fire. They must have dozed, for they were startled by a disturbance at the front door. Sam came in and said that it was the squire, "Drunk as anyfink."

Three footmen were woken to help him to bed, separate from his lady, who would not tolerate him in her

337

room, for the disorganised condition of the lacing on his breeches told her where he had been.

About an hour after Squire Billy, Culpepper returned with a grave face, and informed his master and Lucy that he had delivered the message to Wentworth, not at Portman Square but at D'Aubignys Club. Culpepper had found him there, engaged in a card game it appeared.

"What did the gentleman say?" asked Charles.

"The honourable Giles Wentworth sends his regards to yourself, my lord, and to Miss Emmett, and says that he will call on you here, later this very morning."

Lucy breathed a sigh of relief. It was still possible Wentworth might prefer to apologise.

Once in bed, though, her worries returned, and although the heir slept soundly at her side, her eyes stared out into the darkness. *What if Giles did not apologise? What if he did not step down?* Her tortured brain conjured pictures of the heir lying mortally wounded, blood pouring from his heart, from his head, from his throat; and then it would be Giles, breathing his last.

A grey misty morning saw her numb and exhausted. She hardly touched her breakfast and Charles, who ate heartily, was very concerned. She excused herself, saying she felt a little feverish. And while the heir went off to write a letter to the earl, saying that he hoped to return to Landsdun before the week's end, but saying nothing about the duel, Lucy went to her salon, where she sat by the fire with Mrs. Royalston, Sam, and Magpie for company.

Jemima Royalston embroidered and made light conversation in an attempt to cheer Lucy, but the girl sat in glum silence, staring into the fire with Magpie on her lap. It seemed impossible to Mrs. Royalston that only a short time ago Lucy had been so very happy, full of hope for a future with the heir. "Puss, dear, do not look so sad, I pray. Sam, sing a song to cheer your mistress."

"I don't know nuffink," said Sam, miserably.

"Oh you unaccommodating little wretch," said Jemima Royalston.

Lucy smiled and ruffled Sam's hair. He and Magpie

338

both echoed her dejection. She had begun to wish that she had never come to Pall Mall. Because of her the heir's reputation had been damaged, his position in society threatened, and now he might even die. She tried hard not to think about Giles Wentworth; her feelings towards him were almost too powerful to be contained. She felt anger and hate, and yet she kept seeing his wicked smile, hearing his low laughter, and last night, when she had told him of her scathing remark to Dolly Charrington, how he had delighted in her forthrightness. She knew him to be ruthless, capricious, irresponsible, and cruel, and yet he intrigued and excited her. She loved the heir, of that she had no doubt; where Giles Wentworth was concerned, her feelings, she had to admit, were somewhat ambivalent.

Sam sprang up from the floor and ran to the window. "He's here, miss," he shouted. Lucy was on her feet at once and ran out of the salon. She met Charles at the head of the stairs. "Charles, do not tell me that I cannot hear what you and Wentworth say to one another, I shall not bear to be waiting in my quarters. The worry and the suspense shall kill me. If you say that this is men's business I shall scream," she said, running down the stairs in front of him.

"Good morning, Miss Emmett," said Giles, as she entered the blue drawing room. "By God, you look as jaded as I feel."

Lucy leaned against the door, to get her breath, and studied Giles. She deduced that he had come straight from D'Aubignys, he wore the same clothes as he had worn at Dolly Charrington's, his lace was soiled and crumpled and undone at the throat and wrists. There were dark, dissipated shadows under his mocking green eyes.

"Giles, for heavens sake, apologise to him," begged Lucy. But Wentworth looked past her to the heir, who had arrived at the door.

"Melton, my dear fellow. I have a devilish head, and took the liberty of sending a servant for some brandy and bitters." He walked slowly away from Charles and Lucy and sat down in a chair, stretching out his legs and pushing his hands deep into his coat pockets. He surveyed Lucy, from beneath lowered lids. The butler arrived with a silver tray. Upon it was a Rummer of brandy and bitters. Giles took it without a word and sipped it slowly, still watching Lucy, who had sat down opposite him, feeling very uneasy. The heir shut the door after the butler.

Giles raised his glass to Lucy. "The only cure for too much of this, Miss Emmett, is more of the same. You think me a rake!"

"I *know* you are one," retorted Lucy.

"Oh, such certainty," crowed Wentworth. "Those words have cut me. Beneath this tortured, raddled, and dissipated front, there is a saint, struggling to be released."

"You got my message, Wentworth?" asked Charles.

"Did," smiled Giles.

"And your reply?" He met Wentworth's eyes, and saw them narrow.

"I take you up," said Wentworth, "naturally."

"Giles, no," cried Lucy, her voice full of anguish.

The heir turned to her. "Lucy, please."

But she was on her feet. "Charles, you must let me talk to him. I insist."

Giles laughed. "She insists, Melton, deuced bad form to deny her."

"Giles, I have told the heir all about your visit to Ragby Hall."

"The devil you have."

"Yes I have. He knows everything."

"Everything?" asked Giles, raising an eyebrow.

Lucy blushed. Wentworth was implying there was more to their meeting at Ragby Hall than she had told the heir. He was right. She had not told Charles she was attracted to Wentworth.

"Everything," she repeated emphatically, taking care not to meet his eyes.

"Honest little body, ain't she?" said Wentworth to Charles. "Lucky fellow."

"Now you must know that I am utterly uninterested in you," Lucy went on.

Wentworth groaned. "Cut again," he said mockingly.

"And so you must see that this duel will serve no purpose. I have explained to the heir, that I do not want..."

"What *you* want has nothing to do with it," said Giles, finishing his drink and running his forefinger around the rim of the glass. "The heir asked for satisfaction, and I shall not deny him."

"Giles, you have had your fun," Lucy said.

"I'm damned if I have," he replied. "But I must say, the picture brightens. For look at the turn since last night; there's Dolly Charrington penning a missive full of panic and outrage to Mrs. Stowe in Hampshire. She tells of the heir stewing in a sweaty, lustful bed. I'll wager that at any time, Mrs. Stowe will come pounding down like Boadicea in her chariot. The general will muster troops—or rather troop, namely Dolph—to storm in and drone at you. Miss Stowe will have the vapours, and now there is to be a duel, which will delight the gossips. There may even be a death, which will cheer some lucky coffin merchant."

"Oh Giles, how can you be so flippant?" cried Lucy.

"Damned if I am being," replied Giles. "Being realistic."

"But you enjoy strife," said Lucy.

"Did I deny it? No." Wentworth looked at Charles, who said, "There may be two deaths, Wentworth, you have forgotten the earl. His health has improved somewhat over the past weeks, but his heart will not stand worry or excitement."

"Ah yes, I had forgotten the earl," said Giles. "You will have noticed, Miss Emmett, the reverent tones." He widened his eyes, and spoke in a hushed voice. "The earl. We might be speaking of a deity, might we not? Landsdun. The line. The inheritance. The name."

"Have a care, Wentworth," said Charles, but Giles continued, "Do you realise, Miss Emmett, that if I despatch this fellow, it will be the end of all that?"

"I do," said Lucy, "and that is why I beg you—" But Charles silenced her.

"Do not beg, Lucy. Now, Wentworth, what is it to be, points or pistols?"

"Shall we toss?" asked Giles blithely. They had to call Culpepper and borrow a coin, for neither of them carried money. "Heads for points, tails for pistols," said Wentworth. "Give the coin to Miss Emmett, Culpepper."

Lucy took the coin, and with a sinking heart spun it. It came down tails. She was delighted.

"Oh bad luck," said Giles to the heir.

Lucy laughed. "Bad luck?" She said, "Charles is a dead shot."

"He is," said Giles. "Only one better in the whole of Europe."

"Who's that?" asked Lucy.

"Me," grinned Giles.

After Giles had left, Lucy begged the heir to reconsider; if Wentworth refused to apologise, perhaps Charles should apologise to him. "For what?" the heir had asked.

"Well, couldn't you back down?"

"And be called a coward?"

"I should rather be called a coward than declared dead," said Lucy. But Charles would not be persuaded, and went off to seek out Willie Caruthers and Pinkerton, to ask them if they'd be his seconds.

Five minutes later Lucy walked into her salon, and found Sam there. "Note," he said, handing her a piece of folded paper.

"Who is it from?" she asked, puzzled, for it was grubby and covered with scrawled figures, which appeared to denote sums of money.

"Sir Wentworf," said Sam. "Told me to give it to yer in private." Lucy understood the significance of the figures at once. Obviously Giles had used the paper to scribble down his bets at D'Aubignys. She unfolded it, and read the scrawled message.

"Be mine, and I shall back down."

"Infernal sauce," hissed Lucy, tossing the note onto the fire. Giles had reckoned on her being prepared to give herself to him to save the heir's life. Perhaps she should, but then Wentworth should have won. She sank down on a chair, trying to make up her mind what to do for the best. Her head was in a spin, and to make matters worse Cassie entered with an engraved card, saying, "Lady Charrington waits outside in her carriage. She asks if you will receive her?"

"No, I won't," said Lucy, tossing Lady Charrington's card onto the fire. "Tell the old besom to go away. And you go away too, Sam, and take Magpie with you." Sam looked quite hurt. "Oh, Sam, I am sorry," cried Lucy, hugging him, "but I am in such a turmoil."

"Come along, Sam," said Cassie, taking the boy's hand.

"If the heir does get blown out, shall we be living wiv Sir Wentworf?" Sam asked as he was led to the door. "I've got me living to fink of."

"Did you hear the child?" Cassie cried. "Born in a beggar's shed in Monmouth Street, and he talks about making a living. He earns more than I already. You mercenary little whelp."

Lucy breathed a sigh of relief as the door closed behind them, but her peace was short-lived, for the door burst open only minutes later, and Dolly Charrington swept into the room.

"How *dare* you refuse me," she snapped. "There is not a lady in London who would refuse to entertain me."

"Wrong," replied Lucy. "Here is one who just did." Dolly Charrington did not allow this remark to set her back. "Take my cape," she ordered Cassie, who had run in after her. "I have come here to speak, and speak I shall."

Lucy sighed and nodded to her maid, who took Lady Charrington's cape. Lucy watched as Lady Charrington settled herself on a chair opposite her, noticing that the maquillage was even more garish in the light of day—the thin lips a mere scarlet line, the crepey skin of her throat hung in folds, and her stiff low-cut bodice, displayed ruined breasts. Lady Charrington had painted the backs of her hands with white lead to cover the brown mottling that betrayed her years. The woman looked ridiculous, although she must have been a beauty once, for she had fine, large eyes, chestnut brown and still lustrous.

How age destroys beauty, Lucy thought. *but how vanity destroys dignity*.

Lady Charrington lifted her quizzing glass and peered

at Lucy. "Now Miss Emmett, since last night I have received further intelligence of your antecedents."

"From Giles Wentworth?" Lucy asked.

"The source is immaterial. Suffice it to say that your lineage, if we may call it that, is considerably more suspect than I had even imagined."

"You have heard that I am a bastard," said Lucy. "I suppose Giles told you that as well?"

"I repeat, the source of my information is immaterial, but you will understand that I regard your being couched here with the heir as an extremely grave matter. I feel bound to tell you that I have written to my friend Mrs. Stowe, who is at present engaged in preparing her daughter for a Christmastide marriage to the heir, and it is for Georgiana's sake I am come here today."

"Go on," said Lucy.

"Miss Emmett," continued Lady Charrington, "you are very young and very beautiful, and at first I imagined you were an innocent. But now I perceive that you are possessed of a worldliness beyond your years, so I can only speculate as to the methods used by yourself and those persons who sponsor you, to entrap the heir and cause him to act in such an unseemly manner. For until this time Melton had been a young man of impeccable behaviour. True, he is a blood, and on occasions high spirited, but immoral never, and indiscreet not at all. Now I understand that a creature such as yourself, without position, breeding, and even parentage, must play a clever hand, and even a crooked one—"

"Come to the point," said Lucy, fighting back her fury.

"At once," said Lady Charrington. "I offer you the sum of five hundred guineas, to leave Pall Mall at once, in short leave London, and never see the heir again."

Lucy was stunned. "Why should you offer me money?"

"Let us say that your being here is against my interest, and that I offer it also on behalf of Mrs. Stowe, who would do the same if she were here."

Lucy stood up and pulled the bell to call Cassie. "Have Lady Charrington shown out, will you," she said.

Lady Charrington laughed shrilly. "Very well, six hundred."

"If you do not go," said Lucy, "I shall strike you."

It was not until she heard the door close behind Lady Charrington that she sat down by the fire, covered her face with her hands, and sobbed and sobbed. But she dried her eyes quickly, for there was a knock on the door.

"Enter," she called, trying to compose herself. It was Culpepper.

"Lord Melton is returned, Miss Emmett," he said; then he looked closely at her.

"You are upset?"

"No," said Lucy.

"Shall I call Mrs. Royalston or Cassie to you?"

Lucy shook her head, then burst into tears again. Culpepper at once took her hand, and let her lean her head against his waistcoat, which was soon quite saturated.

"Oh, Culpepper, this is all my fault, I must leave Pall Mall."

"There, there," whispered Culpepper, "you shall leave. Lord Melton will establish you in a house of your own—why there is one in Richmond that sounds as though it will suit very well. Lord Melton shall take you to see it shortly."

"No," sobbed Lucy, "I must go back to Leicestershire."

"What, to that pauper's farm?" asked Culpepper. "It is Lady Charrington who has upset you?"

"She offered me money to leave, Culpepper. Oh I felt so ashamed, she said it was against her interests that I should remain with Charles and that if Mrs. Stowe were here she would do the same."

"Oh, that is to do with the king," said Culpepper.

Lucy recoiled with shock. "The king?"

Culpepper nodded. "Well, this scandal touches the monarchy, you see."

"I do not see," said Lucy. "This is the first time I have heard the king mentioned."

"Well, the king and queen are to attend the wedding, for the earl and the Stowes are well thought of by the crown. Now, both he and the queen are respectable and pious, and he is a devoted son of the Church of England, and obstinate, and narrow-minded to boot. He is mad, as well, but that is beside the point."

"You mean, if the king hears of this, he will disapprove?" Lucy ventured. She felt very confused.

Culpepper nodded. "Worse, Lady Charrington is very close to the queen and she and Mrs. Stowe have set their hearts on Miss Stowe being engaged as a Lady in Waiting at court, once she is Countess of Landsdun. Now any scandal spoils her chances."

"I see," whispered Lucy. "The duel will make matters much worse."

Culpepper nodded. "There will not be much sympathy for Lord Melton nor support," he said. His words proved correct, for when Lucy joined Charles in the blue drawing room, she found him very dejected. All his circle had refused to stand as seconds for him. "Willie will stand for Giles, so will Pinkerton. Plunkett pretended to be out, when I called at Cavendish Square."

"But, Charles, they are your friends."

"Were," said Charles. "Then I tried Clive; 'sorry old fellow, won't be in town,' he said; then I went round to D'Aubignys; cold silence when I walked in. Still I asked a few fellows."

"What happened?"

"Oh, lots of foot shuffling and embarrassed looks. Then lots of excuses. So I have no seconds." He laughed bitterly.

"Oh, it's all because of me," said Lucy.

"No, no," said the heir.

"Charlie, it is. They disapprove so much, they see your conduct as outrageous."

"Lucy, there is not a man among them who is not a rake, a libertine, or an adulterer. I am none of those things, and I am damned if I shall be bowed down by their hypocrisy. I shall fight Wentworth, and then we shall do as we intended, set you up in a house, and then—"

Lucy interrupted. "Charles, we shall never be happy like that. How will our love survive, with me hiding away and you visiting furtively. Your honour means so much to you, and I could not bear the sniggering and the whispering. Charles, I beg you once again to reconsider." The heir just smiled and kissed her, and said he would ask the squire to be one of his seconds, and Peter to be the other, and then left the room to seek them out. To Lucy, there seemed only one thing to be done. She asked Sam to call her a chair, ran upstairs to fetch her bonnet, cape and muff, and very soon was being carried along through the muddy thoroughfares of the metropolis.

There was an extremely haughty butler at Giles Wentworth's house at Portman Square, who was not at all amused by young ladies who ignored the proprieties, pounded upon the door knocker, and said breathlessly, "Lucy Emmett."

"Whom do you wish to see?" asked the towering fellow in a hollow, disdainful voice.

"Mr. Wentworth," said Lucy.

"If you will hand me your card, and then return to your sedan, I will carry the card to the *Honourable* Mr. Wentworth, and ask if he will receive you."

"I have no card," said Lucy, pushing past him, "and he shall receive me, for it is a matter of life and death."

"Congratulations," said Giles. He was lunching alone at a vast polished table.

"For what?" Lucy rapped out.

"Why, for getting past the butler," Giles said, gesturing to a chair at his side. "Fancy some quail?"

"I have not come here to be sociable," retorted Lucy.

Giles laughed and said, "Intimate, perhaps?" Then helped himself to some quail from a silver dish. Lucy noticed he had been shaved, and wore spanking clean lace, red velvet, and his black hair was drawn back and secured with a bow. In spite of the formality of his dress, he looked, as always, rakishly casual.

"I take it you got the line?"

"The line?" Lucy asked.

Giles laughed again and said, "Miss Emmett, if you had not had the line, you would not be here." A deep blush coloured Lucy's cheeks, and she pushed her hands deep into her muff. "Oh, *that* line. Well, yes I did."

"Do sit down, Miss Emmett," sighed Wentworth.

Lucy slammed the palm of her hand down upon the table. "You are setting out to ruin a gentleman of the highest..." Giles did not bat an eyelid at her outburst; he merely interrupted her. "What about some wine?"

Lucy's lips began to quiver, and to her horror she realised she was going to cry. She fought the tears, but they had already begun to flow. "You cannot do this to him," she whispered, sinking onto the chair beside Giles. She lifted her muff and buried her face in it. For a full five minutes she sobbed so bitterly that another man might have felt sorry for her, but Giles Wentworth continued to enjoy his lunch, saying when the loud sobbing had subsided a little, "The solution lies with you, for make no mistake, if it does come to a duel at dawn, I shall kill him. I am determined, and when I am determined, I always have my way." Lucy uncovered her face and looked at him. He smiled at her. "His life is in your hands. Just think, you can so easily save him."

"But only by betraying him," said Lucy, removing a small lace-edged kerchief from the pocket in her muff, and wiping her eyes.

"Mr. Wentworth, I really do not know whether you mean what you say, or whether it is just a source of amusement to you—a game. If it is, I beg you to end it now, for it is quite horrible."

"I do not think that you find me quite horrible," said Giles.

Lucy shook her head. "Oh, I do not know, I am so confused, I do not know what to think, nor what to do."

Giles said calmly, and with some amusement, "I have told you what I want, and I have indicated what you should do." He was leaning back in his chair, dabbing the corner of his mouth with a white damask table napkin. He had been quite unperturbed both by her tears and by her confusion. *How he infuriated her.* "I suppose you always get what you want," she snapped angrily.

"Damned if that ain't true," said Giles brightly. "Can't deny it. Melton told you that I was a winner."

"Yes," said Lucy, "and a ruthless and despicable beast."

"Hah!" crowed Giles. "So ruthless, and so despicable—such a beast, that you come running to me." He lifted his wine glass in a mocking salute, studying her over the rim of the glass.

"You know why I came, because I love Lord Melton," cried Lucy.

"I told you that you would," said Giles, still watching her through half closed lids. "Correct me if I am mistaken, but I believe that I have completely penetrated your armour, and I'm damned if it has not been a good deal easier to achieve than I thought."

"Have you no scruples?" gasped Lucy.

"You talk about scruples, when the sapphires you wore at the theatre are worth a good deal more than Georgiana Stowe's famous emerald ring? I do not imagine that scruples brought you those sapphires, nor that scruples brought you so very far from your very humble, not to say shameful, beginnings."

"You think me entirely mercenary, don't you?" said Lucy.

"You hate riches and luxury, then?" asked Giles.

"I value love more," retorted Lucy.

He smiled, and his face became almost evil for a moment. "I know," he whispered.

Lucy sat and stared at him for a while. He had taken her breath away. She loathed his ruthlessness, but his singlemindedness astounded her; she almost admired it, although she knew that he deployed it to score petty triumphs, and on this occasion, to destroy her union with Charles. He had it in his power to do that. Her heart beat faster. It was because she was afraid of him. How different he was from the heir; at first she had half wished Charles was more like him—more carefree, more scornful of convention, but now she saw that Giles Wentworth's easy, humourous surface had an interior as hard as stone, as cold as ice, and as relentless as an iron trap. The heir often

349

appeared cold, too controlled, but he had shown her he was capable of love and of tenderness, where Giles Wentworth cared only for himself. She spoke at last. "If I refuse to give myself to you and the duel does take place?"

"And I kill Lord Melton?" said Giles.

"Yes, but what will you have gained?"

"You," he replied.

"How?" asked Lucy.

He laughed. "What *would* become of you, dear Miss Emmett, without a gentleman's protection? The *ton* would not tolerate you, and you would be cast out, and would end in strumpetry."

"Never," cried Lucy.

"Oh, that would be your end, I assure you; it is a path that has been trodden by countless poor girls, once as beautiful, spirited and proud as you, Miss Emmett. But you see, for a person such as yourself, without a name or fortune, you must either attach yourself to a gentleman who has both, or marry a fellow who has neither. And after your taste of rich living, I doubt the latter would suit. This scandal will deny you the former, so only the streets remain. If you have any doubts as to the result of that course, take a chair to Star Court in Westminster or go at night to St. James's or Vauxhall, go to Cheapside, and look well—understand what it means to sink into degradation. Watch the whores, many of them younger than you, Miss Emmett, in their filthy rags, their bodies and beauty destroyed, and their brains as well, by the pox. See them shuffling along in the shadows, searching for food in the filth of the gutters, starving, dying, for even the most derelict beggar will avoid them. Or perhaps you need not go. Perhaps for a girl pulled from the womb of a beggar, those scenes can easily be imagined."

"Who told you my mother was a beggar?" Lucy cried.

Giles smiled. "You know that Miss Stowe told me you are a bastard, but your friend, Peter Royalston—that extraordinary antique Macaroni—furnished me with the further details of your unfortunate antecedents."

"And you told Lady Charrington?" Giles took her limp hand in his and nodded.

"I knew it," said Lucy.

Giles raised her hand to his lips and kissed it. "Lady Charrington told me you refused a great deal of money to leave Melton. But remember, whatever happens, she means to destroy you and part you from him. Now you fully comprehend the situation, you will understand the fate that may be avoided if I have my way."

"How fortunate I am that you have my interests at heart," said Lucy.

"Well, there's no doubt you have landed upon your feet." Giles looked confident as Lucy smiled and took a sip of wine from his glass.

"So if I come to your bed now, I can be sure that you will apologise to the heir, back down from the duel, and cease this pursuit of me?" She allowed him to draw closer to her and touch her breasts with the palm of his hand. Then his lips met hers, and on this occasion she was quite unmoved by his kiss. As he drew back from her, smiling, she realised that he was so unconscious of her true feelings, so certain of victory, that he believed his power over her was complete. *Giles Wentworth, you are a fool*, she thought. "How can I be sure that you will keep your word?" she asked.

"You can't," he said. "You will have to trust me." He took her hand and stood up, pulling her to her feet, and pressing his body against hers.

"I do not believe you are to be trusted," said Lucy. He was kissing her throat.

"Knowing whom to trust is damned important," whispered Giles.

"Whom to trust, and *when* to trust," said Lucy. "The poor woman that you got with child—the one who drowned herself—did she love you?"

"Let us not speak of her," groaned Giles, searching for her mouth. "She was a foolish, hysterical creature, and I tired of her."

Lucy turned her face away. "*Did* she trust you?"

He laughed. "Don't know. But, oh, you are different."

Lucy laughed. "Yes I am, I should not drown myself."

"What would you do?" whispered Giles.

"Drown you," said Lucy eluding his embrace.

Giles laughed. "Cut again, Miss Emmett." He watched her raise her hands to the ribbons that secured her bonnet under her chin and untie the bow, with a great show of having made up her mind. Lucy saw his eyes light up.

"Oh, if only Melton knew what you are prepared to sacrifice for love of him," he said, "he would erect a statue to you, and entitle it 'Martyred for love.'" At the door he stopped and turned to extend his hand to her. "And I wonder what he would say if he knew how you *loved* to be martyred?" The confident smile vanished from his face when he realised Lucy had untied her bonnet, only to tie it more securely. She picked up her muff. "Call me a chair, will you?" she asked briskly. "I must return to Pall Mall." For a second Lucy had the pleasure of seeing Giles Wentworth absolutely nonplussed, then he regained his composure.

"My dear Miss Emmett, you think that I bluff. I do not, I assure you."

"Oh, no. I am quite certain you mean to kill the heir in the morning by fair means or foul," said Lucy, walking past him towards the door.

He followed her into the hall. "And you will risk that rather than give me satisfaction? You will regret it when you weep over Melton's corpse in the morning."

Lucy turned to face him. "At least he shall have someone to weep for him," she said. "Whereas if you fall on Parliament Hill fields I'll wager not a tear will be shed."

"Cut, after cut, after cut," said Giles, smiling, though his eyes were hard as nails. "Call Miss Emmett a chair, will you?" he said to the footman.

"Besides, you forget something," said Lucy.

"Enlighten me, then," said Giles.

"Even a winner can lose," said Lucy, as she turned and followed the footman.

"Not *this* winner," called Giles.

Lucy left Portman Square to the sound of his mocking laughter. All the way back to Pall Mall, she suffered the pangs of hell. She had gone to Portman Square, prepared to give herself to Giles Wentworth, if she could but be certain he would stand by his part of the bargain and call off the duel. But her exchange with him had convinced her he was a person entirely without moral scruples and that he could not be relied upon to keep his word. She had to admit that when she had gone there, she had felt a certain attraction—that he did fascinate her, that his embraces would not be abhorrent to her. But for all his outward good looks and dashing charm, Giles Wentworth was the devil. And no wise person made a deal with the devil, for that was a certain way of coming to a bad end. Lucy was determined that her end should not be a bad one, in spite of all the dire prophecies that had been made throughout her young life.

She arrived at Pall Mall, slipped into the house through the back entrance, and ran upstairs by the servants' flight. Not a soul saw her, and soon she was safely in her salon. She sat down by the fire, her chin on her hands. "Oh God, if only I could be sure Charles would win. But Giles is the better shot," she groaned, "and he is utterly ruthless." There was a tap on the door, and Mrs. Royalston entered. "Why, there you are, Puss, where have you been?"

"Out," said Lucy dejectedly. "Has Lord Melton asked for me?" That was another worry. Charles would be wild if he knew she had gone to Portman Square, furious if he learned what she had intended to do there.

Mrs. Royalston shook her head. "No, he has been closeted with his lawyer."

"His lawyer?" Lucy cried, jumping to her feet. Mrs. Royalston nodded, then started to wring her hands. "He's making his will," she whispered.

"His will?" Lucy felt the blood drain from her face.

"Not just a will, Puss, for he has had a Deed of Conveyance drawn up for that house in Richmond. He has bought it for you. The squire and Peter are in there with the heir and the lawyer to witness both documents. My husband says that if the heir does die, you shall be a rich woman, for he has made magnificent provision for you. Oh, he is a saint, that young man. Death confronts him, but his first thought is for you, and your future."

"If only he would understand that I *want* no future without him," Lucy cried. "Why must he fight Mr. Wentworth? Men, oh men. They will do everything except the sensible thing." She paced the floor distractedly. "He says he is going to fight for my honour because he loves me—have you ever heard of anything so foolish? My God, to die for love, when one might live to love for a whole lifetime," cried Lucy.

At that moment the door opened and the heir walked in. Before he could utter a word Lucy had run up to him and slapped him full in the face. "You will not listen to reason will you? Will you? Do you imagine I want your money or a house in Richmond? You are just like Mr. Wentworth and Lady Charrington. You think me altogether mercenary."

"Lucy," Charles ventured, but she wouldn't be stopped. Her expression was furious, but tears poured down her cheeks. "Fancy rising to Giles Wentworth's bait," she went on headlong. "He is not *worth* dueling with. To think you would jeopardise your life and our happiness for that fellow." She had completely dissolved into tears now, but as the heir tried to comfort her she pulled furiously away. "Call it off at once," she said. "Send a note to Mr. Wentworth and tell him you shan't meet him."

"Lucy," said the heir, desperate to get a word in edgewise. "I can't do that. It is a question of honour, and I shall not be called a coward."

For a minute, Lucy stood and said nothing. Then she began to laugh hysterically.

The heir stood perplexed, for she was laughing and crying at the same time. To make matters worse Mrs. Royalston had started to cry too. "Ladies," he began, hoping to calm them.

"Go and meet Mr. Wentworth in the morning. Go and have your head blown off. What an honourable corpse you will make." Then she fled to her bedroom, slamming the door behind her.

The heir looked at Mrs. Royalston and shook his head. "What is to be done?" he asked. To his utter amazement,

Mrs. Royalston jumped to her feet, snatched up a pair of fire tongs and threw them at him. Charles dodged the fire tongs, only to find Mrs. Royalston beating upon his chest with her fists. Then she threw her arms around him, hugged him, slapped his face, and ran sobbing after Lucy into the bedroom.

"There is nothing to be done," said Mrs. Royalston. She and Lucy sat holding hands on Lucy's bed. "Lord Melton is adamant, the carriage is called for five in the morning and his pistols are sent to the gunsmith to be checked and oiled, with express instructions that they be returned tonight. It is inevitable, Puss, a gentleman must do what a gentleman must do . . . even if it is ridiculous," she added.

"And I suppose a woman must sit by and let him," said Lucy. Mrs. Royalston didn't like the thoughtful expression on her face.

"No," Lucy said. "Dammit. I'm not going to sit about and wait for him to get himself killed."

"He might not be killed entirely," ventured Mrs. Royalston. "He might only be maimed. There are a lot of fellows walking about without legs, you know, who were once given up for dead. We must not look only on the black side, Puss. There are a lot of things a man can do even though he has no limbs at all."

"For instance?" asked Lucy.

Mrs. Royalston looked flustered. "I'm only trying to cheer you up," she said. "I mean, men who have been shot full of holes have survived to live useful lives."

"As what?" asked Lucy. "Pepperpots?" Suddenly, she smiled radiantly. "I have a plan. Call Sam," said Lucy, jumping to her feet. "By God, I *have* a way to beat Giles Wentworth and save the heir."

Sam followed Mrs. Royalston into Lucy's bedroom a few minutes later, looked around warily when Lucy locked the bedroom door.

"Wot 'ave I done?" he asked. "Wot, am I to be whipped? Cor, I ain't done nuffink."

Lucy ignored his questioning. "Stand by Mrs. Royalston," she said. Sam was mightily thankful to stand by anyone at that minute.

"Now," said Lucy, after taking a deep breath. "I take it for granted that I can trust you both?"

"Oh, Puss, how could you doubt me," asked Mrs. Royalston. "You are like my own flesh."

"What about you, Sam?" Lucy asked.

"Well, it depends wot it is," said Sam cautiously.

"Very well," said Lucy. "Sam, I want you to promise that everything that passes between us from now on shall go no further. I have a plan to save the heir's life, and it must be kept secret. Swear that you won't utter a word," she said fiercely.

Sam considered solemnly. "I swear." He spat on his forefinger and crossed his heart. "Nuffink wot passes between us shall go no furver," he said. "I won't utter a word, unless I am put to the torture, or burned, or tickled, 'cos tickling gets anyfink out of me."

"Quick," said Lucy. "Have you got a shilling?"

Mrs. Royalston rummaged in her reticule and at last produced the coin. Lucy took it and pressed it into Sam's hand. "Laudanum," she said hastily. "Run out and fetch some. Bring it straight to me, and if anyone should enquire where you are going, tell them that you are taking Magpie to—you know what. Now run along." As soon as the child departed she locked the door and turned in triumph to Jemima, who's face had gone ashen.

"Puss, you aren't going to—?"

"I am," said Lucy. "I shall put the drug into Lord Melton's brandy. He always takes a glass before retiring. *That* will stop him."

"Yes, but even if you do succeed in preventing his meeting Mr. Wentworth in the morning, they are bound to meet on another occasion. There is the matter of honour. Oh, Lucy, think again, you must resign yourself," said Mrs. Royalston.

"Resignation is not my style," said Lucy. "The heir shall not meet Giles Wentworth on another occasion."

"But how can you be sure?" asked Jemima.

"Because *I* shall meet Giles Wentworth in Lord Melton's place," said Lucy, squaring her shoulders. "And it will give me the greatest pleasure in the world to shoot him straight between his lecherous eyes."

Mrs. Royalston opened her mouth to argue further, then began to sway on her feet. Lucy caught her just before she toppled over.

"Charles, I have your brandy here," said Lucy. The heir was sitting up in her bed, his case of dueling pistols on his knee. One of the superb weapons was held up to his right eye, and he was sighting along the barrel. His finger was on the trigger.

"I do not think I shall take any tonight," said Charles. "I shall want a clear head and a steady hand in the morning."

This was just what Lucy had feared. "Charlie, you shall have neither if you don't sleep," she insisted. "Now come, drink the brandy, it will help you."

The heir turned and looked at her worried face and laughed. "My word, you still are in a fret, aren't you? Come, cheer up, this matter between myself and Giles is a trifle and will be over in five minutes."

"That's just what I fear," said Lucy. "Charlie, please, please drink the brandy."

The heir took her hand and pulled her down beside him. "Oh alright, if it will cheer you. But I wish you would not look so distraught—this is not the first skirmish of my life, nor will it be the last. I am quite determined to despatch the swine." He took a long gulp of the brandy. "I shan't be facing him holding a buttercup. This is the finest pair of pistols in London, manufactured for me by Durs Egg. Silver mounted with steel-butt caps and cross hatching. The barrels are exceeding straight, and, look here, the locks are fitted with a revolutionary sliding bar safety catch which reduces the chance of them being accidentally set off." He finished the brandy and put the empty glass down upon the side table.

Good, thought Lucy, slipping into bed beside him. Part one of her plan had been successfully accomplished. Suddenly a terrible thought struck her. *What if I have given the heir too much laudanum? My God*, she thought, *What if I have killed him to save his life?* She sat bolt upright and turned to him.

"Charles, Charles," she cried shaking him. "What is it, my dear?" asked the heir, smiling at her sleepily.

"Well, the thing is," said Lucy, trembling and biting her lip. "If I hadn't done it, you would have come back a corpse tomorrow anyway."

"Done it?" The heir struggled to raise himself, but he was almost too weak to move. "Oh, Lucy." She saw that he comprehended completely. He lifted his arm and pointed at her. "Don't," he said, struggling to fight off sleep. But the battle was in vain—his eyes closed, his head fell to one side, and in a second he was unconscious.

"How much did you give him?" asked Cassie. She was helping her mistress into her clothes at four o'clock of the coldest, darkest, foggiest morning imaginable.

"Half the bottle," said Lucy. "Oh, I pray to God it wasn't too much. He seems alright—I mean he is not dead yet, just very still. Give me half an hour to be on my way, then go in and try and revive him. Oh, hurry, Cassie, or Culpepper will be stirring ready to call him for the duel." Cassie hooked up the back of her mistress' bodice, and shook her head. "Well I doubt that amount will prove lethal, but I still think this is a foolish, madcap scheme."

"And so do I," cried Mrs. Royalston who had not slept a wink all night and was sitting beside the fire in the salon, wringing her hands.

"Doubts, doubts, doubts," snapped Lucy who had enough doubts of her own without Cassie and Mrs. Royalston adding to them. "Positive thought and action are what counts. Doubts I can do without, thank you very much. Where is my cape?"

Cassie sighed and settled the cape around her mistress' shoulders. "Well, it will prove a complete waste of time," said Cassie. "Mr. Wentworth will not duel with you, the

358

quarrel is between him and Lord Melton. Besides, you are a woman—gentlemen do not shoot ladies."

"We'll see," said Lucy grimly. "Because I mean to shoot at him, and he'll be a fool if he imagines I won't."

"I dunnit," said Sam, bursting through the door. "I woke the coachman and said the heir wanted the coach outside earlier, 'cos of the fog. Cor, it's ever so fick, so fick that if you spat at it, the spit'd bounce off it and hit yer in the eye."

Lucy was trying on her bonnet and frowning. "Is Parliament Hill very steep?" she asked Sam.

"Too steep for them skirts."

"I'll hitch 'em up," said Lucy.

"Yer can't hitch 'em up when yer pace for the duel," said Sam sensibly.

"Oh, I shall find a solution to that," said Lucy. "I shall get the hang of it all, have no fear."

"Hanged *for* it, more like," said Sam to Magpie, who was lying by the fire with his nose on his paws, watching his mistress with an expression of complete resignation.

Lucy looked at the clock. "Right," she said to Mrs. Royalston. "Go and wake Peter—tell him he is to be at the front door in five minutes. But do not say that I am going in the heir's place—he will discover that soon enough."

"What about Billy?" asked Mrs. Royalston nervously. "He was to be a second, too."

Lucy nodded her head. "No. Let the squire sleep. Sam and Peter will suffice."

Mrs. Royalston rolled her eyes at Cassie and went off on her mission.

"Hand me that case of pistols, Sam." Lucy said.

"You ain't never goin' to pull it off, yer know," he said. "Yer too small. Sir Wentworth is near as tall as the heir. You'll just shoot off his kneecaps."

"I shall find a molehill to stand on," said Lucy with exaggerated patience.

"It'll 'ave to be a big un," laughed Sam.

Lucy sighed. "Sam, who killed Goliath?"

"David did."

"Who was the larger?"

"Goliath was," replied Sam.

"What did David kill Goliath with?" asked Lucy.

"A sling," said Sam.

"Exactly," said Lucy, removing a pistol from the case. "Sam, I have here, not a sling, but the finest set of pistols in London, made by Durs Egg. See, they have incredibly straight barrels, silver mounted with steel-butt caps and cross hatching. The locks are fitted with a revolutionary sliding bar safety catch which reduces the chance of them being accidentally set off."

"Thank God," breathed Cassie, for Lucy was pointing the heavy pistol directly at her.

"With these superior weapons, I am invincible," said Lucy. Then her brow furrowed, and she took a closer look at the pistol.

"Sam?" she asked. "Have you any idea how to fire one of these things?"

"Cor," said Sam. "Women."

CHAPTER XII

Lovers or Enemies?

In which a duel is fought.

Giles Wentworth was so confident of winning the duel that before leaving his house in Portman Square he ordered that on his return at about half past nine, a couple of celebratory bottles of champagne would accompany a hearty breakfast, and his seconds, Pinkerton and Willie Caruthers, would join him. His personal physician, Sir Phineas Flinch, a gentleman of funereal features, with a crooked head, was not invited to join them. First because his presence at the table would mean the bloods being subjected to the goriest details of his latest surgical adventures; and second, much to the bloods' relief, he had told Giles that he was to deliver an anatomy lecture at ten to some students at The College of Physicians, the subject of which was to be *Disorders, dislocations, and deviations in the neck and spinal column*. A subject Sir Phineas Flinch knew well, for he suffered from a deviation of the neck himself.

The four arrived at Parliament Hill fields at a little

before six, to find the Landsdun coach already there, with the heir's coachman beside it puffing hard on a short clay pipe which refused to ignite due to the damp foggy conditions that prevailed. There was no sign of Lord Melton, or anyone beside the coachman. Willie approached the man. "Morning?" he said. "I suppose the, er, heir and so forth are up on the hill?" asked Willie. "Huh," laughed the coachman mirthlessly, then he shook his head which could have meant anything or nothing, depending on one's interpretation.

"Yes or no?" asked Willie.

"Yus, and no," replied the coachman.

This cryptic reply sent Willie wading back to the Wentworth coach through the long wet grass and thistles. In a short while he was wading back with Wentworth, Pinkerton and Flinch at his side, to start the trek up the hill to the flat ground where the duel was to be fought.

Lucy, shivering in spite of her bonnet, cape, and muff, had been waiting an endless half hour. She had arrived at Parliament Hill believing Wentworth would already be there—that she would simply storm towards him, pistol in hand, say something like, "Alright you swine, say your prayers," and then, "Bang," he would drop dead, simple as that. But of course, no such thing. She had hitched up her skirts to climb the hill, but had arrived at the top out of breath and muddy, with Peter whimpering at her side, Sam telling her she "wasn't half a larf," and Magpie who had been supremely reluctant to get out of the coach trying to skulk back down the hill at every opportunity. "So much for my support," she grumbled, looking about her. "'Tis just as well that Giles Wentworth is *not* here yet, for you lot make a damned poor show, I can tell you. Now stir your shanks and lift your chins, and look as though we are something to be reckoned with. Do I look faint hearted? No." She marched over towards a small tree, unlocked the case of pistols, withdrew one, and pointed it at the trunk.

"Aha, Mr. Wentworth. I see you are surprised." She was about to continue when she realised that she was holding the pistol the wrong way round. She fell at once to cursing the gunsmith for making them so ornate that one didn't know which end to expect the noise from unless one were prepared really to scrutinize it. "The end with the hole is for the shot," she muttered, and this bit I hold, and that bit I squeeze. Dammit *why* is it so heavy? My arm is near dropping off. Durs Egg indeed—he laid a bad one here. Aha, Giles Wentworth, I see you are surprised. And well you might be, you swine. No, for God's sake, get up from your knees. Do not cower—die like a man." She nodded her head with some satisfaction and turned her back on the tree, then swung round and took it by surprise properly. It had no time at all to jump out of her way and was dead when she said, "Bang." "That's the way," she muttered to herself, "just shoot the devil, before he has a chance to say..." she lowered the pistol. Giles Wentworth was walking towards her across grass with a sort of easy swagger. Willie Caruthers was beside him, so was Pinkerton, and a man she didn't recall having seen before who walked as though he had a noose around his neck.

"Morning, Miss Emmett," called Giles, waving to her.

"What's she doing here?" asked Willie. "Damned queer for a female to be lurking around at one of these do's."

Giles laughed, "I am not at all surprised to see Miss Emmett where the action is—'tis not the cut of her to languish in bed on an occasion such as this. Besides, I think she hopes to watch me despatched."

"It's pretty puff of her to venture out in such inclement weather," said Pinkerton, looking around. "No sign of Melton, though."

Lucy had expected Giles to approach her, but he did no such thing. He was walking about whistling, *"My lodging is in the cold ground,"* and his companions appeared to be conducting a close examination of the grass.

"Feels deuced spongey," said Willie to Giles. "A real boot sinker, shouldn't want to attempt a sprint on it." He and Pinkerton stamped about testing the surface while Giles continued his tuneless whistling. "Oh, this is ridiculous," said Lucy. "How long will this footling continue?"

"Lard, I do not know," said Peter, "may experience of deulling, I am relieved to say, is nil."

"Mm well, at this rate we will be here all day." She

363

marched up to Giles, who smiled sardonically. "Ah, Miss Emmett? I did bid you a good morning, did I not, though I think that it is not such a good morning, what with the weather, and the er, rather regrettable circumstances. Still, I believe the fog lifts, the sun fights for prominence and, damme ain't that a blackbird I hear trilling?"

Lucy was taken aback by this almost poetic observation and more by Wentworth's easy smile, but she managed to retain her scornful expression.

"'Tis not a blackbird, 'tis a thrush. Now Mr. Wentworth, I am—"

"Ah, a thrush, of course," said Wentworth to Willie and Pinkerton.

"I hope, Miss Emmett, that you will excuse my ignorance of bird song, but I am not such a country body as yourself. You know Willie, of course?"

Willie made a low bow.

"And Pinkers here?" Pinkerton did likewise.

"But Sir Phineas Flinch you have *not* met, I think." He dropped his voice. "You'll excuse his not bowing, he's a trifle screw necked and inclined to spin like a top, if he attempts it. Physician. Wierd cove as you can see, but a rapid bone setter and lightning with a needle and gut."

Lucy nodded to Phineas Flinch and got a grunt and a snort in return. She turned to speak to Giles, but he had walked away from her, still whistling infuriatingly and was testing the ground at some distance from her with the heel of his boot.

"Not at all bad over here, Willie," he called back. Lucy drew a deep breath, and picked her way across the grass to join him.

"Mr. Wentworth?"

"Mm?" said Giles, his back to her.

"Now I think that we have had enough of this mooching. Arm yourself, and prepare to die." Willie and Pinkerton had arrived beside her just in time to catch this remark. They froze. As did Wentworth. "Aha, Mr. Wentworth," cried Lucy triumphantly, "I see you are sur—"

"Just one minute," said Giles turning slowly to face her. "Is my hearing at fault?"

Lucy laughed and raised her arm to show that she did indeed mean business.

His green eyes met her blue ones, and for an instant they were locked in silent combat.

"I am here in Lord Melton's place," said Lucy, tilting her chin.

Giles' eyes travelled from her face to her hands. "I see," he said solemnly. "And am I to be shot with a muff?"

Lucy quickly lowered the arm with the muff at the end of it, and raised the arm with the heavy pistol at the end of it.

The pistol was tilted at an angle that would, if it had been fired at that moment, have planted a shot somewhere near the toe of Giles Wentworth's right foot. He rubbed the side of his nose and judged the angle. "So, Miss Emmett, you mean to destroy my boot? Very well, proceed."

"I have told you to arm yourself," said Lucy.

"Hey," cried Willie who was just getting over the shock of hearing Lucy say she was there in Lord Melton's place. "What the hell is going on, excuse my language, Miss Emmett, but I mean where is Melton?"

"What's all this buffoonery about shooting boots?" asked Pinkerton. "Damned if I thought we were here to shoot at boots, bit of a rum touch, ain't it, boot shooting?"

Giles laughed and shook his head. "Well, my dear fellows, I declare that I am as much in the dark as you two. But I can only deduce from Miss Emmett's peculiarly threatening behaviour that what she says is true. Melton has had an attack of the nidgits—in short done a 'jitter and a shirk'—and that he has sent her to act the man for him."

Nothing could have infuriated Lucy more than the suggestion that the heir was a coward. "Damned lies," she cried, "you know very well, Mr. Wentworth, that the heir has the reddest liver of any man on earth. He was all ready to come here today and meet you. He is only absent because I prevented it."

"Good God, did a Delilah, did you?" laughed Giles. "Snipped off his locks?"

"Mr. Wentworth, you are beneath contempt. Get ready

to die, sir." For some reason this remark did not have the effect Lucy had intended.

Giles Wentworth roared with laughter and slapped his knees, as did Willie and Pinkerton. For a full minute the three of them leant against each other, laughing until they were weak. Lucy, watching this exhibition with high hauteur, tapping her muddy shoe on the grass and saying with a small smile and in an exaggeratedly patient voice. "Alright, alright, laugh away. I shall not begrudge you your bit of fun, Mr. Wentworth, for there is little laughter where you are going. Oh, no. Plenty of weeping and wailing though and gnashing of teeth. Old Nick's not much of a prankster, I hear. He keeps his prisoners pretty busy stoking the fires."

Wentworth, Willie and Pinkerton only roared louder at this.

"Ain't she a bit of a rip though?" wailed Willie, wiping the tears from his eyes. "Damned if I ever met a female party like her."

"Old Nick," wept Pinkerton.

"Gnashing of teeth," hiccoughed Willie. "Oh, what a jape. Wait 'til we tell 'em at D'Aubignys."

"Have you quite done?" asked Lucy.

The three stopped laughing, and grinned at her, then Giles said, "Oh, come on, fellows, the joke is done, Melton ain't here, the duel is off. Let's return to Portman Square for our breakfast. Perhaps Miss Emmett may care to join us and entertain us further?" Lucy dropped the muff, raised the pistol, held it with both hands and aimed it at a spot dead between Wentworth's eyes. "Mr. Wentworth, I am calling you out. I think you a mischief maker, a scandal monger, a cheat, and a rake. Now arm yourself, or I shall be forced to shoot you where you stand."

Wentworth's smile departed, and for a second she saw his eyes flicker. She could see she had scored a hit and his temper was up.

His eyes narrowed, he studied her for a while. "You bluff," he said.

"Oh, no," replied Lucy. "I can be relied upon to keep my word." She held the gun quite steady.

"Very well," said Giles. "If you will lower your weapon, Miss Emmett, we will go through the proper procedure. Since you say that you are ready to act the man, I take it you will be ready to act the gentleman, and conduct yourself as the heir would have done, were he here, according to custom and rule?"

Lucy was slightly non-plussed by this, having imagined all that was required was that the two duellists should swing and face each other, and that the fastest shot would win. So much for her surprise attack on the tree. She lowered the pistol, and her knees began to shake. But by a supreme effort of will she hid her fear from the men.

"I am prepared to abide by the rules of the duel, whatever they may be. But first, I wish to make a few matters clear and understood, for I realise that I may die very soon."

There was complete silence as she continued.

"First, Lord Melton is not a coward. I prevented his coming today by administering a drug. He was ready to defend my honour against the evil gossip of the town. You, the Honourable Giles Wentworth, may smile at that, since I know you cannot believe that a country girl born out of wedlock may be worth defending. But the heir is different. He values me and loves me, even understands me, as I value, love and understand him. We have both felt alone in the world for separate reasons—I, because I was born a bastard, and must carry that heavy burden, while he, despite his worldly advantages, is the last of a great line and carries the name and future of that illustrious line upon his back. We both have our burdens, he and I, and we both have our honour, too. Now it has been put about that I am nothing but a whore, a low mercenary creature, a mere money-grubber. And the Honourable Giles Wentworth has fanned the flames of gossip for his own ends. The heir's name and honour are besmirched because of that gossip, and not one friend could he find in all London to come here with him today. Not from what is called the Quality at any rate."

This caused Willie and Pinkerton to blush. But Lucy had not finished yet. "So, gentlemen, I am here today, not to

367

act the man, or to take Lord Melton's place, but rather as myself: Lucy Emmett, a person of honour who prefers to defend that honour herself rather than allow the man she loves to die on her behalf. Since the rules of this 'sport' are man-made, as is the gun I hold, I am, I agree, at a slight disadvantage and fully understand your finding me comical. The ignorant and unskilled in the ways of the fashionable world are often comical to more knowledgeable mortals. But if the proper rules and procedure are explained to me, I am certain I shall acquit myself, not as a *gentleman*, but rather I think, as a *lady*."

There was loud applause at the end of this speech from Willie, Pinkerton, Sam and Peter. Magpie wagged his tail, and even Flinch managed a low "hurrah." Only Wentworth stood apart, on his face a cynical smile. When the hubbub had died down, and Willie and Pinkerton had finished shaking Lucy's hand and congratulating her on "A damned fine speech," they said, "One has to be *born* a lady, Miss Emmett."

"Oh, no," retorted Lucy. "I think one might become a lady very easily, even if one were born a bastard, for you were born a gentleman and see how easily you have become a bastard."

Willie and Pinkerton could not help noticing that Giles had not taken this remark with his customary aplomb.

"The duel is on," he said coldly. "Consult with your seconds."

"I'll just trot along and explain the finer points," said Pinkerton.

"You," said Giles, "are supposed to be *my* second."

"Er, quite," said Pinkerton. "But thing is, the lady's seconds ain't much of a trump, are they?" Before Wentworth could complain further Pinkerton was off.

Willie Caruthers was not at all keen on the idea of a duel between Lucy and Giles and he said so. "Thing is, I shan't be a party to your shooting her. And she is right—you *have* been spreading a stink about her and Melton. And the further thing is, well, they have had damned shabby treatment one way and another. I ain't sayin' Melton ain't

368

gone and behaved like a flat, showing her off before he's got himself hitched to Miss Stowe. He ain't been discreet. But I'm damned if I don't believe that she loves the fellow and he loves her."

"Willie," said Giles. "You know how I loathe mawkish sentiment. I did not start this business, Melton did, and now his doxy has demanded satisfaction. Well, I was never one for refusing a female satisfaction."

"But she ain't no match for you," said Willie. "Now, you and the heir, that was different, though you boast of being the better shot."

Giles smiled. "Willie, she has come here today to scupper me, and I am not to be scuppered, as you well know. All I mean to do is to teach her a lesson, for I assure you she bluffs. When it comes to the point, she will not shoot—she will never have the nerve. She has a lot in her, but not *that* amount of steel." He patted Willie on the back good naturedly and laughed. "Quit worrying," he said. "I know I have my share of faults, Willie. But do you imagine that I would shoot at a mere girl?"

Pinkerton was standing very close to Lucy, demonstrating the workings of the pistol for her when Willie came across and told them, "Wentworth is ready when you are."

"I am quite ready," said Lucy.

"You have the rules in your head?" asked Willie.

Lucy nodded. "I have." Then she turned to her companions. She kissed Sam, hugged Peter, and told them both to tell the heir that she had loved him well and had acquitted herself with proper dignity. Then she took leave of her dog, and this so moved Pinkerton and Willie that it nearly sent them into a seizure of weeping.

"Did you ever see a hound look so mournful?" sniffed Pinkerton.

"Never," replied Willie. "I am almost persuaded to believe that she is about to take her leave of this life."

"Of course she ain't, though," said Pinkerton. "Wentworth may be a rough slouch in many ways, but he'll never shoot a female. No. I mean Wentworth is a gentleman, for God's sake. A blood."

"Absolutely," said Willie.

Lucy and Giles stood back to back at the centre of the ground, pistols primed.

Wentworth's stance was easy, relaxed, almost nonchalant.

Lucy stood shoulders squared, head erect. But Giles could feel her trembling against him.

"Pity it had to come to this, Miss Emmett," he murmured, as they waited for Willie to tell them to start.

"Yes, it is a pity," agreed Lucy. "When first I met you, I thought we might be friends."

Giles laughed. "There was never any chance of that. Lovers or enemies, that is what it had to be."

"You could never be capable of the former emotion," said Lucy quietly. "You mistake lust for love, possessiveness for affection, and I know you to be untrustworthy. If I had given myself to you it would not have saved the heir, nor our love. And what if you had possessed me?"

Giles laughed again. "Ah then, Miss Emmett . . . But what use to speculate?" he sighed.

"I have no need to speculate; once you possessed me, once you had entirely had your way, then your interest in me would have ceased, you would have turned to another woman so that you might break her heart."

"Oh. Have I broken your heart, then?" asked Giles mockingly.

"No. You have not that satisfaction."

"But I still mean to have you," said Giles.

"What, by killing me?" This time Lucy laughed.

"Are you both ready?" called Willie.

"Why, all you will have achieved is to prevent the heir from having me. Will that give you satisfaction? Do you call that winning?"

"Sometimes," said Giles. "Even I am prepared to settle for a little less of a victory. Ready." He called back to Willie. "What about you, Miss Emmett. Are you ready?"

Lucy's legs had turned to liquid. "Ready," she called.

"Proceed," shouted Willie.

"Well, Miss Emmett. This is goodbye then," Giles said with finality.

They started to pace. Lucy counted off the paces, the perspiration springing out on her forehead. She took the longest strides she could, considering that she was hampered by skirts. "Two, three, four." She had to count ten strides. She felt weak and altogether ridiculous. *Was it possible that two rational beings could find themselves in such a preposterous situation?* "Five, six." Her mind was racing ahead of her. *When she stopped, would she be able to turn and shoot?*

"Well, Miss Emmett, this is goodbye," Giles Wentworth's voice was with her every inch of the way. "Seven." *She was seventeen years of age, she had been away from Ragby only a short time, she was in love, and here she was involved in a duel. Here was the bad end predicted.* "Eight, nine, ten."

"Halt," called Willie.

Lucy lifted her free hand and touched one of her mother's gold earrings for luck, then said a quick prayer.

"Turn," she heard Willie shout. She turned and faced Giles. He was grinning at her. Their eyes met across the distance and she knew what he was thinking. That he had already won.

"Raise your pistols," shouted Willie. Lucy raised the heir's heavy duelling pistol with both hands. She shook like an aspen—the muscles in her shoulders ached. There was a long pause, it seemed endless. She waited and waited, so did Wentworth. The pause was due to Willie having lost his nerve. The next command would be, "Take aim."

"What the hell am I to do?" he asked Pinkerton. "I mean I had thought she would have run weeping off the pitch by now."

"Some problem, Willie?" called Giles, impatiently.

"Take aim," shouted Willie. He and the rest watched as Giles pointed his pistol carefully at Lucy's head.

"*Now*, she will give up," said Pinkerton. But Lucy did not. Instead she adjusted her aim, lowered it, and pointed

371

her pistol directly at Wentworth's heart. Suddenly Lucy's dog broke free from Sam, and Pinkerton watched the fat little animal run howling into the brambles.

Lucy turned her head for a second; she looked quite startled.

"Oh, come on, get this over with," hissed Pinkerton. "It's all bluff, for God's sake."

"Fire," shouted Willie.

To his horror, two loud reports rang out, and both Lucy and Wentworth fell to the ground.

Flinch was at Wentworth's side in an instant. He found him unconscious, blood pouring from a wound in his shoulder, but everyone else had run to Lucy Emmett.

"Oh Lard—she's demised," howled Peter. Sam, Pinkerton and Willie were down on their knees at her side. She lay quite still, her face death white and her black hair sticky with blood.

"The swine," hissed Pinkerton. "He shot at her." He was about to lift Lucy's head onto his knee, but Willie stopped him.

"No, let's get the physician over here," he said. "You, what's your name, run and tell Sir Phineas Flinch to come quickly."

Sam shot off like a projectile. Caruthers tried to part the heavy mass of dark curls so he could find the wound.

"Has he done for her?" asked Pinkerton.

Willie shook his head sadly and shrugged his shoulders, and before long Sam appeared. "Sir Wentworf is turning up his toes and will soon be dead as a herring." This piece of news was not substantiated by Sir Phineas Flinch, who reported Giles Wentworth's shoulder was shattered, but that he was not in fact dying. "But is the young lady in *articulo mortis?*" he enquired.

"Don't know where the *'articulo'* is, Old Twig," said Willie, "but if it's around the head, well, that's where she's been shot, in the damned *'articulo!'*"

The physician conducted a very close examination of the wound and declared it "a mere graze," much to everyone's relief.

"Just winged?" asked Willie.

"And a mite concussed," said Flinch. He selected a small, tightly sealed blue bottle from his black bag, uncorked it, and passed it three times under Lucy's nose with a magician's flourish. Almost at once a tiny sigh escaped from her pale lips, her eyelashes fluttered, her hand moved slowly to her head, and then, glory, her eyes opened. There was a burst of applause for Flinch, which he accepted calmly as his due. The first sight to greet Lucy when the cloud of insensibility passed from her eyes was the skull-like grin of the screw-necked physician. "I am dead," she gasped. "Oh. It is not fair."

"No, no, you ain't dead," said Willie. "But you must lie still." For Lucy was already trying to sit up.

"Help me to my feet," she commanded. "I am quite alright. In the part of society I spring from, if you lie down too long, they will lay you out as soon as look at you."

"She ain't arf right an' all," observed Sam, taking his mistress's arm to help her up. "Take my farver for an example."

"What about your father," asked Willie, who, never having come in close contact with an urchin from the lower classes before, found Sam intriguing.

"Well my farver lay drunk for two days, and woke to find hiself, chucked in a poor hole wivout a box nor a shroud. Stark, bum bare he was—some villain had stole is cloves."

"What, buried naked?" asked Pinkerton.

"Not buried," scoffed Sam. "They 'adn't filled the poor hole in—they don't till they're full." He brushed some of the mud off Lucy's skirts.

"Terrible smell from those open poor holes in summer," observed Willie.

"Severe health risk. Keep clear of all bone yards myself."

"Well, I'll tell yer what he did," said Sam, rescuing Lucy's bonnet from the ground. "He waited till nightfall, crept down Fleet Passage, lurked there for a well-cloved cove, and when one swung by he frottled him for his boots and breeches."

"Murdered a man?" asked Pinkerton.

"Hanged for it," said Sam proudly. "Then he was back in the poor hole, but we ate for a week on what me muvver got for the sale of the cloves, so all is well wot ends well, as they say."

Lucy's colour had returned, and she asked if Wentworth were dead.

"Not dead, but pretty wrecked, I hear," said Willie.

Giles was indeed wrecked. He lay on the grass, his head propped up on his folded cloak. Blood still poured from the wound in his shoulder, but he was conscious and smiled a slow smile when he saw Lucy bending over him. "Ah. Good morning again, Miss Emmett. I hope you will excuse my not rising, for it appears that I have been scuppered. How is your head?"

"It aches tolerably well, thank you. How about you? Much pain?" asked Lucy.

"Yes, thank you," said Giles. "First-class agony. I am enjoying it thoroughly."

"And you deserve every bit," said Willie. "You are a swine, Giles. You said you would not fire at her."

"Didn't believe she'd fire at me," said Giles. "Didn't mean to hit her though—fired wide."

Lucy's temper was up. "You *did* mean to hit me, Mr. Wentworth. I saw it in your eyes as I faced you. I have won this duel with no concessions made to my sex, and you must thank God that I was put off my stroke by Magpie bolting, or that shot would have gone right through your evil heart."

"You meant to kill me?" asked Giles.

"Certainly," said Lucy.

"Well, now you have your chance," said Giles, "for you can shoot again and have that satisfaction."

Lucy paled. It was obvious the finer points of duelling had not been thoroughly explained to her. "What, you mean kill you like this?" she asked Wentworth.

"No, no," said Giles. "They will haul me onto my feet."

To her horror, Lucy realised that Willie was priming a pistol for her. "Do I have to?" she asked.

"Don't *have* to," said Willie. "But it is customary." He

374

handed her the pistol and then he and Pinkerton started to help Giles to his feet.

"No," cried Lucy. "Leave him, I . . . well . . ."

"Changed your mind, Miss Emmett?" asked Giles. "Now ain't that just like a woman?" Lucy turned away from him, in anger told Sam to find Magpie. Wentworth was laughing at her, and though she felt furious with him, she couldn't bring herself to kill him now. It had been different when they had faced each other earlier. Then she had been frightened and had fought for her life. But to shoot a person when he was almost helpless, that was different. Besides, she had no taste for killing, and in her heart she was glad she had not been responsible for Wentworth's death.

"Miss Emmett?" She turned back to Giles. "Might I have a word?" She sighed and walked back to him. "Privately," he said. The others stepped back, and he asked, "Why didn't you finish me? A gentleman would not have gone away without complete satisfaction."

"I am not a gentleman," said Lucy.

"No you are not," said Giles. "You have a lot of steel, but not quite enough."

Lucy smiled. "Well, from what I have learned here today, I'll own that gentleman are superior killers. I mean they have elevated it to an art, have they not? But that does not mean they are altogether superior, and you might learn something too, Giles Wentworth. Because a person is soft, and even compassionate, it does not mean that they are weak."

To her surprise Giles extended his hand. She took it. "How old are you, Miss Emmett?"

"Seventeen," said Lucy.

"I hope to live to see what you are, when you are seven and twenty," said Giles.

"So do I," laughed Lucy. "I hope I am not so hasty, nor so headstrong."

"Oh I hope you are," said Giles, "For think how dull my life would be if you were to change? I should not want to have you, if you were dull."

Lucy quickly withdrew her hand. "Mr. Wentworth," she hissed. "I thought that you would have given up by this time."

"Can't," laughed Giles. "It ain't in me, and it ain't in you either."

Culpepper met Lucy in the hall at Pall Mall, and Cassie came running down the stairs, shocked to see her mistress so mud-spattered and bloody.

Lucy's first thought was of the heir. Culpepper told her they had managed to revive him with alternate hot and cold towels, but that it had taken an age. And as soon as he'd learned that Lucy had gone to meet Giles Wentworth in his place, he'd shouted for a horse to be saddled and had gone off after her to Parliament Hill fields, taking Billy Royalston with him.

"Odd you missed him," said Culpepper. "He must have taken a different route."

"Was he wild?" asked Lucy. Culpepper had no need to reply, his face told the whole story. Lucy felt suddenly very weary and needed to summon all her dwindling reserves simply to climb the stairs.

Culpepper and Cassie followed her, with Peter, Sam and Magpie bringing up the rear. Sam and Peter excitedly furnished the two servants with full details of her morning's exploits, and by the time she arrived at the top of the stairs the details of the duel had been so exaggerated she began to wonder whether she had been involved in it at all.

Mrs. Royalston kept saying, "Puss, you have the heart of a lion." Lucy collapsed onto her bed and shut her eyes. "What an exhausting day it has been," she sighed. "And it's not even time for luncheon yet." Then she must have slept, for when next she opened her eyes it was to see Lord Melton glaring down at her.

"Alright," said Lucy, "I'm sorry." Then seeing that an apology was not going to suffice, she closed her eyes again, feigned extreme exhaustion and heard Mrs. Royalston send Charles from the room. It was four o'clock, and she had slept soundly by the time a tray of tea was brought to her. The heir came with it. This time he did not look as black. He sat on the bed. "Well, I've heard the whole story, and I'm amazed."

"So am I," said Lucy, peeping demurely over the top of her teacup.

"You certainly mangled Wentworth."

"Have you seen him?"

"Just come from Portman Square."

"You spoke to him, then?"

"No, he's sedated. Flinch has set his arm."

"Will he be crippled?"

Charles shrugged. "Gangrene may set in."

"Oh my," whispered Lucy with humor. "To tell the truth, I regret the whole episode."

"So you should," said Charles. "I am very angry with you, you know."

Lucy shrank down in the bed. "I thought he'd kill you."

Charles laughed caustically, "Kill me?"

"Well, he said he was the better shot."

"Bluff," said the heir. "I am by far the superior shot. Wentworth is all bluff. Besides, *you* damn near killed me with the laudanum." Lucy studied the tea leaves at the bottom of her cup. "Charles, I *am* sorry. It must have been awful being drugged."

"It was terrible," said the heir. "I still feel as though I have wool in my veins instead of blood. How is your head, anyway?"

"Dreadful," wailed Lucy. "Mrs. Royalston cut off some of my hair to bathe the wound." Tears started to spill from her eyes. The heir took her teacup from her hands, then kissed her hard on the lips. "Promise you won't drug me again?" asked Charles.

"Promise," said Lucy. "Oh, kiss me again."

Charles did and, as usual, one kiss led to another. "Is there room in that bed, for another casualty?" he murmured.

The singularly desirable freehold residence of the late

Thomas Mullet, Esq, in a situation particularly eligible at Richmond, containing cheerful sitting apartments of excellent dimensions, finished in a style peculiarly tasteful. Airy principal and secondary sleeping rooms and an arrangement of domestic offices adapted to meet the requirements of a family of Quality. Lucy hugged herself and read on. *The detached offices, which are in a spacious stable yard secluded from the residence, consist of a coach house and stabling for six horses.*

"Six?" cried Mrs. Royalston. "Oh, Puss, I can't wait to see it. Go on—go on."

There is a forage loft, rooms for four male servants, harness rooms and minor offices, extensive pleasure grounds. Immediate view of the principal apartments, tastefully diversified by plantations of choice shrubs in a state of most luxuriant growth, a large vegetable and fruit garden, and two paddocks of rich land, containing in the whole some twenty acres.

"When are we to go?" asked Mrs. Royalston when Lucy had finished reading the details of the house the heir had given her.

"Tomorrow," sang Lucy gaily. "We shall all whiz down to Richmond." It was the most perfect day. The sun shone, frost glistened on the hedgerows, the sky was clear, the roads firm, and the horses fast. Everyone was in tremendous spirits. Even the surly coachman up on the box was moved to song.

> Young Tom the coachman's tongue was slow
> A sorry gift of speech had he,
> He'd rather let his horses know his secret thoughts
>   than you or me,
> He whistled, whistled, whistled daily, whether good
>   or ill befell.

"I know that song," shouted the squire from the coach window to the man on the box. "I'll join yer." And he did, singing in a fine basso profundo:

> He whistled sadly, whistled gaily while his horses
>   marked him well—

Soon everyone in the coach was singing and whistling. Even the heir joined in the harmony. They were still singing when they arrived. The house directly overlooked the river. "Look, swans," cried Lucy.

"There's a black un," shouted Sam. "Cor!"

"Do you like the house?" asked the heir.

"Like it," cried Lucy, "I love it." She ran in and out of every room with the rest of the party hard pressed to keep up with her, and she talked all the time, exclaiming at the fine fireplaces, the beautiful mouldings around the ceilings, and the views from every window. She was in the attics, in the kitchens, in the pantries, under the stairs, then down in the cellars, then up again, then out across the yard into the stables, up in the forage loft, and down into the coach house, then back to the house, and into the coach house, then back to the house, and into the hall.

"When shall I move in?"

"When you please," said the heir.

"At once," said Lucy. Then, "Oh! No furniture."

"Money provided," said the heir. They danced round and round the hall watched by the Royalstons, Sam, Magpie, Culpepper and Cassie, who were all delighted to see them so happy.

"What a fine Christmas we shall have," said Lucy and then remembered the heir would not be spending Christmas with her. She withdrew from him. At the end of the week he was going to Leicestershire—at Christmas he would be married to Georgiana Stowe. "Well, perhaps next Christmas," she said, taking his hand. But she did not believe it. He would never be with her at Christmas. For every Christmas he would be at Landsdun with his wife, and there would be children...her eyes met his, she smiled and squeezed his hand. "I shall be ever so happy here," she said. "Promise."

It was dark when they got back to Pall Mall. It had just started to snow and huge feathery flakes were falling so thick and fast that everyone was covered with it, even though it was only a step out of the coach and into the hall. Sam had stayed outside for a minute to throw snowballs at the coachman as he drove away to the stables, but the heir collared him and pulled him aside. "Do you think you will like to live in Richmond, Sam?" he asked.

"Like anyfink," said Sam. "So shall Magpie. He shall chase the swans."

Lucy had gone upstairs with Cassie and the Royalstons, so that they could prepare for dinner. "And will you watch over Miss Emmett for me while I am away?" asked Charles.

"Cawse," said Sam, "ain't I always watched over her?" Charles patted the boy on the shoulder and smiled. "You're a good fellow, Sam."

"Will you be away long, my lord?" asked Sam, following the heir into the blue drawing room. "'Cos if you are, I fink Miss Emmett will pine."

The heir warmed his hands by the fire. "Well, I have to get married, Sam, and then go to Europe."

"Europe?" Sam frowned. "Ain't that away somewheres?"

Lord Melton nodded.

"You don't want to go," said Sam.

"No I don't," said the heir.

"Don't go, then," said Sam. "If I was quality, I shouldn't do nuffink wot I didn't want to do."

The heir laughed dryly. "Well Sam, when you are quality, you often find that you do things, not because you want to, but because it is expected of you—because, in short, it is your duty. I mean everyone has a duty, yours is to Miss Emmett, and mine..."

"Excuse me, sir," said Culpepper. The heir looked across at his man.

"Miss Stowe is here," said Culpepper.

It was typical of Georgiana that she had not come alone. The hall was full of Stowes, or so it seemed. Mrs. Stowe was there, so was the general, so was Dolph, so was Emma. Dolly Charrington was there, too.

"You know what to do," said Charles to Culpepper. Culpepper bowed, and went straight upstairs to tell Lucy and the Royalstons that dinner would be late, that the heir had visitors and would they please remain upstairs. Sam followed him, Magpie hidden under his coat according to the heir's instructions. The silence seemed interminable. At last it got too much for Dolph. "Er. How de do, Melton," he said, making a move towards the heir.

"Dolph," barked Mrs. Stowe. Dolph came to an abrupt halt, and grinned weakly. "Are we to stand here forever?" asked Dolly.

Charles looked at Georgiana. She was veiled, and her hand was upon her father's arm, for support. She was the picture of the wronged woman. Charles drew a deep, deep breath, then turned and walked back into the blue drawing room. No sooner had the footman closed the door than Georgiana burst into tears.

"There, there," said the general.

"He knows what he has done," said Dolly Charrington. "Caused a hum. You know that the king is beside himself?"

"How could you," wept Georgiana, "with *that* girl?"

"A letter has gone to the earl," said Lady Charrington.

"Did you have to involve my father?" asked Charles coldly.

"Huh," said Lady Charrington. "Do you think the earl would have thanked me for staying silent? No. The earl *should* know. He should know his heir is disgracing the line—with a bastard, that has not only been bare-faced enough to parade in his carriage and stewed in his house, but has also shot Giles Wentworth."

"Yes, and she has been bought sapphires from the king's jeweler and has been to Madame Blanche for gowns," wept Georgiana. "How *could* you, Melton? Madame Blanch is making my wedding gown."

"I was ignorant of that," said Charles.

"What? Shot old Wentworth?" asked Dolph.

"Yes," snapped Lady Charrington.

"How?" asked Dolph.

"In a duel," said Lady Charrington.

"My word," said Dolph. "How is old Wentworth, by the way?"

"Shot," said Charles.

"My word," said Dolph. "Imagine? Old Wentworth's been shot? Should I slip 'round to Portman Square, say How de do?" He made for the door, so did the general. "Capital idea," he said.

"Bunty! Dolph!" Mrs. Stowe blocked their escape. Both men returned in misery, and stood as far away from the ladies as they could. Georgiana had sunk down on a couch and was still weeping behind her veil as Emma tried to comfort her. Mrs. Stowe and Dolly stood imperiously in the centre of the room facing Charles who had his back to the fire.

"Well?" asked Mrs. Stowe.

"Well?" asked the heir.

"My word, you have a front," said Mrs. Stowe.

"Look," said Charles. "From what I have gleaned since your arrival, Lady Charrington has written to you in Hampshire and has told you Lucy Emmett is my mistress."

"And written to the earl," said Lady Charrington.

Charles ignored her. "And you have hot-footed it up from Hampshire to what?"

Mrs. Stowe was outraged. "To tell you to drop her."

"That is impossible," said Charles. "I love her."

"Love her?" screamed Georgiana. "Love her?"

"Love her," said Charles, emphatically.

There was a long silence, then Mrs. Stowe said, "Bunty?"

The general coughed. "Now look here, Melton, er, it's like this, do ye see. Georgiana here is pretty desolated."

"Desolated?" cried Georgiana. "I am a laughing stock. We are to be married at Christmas, and I am to go to the alter with this scandal hanging over our union?"

"I had not meant there to be a scandal," said Charles. "I own I have been indiscreet, but it is done. If you wish to step down, well I shall understand it. I mean it shall not break my heart or anything, Miss Stowe."

"You will not get out of marrying Georgiana," said Mrs. Stowe quickly. "The world knows you have promised to marry her, and you shall be held to it, shan't he, Bunty?"

"Oh, yes," said the general.

"Mrs. Stowe," said the heir. "I was weak enough to have allowed yourself and your daughter to enveigle me into a proposal of marriage. At the time, well, nothing seemed worth fighting for. I was resigned, if you like, to a convenient social contract with someone or other suitable one day to be Countess of Landsdun. I mean the earl required it, the line demands it, and it might as well be Miss Stowe as anyone. I have sworn that I shall marry you, Miss Stowe, and I shall not go back on my word. But since that contract was made, I have grown to love Lucy Emmett, and by my life she is the only woman I have ever loved, or ever will. I shall not give her up—nothing shall compel me—so I am afraid that you will have either to refuse to marry me—and I truly cannot see you relinquishing a title or the wealth that goes with that title—or you will have to accept that Lucy Emmett is to be my mistress while I live. And more than that, Miss Stowe, she will be the wife of my heart."

Nothing was said for a minute, but then Lady Charrington spoke. "Well, very brave. Very brave, to shame a young lady of quality, by declaring that you prefer the embraces of a lowborn bastard wench of questionable morals. For all you know, she may be the wife of Giles Wentworth's heart, or any man's heart, I do declare." Her thin lips spread into a smile. "Oh Melton, dear, dear, did you never think there might be some smidgeon of truth in what the *ton* says? They say that there is no smoke without a fire having been lit, and Wentworth does burn, I assure you."

The heir walked slowly over to the door, and opened it. He said, "I have not yet dined, so I hope you will excuse me. I am here at Pall Mall until the day after tomorrow. On Saturday I am going to Landsdun, to make my preparation for the wedding. I have told you how things stand. If you, Miss Stowe, feel that you cannot under the circumstances marry me, then I hope you will so inform me before I leave." He bowed and took his leave, in a moment a footman appeared to show them all out.

Lucy had been on pins, waiting for the heir to come u to her salon and when at last he appeared she searched h face anxiously. "What happened?"

He shrugged. "Nothing significant."

"What did they say?"

He sighed. "Asked me to drop you."

She nodded. "Will you?"

He laughed. "Did you really think I would?"

"No, but I should have understood. If you had, I mean, said Lucy quickly. "It seems wrong, really, and not hones I believe that if I were Miss Stowe, I should feel quit desperate."

"You don't know Georgiana," said Charles. "Do n waste your pity on her. She is quite formidable in her ow way, I assure you. My only regrets in all this are that w couldn't have quietly moved you to Richmond and tha the earl is informed. I meant to tell him, of course, bu later." He laughed. "I have been so naive. Off my head with love, I suppose." He put his arm around her. "And thank God for it. But, now, wife of my heart, let's to ou dinner and then early to bed, for you shall be busy furnishing your establishment, and setting it in order. No, he went on, when Lucy tried to question him further, " refuse to have my dinner spoilt." But later when they wer in bed, he asked her a question. "Lucy, I have to ask if ther is anything between yourself and Wentworth. Anything a all?"

Lucy didn't answer at once, and then she asked "Anything at all?"

"Anything at all?" asked the heir.

"Well, there is something," said Lucy. "I cannot for the life of me think what it is. But it's not love."

"And you have not let him love you?" asked the heir.

"No," said Lucy. "I should have told you if I had."

"Promise?" asked the heir.

Lucy thought about her visit to Portman Square when she had thought she would give herself to Giles if by doing so she could stop the duel. Would she have told the heir? No she wouldn't.

"I have not given myself to Giles Wentworth," said

Lucy, "and I do not mean to give myself to Giles Wentworth. But if by any chance or trick of fate, I find that I have given myself to Giles Wentworth I shall tell you."

The heir smiled and drew her to him. "Listen, if by any chance or trick of fate, you *should* give yourself to Giles Wentworth, I want you to promise me something."

"What?" murmured Lucy.

"Don't, for God's sake, tell me," groaned Charles.

"Promise," whispered Lucy as her lips met his.

CHAPTER XIII

Revolution Now!

In which pickled walnuts and bricks lead Charles to make a revolutionary decision.

Charles woke early the next morning to find Lucy's place in the bed empty and cold though a glance at the clock told him it was not yet eight. The air in the room was chill because the fire had gone out. Normally he would have rung for Culpepper to bring him a warm robe before venturing out of bed, but sounds of laughter from the street outside caused him to rise shivering, wrap a cover around his shoulders, and go to the window to investigate. He drew back the drapes and looked out over the city. A glorious sight met his eyes—a big, vibrant, orange gong of a Winter sun sat in a pale grey sky, suffused with pink. It must have snowed all through the night, for every roof and spire, every tower and tree, was decked like a bride in virgin white. It was knee deep in the streets and looking down, he saw the source of the laughter. It came from Lucy and Sam who were engaged in building a snowman in front of the house. It was going to be a monster snowman by the look of it. Sam was constructing a giant snowball for its head, while Lucy built the body patting away at a huge heap of snow only stopping once in a while to blow on her hands. Magpie was out there, too, in a huddled hump, hating the flimsy, freezing white flakes that clung to his thick coat.

Well, Lucy shall not get to Richmond today, Charles thought. *No coach shall get through that. And if it does not clear by Saturday, I shall not be able to venture to Leicestershire.* He rang for Culpepper, who came in with his robe and helped his master into it.

"I see Miss Emmett is in fine form this morning," said the heir.

"Now she is," said Culpepper, "but was not so earlier this morning."

"How so?"

"I hear that she was sick, my lord."

"Sick?"

Charles went to the window to conduct a closer examination of Lucy. She looked exceedingly well, if a trifle red nosed.

"Cassie tells me she rang for her at six, my lord. I believe she was a trifle indisposed."

"Mm," murmured Charles, frowning.

"Your bath water is arriving, my lord," said Culpepper.

"Has Miss Emmett bathed already?"

"Yes, sir."

"Without me? Well, well. Did Cassie say more?"

"Er, no, my lord. I did not think it prudent to enquire further," said Culpepper.

"No, no. Quite right," said the heir, following his man out of the bedroom. "These, er, matters that concern ladies, should not draw question, or comment from gentlemen." Still Charles did feel curious as to the nature of Lucy's indisposition. There was a vast, mysterious part of the female condition that gentlemen were excluded from—strange ailments, pips and vapours, faintings, and so forth. These all came under the heading "feminine dispositions," and usually did not only cause inconvenience or discomfort to a lady. *How often,* Charles thought, *he had called on ladies in the past for, to be blunt, copulatory purposes, only to have a maid inform him . . . "My mistress says, sir, that she is indisposed, but that if you would care to call again after a few days, why then she will be delighted to entertain you."*

Because when ladies were "indisposed" their feelings were known to be acutely delicate, Charles said nothing to Lucy that morning at breakfast that might distress her; in short he did not mention that he had ordered Culpepper to air his own bed in case he should suddenly find himself banished from Lucy's. He was naturally put out at the idea he might have to sleep alone, for he had got used to the comforts, not to say the delights, of sharing Lucy's bed. He had to admit to himself, though, that she looked very well, not a bit peaky. She was highly excited when he told her the attics at Pall Mall were full of fine furniture and paintings, and that she might find some articles among them that would suit the house in Richmond. When they had finished breakfasting, she was off to the attics at once with Mrs. Royalston.

Lucy had been slightly alarmed at her morning sickness, but it had only lasted about an hour, and she had eaten an enormous number of pickled walnuts at dinner the previous evening. *Pickled walnuts! Pickled walnuts!* she thought as she carefully marked a very pretty walnut and brass inlaid side table with a chalk cross. *Pickled walnuts!* she thought, as she marked six hall chairs, with a cross each, so that they would be taken to Richmond.

"Walnut," observed Mrs. Royalston, "with nice cabriole legs, and the embroidery on the seats and backs is very fine. They will do splendidly in the hall at Richmond with the walnut side table."

Walnuts, thought Lucy. *Pickled walnuts.* She had an overwhelming desire for walnuts, pickled, an obsession for small black pickled walnuts in vinegar. She could hardly wait for luncheon.

She ordered pickled walnuts after her mutton, and more pickled walnuts after the pickled walnuts, then more pickled walnuts. A message sent up from the kitchens by a bewildered cook said that Miss Emmett had quite cleared the pantry of pickled walnuts, whereupon Miss Emmett at once sent a message back to the cook, saying that more pickled walnuts should be purchased at once, since she rather fancied she might rather fancy some pickled walnuts after her dinner.

Lord Melton, being a gentleman, put this fanatical fad for pickled walnuts down to Lucy's indisposition, whatever it might be. *Perhaps*, he mused, *pickled walnuts have some sort of therapeutic value? Perhaps if a lady eats sufficient pickled walnuts, her indisposition will disappear?* He had heard of stranger things, for instance one lady he had known had swallowed great quantities of wood lice to keep her blood pure.

However, Mrs. Royalston, being a lady, was driven to ask a question. "Puss?"

"Yes, dear?" replied Lucy.

"Are you quite in the pink?"

"Oh quite," said Lucy quickly.

"Not been a trifle..." Mrs. Royalston blushed and the heir looked away to save her embarrassment. Only the fop lacked the good sense to pretend he was not curious.

"Indisposed?" asked Mrs. Royalston.

Lucy laughed. "Indisposed? No. Never felt better in my life."

Her answer puzzled the heir, but he put it down to a lady's natural bashfulness. He was alarmed, though, when he noticed that she was sniffing longingly at the vinegar in which the pickled walnuts had been served. "Good God. You shan't drink that, shall you?" he asked.

"Of course not," laughed Lucy. But after lunch she quickly excused herself, sped down the backstairs to the kitchens, and to the utter amazement of the cooks and scullions, rescued the vinegar, before it could be thrown away, and drank it all straight from the serving dish.

It snowed again that afternoon then started to freeze. It was far too cold to remain in the attics, so Mrs. Royalston and Cassie and Sam and Magpie all joined Lucy in her salon to continue planning the furnishing of the Richmond house. The fires at Pall Mall were built up so high there was a danger of chimney fires. Heavy curtains and draught stops were pulled over and against the doors. But the rooms were large and the ceilings lofty and when one got only a short distance from one of these roaring fires it felt as though "Jack Frost had yer caught by the bollocks." This observation was made by the squire, who had started a card game in the blue drawing room with Charles, the fop, and Culpepper to make a fourth hand.

They had the card table right in front of the fire, and a good bottle of brandy to keep out any aggressive cold. Charles was glad of more snow, even glad of the freeze. To be prevented from returning to Leicestershire did not cause him any despair, especially since it meant his remaining with Lucy a little longer. He would have to go to Landsdun when it thawed, of course, and the snow kept Georgiana in London as well. The Stowes' London house was only a few doors distant down Pall Mall, but Charles had a feeling he would not see any of them until the wedding. He had made his feelings about Lucy quite clear on the previous evening. Mrs. Stowe would not allow Georgiana to do anything that might lose her such an eligible bridegroom, so for the present, he was content to enjoy a game of cards, a glass of brandy, a warm fire, and later, who could tell, perhaps even the warmer embraces of his mistress, if her disposition allowed, of course.

"*More* pickled walnuts?" cried Mrs. Royalston at dinner that evening. "Pussy, are you absolutely insatiable in that direction?"

"Lard," said the fop, making a sour face. "Your innards shall be quate devastated."

"Rot," said the squire. "Something of what yer fancy can do yer nothing but good."

"There speaks a man," said Mrs. Royalston, who was quite flushed from four glasses of claret to keep out chills, "who has had far too much of what he fancies for years. And if any person here presents doubts that a surfeit of appetite of *any* description is ruinous, I repeat ruinous, then I draw their attention to my husband's vast bulk, his rubificant face, and the lust-spawned tremour which shakes his shanks."

"All hereditary," beamed Billy.

"Inherited from *whom*?" asked his wife pointedly. "Not from *near* relationships, oh no. Near relationships, no matter how mischievous, cannot be held responsible for *all* your afflictions. The portly build, perhaps. The ruddy countenance, maybe. The gout, at a pinch. But that hidden malady in the nether regions? Never, unless you, Billy, had relations of Italian extraction. Have you, I wonder, a Signor in your ancestry that I am ignorant of?"

Everyone knew she was referring to the pox, but everyone pretended they didn't.

"Drunk," said the squire to Charles.

"Oh, monstrous insinuation," cried Jemima. "I am the most temperate of beings." But then she saw three Billys, three fops, three heirs, and three Lucys all melting into one another and at once excused herself from the table.

The heir had no sooner watched her totter from the dining room when a question from Lucy set him back.

"Do you think that I might have some pickled walnuts upstairs?" she asked.

"What? Shall you eat them all night?" he asked later, pointing to the small dish of pickled walnuts on the table beside Lucy's bed.

"Not *all* night," said Lucy, wrapping her arms around his neck.

So much for that slight indisposition, thought the heir, joining her in her bed with a smile. Obviously, the pickled walnuts had done the trick.

"Charles, Oh Charles, Oh God!"

The wailing seemed to come from a long way away, the heir struggled out of sleep into consciousness with the desperation of a drowning man trying to achieve the surface of a murky millpond.

"Charles?"

He opened his eyes. She was hanging over him, her face as white as the sheet that covered him.

392

"I am sick," she wept. The heir's eyes moved warily over to the saucer on the bedside table. The pickled walnuts had vanished.

"What shall I do?"

"Call Cassie."

"Call Cassie. Right. I shall. At once." He ran out of the bedroom across the salon, opened the door and found Sam lying on the floor in his usual place. He administered a sharp kick to the urchin's lean backside, nearly dislocating the toe on his right foot, and said, "Cassie, at once."

At once the heir was banished from Lucy's bedroom and the door shut on him. He could hear yelpings and moanings from behind the bedroom door.

"Ooh, ooh, oh," cried Lucy, who felt as though she were about to be turned inside out with retching and would remain in that uncomfortable position for the rest of her life. She prayed to die at once, and when she didn't she complained louder.

"Indisposed again?" asked Culpepper who had also been called on the heir's instructions.

Charles nodded. "God, how I wish I had the services of Sir James Robertson here," he said, pacing the room. "It must be something dire," he told Culpepper. "I mean, she's not one to set up a howling like that for a trifle, is she?"

"What about Flinch?" asked Culpepper.

"This is 'a feminine indisposition,'" said the heir. "I mean, that's not a blood in there who's taken a tumble off his horse."

Culpepper shrugged and let the heir pace for a moment.

"Ooh, let me die," cried Lucy again.

"That's it," said the heir. "Send for Flinch."

Because of the snow it was almost two hours before Flinch arrived, and when he did he was told off in no uncertain terms by the heir, who said that he was "too late."

"*In articulo mortis*?" asked Flinch.

"Recovered, you lopsided quack," said the heir. The peculiar angle of Flinch's head was not altogether a disability, in that it did allow him to look directly around Lucy's door. She was sitting up in bed looking quite pert.

"Any clue as the cause of nauseum?" asked Flinch.

"Pickled nuts," replied the heir.

"Many?" asked Flinch.

"A ton," replied Charles.

"Craving," commented Flinch.

"Mad for them," said Charles.

"Examination," said Flinch, wending his way towards Lucy. He was ten minutes, and then back with Charles. "Diagnosis," he said. Charles waited. The fellow looked grim, but then he always looked grim. "Well?" asked Charles.

Flinch closed the bedroom door. "With child," he said. He allowed the heir a minute to recover from this news. "Early stages, not much advanced."

The heir nodded and smiled. "Oh well. I mean, early stages. It will advance, though, I mean she's strong and able I think."

"It will indeed advance," said Flinch with about as much joy in his voice as a grave robber who'd just dug up an empty coffin, "unless of course it is removed, which under the circumstances...."

Culpepper marched him from the room before the heir could grab him. Culpepper knew Flinch was only suggesting a discreet course of action, but as he explained to the physician as he saw him out through the front door, "Wrong time, wrong place, wrong man—wrong woman, too."

If Charles had expected to find a radiant mother-to-be waiting for him, then he was disappointed. Not that Lucy looked miserable or was in a pet, she was just subdued and thoughtful. The broad smile and the shining eyes belonged to the heir, who accepted congratulations from Cassie and Sam with a grin that was almost triumphant then fell to kissing Lucy so hard, and so repeatedly that Sam wondered whether she wouldn't emerge bruised.

394

"You are pleased?" Lucy asked.

"Pleased?" asked the heir. "Well I'm cock-a-hoop."

"Promise?" asked Lucy.

"Did you hear that, Culpepper?" asked Charles as the man entered Lucy's room.

"I did, sir," said Culpepper.

"What am I, Culpepper?" asked the heir.

"I believe you said you were cock-a-hoop, my lord," replied Culpepper.

"You heard right, Culpepper," said Charles. "Now send a servant down to the cellars, and let's have a bottle of the best champagne up here, so that we may drink a toast to Miss Emmett and to the future of our child."

Lucy had suspected for some time that she might in fact have been in *that* condition, but she had turned a blind eye for many reasons, not least the belief the heir might view her condition as an embarrassment. Now she wondered how she could ever have doubted that he would be pleased, and when he had pressed more kisses on her she began to glow, then to smile. Even the prospect of continuing morning sickness did not put her off. It was not every day one was told one was to be a mother, and she was loved and had a home waiting for her in Richmond. What more could a bastard girl want? What more indeed, unless it was not to have a bastard, but a legitimate child?

Unlike his master, Culpepper was very discreet. He did not send a servant for the champagne, but went himself. It would not do at all if it were to become widely known that Miss Emmett was to have a chance child, especially since Miss Georgiana Stowe was supposed to produce the first *public* fruit from the heir's loins. Culpepper knew he could trust Sam and Cassie to remain silent, the squire and Mrs. Royalston, too, would comprehend why the news should be kept under the blanket. As to Flinch? Well he hoped the physician's oath to medicine would keep him mum. But the fop was not to be told, nor were any of the lower servants. As soon as there was a thaw, the heir would be off from prying eyes and the sharp tongues of the *ton*. Culpepper did not care for Georgiana Stowe, but until the heir said otherwise he would continue to do his duty, as he saw it.

In fact, Flinch did keep mum, after a fashion. From Pall Mall he went to Portman Square to attend Giles Wentworth who was still kept in his bed waiting for his shoulder to heal.

Giles was surprised to see Flinch so early in the day. "I thought you preferred to dissect your corpses straight after breakfast?" he said while Flinch stood waiting for the woman engaged to nurse Giles to remove the bandages.

"Have not taken breakfast yet," said Flinch, making a close examination of the arm and shoulder. "Called out to Pall Mall. Emergency of sorts."

"Where in Pall Mall?" asked Giles, wincing as Flinch probed his shoulder with a long pair of tweezers.

"Mm. Good, no pus," said Flinch.

"Where in Pall Mall?" repeated Giles.

"Melton's," replied Flinch. "Clench the fist."

Giles clenched the fist of his left hand. "The heir?" asked Giles.

"The mistress," said Flinch.

"What ails her?" asked Giles, looking worried. "Not that head wound—you said it was—?"

Flinch said, "No, no. Just sick."

"What manner of sickness?" asked Giles, as the nurse began to replace the bandages.

"Oh, a feminine indisposition," said Flinch.

Giles had not the heir's gentlemanly approach to matters feminine. "What manner of damned feminine indisposition?" he shouted as Flinch put the tweezers back in his bag. "Flinch, why the hell are you being so evasive? What *manner* of sickness?"

Flinch picked up his bag. "What part of the day is it?" he asked Giles.

"Morning," Giles replied, then he smiled. "You mean she's . . . ?" He searched Flinch's face to see if he had guessed right. He got a nod—only the merest nod, but a nod none-the-less. Giles shouted with laughter. "Well, I'll be damned. Oh I would give a thousand guineas to see

Georgiana's face when she hears about this. Hey, Flinch, what a subject for a lampoon, eh? What a subject for a cartoon? Dear Miss Emmett, that girl has a remarkable talent for stirring up hornets' nests."

Giles received the cartoon later in the day from Pinkerton who had come with Willie and Plunkett. "That was quick," said Giles, as he received the pamphlet. "How the hell did they get it so fast?"

"These are printed by a group attached to the Society for Constitutional Information," said Pinkerton, "and they have spies everywhere, as you know." Giles knew well enough. The Society for Constitutional Information was an organisation formed to spread revolutionary doctrines and agitation among the lower classes. He looked at the nurse, who was just leaving the room: she might have talked to the revolutionary press, or perhaps Flinch had—no, surely not Flinch—or perhaps one of the servants at Pall Mall had talked?

"I tell you something," said Willie, "this country is going to go to the dogs just like France. One cannot even rely on one's servants to be discreet. Anyway, just wait 'til Farmer George sees that."

Giles studied the cartoon and saw exactly what Willie meant. The cartoonist had called his work, "A solemnisation of Matrimony among the nobility." Lord Melton and Georgiana Stowe wildly caricatured stood before a minister of the Protestant church. A bubble came from the minister's mouth and it was written, "Does any man here know of any impediment that should prevent these two from being coupled together in Matrimony, by God's law, or the law of the Realm?" Giles laughed. The king had been caricatured as a farmer, with a straw sticking out from under his wig. A bubble came from his mouth. "Hay? hay? what impediment?" The *impediment* was the figure of a ragged girl, who stood in the centre of the aisle, her belly bulging. She wore a gag around her mouth, and on the gag was written "Ignorance." Her hands were bound with ropes, and on the ropes was written "Poverty." She had chains around her legs, and a ball was attached to the chains. On the ball, the cartoonist had written "Degradation."

There was no mistaking the girl's identity. It was Lucy Emmett. Giles laughed. "You are right," he said to Willie. "I should think the Farmer will run mad for a month when he sees this. But I wonder how Miss Emmett will feel when she discovers she is a heroine of the lower classes?"

It was Culpepper who handed the cartoon to Lucy. She was thunderstruck. "Where did this come from?"

"Sam found it in the kitchens," said Culpepper. "I never thought to see literature against the monarchy in Pall Mall. This is political propaganda of the worst kind—aimed directly at the lower classes who cannot read. You see what these enemies of the state imply?"

Lucy could see only too clearly. To the poor of London it appeared as though she, like them, was a victim of the wealthy upper classes. And in a way she agreed with them. Ture, she was not to be cast out on the streets to die of starvation, and her child would be brought up in comfort. But ignorance and poverty was what she had sprung from, and perhaps to be thought "unsuitable" to marry the man one loved not because of some basic lack in one's character, but because one had the misfortune to be born a bastard in poverty and ignorance *was* a sort of degradation.

"I wonder?" asked Lucy, "which are the greatest enemies of the state, these so-called political propagandists, or the king and the quality?"

Culpepper was astounded. "Why, Miss Emmett, that is an improper question," he said.

"I do not believe there is any such thing as an improper question," said Lucy. "All questioning is proper and healthy, dammit. Well I shall tell you what I think. Both the propagandists and the quality are to blame, for both manipulate the people for their own ends. And I tell you this, the sooner the lower classes are taught to read, the better, for then they shall no longer be ignorant, may escape from poverty, and will no longer live in degradation."

Culpepper was speechless. "What, educate the lower classes?" he asked. "Do you want a revolution? Blood, murder, and carnage in the streets?"

"I am the lower classes, and I can read," said Lucy, "and there has not been a revolution yet, has there?"

At that moment the window of the blue drawing room was smashed by a projectile. Splinters of glass flew across the room. Culpepper calmly bent down and lifted a large brick from the floor and untied the piece of paper that was wrapped around it. It was a copy of the cartoon, and across it someone had scrawled a message in charcoal. Culpepper handed it to Lucy.

Revolution now, she read.

Only a couple of minutes after the window of the Landsdun house was smashed, a brick flew though Mrs. Stowe's sitting room window and might have hit Dolph on the head and killed him, if he had not got up from his chair at that precise moment to help himself to a hot muffin from the dish by the fire.

"My word," said Dolph, undercutting the screams of Mrs. Stowe, Georgiana and Emma. "It looks like a brick."

"What's up?" asked the general, marching into the room. In common with most generals he made a point of arriving at the scene of the action only after the battle had taken place.

"Brick," said Dolph, reporting.

"My word," said the general. "There's a message on it." He unwrapped the piece of paper. "What is it?" cried Mrs. Stowe.

"Brick," said Dolph.

"My word," said the general, after a close look at the pamphlet.

"What is it?" cried Mrs. Stowe. "Bunty, bring it here at once." Bunty brought it, Mrs. Stowe saw it and so did Georgiana who fainted at once.

"Oh what is it?" wailed Emma, running to Georgiana's aid.

"Brick," said Dolph.

"This is by Gillray," said Charles when he was shown the cartoon.

"Surely not," said Culpepper. "I thought that Gillray was under a positive engagement to Mrs. Humphrey the Publisher; surely, sir, he would not work for such unscrupulous persons?"

"For strong liquor," said Charles, "Gillray would work for anyone. No, he has tried to disguise his style, but this is Gillray's work, right enough. Just look at the caricature of the Farmer. Who else could capture the awkward shuffling gait, the undignified carriage, that fatuous countenance?" He looked at the broken window and said, "Better call a man to mend that."

"Are you not put out?" asked Lucy.

"No," said the heir, "but the window is."

"What," asked Mrs. Stowe, producing the cartoon from her reticule, "do you have to say about this?"

"Gillray," said Charles. "Unmistakably Gillray."

Mrs. Stowe was astounded. "We have just had our windows put out," she said.

"With a brick," said Dolph. All the Stowes, including Georgiana who was only just vertical due to the smelling salts Emma held under her nose, had arrived to do battle.

"Bunty," commanded Mrs. Stowe. "You know what to do."

The general coughed.

"Is it true that *that girl* is with child?" asked Mrs. Stowe. Lucy was still in the blue drawing room and could hear every word.

"With a brick?" asked Dolph.

"What?" asked Charles.

"Well, my word, imagine," said Dolph. "With a brick, landed in me chair! Should have been killed if it hadn't been for the muffins, shouldn't I, Ma?"

"Silence," hissed Mrs. Stowe.

"Well?"

"Well?" asked the heir.

"My word. You *have* got a front," said Mrs. Stowe. "But I warn you, if this is true, you shall have the king on you. For Georgiana is named for the king. And the king shan't have a lady named after him shamed in this manner, no indeed, not by your dealings with a lowborn bastard who is no doubt in league with revolutionary factions."

"You are not content to make me a laughingstock among the *ton*, but now I am become an object of ridicule among the lower order," wept Georgiana.

"So is the king," said Mrs. Stowe, "and the church."

"It wouldn't be the first time," said Charles, referring to the cartoon.

"Oh isn't it?" snapped Mrs. Stowe. "You have *more* bastards who have given you bastards, have you?"

It was at that moment that Dolph, unseen by anyone, slid into the blue drawing room.

"Ah," he said when he saw Lucy standing a little behind the door. "How de do?"

"Hello," said Lucy.

"See the window's been put out."

"Yes," said Lucy. She did feel embarrassed because Charles had asked her to keep out of sight, but Dolph had stumbled on her. "With a brick?" asked Dolph. Lucy nodded. "My word, what a coincidence," said Dolph.

"That girl's in there," gasped Mrs. Stowe, overhearing voices from the blue room. "I want a word with her." She pushed past the heir. "Ah. There you are," said Mrs. Stowe.

"Ma," said Dolph. "Melton's had his window put out, too."

"I shall put out your tongue if you don't hold it," snapped Mrs. Stowe. "Now, my girl. I wish to know exactly what your game is?"

"It's alright, Charlie," said Lucy, when she saw the heir's face growing dark. "I can handle her. If I can handle Lady Charrington, well this one is no bother to me."

"Bunty." The general looked at his wife. "What are you going to do?" she asked.

"Talk to her," said the general.

"There," said Mrs. Stowe to Lucy. "The general is going

401

to talk to you now." She made herself comfortable in a chair, and patted at her bonnet triumphantly, while Georgiana sank onto a couch with Emma at her side. Lucy waited for the general, but nothing happened. He just stood like a statue staring at the ceiling. She could feel herself growing redder and redder, desperately wanting to laugh. She peeped at the heir who was looking at the buckles on his shoes. Lucy looked quickly away. He was shaking with suppressed laughter, too, and if he caught her eye she knew they would both explode.

"With a brick, Ma," said Dolph, and Charles and Lucy both exploded, lurching about the room shrieking with laughter and making so much noise that Mrs. Royalston, the squire, Peter Royalston, Sam and Magpie, Culpepper and Cassie all rushed in convinced the revolution had started.

"Oh Pussy," cried Mrs. Royalston when she saw Lucy clinging to Charles for support with tears streaming down her face. "You are not to do anything too extreme in your condition."

"So it *is* true," said Mrs. Stowe. "And you, ma'm, I presume, are the person Lady Charrington mentioned. You are the unscrupulous person who has pushed this wretched creature forward. You are the evil genius behind this plot?"

"Evil genius?" gasped Mrs. Royalston.

"How dare you pose as an Englishwoman," snapped Mrs. Stowe. "What do you know of the Society for Constitutional Information?"

"The what?" asked an amazed Mrs. Royalston.

"You have just hurled a brick though my window," said Mrs. Stowe.

"Oh," wailed Jemima. "How could I have done such a thing without leaving my room?"

"Easily," said Mrs. Stowe. "Persons of your type can do anything if it will further their own desperate revolutionary ends. Come, own up—your heavily disguised accent fools no one. You are French, madam, and determined to topple the monarchy. You are the scourge of the nobility and should be hanged."

At the mention of hanging, Peter Royalston fled the room, colliding with a footman as he did so.

"You shouldn't throw bricks," said Dolph to Mrs. Royalston. "I might have been killed if it wasn't for the muffins."

"Lady Charrington, sir," said the footman. Everyone turned towards the door and Lady Charrington swept in, looking powerfully vindictive. "I was just stepping into my coach at Berkeley Square, on my way to see Mrs. Stowe, when this," she hissed at Charles, "was pressed into my hand by an anonymous person who fled before he could be apprehended." She handed Charles the cartoon. "Is it true—is that entirely unsuitable person with child?"

It was Lucy who answered. "I am with child, and believe myself to be as *suitable* to have one as any other person in this world."

Lady Charrington laughed, and asked spitefully, "Might one enquire, by whom?"

"Dolly," said Charles warningly, but Lady Charrington would not be called off.

"I suppose you, poor dear, are absolutely confident you are the father? I wonder if Miss Emmett here is so confident? I wonder, too, if Giles Wentworth isn't damnably relieved that you are so confident. Being the youngest son of a family not so richly endowed with wealth as your own, and very much in debt already, I hear, due to reckless gaming and even more reckless amorous intrigues, I doubt very much that he could find the funds to silence a scandal of this proportion. Certainly he could never reach Miss Emmett's price. I myself offered her six hundred guineas, but of course, 'twas not enough."

"You—offered her money?" Charles looked at Lucy. "Lucy, why didn't you tell me?"

Lucy lowered her eyes. She felt sick with mortification at Lady Charrington's insinuations.

"No, Giles, I am sure, shall be enjoying himself hugely over all this. You know what a one he is for all kinds of devilment," laughed Dolly. "No, he is laughing like a drain, I should imagine. Dear Giles, to think he planted the seed, and another man shall foot the cost of rearing, upon my word, oh that shall tickle him vastly. And to think that you have paid so handsomely, too. Why, a house in Richmond, no mean abode, several acres of land, and a large living for that bastard girl throughout her life. Not bad, eh, Miss Emmett? Not a bad payment for strumpetry, I think? Oh, and Giles may benefit further from you, Charles, when you are not in the love nest." She winked at Lucy. "All shall be laid on and laid out for him."

Both Lucy and Charles were quite speechless.

"Do you mean he has given that girl property and money, as well as buying her jewels and gowns?" gasped Georgiana, forgetting her vapours and rising from the couch to face Lucy.

"Property and money, from an inheritance that should properly belong to your children," said Dolly.

"From the inheritance?" asked Georgiana. She was glaring at Lucy, and Lucy was glaring back.

"I do not know where you got that information, Dolly," said Charles. "From gossip I suppose, and you know how unreliable that is. Neither the house at Richmond nor the money that I settled on Lucy came from the inheritance. You forget I have not yet inherited. It came from my personal fortune—every penny came from that source."

Georgiana was circling around Lucy, looking her up and down, a sneering smile on her face. "My word, you have done well for yourself, haven't you? To think that when I first saw you in Ragby churchyard you were barefoot and in rags. Now, I warrant, you are better dressed and better shod than I, and a person of property, and fortune, too. Yes you have done very well for yourself by such devious and unscrupulous means."

"*You* call her unscrupulous and devious?" said Charles, "When you and your mother arranged that disgusting scene at Landsdun?" The heir was white with fury. Lucy could never remember having seen him look so pale before. "By God, madam, you had better stop sniping at her or that shall become common knowledge. Up 'til now my own shame at allowing myself to be so easily inveigled into proposing to you has prevented me from disclosing the full details of that disgusting exhibition—entering my quarters half-dressed, madam, and begging me to take you."

"And you did," cried Georgiana. "My mother knows, so does the earl, so does Sir James Robertson."

"Because you led them to believe it," shouted Charles, "and because I did not altogether deny it, because I was a fool and resigned."

Mrs. Stowe was quick, she was not going to allow the title, the fortune or the influential position at court to escape her family now.

"You shall not back down from this marriage, Melton, for if this matter came before the king or before the House of Peers, you should be entirely discredited. For if necessary I can produce a document from a reputable physician which declares that after our visit to Landsdun, Georgiana was no longer *in virgo intacti*."

Charles smiled. He might have known Mrs. Stowe would go to any lengths to prove he had taken Georgiana's maidenhead, so that he would be honour bound to marry her. "I daresay you could, madam, produce such a document, but if Miss Stowe is no longer *in virgo intacti*, she was in that condition before she came to Landsdun, for I did not do the deed and can only believe some other man had that questionable pleasure," said Charles.

The gale from the gasp of horror that left Lady Charrington and Mrs. Stowe could have beached a British man-o'-war. Dolly spoke, her voice cutting. "Are you, sir, suggesting that a young lady of quality, so carefully reared by so devoted a mother"—Mrs. Stowe was now crying with fury—"would stoop so low?" continued Lady Charrington, "as to toss away her maidenhead before her marriage?"

"You may read what you please into what I have said," snapped Charles.

"Just because your bastard doxy there is not so careful of her virtue, sir, do not please assume that all female creatures are whores," said Lady Charrington.

"I did not seduce her," said Charles.

"You would go before your Peers and say that?" cried Mrs. Stowe. "I should go before God and say it," said Charles. "I did not seduce her."

"She has seduced you, the dirty cheating little trollop," said Georgiana, and then she spat full in Lucy's face. For a minute there was an awful silence while everyone waited for Lucy's reaction.

Her eyes met Georgiana's, she tilted her chin, and smiled. "That is the first and last time that I shall be spat upon," she said. "Charlie, I shall not remain here, to be spat upon, not by any person on earth."

The heir crossed to her to take her hand, but Georgiana came between them. "Where will you go, eh?" she asked taking hold of Lucy's arm, and pulling her round to face her. "Richmond? Will you go to Richmond? Oh you have made sure you shall be well provided for, and that the bastard that grows in you shall be well provided for no matter who fathered it. Well, do not imagine you shall live snug and secure in Richmond, miss. No, do not imagine that for a minute. There are still ways to make you miserable."

Lucy shook herself free and walked slowly to the door.

"Quite right," Lady Charrington shouted after her. "Neither you nor that brat shall be allowed to stay there. All respectable people shall shun you. No tradesman will dare cater for you. No, Richmond is too close by far to London, miss. You and your offspring shall be driven out in shame, and if you have any doubts, miss, well remember that it is people such as myself who keep the upper hand, thank God. And it is people such as myself who shall not rest until people such as yourself are put back in their place."

Lucy was almost at the door when she turned. "And where might that be?" she asked quietly.

"In the gutter," screamed Georgiana.

Lucy smiled and walked back. She stood directly in front of Georgiana and said in an easy, pleasant voice, "When first I saw you, in Ragby churchyard, Miss Stowe, it is true that I was ragged and barefoot, poor, and ignorant. To me you appeared wonderful—you were so perfect in your dress, so delicate in your movements, and I thought *Oh, that is a lady of quality*. But now I think I mistook fine clothes and pretty manners for signs of quality, instead of thinking of quality of character."

Georgiana turned her back on Lucy, but Lucy continued quietly, "For a long time, too, I felt very guilty about you. I imagined that the heir and myself had behaved badly towards you, thought that you must be hurt, that you must feel abused, because I was ignorant of your true character. I did think you were a more *suitable* person for him than I, and although he did not love you, that he did owe you a duty."

"And so he does," hissed Georgiana, spinning round on her. "He does owe me a duty."

"I think not," said Lucy, her voice becoming hard. "For by meeting you, front to front for the first time, by watching you, by listening to you, and after hearing that you tricked the heir into offering you marriage, why I am persuaded that *you* will stoop to any depths to further your greed and ambition."

"Bunty," snapped Mrs. Stowe, but Bunty, like everyone else, was too busy listening to Lucy to hear.

"I laugh when I think of the mortification and pain that I have felt through my life because I am a bastard and because I have not good blood nor good breeding. For now that I have met persons who are endowed with both and have wealth besides—who have, in short, all advantages...persons of quality, Lady Charrington. Those persons who have the upper hand, as you say. Well, do you know what I say? By God I say, if you," she pointed to Lady Charrington and the Stowes, "are representative of the quality, then to hell with all of you and send the revolution."

"I told you," cried Mrs. Stowe. "I told you, that girl is against the king, against the realm, and against the aristocracy."

"Perhaps this realm might benefit from a new

407

aristocracy," said Lucy, "made of persons like Sam and myself, and good honest gentry like the squire and Mrs. Royalston. For we are all better persons in character than you by a long chalk, and I swear there is not a pox-ridden whore in the world who is not more honest than Miss Stowe. If one asked a whore, no matter how mean, what her profession was she should answer straight and honest that she was a whore, not that she was a lady of quality." She turned on Charles and pointed to Georgiana. "So, sir, if that is *suitable* to be your wife, and to bring forth children to carry your name through the centuries, then you had better find a person *suitable* to be your mistress, for I shall not play second fiddle to her, nor shall my child be spat upon by hers. I might have been content to be your mistress had I thought your wife so wonderfully superior. But I am damned if I shall be your mistress now. If I were in your shoes, Charlie, why I'd as lief marry a dishclout, and a greasy one at that." Having delivered this speech, she walked quickly from the room followed by Squire Billy, Jemima, Sam and Magpie, and Cassie. Culpepper stayed to attend to his master, if he should be needed.

For a long time the heir just stood quietly, with his head down and a very thoughtful frown on his brow, and then he lifted his head, looked at Georgiana and said, with cold deliberation, "Culpepper, I wish you to word a notice that shall be printed in the *Times* tomorrow."

"Yes, sir?" said Culpepper hopefully.

"It shall say," said the heir, "that Lord Melton shall not after all be marrying Miss Georgiana Stowe at Christmas-time." There was a gasp of horror from the Stowes and Lady Charrington. "I trust you, of course, to word it more formally."

"Oh, of course, sir," said Culpepper gravely bowing to his master.

"Have a footman come and show these persons out, Culpepper," said Charles, walking from the room, "and for God's sake let us have that window mended, the draught in there, is insupportable."

"You shall come before The House of Peers for breach

of promise," screamed Mrs. Stowe. "It will cost you everything."

Charles ignored this, and walked across the hall. Culpepper gave quick instructions to the footman, then hurried to the heir who had paused at the foot of the staircase.

"My lord?"

"Yes, Culpepper?"

"The notice in the *Times*, my lord, would it be proper, my lord, if the reason for your match with Miss Stowe being off were given, my lord; it would be a slap in the eye for those Revolutionaries, my lord?"

Charles smiled and walked slowly up the stairs. "I think that we would be a little presumptuous, Culpepper. After all, I have not yet asked Miss Emmett if she will have me."

CHAPTER XIV

Esmeralda's Rings

*In which Lucy and Charles are joined, and Roger's secret
is disclosed.*

Culpepper went off to compose the notice for the
Times, well aware that the reasons behind Lord Melton's
cautionary reply were complex. Breaking off his engagement to Georgiana Stowe was one thing—that in itself
would cause a terrible scandal—but if he were to marry
Lucy Emmett, well, that would cause the scandal of the
century. The idea that he had rejected a young lady of
Quality for a poor country bastard girl might be a popular
move with the agitant factions among the lower classes,
but in the present political climate, such a match would be
viewed with the utmost suspicion among the ruling
classes. Mrs. Stowe's wild outbursts about the Society for
Constitutional Information had proved that.

The confidence of the British ruling class had been dealt
a mortal blow by the American rebels a few years earlier
when they had forced the British out of those Colonies.
The sense of unease, of impending doom and revolution,
had lately been exacerbated by the rumblings from
France. There the underprivileged were rising to over-

411

throw the artistocracy, armed among other things with Tom Paine's *Declaration on the Rights of Man.* "All human beings are born free, and equal in dignity and rights," was the message from the American Revolution.

Though "Farmer George" had declared he would never go to the assistance of the French king, because he believed the French troubles were a divine punishment for their having supported the American rebels, he was not ignorant that the same desire to overthrow the monarchy was growing in Great Britian, and that any success for the French Revolutionaries fired the cause in Britain. As the confidence of the lower classes grew, the confidence of the ruling class waned, and Culpepper knew that if Charles, who was a diamond in the crown of the British nobility, were to take a wife from the lower orders, it was bound to be viewed as sinisterly significant.

If Lord Melton did ask Lucy Emmett to become his wife, and if she agreed, Culpepper wondered whether the young man would have the courage to face the avalanche of censure that would be directed against him. And he wondered, too, whether Lucy Emmett would have the stamina to stand at his side and take it.

Charles had asked himself these questions a thousand times, and had come to the conclusion that none of them could be answered. The future was so uncertain, the world was in a state of flux and of change, and one could be certain of nothing. He knew, though, that he must ask Lucy to be his wife. He could not be sure that her answer would be yes. She had refused to be his mistress, perhaps she would refuse to be his wife. He knocked on the door of her salon and entered. There were traces of tears on her cheeks. He thought how typical it was of her not to have wept in front of Georgiana Stowe.

"I have something to ask you. Might we be alone for a while?" She nodded to Mrs. Royalston and Cassie to leave.

"Charlie, before you say anything, I must tell you that I meant what I said about not being your mistress. I shall not go to Richmond. I shall go back to Leicestershire with the

Royalstons, at least until after the child is born."

The heir sat down on the bed and frowned. "I see."

"It is not that I do not love you, or because I am not fond, you know I am. But it is just that my pride will not allow me to remain to be slandered by all and sundry. When you are married it will just be worse, and we should never be happy."

"You don't believe that love, like faith, can conquer anything?" asked the heir.

Lucy sighed, "Well, I should love to have the faith to believe, but truly I think that the strongest love in the world would dwindle, at last, into mere toleration, if everyone in the world regards it as shameful."

"We don't regard it as shameful," said the heir.

"We know it's not," said Lucy, "but, oh, it would begin to feel shameful, if it were reduced to furtive meetings, and stolen moments. If we are in love, then why haven't we the courage to love openly? Why do we allow convention to come between us?"

"Come sit here by me," said Charles, patting a place on the bed beside him.

"No," said Lucy. "You will try and change my mind, and it is quite made up. I may not be a lady, but I have pride, and I shall not remain anywhere near London, for I am sick of the whole shoot, that is the truth."

Charles extended his hand. "Please," he said.

Lucy looked at him. "If I come and sit with you, promise that you will not touch me?"

"Promise," said the heir, smiling, and folding his hands in his lap. Lucy hung back for a minute, and then tilted her chin, and walked across to the bed and sat at what she considered was a safe distance. She knew that if he touched her, all her resolution would melt, for the last thing in the world she wanted, was to be away from him for a moment. He had turned to look at her, and she felt a flush colour her cheeks.

"May I not even hold a finger?"

"No," she said sharply.

"Oh, Lucy, how am I to ask what I have to ask, unless I touch you?"

413

"Persons do communicate without touching each other," she replied, rather primly. He laughed, and caught her hand before she could draw it away.

He raised it to his lips, and kissed it, and then gently bit the tips of her fingers.

Lucy closed her eyes. "Oh, you promised," she whispered, as she felt his arms around her, and his mouth meeting hers. *So much for resolution*, she thought.

"Lucy?"

Lucy opened her eyes.

"I have broken off my engagement to Georgiana Stowe."

He kissed her throat, then her shoulders.

"When?" she asked.

"A short time ago. Culpepper is drafting a notice for the *Times*. Aren't you pleased?"

"Why, yes. But what will the earl say?"

"I shall tell him I will not marry her under any circumstances, and there is only one lady in the world that I will marry." He pushed her gently back on the bed, and kissed her surprised mouth then said, "You."

"Me?" cried Lucy, pushing him away from her.

"Will you?" he asked. "No buts," murmured the heir. "Say yes, my love."

"But you can't mean it."

The heir sat up. "Would I ask you if I didn't mean it?"

"I don't know," said Lucy, frowning and studying his face. He slipped his arm around her, and rubbed his cheek against her. "You *know* I wouldn't," he whispered.

Lucy averted her eyes, "You wouldn't joke about such a thing? Me? Your wife?"

He nodded and touched her chin with the tip of his finger. "You. Lucy Emmett."

"Your wife?" she asked again, peeping at him. "And the child shall not be a bastard?" Her voice was quivering so was her lower lip.

"If you do not believe me, then I shall make a formal proposal," said the heir, jumping off the bed and falling on one knee. He took her hand and said, very solemnly, "My dear Miss Emmett—"

"Oh no," laughed Lucy, "oh, get up."

But Charles went on, "I have loved, admired, and respected you for a very long time. Would you make me a happy man, and do me the honour of becoming my wife?" He waited for a reply, watched her face. Her eyes were lowered, and he could see bright tears forcing their way between her dark lashes. His own eyes pricked, and his voice when he spoke was husky with emotion. "Oh, Lucy, say yes. You shall never regret it, I promise."

"But, *you* may," she whispered.

"Never," said the heir emphatically.

"Oh, Charlie, you may." She broke down and wept, leaning her head on his shoulder. "People shall never accept it, never."

He kissed the top of her head, and said, "I care nothing for people. I care for you."

"But I know nothing of managing grand houses and servants, I mean—"

"Lucy, those things can be learnt, but they are of the most miniscule importance. What *is* important, is that we love each other, you and I, and were meant for each other. You know it, and I know it, and that is all that matters."

Lucy smiled, and raised her head. "It is madness though," she said through her tears.

The heir laughed. "Yes, it is," he replied, "absolute madness, heaven alone knows. But I am resigned to being mad for the rest of my days, even into extreme old age. More. To my grave. We shall be mad together, you and I."

"Madly happy?" asked Lucy.

The heir nodded. "Madly, madly happy."

"In spite of the world?" asked Lucy, looking intently at him. She still wasn't sure whether she was dreaming or not.

"In spite of the world. What do you say? Is it yes?" He searched her face eagerly. "Come, be mad, say yes. Do not tell me that when at last I have learnt to be impetuous, you have turned careful."

Lucy laughed. "Me? Careful? Dammit, not at all. To hell with the world, that's what I say. Oh, I shall make you the best, the loyalest, the strongest, the most *everything* wife on earth," she cried, "I promise."

The heir carried her out of the bedroom and across the salon. "I know," he said, "that is why I asked you. I am not a *complete* fool." He took her in his arms to the top of the staircase, and shouted, "Culpepper!" The manservant ran out of one of the downstairs rooms and into the centre of the hall, his quill pen dripping ink on the rich rugs. He looked up at his master, and smiled expectantly.

"Yes, my lord."

"Yes, Culpepper," shouted the heir. "The answer *is* yes."

"Shall I announce it in the notice, my lord?" asked Culpepper.

"Why not?" said the heir. "You may say that Miss Lucy Emmett has done me the honour of agreeing to become my wife. I shall expect you to word it more formally, of course."

"Of course, my lord," smiled Culpepper. "Champagne, sir?"

"A bottle," said Charles triumphantly. "No, ten bottles, for this is the merriest day of my life."

No matter what trials and tribulations the rest of the world was engaged in that night, the Landsdun house at Pall Mall was immune to them. There the scene was of the utmost jollity. Champagne flowed not just upstairs, but downstairs too. Master, guests, and servants celebrated as one. They danced, they sang, they laughed. The house was bright with music, lights, warmth, and good-hearted people. Brightest of all the company were Lord Melton and Lucy Emmett. Everyone had gathered in the music room, where a large fire had been lit. Lucy sat with Magpie on her knee, the squire and Sam on either side. Peter had been found hiding in one of the upstairs closets, when Mrs. Stowe and her war party had departed, and he had been assured he was not to be hanged. He was present in the room, as were most of the servants, who sat around in the candlelight, some of them on the floor, listening with rapt attention as Mrs. Royalston accompanied the heir on the piano, while he sang in a fine clear baritone. His reserve had been completely broken down, by love and a little champagne, and the song he sang might have been written just for Lucy Emmett.

> Can love be controlled by advice?
> Can madness and reason agree?
> Oh, Lucy, who'd ever be wise
> If madness be loving thee?
>
> Let sages pretend to despise
> the joys they want spirit to taste,
> Let us seize old time as he flies,
> And the blessings of life while they last.
>
> Dull wisdom but adds to our cares,
> Bright love will improve ev'ry joy.
> Too soon we may meet with grey hairs,
> Too soon may repent being coy.
>
> Then, Lucy, for what should we stay
> 'Til our best blood begins to run cold?
> Our youth we can have but today.
> We may always find time to grow old.

Charles sang the song with such conviction that there was not a dry eye left in the room; even the squire was moved to say that he must have a cold coming on, his eyes watered so profusely.

"Shame on you for a romantic," sniffed Lucy when Charles joined her after the song. He smiled, and handed her his kerchief. "What is the date?" he whispered.

"Why, the twentieth day of December," said Lucy.

He took her hand, pulled her to her feet, sat down on her chair, and took her on his knee. "I will sing it for you on this date for the rest of my life," he said.

"Promise?" asked Lucy.

"Promise," said the heir, "but you shall have to pour champagne into me, or I shall be too bashful."

Lucy laughed. "Promise," she said.

"May Lard?" called Peter. Charles and Lucy looked

towards the piano. He was standing there smiling across at them.

"Oh no," groaned the squire. "He ain't goin' ter warble, is he?" But it looked dangerously like it, for the fop had arranged himself on one toe, with his arms spread out like wings and Mrs. Royalston's hands were in the air, ready to strike a chord.

"May Lard. I am here to entertain with a song, suitable I believe for such a paradisiac and concordant occasion." He ignored the groans from his audience and continued, his peaky, flour-white face wreathed in a toothy smile.

"I believe that it is not generally known, that I was responsible for bringing these two together," he simpered towards Lucy and Charles. "Might I call you children of Aphrodite?" This brought a laugh from Charles who called, "Cupid, proceed."

"May lard, I will, if you will permit me, and I am, may Lard, your lardship's most dutiful, eager, and most voraciously obedient sarvant in all matters of the heart." He bowed very low, Mrs. Royalston struck the chord, and he was away.

> Bid your faithful Cupid fly,
> to the farthest Indian sky . . .

"I did not know yer were planning ter leave the country," shouted the squire. "The sooner the better, if yer ask me." The fop was too intent on his song to bother with that. He looked as fierce and determined as he was capable of looking, and continued.

> And then at thy fresh command,
> I'll traverse oe'r the silver sand.
> I'll climb the mountains, plunge the deep. I like mortals never sleep
> I, like mor . . . tals, ne . . . ver sleep.

A loud, shuddering snore from Magpie accompanied his flutterings around the piano.

"What time do we set out for Landsdun in the morning?" Lucy whispered to Charles.

"At dawn," he whispered back, "weather permitting."

"Then perhaps we should not be too late retiring?" Lucy whispered back. Their eyes met, she had no need to elaborate. They rose stealthily and crept from the room together, leaving everyone else listening to Peter. Soon they were in Lucy's bed with their arms around each other, two children of Aphrodite.

The weather did permit, the thaw had set in and just after dawn Charles, Lucy, the Royalstons, Peter, Cassie, Culpepper, Sam and Magpie set out in two fine coaches for Leicestershire. Charles was going to put his case to the earl, but he had sworn he would marry Lucy with or without his father's blessing. If he got it, he and Lucy would live at Landsdun, but if not, Charles had said they would return to the house in Richmond. He would not allow any grey thoughts to cloud their happiness, but he did admit to Lucy that his father's blessing would make his happiness complete.

Their departure from London meant that they escaped the hum the announcement in that day's *Times* caused among the fashionable. Lady Charrington read it and went straight to the Stowes' house at Pall Mall, her face and clothes in complete disorder, to find Georgiana would enter a Protestant convent. The general and Dolph heard the news at D'Aubignys club from Willie Caruthers, who was there with Pinkerton and Plunkett. The three bloods piled into a coach and went off to Portman Square to tell Giles.

Wentworth was sitting up in his bed, a copy of the *Times* on his lap, when they were shown in. He looked black as thunder.

"Ain't that a rub?" said Willie, pointing to the announcement, "he's going to marry her, it says. Marry her? Well, that ain't straight. I mean she's a pert enough creature, but she ain't got no folks."

"How shall he marry her with no folks?" asked Pinkerton.

"Thing is," said Willie, casting an eye at Giles who hadn't said a word, "should we let Melton make a complete flat of himself over this? I mean, he is a blood, was rather. What I mean, Wentworth, is shouldn't you come clean?"

Giles glared at him. "Come clean?"

Willie looked embarrassed and scratched the hair under his wig. "What I mean is play the game."

Giles sighed, screwed his copy of the *Times* into a ball and threw it across the room.

"Willie, why don't *you* damn well come clean and tell me what you are babbling about?"

"Come clean with Melton," said Willie. "I mean everyone knows, it's all over the *ton*." Willie was growing more scarlet by the minute and Pinkerton and Plunkett were looking mighty flushed too.

Giles was losing his patience. "Out with it, Willie!" he roared, his green eyes flashing.

"Very well," Willie shouted back. "Thing is, Melton's always been a stickler for doin' the right thing, duty and all that. But he's lost his loft over this party, quite bust his noodle. Thing is, the poor fellow will live to regret it, for the Stowes are talking about taking him before the House of Peers. Seems Georgiana Stowe ain't intact anymore owing to Melton having seduced her earlier, first fellow on the spot if you catch my drift."

"Not true," said Giles smoothly.

"What?" asked Willie who hadn't paused for breath during the previous speech.

"Not true," repeated Giles, "that Melton was the first fellow on the spot."

"How do you know?" asked Pinkerton.

Giles smiled and studied the fingernails on his right hand. "Because I was," he said, "I had that pleasure myself earlier in the year. I perpetrated the penetration."

"You did?" grinned Willie admiringly. "By God, Wentworth, ain't you a devil of a fellow?"

Giles smiled and looked at the rapturous bloods from

420

under lowered lids. "Well, I'm damned if I shall allow Melton to take the credit for my seduction of Miss Stowe, nor shall I allow Miss Stowe to damage my reputation as a seducer of ladies merely because it suits her convenience."

"What about the Emmett girl?" asked Willie.

"You mean, have I had the pleasure of Miss Emmett?" Giles asked. There was a long, breathless pause while the bloods crept closer to him, waiting for the reply. Giles laughed. "Have I had the pleasure of Miss Emmett," he repeated and then started whistling under his breath.

"Look here, Wentworth," said Willie. "If you have, you should come clean with Melton. He means to marry her because he believes her to be with child by him. You should do your duty by the fellow."

At the mention of the word duty Giles ceased to look quite so pleased with himself.

"You should go round to Pall Mall directly and put the cards on the table—tell all, get him to call it off. For there's one hell of a huff goin' around about this. If he marries her, he shall be *persona non grata* everywhere. It's your responsibility as a gentleman to go to Pall Mall and tell the fellow what he's letting himself in for. If you don't, well we shall. Shan't we fellows?"

There were murmurs of agreement from Plunkett and Pinkerton who, like Willie, were still not completely sober after their night of carousal at D'Aubignys.

Giles shrugged and sighed, "Very well, if you insist I shall drag myself out of this bed, and go to Pall Mall, but Melton will never believe me, I promise you." As Giles waited for his manservant to help him into his clothes he pondered upon what a dreadfully tedious business it was, to have a reputation as a lady killer, and to have to near kill oneself to keep it. Still, shattered arm or no shattered arm, that *was* his reputation—and being a first class blood he was supposed to prefer death to the loss of it.

The trip from Portman Square to Pall Mall was a painful experience for Giles. He was mightily relieved when the coach stopped before Melton's house at Pall Mall. He had resolved to bluff it out with the heir. He would not say that he had enjoyed Miss Emmett's favours, but on the other hand he would not deny it. He'd leave the question tantalizingly open. That would be sufficient to madden the heir and might well be sufficient to drive the delectable Miss Emmett into his arms, or rather arm. He laughed to himself smugly. *Yes, she would be unprotected and with child, cast out on the streets, just as he had prophesied—but not too big with child to be enjoyed, and besides, he liked her more for shooting him than for anything else.*

As Willie jumped out of the coach and went up to the door, Giles Wentworth shuddered. He began to have a slight suspicion that he might be in love with Lucy Emmett, and the thought set him back a bit. That didn't suit the reputation at all. Just as he was beginning to suffer what could only be described as severe cold feet, Willie leapt back into the coach flushed and breathless and gasped, "Landsdun, they've gone to the seat, we must stop them." He shoved his face out the coach window and yelled, "Leicestershire," to the amazed coachman.

"Er, just a minute, Willie," started Giles.

"Duty," said Willie as the coach moved forward at a lick.

"Let me out," shouted Wentworth.

"Like hell," said Willie grimly settling himself on the seat opposite and folding his arms. "You're goin' to come clean."

Just as they flew past Buck House Giles fainted, probably from pain, which Willie observed to the other bloods was just as well for it was going to be a long journey, though he had every hope they would catch up with the heir at one of the many inns on the way. "But it don't much matter if we don't," he told Pinkerton and Plunkett, as he raised his boots and rested them on Wentworth's lap, "for it's a huge jape, bound to be an adventure, and what a stir it will cause when we return to D'Aubignys with the tale?"

As it happened they didn't catch up with the heir's party that night because one of the horses threw a shoe in the wilds of Bedforshire and they were forced to stop at the nearest hostelry. Giles was all for turning back to the metropolis, but the other bloods wouldn't hear of it, for fear of losing face.

So Giles, for the sake of his reputation, spent the night in a damp flea-infested bed, after a dinner of the foulest food it had ever been his misfortune to swallow, and woke before the sun, itching like a Deptford rat, with a rumbling stomach, a throbbing shoulder, to the sounds of Willie's tuneless snoring from the pillow beside his head.

It was one of those occasions when a gentleman is driven to ask himself several questions, the first of which is always... "What am I doing here?"

Lucy and Charles passed the River Soar and entered Leicestershire in the late afternoon of the next day, after a wonderful journey. The weather they had met upon the roads had been more like Spring than Winter. Bright sun from early in the morning had left only the odd trace of snow on the grass verges.

"I know we are near home," said Lucy who was excited not just because she was travelling to become Lord Melton's wife, but because she would see Roger Emmett, and Toby and John again. She had so much to tell them, so many plans for their future were buzzing in her head. She was going to see if the squire would sell Ridge Farm. She had discussed it with the heir, in bed in the coaching inn where they'd stayed the previous night. He had asked her what would make her happier than she was already, and she had said she would like to be married with the earl's blessing, and she would like to come by a way to make Roger Emmett his own master. And Charles had said, "Very well, let us see if we can do that."

Lucy was thrilled, for if the squire could be persuaded to part with the farm, it would make Roger Emmett a man of property at a stroke, and would mean that he could leave the farm to Toby and John when he died. It pleased her to think this was possible. There had always been Emmetts at Ridge Farm, toiling away on land that belonged to others. It seemed right to think that there should always be Emmetts at Ridge Farm, but that from

423

now on they would toil for themselves. The only thing she was sorry for was that Margaret Emmett couldn't have been spared to see her returning home with such high hopes for everyone. But then, if Margaret had been spared, she might never have run away, might never have met Charles . . .

"What are you thinking?" asked the heir, taking her hand.

"Oh," Lucy sighed. "Funny, bittersweet thoughts." She smiled, but there was a lump in her throat all the same. "Charlie, would you mind if I stayed at Ridge Farm tonight, instead of coming straight to Landsdun? It would be better, I think, for you to speak to your father without my being present. And to tell you the truth, I long to see Roger Emmett and my brothers again." Of course Elizabeth, Roger's wife, would have to be got past, but then there was always a hitch.

"Do you really want to?" Charles asked.

She nodded. "Really, it will probably be the last time I spend a night under that roof and it seems right I should."

"Then you shall," said Charles gently.

The Royalstons were dropped off at Ragby Hall, and so was Peter, much to his chagrin—he had imagined that he, since he was Cupid and Godlike, would be carried straight to Landsdun with the heir to enjoy grander surroundings than Ragby Hall could offer. Only when Charles promised him he would not be left there indefinitely, but would be his and Lucy's close companion in the future wherever they went, did he cease grumbling and hanging onto the door of the coach.

It was very dark when the two coaches drew up before the gates of Ridge Farm, and Magpie who had slept on Sam's knee for almost the entire journey lifted his nose and sniffed deeply. *Shrews*, he thought. Then he whined, slid sleepily onto the floor, and waited to be let out.

Sam had to be shaken awake. "Come on," Lucy said, "you shall spend the night at Ridge Farm with Magpie and me." Sam yawned, and rubbed his eyes, then lifted Magpie into his arms. Lucy kissed Charles fondly, and whispered, "Good luck with the earl."

"Be at the gates here early in the morning, for I shall

424

come to you as soon as it is light," said Charles, kissing her.

She nodded, the coachman opened the door, and she stepped out into the night. At once she was surrounded by the sounds, smells, and feelings of her earliest memories. Cassie had got out of the second coach, thinking she was to stay with her mistress, but Lucy bade her go to Landsdun, because Ridge Farm was far to humble a place for a lady's maid. She and Sam stood and watched the lights of the coaches disappear towards the Charnwood. Owls were hooting, and when coach wheels were silent, that was the only sound left to stir the velvet night, apart from the soft rustling of the trees and hedgerows, and the gentle sighing of the country breeze.

She took Sam's hand in hers, and turned towards the house, letting Magpie walk before them across the yard. There was a dim light showing from the window, and when she arrived at the door she tapped lightly. Her heart was beating heavily; she had an odd feeling that if she knocked too hard, Ridge Farm would disappear like a house in a dream, and with it would go her whole reality.

Roger Emmett was sitting alone by the fire, staring into the flames. He was smoking one of his short clay pipes, and thinking, as he often did when he was alone, of Esmeralda Lee. The tap on the door disturbed him. He raised his chin and turned his head towards the sound. Toby and John were out in the village, courting seriously at last, thank God. If it was either of them, they wouldn't knock, they would just walk in. Perhaps it had been his imagination, and there was no one outside. It was too late for callers. He turned back to the fire and examined the bowl of his pipe. He felt sleepy but, wait, there was another knock. He clenched his pipe between his teeth, shook his old grey head, hauled himself out of the inglenook with a groan, made his way slowly to the door and, opening the door, looked out into the darkness. What he saw, turned him cold. Esmeralda Lee's face looked back at him from the night. There were the large lustrous eyes, there was the mane of black hair, with two bright golden earrings, dancing among the curls. "Esmeralda," he whispered at the ghost.

"Roger Emmett. It's me. Lucy."

He blinked. "Lucy?" She was in his arms. It took Roger Emmett a full ten minutes to come to terms with the situation. Lucy had to sit him down and fill a tankard full of ale to revive him from the shock. He kept saying "'Tis Lucy Emmett, come back from London looking like a lady."

"Silly. It's just the clothes. I am the same girl underneath." She was astonished at how much Roger had aged because, while she had been away, her memory had kept him as he'd been when she was a child. Whenever she'd seen him in her mind's eye, she had seen the blond blue-eyed giant who had carried her under his coat.

"I thought you'd never come back," said Roger.

Lucy laughed. "You'd think that I'd been away for years."

"That is how it feels to me," said Roger.

"This is Sam," said Lucy, bringing the boy to the fire to be introduced.

"How are you, Sam?" Roger asked, stretching out his big, workworn hand.

Sam grinned and took it. "Pretty well, fanks," he said. "How's yourself?"

Roger laughed and slapped his knee. "Well as God is my witness," he roared, "that is the oddest spoken boy I've ever heard. And if it isn't, well, let my boots be burned under me."

"I'm from Monmouf Street," explained Sam, as though that would make his accent seem less strange. But the "Country cove" just looked more bewildered, and Sam came to the conclusion that *Fings go slower the furver you get from London. Brains, in pertikler.* "Are you her farver?" Sam asked, nodding towards Lucy.

Roger was about to answer, but Lucy said, "Not my *real* rather, Sam, but *like* a real father. I am his adopted daughter." Her smiling eyes met Roger's for an instant, and then for some reason she noticed that a shadow of pain crossed his face, and he looked away from her again and studied the bowl of his pipe.

"Mine's hanged," said Sam, puffing out his chest.

Afraid both she and Roger were about to be treated to

the full story of Sam's father's adventures in the poor hole, and his attack on the "cove wiv no cloves," Lucy asked quickly, "Where is your wife?"

"Gone," Roger told her. "Back to her family." He sighed. "I doubt she will return." Lucy patted his shoulder to comfort him. She had never cared for Elizabeth, but it was a sad thing to see a man without a wife to keep him company in his old age. "I'll get some supper," she said. Obviously she wasn't the only person with a tale to tell at Ridge Farm that night.

It had been the earl's idea that his son and Georgiana Stowe should be married on the twenty-sixth of December. Theirs had of necessity to be a short engagement, for the earl knew his health was growing poorer by the day. More and more of his time was spent lying in his bed. Walking exhausted him, for his heart was weak. But his determination to live at least until he saw his only son married was strong. It was for reasons of his health, that the wedding was to be held at Landsdun, for normally the heir would have been married in London and the earl thought it a most flattering sign of George's respect for him, that the monarch was prepared to leave his capital to travel to Leicestershire in mid-winter to be present at the wedding.

For two weeks prior to the heir's arrival, Landsdun had been preparing to entertain the king and queen and over a hundred guests. When Charles climbed out of his coach and mounted the long flight of steps to the front door, the house was still ablaze with lights and gave every sign of bustle. When he walked into the grand hall, his heart sank. It was decked with holly, ivy, and fir. Garlands of hothouse flowers festooned the doors and staircases to greet the guests. Everywhere he looked Charles saw his and Georgiana's initials picked out in gold among the blooms and foliage. The Landsdun and the Stowe family crests were everywhere. He walked through the doors that led into the ballroom anteroom, and saw that the tables in there groaned with wedding presents. Culpepper followed him, and when their eyes met, the servant sighed and shrugged.

"I suppose I had better go and see the earl?" Charles said.

"Better get it over with, my lord," Culpepper replied.

"I hope to God no guests have arrived yet; that would really be too embarrassing," said Charles walking towards the ballroom.

"The snow will have stopped them, my lord, and the notice in the *Times*."

"I sincerely hope so," Charles sighed, throwing open the gilded doors to the ballroom. To his horror, a dais had been erected at the far end of the room; upon it were two carved gilt chairs. The dais and the steps leading to it had been covered with red carpet.

"For their Majesties," whispered Culpepper, craning his head to peer over his master's shoulder. Servants were rushing around, carrying candles for the huge crystal chandeliers that had been lowered almost to the floor. A very effeminate-looking stranger was walking around with a fleet of servants at his heels. He was obviously the person in charge of the decor, for the servants behind him carried bows of silk ribbons and boxes of pins. As Charles hurriedly shut the door on the scene, the dandy fellow was supervising the pinning of the bows to the edge of the red carpet.

Charles felt even more depressed as he and Culpepper arrived in the great hall again. *All this frenzied preparation for his wedding to Georgiana, a wedding that would never take place.*

He began to wish he had taken the coward's way out. He could have eloped with Lucy and married her quietly, perhaps on the Continent. They might have gone to Italy, or Austria. But it was not his way to sneak off and leave the earl to face the shame that an action of that sort would have brought. Although he did not relish the idea of breaking the news of his jilting of Georgiana and his plan to marry Lucy Emmett to his father, he knew that it was the only honourable thing to do.

Lacey the footman met them in the hall, all smiles.

When he had welcomed the heir home, he told him, "The earl and Sir James Robertson have been informed of your arrival, my lord, and say that they await you in the earl's quarters. Supper shall be served at your convenience."

"I may not be here for supper," murmured Charles, as he climbed the stairs to break the news to the earl.

Culpepper didn't offer Lacey any explanation for his master's glum statement, but told the footman to go down to the servants' quarters and make sure Cassie was looked after. Then he followed Charles towards the upper regions of the house.

When Lacey got to the servants' hall he found a pretty Irishwoman there surrounded by kitchen staff, who were all cross-questioning her. It was not long before he heard that Cassie had been engaged as a maid to Miss Lucy Emmett at Pall Mall, and that the marriage of the heir to Miss Stowe was off.

"Off?" asked the amazed Lacey. "Why?" Cassie told him, and in less than ten minutes he was a wiser man than almost anyone at Landsdun, except of course the heir and Mr. Culpepper.

Meanwhile these two gentlemen had arrived at the door to the earl's room, and while Charles waited to be announced, Culpepper took the opportunity of straightening the lace around his master's throat. He also whisked his handkerchief over the heir's boots, for they were dusty from the journey. "Shouldn't you perhaps change, my lord?" he ventured, feeling that his master would be better equipped to put his case to the earl if he looked sprucer.

"Clean lace and linen, sir, a dash of toilette water, my lord?"

His suggestion was ignored, as he knew it would be. The only thing on the heir's mind was to get this unpleasant task over with as quickly as possible.

"Ah, my boy, welcome home," beamed Sir James Robertson who met Charles by the door.

"We expected you earlier, but the snow, of course." He shook the heir's hand heartily, then whispered, conspiratorially, "Lady Charrington wrote."

"I know," whispered Charles. The physician winked

and nodded towards the earl's bed. "Say nothing about it to him."

"Didn't he read it?"

The old man shook his head and answered Charles' question, in a whisper. "Eyesight's bad, Dolly scrawls. Asked me to read it and I did." Charles understood at once. Sir James had been anxious to save distressing the earl and had not disclosed the full contents of Dolly's letter.

"I am much obliged to you," said Charles. The older man laughed, and his eyes twinkled. "Well, we all know how Lady Charrington exaggerates and who would blame a young man for sowing a few wild oats before tieing the knot?" Charles did not have the opportunity to tell the physician that he had been sowing rather more than wild oats at Pall Mall, for the earl's voice interrupted him.

"Jamie, what are you two whispering about over there?"

Charles turned and approached the huge canopied bed, and as he did so, Rex and Regina, the earl's hounds who reclined at their master's feet, raised their imperious, long-nosed heads, in silent greeting. As Charles sat down behind the bed, his father turned his face towards him and smiled. His appearance was a shock to the heir. He looked incredibly frail. The skin that hung in folds over his fine-boned face was so pale it was almost transparent. His lips were colourless, his eyes, once bright and intelligent, were clouded. His white hair, spread out on the lace-edged pillows, shone like a soft silver halo in the flickering candlelight.

"Surprised that I still live?" asked the earl in a weak, but mocking voice.

"Well, sir," started Charles.

The earl laughed. "I am surprised," he said. "I think the grim reaper is, too, surprised that I have managed to dodge his scythe for so long. Perhaps the fellow is drunk, eh?" Charles smiled, pleased his father's sense of humor was still sharp, "Or perhaps he is reluctant to cut you down because he enjoys the game, sir?"

"Don't you think it curious, though?" asked the earl,

"that a man spends the best part of his youth courting death in sport and battle and the whole of his old age trying to avoid it?" He closed his eyes and was silent for a while. Charles could see that even such a brief burst of conversation fatigued him. His chest tightened with panic. He had expected to find the earl ill, but not *so* ill. When his eyes were closed he looked as though he were already dead. "I thought Georgiana would be here by now. Did you see her in London?"

"Er. Yes, sir," said Charles, trying to hide his distress.

"Dear Miss Stowe," the earl said fondly. "No guests are here yet. I expected guests to be here before today."

I must tell him, thought Charles, but even as he thought it he knew he couldn't.

"The snow, Edward," said Sir James who had approached the bed. "The country has been snowbound. Just be patient. They will start to arrive now the thaw is nearly complete."

"Ah, yes, the snow to be sure. I am quite out of touch. You know, Charles, when one is bedridden as I am, one relies on others to carry the news to one. The weather is nothing to me. I do not see it. I see little . . . less everyday." He sighed and stretched out his hand to his son. Charles grasped his father's hand and a lump came into his throat, for the hand he held felt small and weak like a child's.

"I had dearly hoped I would be present in the chapel for your wedding, but oh, I fear I shall never see you and your bride at the altar."

The sinking feeling in Charles Landsdun's heart had become acute. He half wished Sir James *had* read out the entire contents of Lady Charrington's letter. At least his father would have been prepared for his son's change of mind, but as it was, the earl's innocence of everything that had transpired between him and Lucy and the Stowes made the heir's task almost impossible. "Sir, I can see conversation tires you. Perhaps you would care to rest a while? I shall go and change my linen, take some supper, and then if I may, I shall call on you again before I retire," said Charles rising from his chair. *It was no good, he could not bring himself to tell the earl he intended to marry Lucy*

431

Emmett—not for the moment anyway. He needed guidance badly, and to this end he asked Sir James Robertson if he would join him in the library later.

Charles left the room in an agony of indecision. His only hope was that Sir James Robertson, in his wisdom, might be able to advise him on a proper course of action. He knew he must tell the physician everything, and later, over supper he did. It took him two hours to tell the story, and during that time not a morsel of food passed their lips. Sir James listened in silence, his expression grave, as Charles spoke of his first meeting with Lucy and of the love and passion he had felt for her from the first moment. He spoke of the way he'd tried to deny his emotions, of how Mrs. Stowe and Georgiana had staged a seduction scene to force him to propose. He told Sir James of Lucy's stay at Pall Mall, of the scandalmongering of the *ton*, of her duel with Giles Wentworth and how he had learned she was expecting his child; and finally he came at last to the decision to throw over Georgiana Stowe. "I realised that if I married Georgiana I would regret it for the rest of my life. The only thing that had prevented the thought of marrying her being absolutely abhorrent to me was the knowledge that I should have Lucy for my mistress. But when she said she would not be mistress if I married Miss Stowe, I realised how unfairly I had treated her, and how very selfish I had been. I asked her to marry me and to my joy, she agreed."

"And then you put the notice in the *Times*?" asked Sir James, removing his wig and mopping his bare head with a handkerchief.

Charles nodded. "Yes. I knew it would cause an even bigger scandal but I am prepared to weather that rather than lose her. I came to Landsdun to tell all this to the earl. I felt I should be honest with him, and I meant to be. But when I saw him—so fragile, so near death—my resolution failed." He rose from his chair and began to pace. "I realise that my behaviour throughout this affair has been stupid and ill-considered, and I can make no excuse for it, except to say that I tried to observe the conventions of my class. I strained to please everyone, except myself and Miss Emmett."

"There is no question of your changing your mind about her?" asked Sir James.

"No question," said Charles. "I know it is a match that will be considered outrageous by everyone, but I intend to marry her, for I will take no other woman to wife. But should I tell the earl? I think that I must, for he will know sooner or later. Miss Stowe will not arrive here, neither will the king, nor the other guests. The thing is, how? How am I to tell him without..."

Sir James interrupted him. "There is no way to tell him that will save him suffering. But you are right, he has to know." The old man poured himself a glass of wine and sipped it thoughtfully for a while. Then he smiled and laughed. "You say she shot Giles Wentworth?"

Charles nodded. "In the shoulder."

Sir James seemed much amused and replaced his wig, muttering that it was time a female taught that young fellow a lesson. "Now look, my boy," he said, rising to his feet, "I do not pretend to understand all this, because I, like your father, am an old man with very set ideas of how a young noble gentleman should conduct his life. But, well, things change. Whether the change is for the better, or worse, is beside the point. He and I are of the past—the future belongs to you. I will go and speak to him. I will tell him everything you have told me. If he wants to see you, well I will have you called. If not..." Sir James shrugged and smiled at Charles, "I will have tried, and you must go your way, for a man can only act according to his nature." Having said this he left the room, leaving the young man pacing the floor.

It was a terrible wait. When he had finished pacing Charles sat by the fire, raising his eyes from time to time to look at the clock. The hands moved from ten to eleven o'clock. Supper was cleared away untouched. The hands of the clock crept to midnight, the fire died, the candles burnt low, and still he was not sent for. It was almost twenty minutes to one when the library door opened and

Sir James stood there. Charles leapt to his feet, and said, "Am I to come to him?"

Sir James looked haggard. He closed the door. "No. I gave him a drug to help him sleep."

Charles sank back into his chair and covered his face with his hands. "You told him everything?" he asked through his fingers.

"Everything," said Sir James.

"He will not forgive me for this," said Charles, removing his hands from his face and leaning his head against the back of his chair. "He will die without forgiving me. Oh, if only he had been well it would have been so much easier. Anger, I could have faced . . ."

"He was angry," said Sir James, sitting opposite the young man. "It is possible for a man to feel anger, even with death breathing down his neck. At first he was going to disinherit you, but I pointed out that if he did, one of your dead uncle's bastards from the Americas would inherit. That quieted him, and made him slightly more reasonable. When he had got over the initial shock and sense of outrage, he asked me about Miss Emmett. I told him he had met her briefly at the ball. He remembered being impressed by her beauty. Then I told him she had fought a duel with Giles Wentworth, and he said that he was impressed by her spirit. When I told him she was carrying your child, he seemed impressed by her fecundity."

"Yes, but what did he say?" asked Charles. "Am I to marry with his blessing or not?"

"He will reserve judgement until he meets Miss Emmett again," replied Sir James.

"When will that be?" asked Charles.

"First thing in the morning, if you have any sense," replied the good doctor. "Have her here in her best bonnet after breakfast."

Charles jumped to his feet and shook the old man's hand. "I will have Jupiter saddled at dawn," he said, racing towards the door to find Culpepper and send him out to the stables to inform the groom. "Oh, and that's another thing," called the physician.

"What?" asked Charles, turning from the door, relief written all over his face.

"The earl said that a coach should be sent for her. It would not be proper if she were bumped about on horseback—not if she's carrying a child, my boy."

Lucy was waiting at the gate of Ridge Farm at first light with Sam, Roger, Toby and John. She was in a state of some agitation, because although she had told her family she was going to be the heir of Landsdun's wife, she still wasn't quite convinced of it herself. *What if the earl had changed Charles' mind? What if having returned to his family seat, the heir had started to regret his impulsiveness?* She had lain all night on a straw mattress by the fire unable to sleep. When she saw the Landsdun coach come careering down the road from the direction of the Charnwood, she experienced a moment of extreme panic. *What if Charles was not in the coach? What if it was a messenger from Landsdun to say the heir had changed his mind? And why shouldn't he change his mind?* "And why have you such a small amount of faith, Lucy Emmett?" she asked herself angrily, as the coach came to a halt.

The door was flung open and Charles jumped out. Before she knew it, she was in his arms, all doubts dispelled. He told her she was to go to Landsdun with him directly.

"What, to speak with the earl?" Lucy asked. He nodded. "Does he give us his blessing then?" Lucy asked.

"That is a question I cannot answer," said Charles. "But I am glad to be with you again. I have not slept all night."

"Neither have I," laughed Lucy, leading him to meet Roger and her brothers. Charles liked Roger Emmett and his sons on sight, and after the three countrymen's natural reserve had been broken down, they conversed easily with him. Sam had elected to stay at Ridge Farm with Magpie and the Emmetts, while Lucy went with Charles to Landsdun. So it was only the two of them in the coach, and on the journey Charles told Lucy everything that had happened on the previous night.

Sir James Robertson met them at the door, and after greeting Lucy with a kindly smile, he informed them the earl had expressed a desire to speak to Lucy on her own. It was with trembling knees that she followed the heir and Sir James up the vast staircase, and by the time she got to the door of his room she felt quite faint. So much depended on the impression she made. Charles kissed her, and told her he would be outside waiting for her, and Sir James told her not to worry, that the earl was not an ogre. But these statements did nothing to comfort her, as she entered the huge bedroom and found herself confronted by an immense canopied bed. Two elegant hounds stepped forward to sniff at her, as she waited for some sign from the motionless figure on the bed. She felt as though she should fall on her knees but she managed to stay upright. She saw a hand raised. It gestured towards a chair.

"Is that Miss Emmett?" asked the earl, turning in her direction. She dropped a curtsey and said in a voice that broke with fear. "Yes, my lord. It is Lucy Emmett." She hurried to the chair and sat down quickly, keeping her eyes lowered. She was afraid that if she looked into the earl's face, she would see nothing but acute displeasure.

"I hear, Miss Emmett, that my son wishes to marry you?"

"Yes, my lord, if it pleases you," whispered Lucy.

"Well, it appears that he means to marry you whether it pleases me or no," returned the earl sharply.

Lucy raised her eyes and looked at him. What she saw was a poor, ailing old man.

"Pull your chair closer, I can't see you properly," said the earl.

Lucy quickly did as she was told. The earl might be old and ailing, but there was no mistaking the authority in his voice. He was used to being obeyed. When she was closer to him, he said, "Yes, you are quite as comely as I remembered you to be. The velvet and sables become you."

"Thank you, my lord," said Lucy, feeling herself blushing, "but you have not called me here to pay me compliments I think?" She wished she had bitten her tongue. As usual when nervous she had been blunt when she should have accepted the compliment gracefully.

To her surprise the earl laughed. "I see that you are a young lady who prefers to keep to the point. Very well, we shall pursue our business. What is your opinion of my son wishing to marry you?"

"Well, of course I am pleased, and I believe that he will marry me with or without your blessing, but—"

"But what?" asked the earl, watching her face closely.

"Well, I do not know whether I could marry him in those circumstances because I think he might feel guilty through his life, and grow bitter through the years, and I should hate to come between a father and his son. Your blessing would make us both very happy. It would put the seal on our joy."

There was silence for a minute while the earl considered what she had said. "You are a bastard girl, I hear?"

"Yes, my lord," said Lucy.

"No knowledge of your parents?"

"None, my lord."

The earl sighed.

"I know what you are thinking, my lord," Lucy said hurriedly. "And if I could have produced two parents, I would have. I lack proper birth and breeding, and I know Charlie should marry a young lady of similar background to himself. But the fact is he loves me and I love him. The thing is, that I have apologised endlessly for my parentless state, and I do not intend to continue to apologise. It is not my fault. We do not choose where or how we are born, I am sure though that if a person could choose, they would choose to be born legitimate, with two living parents, preferably in wealthy surroundings such as these." She broke off suddenly, thinking she had gone too far. But the earl seemed impressed, and said, "No. Miss Emmett, pray continue, I am very interested in your opinions."

"Well," said Lucy after taking a deep breath, "I am not an ideal person for your son to marry, but then *is* there such a person? Georgiana Stowe was far less ideal, I think. She did not love your son, she loved the title and the fortune that marrying him would bring. She would not have strived to have made him happy, would she?"

437

"I must admit I was mistaken about Georgiana Stowe," said the earl sadly.

Lucy hesitated, then covered his hand with hers. "My lord. I own that I am far from perfect and that I am young and have a lot to learn. But I do *think*, you know, and I thought a lot before I agreed to be Charlie's wife. I have had my share of doubts, I can tell you. I do not relish the idea of being scorned and ridiculed for the rest of my life by the people who are known as society people. I shall fee neither fish nor fowl for a long time. Very uncomfortable, you know."

The earl nodded. "Those people may never accept you as Countess of Landsdun."

Lucy sighed and let go of his hand, but he took hers, and held it. "Perhaps you are wise beyond your years, Lucy Perhaps you have already learned what it has taken me a lifetime to learn?"

"What is that?" asked Lucy.

"Nothing matters very much," replied the earl with a smile. "Things do matter, but not *terribly*, if you understand me, especially not when, like me, you prepare to meet your maker."

Lucy nodded; she understood completely. The earl sighed, and squeezed her hand. "Tell me why my son did not come to me and speak plainly to me?" he asked her "He should have come to me, like a man, and told me the truth."

"He did try," said Lucy, "but in order to be a man, he had to stop being your son, it seems. That is a very agonising thing, especially for a person who has been so drilled in discipline."

The earl's eyes clouded with tears and he let go of Lucy's hand and covered his face for a minute. When he looked at her again he was smiling, and he asked gruffly, "Have you breakfasted yet, Lucy?"

"Yes, but I am still hungry," she replied. The earl smiled, "Ring that bell," he said, pointing to a cord beside the bed, "and a servant will appear to fetch you something." Lucy did as she was told. "Now. Call in my son, and let's have an end to this misery." Lucy went straight to the door and opened it. Both Charles and Sir James were standing there, looking worried.

"Come along in," Lucy said to them.

When the three of them arrived beside the earl, he addressed his son. "I have spoken to this young lady, and she has been very straight with me. I hope you will be as straight. Do you intend to marry her whether I approve or not?"

Lucy looked at Charles and saw him straighten his shoulders. "Sir, I do," he answered unhesitatingly. For a moment, nothing was said, and then the earl stretched out his hand. "Spoken like a man. I am proud of you," he said.

Charles took his father's hand and shook it. He was smiling with pleasure, and relief. "Does this mean we have your blessing, sir?"

"Of course you have my blessing," said the earl. "Marry her and quickly, for the sooner she takes you in hand the better." Before he had quite finished, Lucy had thrown her arms around his neck and had kissed his cheek fondly. It was at that moment that Lacey answered the bell. "I think that Miss Emmett wishes to order some breakfast," said the earl.

"Er, yes, my lord, but . . . ," he turned to Charles, "The bloods have arrived, sir. The honourable Giles Wentworth, and . . ."

"Pinkerton, Plunkett, and Willie Caruthers?" asked the heir with a frown.

"Yes, my lord, and I think that Sir James better have a look at the Honourable Giles," said Lacey.

"Oh, Charles," cried Lucy, "his shoulder."

The bloods had been shown into the red drawing room. Wentworth was lying on a couch, looking quite green and groaning. Sir James Robertson entered the room first, carrying his bag of instruments. Lucy and Charles followed him. As soon as Lucy saw Giles she let out a cry, rushed over to the couch, knelt at his side, and said angrily, "Oh, Mr. Wentworth, what are you doing here, in this condition?"

Slowly, the wicked hooded eyes opened, and he smiled. "A very good question, Miss Emmett. A question I have asked myself over every bump, and through every rut on the way. What am I doing here? I have asked with a sort of bewildered wonderment. Mind you, now that I am here and gazing on your exquisite face, I am not at all sorry. The discomfort was well worth it."

"We have a very important mission here," said Willie, looking stern.

"Oh, do shut up, Caruthers," groaned Giles, as Sir James started to examine his shoulder.

"What mission?" asked the heir. "I thought you had come for the wedding."

Giles whispered to Lucy, "Be a dear, and stroke my head, Miss Emmett."

"Have you come here to make mischief?" Lucy whispered back, ignoring his request.

"Me, make mischief?" Giles asked, looking amazed. "Ouch, take care, Robertson; Flinch has set that shoulder."

"No doubt," observed the physician dryly, "but it has unset itself. I think we should have you carried to a bed. I shall have to set it again."

While Sir James and Lucy were seeing to Giles, the other bloods had joined Charles. "Read the announcement in the *Times*," said Willie out of the corner of his mouth, "set out at once, to save you."

"Save me?" Charles asked looking puzzled. "What am I to be saved from?"

"From yourself old fellow," Willie replied, "couldn't let you go through with it. Would have it on our consciences for the rest of our puffs, wouldn't we, fellows?" Pinkerton and Plunkett murmured their agreement. "Wentworth don't care, no scruples," said Willie, "couldn't have you marryin' the girl, and ruinin' yourself."

"Well, if you have come to stop me marrying Miss Emmett I am afraid it has been a fool's errand," said Charles, "because I am to marry her, and with the earl's blessing." He walked away from the three of them and joined Lucy at Giles Wentworth's side. "We are to be married as soon as possible," he said, taking her hand.

"So it is true," cried Giles in a mock tragic voice, "I have lost you, Miss Emmett. Quick, fetch a pistol."

"What for?" asked Lucy. Giles pointed to his heart and said with a bleak smile, "Finish me."

Both Lucy and Charles laughed. "Listen, Wentworth," said the heir, "if you can stagger to your feet on the twenty-sixth, why don't you be my best man?"

Willie and the other bloods gaped. Obviously Melton was completely ignorant that Wentworth and Lucy Emmett had been lovers, that or he was so out of his loft with love, that he didn't care.

"Listen here, Wentworth, you better come clean, or I'll shoot you myself," said Willie.

Wentworth sighed, and looked first at Lucy, then at Charles; they both looked blissfully happy.

"Oh, Giles, do say yes," said Lucy. "It would make me so happy if we three could be friends."

"Not lovers or enemies?" Giles asked.

"But you have been lovers," said Willie. Giles looked solemn. "Yes, it is true, Melton, I have been Miss Emmett's lover."

"Giles Wentworth," gasped Lucy. "But only," said Giles, raising his hand, "on a purely spiritual level."

Lucy laughed, bent over him, and kissed his cheek. He caught her hand and whispered, "I hope to enjoy you on a physical level, as soon as my health and the occasion permit." As she drew away from him he said in a loud voice, "I shall be honoured to be your best man, Melton, for I am certainly the best man for the job." Lucy was both angry and excited by what Wentworth had said to her—angry because it appeared he still refused to believe he could never have her, and excited—*Why* she asked herself under her breath. *Was it because she would have been disappointed if Giles had stopped being determined to have her?* His voice interrupted her thoughts. "There is one proviso in my agreeing to be best man."

"What is that?" asked Charles, slipping his arm around Lucy's waist.

"I shall demand the first kiss from the bride after the ceremony," said Giles.

Charles laughed, and Lucy felt him pull her closer. "The first kiss is mine," he replied, "but you, Wentworth, may

441

have the second. With one proviso, that you are strictly supervised."

Giles laughed heartily at his reply, and declared it to be one of the most handsome compliments to his prowess as a lady killer that had ever been paid. But when Lucy smilingly stretched out her hand and asked, "Are we friends then, Giles?" he groaned, looked miserable and asked, "Oh, Miss Emmett. Is that all that we are to be to each other, you and I? Merely friends?" And as he took her hand and raised it to his lips he whispered in a voice full of regret, "Broken hearted."

Suddenly, Pinkerton, who like the other bloods had remained silent and quite perplexed throughout the proceedings, turned on Willie, and asked irately, "I say, Caruthers. Does this mean that our trip here has been a waste of time?"

Charles laughed, because he knew very well why they had come, although he did not intend to admit it. He put his arm around Pinkerton's shoulder, and said, "A waste of time, Pinkers, not at all. For if you bloods will stay to my wedding I think I can promise you one of the smallest but one of the merriest parties this grand old house has ever seen."

More snow came that night, and with the snow came the young clergyman from York who had been engaged to officiate at the wedding of Lord Melton and Miss Georgiana Stowe. He was a bit puzzled when he discovered that the bride to be was now called Miss Lucy Emmett. "Not Miss Georgiana Stowe?" he asked the heir.

"No," replied Charles. "It *was* Miss Georgiana Stowe, but now it is Miss Lucy Emmett." The clergyman smiled weakly and made a quick mental note of the change of name. Then he was told that the wedding was not to be held in the private chapel at Landsdun as he'd thought, but in the parish church at Ragby. It seemed that it was the bride's preference. He made a quick mental note of the change of location, shrugged, and was heard to comment as he was shown out of the red drawing room, that the nobility like God moved in mysterious ways. It snowed through the next day, in fact it snowed right through the

442

preparations for the wedding, causing everyone at Landsdun to look out of the windows and wonder if it would ever stop.

On the morning of the twenty-sixth of December it was still snowing, and it had piled into drifts so deep that if you walked into them "they'd be over your ears, and up your nose." This remark was made by Roger Emmett who as usual at that time of the morning and at that time of year, was out in the big field that led to the Charnwood. The remark was made to Sam, who accompanied him on his inspection of the ewes with Magpie, who had point blank refused to walk and had to be carried by Sam. So deep was the snow, and so raw the morning, that Roger was put in mind of the winter of seventy-two.

"The winter of seventy-two?" Sam asked.

"Winter of seventy-two," replied Roger. "That was a bad un that was, a real freezer, snowed for weeks with no let up, stock and fowls dropping dead like swatted flies, and the pond in the village froze over so fast the ducks was trapped in the ice and had to be rescued or they'd have perished."

"Go on," said Sam, "pull the other leg. It's got bells on it."

"You don't believe me, but it's true, as God is my witness," said Roger, leaning on his stick, and surveying his ewes. "Oh, I have cause to remember that winter, especially a January morning in that winter. I was out after rabbits in those woods, and I caught a young girl in a trap."

Sam laughed. "Caught a girl in a trap? Was she pretty?"

Roger rolled his eyes, leant on his stick and drew an especially curvaceous female form in the air with both his hands. "Pretty? By God, she was a dazzler, a real picture. A Gypsy girl with long curling black hair. Just like pure black silk it was."

"Like Miss Emmett's?" asked Sam.

"Now, it's funny that you should say that, Sam," said Roger, "because that young girl was the spittin' image of Lucy Emmett, so near in looks and ways to her they could be very near relations."

He looked thoughtfully at the Charnwood for a minute,

and Sam thought he had fallen asleep standing up. But he needn't have worried, for the queer old cove walked on across the crisp white ground, saying, "Let's see to my stock, and quick, for at eleven this day I must be at Ragby church to give Lucy Emmett to Lord Melton. That's if the snow will let us get there."

They all got there in spite of the snow—Lucy, and Charles, Giles with his arm in a splint and a sling. The three bloods went, too, so did Mr. Culpepper, and Cassie, Roger, Sam and Magpie, Toby and John with their two round, apple-faced country girls, Dora and Margery, who would be their brides in the spring. Squire Billy was there, so was Jemima, and the fop was there, too, resplendent in his extravagant silken pantaloons and his vividly striped stockings, crowned as usual with the minute *chapeau bas*. Wilchup and Betsey the slattern from Ragby Hall were there, so was the landlord from the Hare and Hounds. Boost the blacksmith was there, with all his noisy, sprawling, brawling children. Barney Cowper, the wheelwright's apprentice turned up, as did *the* Miss Parson Brown, picking her way through the snow-covered graves like a black bonneted spider, with her brother at her side, complete with dew drop and dazed expression. In fact, the whole village turned out, in its best clothing, to see Lucy Emmett given to Lord Melton.

The earl could not leave his bed, but Lucy and Charles had promised that the sexton would ring the bell as soon as they were married so that the earl should have the news as soon as everyone else.

The little church was bursting at the seams with rednosed, frozen-toed, but excited people, as Lucy was led in on Roger Emmett's arm, and they all agreed that they had never seen a lovelier bride. Lucy, her face glowing with happiness, walked slowly down the aisle, wearing her wine velvet gown, and the cape with the sable trim, and the bonnet that covered her glossy black curls matched the gown exactly. She was a positive picture. Even Miss Parson Brown had to concede this, as she turned her attention away from the girl, who she had sworn

444

would come to a bad end and pressed her black mittened hands together.

Charles stood at the altar steps, splendid in his suit of silver brocade, his hair carefully powdered for the occasion at Culpepper's insistence.

Giles stood beside him, not a whit less broken-hearted, but still as rakish and casual as ever. His green eyes were filled with amusement as he surveyed the hotch-potch congregation of villagers, and in his right hand he held a small leather box, the contents of which had amused him even more.

The box held Lucy's gold earrings, and it seemed that they were to be used in lieu of wedding rings, until Lucy and Charles could have proper rings made.

"That's a bit of an eccentric touch," he had declared when Charles had handed him the earrings. "But then the whole damned scheme is a touch eccentric, my dear fellow, so perhaps it ain't so eccentric to be married with earrings after all."

As Lucy stood at Charles' side and listened to the solemn words spoken by the clergyman she could not help wondering at the fate that had decreed that a poor girl taken from the womb of a beggar should one day stand at the side of the heir to a great estate and an illustrious name, to be made his wife.

"I require and charge you both, as ye will answer at the dreadful day of judgment, when the secrets of all hearts shall be disclosed, that if either of you know any impediment why ye may not be joined together . . ." Lucy felt the heir's hand searching for hers; her fingers met his, and they held hands tightly.

"Wilt thou have this woman to be thy wedded wife, to live together . . ."

Lucy couldn't believe it, there had been no impediment, and it was happening.

"I do," she heard Charles say, and his grip on her hand tightened.

"Wilt thou have this man to thy wedded husband, to live together after God's ordinance in the Holy estate of

445

matrimony? Wilt thou obey him and serve him, love
honour and keep him, in sickness and in health, and
forsaking all others keep thee only unto him, as long as y
both shall live?"

Lucy thought, what a heavy and solemn vow that wa
for a girl of seventeen to make; but she wanted with all he
full, young heart to keep it. "I will," she replied.

"Who giveth this woman to be married to this man?

Roger Emmett, sure the secrets of all hearts would b
disclosed on the day of judgment, stepped forward wit
tears running down his weathered cheeks and touched he
arm. It was when he saw Esmeralda Lee's golden earring
shining in the light from the altar candles that he knew a
last that his secret must be disclosed.

In the high tower of Ragby church the heavy bell wa
tolled. Its message rang out across the snow-covered
fields and hedges, over the oaks of the Charnwood, across
the ridge to Landsdun to tell the earl that the ancient lin
was secured. Only then did he close his eyes and offer hi
soul to God, certain whether he received it or not, that h
had life everlasting.

Lucy had gone into the vestry to sign the register an
while Charles signed his name and the name of his parents
she thought what a sad thing it would be to sign Lucy
Emmett there, and then to have no name for her parents

"Write Roger Emmett and Esmeralda Lee," whispered
Roger in her ear. She turned and looked at him with acut
surprise.

"Just write that down," said the old man, nodding hi
head vigourously, and she did. She did not question him a
all. She wrote not Lucy Emmett, but Lucy Melton
because that was her new name; and underneath, in he
most flourishing script, she wrote, "Roger Emmett" an
then "Esmeralda Lee." "There," she said, with a smile
"Now I have a father and a mother and a husband, all on
one day." As she said it, she felt her child move inside her
It was the slightest flutter, like the movement a butterfl
makes when it is held in your palm. But it was lif
quickening nontheless, and as she walked out of the vestr
between Charles and her father and into the flurryin

snow, she thought of all the adventures she had been through since the Ragby bell last tolled for her. Slipping one arm through Roger's and another through the arm of her husband, she walked out through the gates of the churchyard with the snow covering her like confetti, and knew that her life lay before her—and that promised to be the greatest adventure of all.